U0000907

一次戰勝新制多益

TOEIC
必考核心單字

蔡馨慧 Nicole 著

要背就背必考的！

NEW TOEIC VOCABULARY

如何使用本書
How to use this book

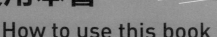

★符合多益官方 13 大情境

本書按照多益官方頒訂的13大情境所規劃，依照這些情境延伸出20個單元，所有單字及例句完全符合多益考試必考情境，讓你用最寶貴的時間學到最必要的單字！

★學前預習抓重點

每個人都知道多益考試需要不斷複習單字，卻忽略了學前預習才最能抓出重點！本書每個章節一開始皆有自我檢測，先抓出自己在本章節最不熟悉的單字，用最少的時間對症下藥！

★分段學習，分段測驗

本書每個章節最後皆會有小測驗，包含混合題型及完全擬真多益考試的題型。分段學習，分段吸收，才不會一次囫圇吞棗，學到後面忘了前面。分段測驗，學完馬上驗收，才能知道自己的強項和弱項在哪！

point

特別收錄學習計畫表

學習計畫表專為考生量身打造，無論你是需要考前衝刺的上班族，或是有較充裕的時間準備考試的學生，亦或是想要穩紮穩打、考好考滿的考生，都可以依照學習計畫表自行規劃學習時程！（請翻至 p.004）

★星號表示出題頻率

★星號表示出題頻率

本書每個單字皆有標示星號，從一顆星到三顆星，星號越多，出題頻率越高！平常學習時可以根據星號加強記憶重要單字，也可以在進考場前針對標有三顆星的單字重點複習！

★美、英口音單字與例句 MP3，隨掃隨聽

本書特別邀請美籍及英籍名師，為考生錄製最接近真實考試速度的全書單字及例句MP3，除了免費附贈一片CD，還特別收錄了單字及例句的音檔QR碼，就算出門在外，也能隨時隨地用手機掃描QR碼收聽音檔，讓你走到哪聽到哪！

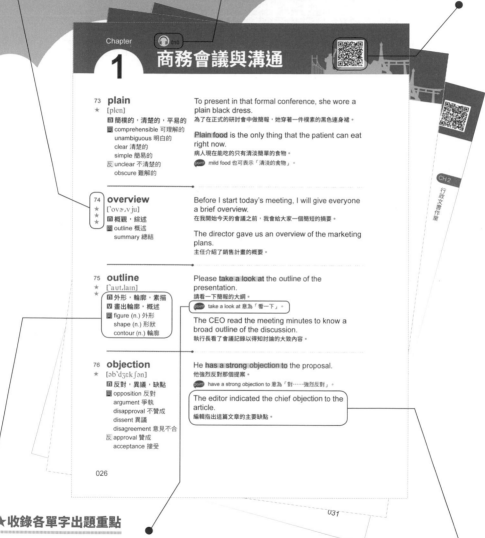

Chapter 1 商務會議與溝通 010

73 **plain**
★
[plen]
形 簡樸的，清楚的，平易的
同 comprehensible 可理解的
unambiguous 明白的
clear 清楚的
simple 簡易的
反 unclear 不清楚的
obscure 難解的

To present in that formal conference, she wore a plain black dress.
為了在正式的研討會中做簡報，她穿著一件樸素的黑色連身裙。

Plain food is the only thing that the patient can eat right now.
病人現在能吃的只有清淡簡單的食物。

point mild food 也可表示「清淡的食物」。

74 **overview**
★★★
[`ovəˌvju]
名 概觀，綜述
同 outline 概述
summary 總結

Before I start today's meeting, I will give everyone a brief overview.
在我開始今天的會議之前，我會給大家一個簡短的摘要。

The director gave us an overview of the marketing plans.
主任介紹了銷售計畫的概要。

75 **outline**
★★
[`autˌlaɪn]
名 外形，輪廓，素描
動 畫出輪廓，概述
同 figure (n.) 外形
shape (n.) 形狀
contour (n.) 輪廓

Please take a look at the outline of the presentation.
請看一下簡報的大綱。

point take a look at 意為「看一下」。

The CEO read the meeting minutes to know a broad outline of the discussion.
執行長看了會議記錄以得知討論的大致內容。

76 **objection**
★
[əb`dʒɛkʃən]
名 反對，異議，缺點
同 opposition 反對
argument 爭執
disapproval 不贊成
dissent 異議
disagreement 意見不合
反 approval 贊成
acceptance 接受

He has a strong objection to the proposal.
他強烈反對那個提案。

point have a strong objection to 意為「對……強烈反對」。

The editor indicated the chief objection to the article.
編輯指出這篇文章的主要缺點。

CH.2 行政文書作業

026

031

★收錄各單字出題重點

Nicole老師在本書中一次匯整了出題重點，包含文法重點、同義詞、反義詞、衍生字、搭配詞，並秉持其一貫的教學精神，提出各種專為考生設計的必背考點整理！

★例句模仿多益考題

除了完全擬真多益考試的小測驗之外，Nicole老師撰寫此書的例句時，也完全按照多益考試題目的敘述方式，讓你在背單字的同時，讀例句也能自然而然地學會如何作答多益考試！

學習計畫表

1. 需要考前衝刺、重點複習的考生：推薦 **30天計畫**
2. 有較充裕的時間準備考試的考生：推薦 **45天計畫**
3. 想要穩紮穩打、考好考滿的考生：推薦 **60天計畫**

多益測驗考試日期：　　　月　　　日

學習內容	預定學習日		實際完成日		學習內容	預定學習日		實際完成日	
Chapter 1	月	日	月	日	Chapter 11	月	日	月	日
Chapter 2	月	日	月	日	Chapter 12	月	日	月	日
Chapter 3	月	日	月	日	Chapter 13	月	日	月	日
Chapter 4	月	日	月	日	Chapter 14	月	日	月	日
Chapter 5	月	日	月	日	Chapter 15	月	日	月	日
Chapter 6	月	日	月	日	Chapter 16	月	日	月	日
Chapter 7	月	日	月	日	Chapter 17	月	日	月	日
Chapter 8	月	日	月	日	Chapter 18	月	日	月	日
Chapter 9	月	日	月	日	Chapter 19	月	日	月	日
Chapter 10	月	日	月	日	Chapter 20	月	日	月	日

我只寫我會教的內容，我只寫學生在多益考試中會需要的內容。

從事教學十年，依然熱愛得很，不管教什麼科目、什麼類型的課、什麼行業的學生，「有效教學」對我而言是一個最重要的原則。坊間的書縱使有些是以語料庫來篩選單字，但隨著多益考試的演進，書中還是收錄了不少多餘的單字。辛苦的考生買了書回去讀，也不知道這些單字在真正的多益考試裡是怎麼呈現，往往前幾天認真背了幾回，就開始萌生「沒方向感」、「到底哪個會考」、「單字海」的感覺，最後書就被擺在角落。等到下次有人介紹了某本單字書，心想「可能會有所不同，再給自己一次機會吧」，買了之後，在沒有老師的教學介入下，往往又重蹈覆轍。

有時聽學生分享自己學習時的挫敗感真的讓我很揪心，但確實不是每個學習者都有時間和預算上課，因此，「把教學帶著走」的想法促成了這本書的誕生。為了讓讀者能夠透過這本書有效學習，我在編寫單字書時的理念就是：「讓讀者知道這個單字在多益中常考的樣子為何」，並藉由以下幾點盡力達成這個目標。

1. **全書例句依照多益出題的方式撰寫**：讀例句時就像是在讀題目，提早熟悉多益的樣子，讓準備時期看到的素材跟真正考試的差別不大，無縫接軌。

2. **補充常與此單字一起出現的搭配詞**：這樣就更能預期看到此字時還會遇到哪些字啦！

3. **單字在多益中出現的常用情境走向**：對音檔或文章的背景知識越多，即使遇到不熟的單字，也還是能夠預測或推敲出可能的內容唷！

4. **補充最常在多益中出現的文法**：英文文法那麼多，直接幫讀者點出來誰就是特別愛在多益考試裡出現，省時省力，是不是該讀一下！

5. **每個單字幾乎都有兩個不同程度的例句**：有些讀者在熟悉單字時需要搭配例句一起學習，本書每個單字幾乎都有兩個例句，幫你節省額外查例句的時間！如果時間有限，挑著附近的鄰居（搭配詞）先讀吧！

6. **分段測驗的多元驗收方式**：每一章節後面都有收錄測驗，有仿真題目的形式，也有混合題目的形式，目的就是要讓讀者讀完後，能有跟單字互動的機會。有互動才有機會印象深刻唷！再者，額外抽出來當題目的字絕對是精華中的精華！

作者的靈魂就住在書裡，這絕對是一本負責任的單字書。考生時間寶貴，我們只做有效且最有效率的學習，希望讀者們都能夠順利通過多益考試，讓這個考試成為你進入人生下一階段的 golden ticket！

With Love,
Nicole

目錄 contents

如何使用本書 ⋯⋯⋯⋯⋯⋯⋯⋯⋯⋯⋯⋯⋯⋯⋯⋯⋯⋯⋯ 002

學習計畫表 ⋯⋯⋯⋯⋯⋯⋯⋯⋯⋯⋯⋯⋯⋯⋯⋯⋯⋯⋯⋯ 004

作者序 ⋯⋯⋯⋯⋯⋯⋯⋯⋯⋯⋯⋯⋯⋯⋯⋯⋯⋯⋯⋯⋯⋯⋯ 005

Chapter 1 商務會議與溝通 Business Conference & Communication ⋯⋯ 007

Chapter 2 行政文書作業 Administrative Paperwork ⋯⋯⋯⋯ 029

Chapter 3 調查研究 Investigation & Research ⋯⋯⋯⋯⋯⋯ 051

Chapter 4 投資與設備 Investment & Equipment ⋯⋯⋯⋯⋯ 073

Chapter 5 科技研發 Technology & Development ⋯⋯⋯⋯⋯ 095

Chapter 6 金融財務 Finance & Accounting ⋯⋯⋯⋯⋯⋯⋯ 117

Chapter 7 經營管理 Business Management ⋯⋯⋯⋯⋯⋯⋯ 139

Chapter 8 生產製造與品管 Manufacturing & Quality Control ⋯⋯⋯ 161

Chapter 9 人事組織 Human Resources & Organization ⋯⋯⋯ 183

Chapter 10 物流運輸與貿易 Logistics & Trade ⋯⋯⋯⋯⋯⋯⋯ 205

Chapter 11 零售購物與訂單 Shopping & Orders ⋯⋯⋯⋯⋯⋯ 227

Chapter 12 行銷銷售 Marketing & Sales ⋯⋯⋯⋯⋯⋯⋯⋯ 249

Chapter 13 社會經濟 Society & Economy ⋯⋯⋯⋯⋯⋯⋯⋯ 271

Chapter 14 餐飲住宿 Catering & Accommodation ⋯⋯⋯⋯⋯ 293

Chapter 15 交通觀光 Transportation & Tourism ⋯⋯⋯⋯⋯⋯ 315

Chapter 16 醫療健康 Medical Treatment & Health ⋯⋯⋯⋯⋯ 337

Chapter 17 展覽表演 Exhibitions & Performances ⋯⋯⋯⋯⋯ 359

Chapter 18 表達與演講 Expression & Speech ⋯⋯⋯⋯⋯⋯ 381

Chapter 19 傳播媒體 Mass Media ⋯⋯⋯⋯⋯⋯⋯⋯⋯⋯ 403

Chapter 20 日常生活 Daily Life ⋯⋯⋯⋯⋯⋯⋯⋯⋯⋯⋯ 425

Chapter 1
商務會議與溝通

以下多益必考單字，你認識哪些？

☐ discussion (p.011) ☐ inconvenient (p.020) ☐ section (p.019)

☐ upcoming (p.013) ☐ seminar (p.009) ☐ figure (p.013)

☐ supervisory (p.009) ☐ reception (p.008) ☐ remind (p.010)

☐ compromise (p.018) ☐ supportive (p.008) ☐ permit (p.013)

☐ boardroom (p.008) ☐ overview (p.026) ☐ budget (p.013)

☐ finalize (p.021) ☐ conference (p.012) ☐ attendance (p.012)

1 商務會議與溝通

---

01 boardroom
★
★ [`bord͵rum]
★
n 會議室
同 meeting room 會議室
conference room 會議室

The boardroom will be renovated next month.
會議室下個月會被重新整修。

The boardroom is well-designed and equipped with advanced facilities.
會議室設計良好且具備了先進的設施。

point be equipped with 意為「具備著」。

---

02 reception
★
★ [rɪ`sɛpʃən]
★
n 接待，招待會，接待處
衍 receptionist
(n.) 接待員；傳達員
recipient (n.) 接受者

I signed up for the conference at the reception desk.
我在接待處報名了這場討論會。

point sign up 意為「報名」。

The guests were waiting in the reception room because the manager was still in the meeting.
訪客正在接待室等待，因為經理還在開會中。

point reception room 意為「接待室」。

---

03 supportive
★
★ [sə`pɔrtɪv]

a 支援的，贊助的
同 encouraging
鼓勵的；贊助的
反 discouraging
令人沮喪的；阻止的
opposed to 反對的
衍 support (v.) 支持，贊成

Employees with supportive supervisors usually perform well.
有上司支持的員工通常表現得很好。

People who are supportive of the plan all attended the meeting.
支持計畫的人們都出席了會議。

---

04 hallway
★
★ [`hɔl͵we]

n 玄關，門廳，走廊
同 corridor 走廊
passageway 通道

The conference room is at the end of the hallway.
會議室在走廊的盡頭。

point 易混淆字：halfway (adv.) 中途地。

There are many portraits and introductions of the chief founders hanging on the walls of the hallway so that visitors can know the history of the company.
走廊牆上掛著許多主要創辦人的肖像及介紹，如此一來訪客能夠了解公司的歷史。

point so that 意為「如此一來」，so... that... 意為「太……以至於……」。

05 **seminar**
★★★
['sɛmə͵nɑr]
n 研討班，專題發表會
同 meeting 會議
conference 會議
session 會議
convention 大會

There will be an addition to today's seminar.
今天的研討會將會有一項新增的行程。

point 多益測驗中出現的會議或演講常常會有新增的行程，常以 addition 表示。

Two managers in Marketing Department confirmed to present in the seminar.
兩位行銷部的經理已經確認會在研討會中發表。

06 **leader**
★★
['lidɚ]
n 領袖，領導者
同 chief 首領
principal 首長
反 follower 跟隨者
supporter 支持者
衍 leading (a.) 領導的

The team leader had distributed the work to his subordinates before he took leave.
組長在請假前就已經分配好工作給他的下屬。

The leader announced the revised schedule and the new meeting venue.
領導者宣布修改的行程以及新的會議場所。

point venue, location, spot, premises 皆可指「地點」。

07 **supervisory**
★★
[͵supɚ'vaɪzərɪ]
a 管理的，監督的
同 managing 管理的
controlling 控制的
regulatory 管理的
衍 supervisor (n.) 監督者

The supervisory institution will have a meeting tomorrow.
監察機構明天會開會。

The interviewer asked the interviewee what supervisory roles he had played.
面試官問面試者以前做過什麼監察工作。

08 **during**
★★★
['djurɪŋ]
prep 在……期間
同 throughout 從頭到尾

All the guests enjoyed refreshments during the break in the session.
所有的來賓都很享受會議休息時間的茶點。

point refreshments 為茶點，是多益測驗於會議行程中描述休息時間時的常見單字。

The company tried to attract more potential customers by holding a clearance sale during off-peak season.
公司試著吸引更多潛在客人藉由在淡季時舉辦清倉特賣會。

point off-peak season = slack season = low season 意為「淡季」、peak season = high season 意為「旺季」。

Chapter 002

1 商務會議與溝通

09 director
★
★★
★

[dəˋrɛktɚ]

回 主管，經理，導演

同 administrator 管理人
manager 經理
chairman 主席
chairperson 主席

衍 directory (n.) 目錄
direction (n.) 方向
directly (adv.) 直接地

My director **appointed** him **to** be responsible for making meeting arrangements.
我的主任指派他負責會議的安排。

(point) appoint sb. to 意為「指派」。

The director takes training courses regularly so that he can teach his employees new knowledge.
那位主任規律地上訓練課程，所以他才能夠教他的下屬新知。

10 accept
★
★★
★

[əkˋsɛpt]

V 接受，答應，認可

同 agree 同意
approve 贊成

反 reject 拒絕
refuse 拒絕
oppose 反對

衍 acceptable (a.) 可接受的
acceptance (n.) 接受

He accepted your proposal **since** it would reduce the cost of materials.
他接受了你的提案，因為這會減少原料的成本。

(point) since, because, as 皆可表達「因為」，皆為連接詞。

The assistant was surprised that her supervisor accepted her suggestion and reported it in the monthly meeting.
助理非常驚訝上司接受了她的意見，還在每月的會議中提出。

11 clarify
★
★

[ˋklærəˌfaɪ]

V 澄清，闡明，得到淨化

同 make clear 弄清楚
simplify 使單純
explain 闡明
refine 精煉

He tried to clarify the point in another way.
他試著用另一種方式闡明論點。

The **water filter** can clarify water.
濾水器能淨化水。

(point) water filter 意為「濾水器」。

12 remind
★
★

[rɪˋmaɪnd]

V 提醒，使想起

同 refresh someone's memory
喚起某人的記憶
help someone remember
幫助某人想起

The secretary **reminded** her supervisor **to** attend the seminar.
祕書提醒她的上司出席研討會。

(point) remind sb. to + V 意為「提醒（某人）做某事」。

The student **reminded** the coach **of** another promising athlete.
這名學生使教練想起了另一名有潛力的運動員。

(point) remind sb. of sth. / sb. 意為「使想起（類似的人或物）」。

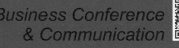
13 equip

★
★

[ɪˋkwɪp]

V 裝備，配備

同 provide 提供
　　furnish 配置
　　supply 供給

衍 equipment (n.) 裝備

The conference room that is equipped with computers and Internet access should be booked in advance.

有電腦即可上網的那間會議室必須要事先預約。

point in advance 意為「事先」。

The orientation equipped our newcomers with background about the company and the related field.

新進員工訓練使新員工具備了公司及相關領域的知識。

14 discuss

★
★
★

[dɪˋskʌs]

V 討論，商談，論述

同 consider 考慮
　　examine 審問
　　explore 探索
　　study 細察
　　analyze 解析

Let's discuss the details of that proposal in person.

我們當面再討論那個提案的細節吧。

point in person 意為「當面」。

After discussing with our interior designer, we were determined to build an extension to our house.

在和我們的室內設計師討論過後，我們決定對房屋進行擴建。

point be determined to 意為「下定決心」。

15 discussion

★
★
★

[dɪˋskʌʃən]

n 討論，商討，談論

同 conversation 會話
　　talk 談話
　　exchange of views
　　交流看法
　　consultation 諮詢

The coordinator led the discussion and made a conclusion according to it.

協調者引導討論並根據討論內容做出結論。

point according to 意為「根據」。

The panel will have discussions about the emergent issue that happened last week.

專家小組將會討論上週發生的緊急議題。

point panel (n.) 專家小組；儀表板；操縱台。

16 attend

★
★
★

[əˋtɛnd]

V 出席，參加，照料，伴隨

同 be present 出席
　　go to 前往
　　join 參加

反 absent (a.) 缺席的

Will you attend the board meeting tomorrow, Jason?

你明天會去委員會會議嗎，傑森？

point attend 當「出席」時不加 to。

To update my knowledge, I attend seminars regularly.

為了更新我的知識，我規律性地參加研討會。

point regularly = frequently = on a regular basis 皆意為「經常地；規律地」。

商務會議與溝通

17 attendance

★
★
★

[ə`tɛndəns]

n 到場，出席，出席人數

同 presence 出席
appearance 出現
turnout 出席者

反 absence 缺席

Having a good attendance record is crucial since it somehow reflects your attitude to work.
有好的出席紀錄是重要的，因為這多少會反映出你對工作的態度。

(point) attendance record 意為「出缺席紀錄」。

Attendance at the luncheon is optional.
出席午餐宴會是自由選擇的。

(point) 與 optional 相反的詞為 mandatory，意為「必要的；強制的」。

18 convention

★
★

[kən`vɛnʃən]

n 會議，大會，習俗

同 conference 會議
congress 代表大會
assembly 與會者，集會
gathering 集會

衍 conventional
(a.) 習慣的，常見的

It is a convention to hold wedding banquets in many countries.
舉辦婚宴是許多國家的習俗。

(point) 易混淆字：banquet (n.) 宴席／bouquet (n.) 花束。

The receptionist led the guests to the meeting room for the party convention.
接待人員將訪客帶到黨員大會的會議室。

19 conference

★
★
★

[`kɑnfərəns]

n 會議，協商會，會談

同 congress 代表大會
meeting 會議
seminar 研討會
forum 討論會

We reserved a conference room for 100 people.
我們訂了一間可容納一百個人的會議室。

(point) 相關訂位用語：reserve a table for 4 意為「訂四人位」。

Jackson will be out of town to attend the annual economic conference.
傑克森將會出城參加一年一度的經濟研討會。

20 focus

★
★
★

[`fokəs]

v 集中，使聚焦

n 焦點，重點

同 center (n.) 中心
emphasis (n.) 強調
priority (n.) 優先
attention (n.) 注意
concentration (n.) 專心

反 out of focus 失焦

Let's discuss the issues one by one so that we won't lose focus.
讓我們一個一個議題來討論，這樣才不會失焦。

(point) lose focus 意為「失焦」。

In today's workshop, we will focus on how to lead your team members to brainstorm the project.
在今天的工作坊，我們將會聚焦在如何引導你的小組成員來為專案腦力激盪。

21 **permit**
★
★
[`pɝmɪt]
n 許可證，執照
[pɚ`mɪt]
v 許可，允許
同 license (n.) 許可證
certification (n.) 證明
grant (v.) 授予
enable (v.) 賦予
反 forbid (v.) 禁止
prohibit (v.) 禁止

Photography is not permitted in the museum.
博物館裡不允許照相。

point 多益測驗中會提到在博物館禁止做的事情還有：不能飲食。

Without our manager's permit, you are not allowed to enter the board meeting room.
沒有我們經理的同意，你不能進入委員會會議室。

point be not allowed to 意為「不被允許」，為多益測驗在規定類事項的常見寫法。

---

22 **upcoming**
★
★
[`ʌp͵kʌmɪŋ]
a 即將來臨的
同 forthcoming 即將到來的
approaching 接近的
coming 即將到來的

He is packing for the upcoming business trip.
他正在為即將到來的出差打包行李。

The manager couldn't attend the upcoming seminar due to schedule conflicts.
因為行程衝突，經理沒辦法參加即將召開的研討會。

point schedule conflicts 意為「行程衝突」。

---

23 **budget**
★
★
★
[`bʌdʒɪt]
n 預算，經費
v 將……編入預算，安排
a 低廉的
同 ration (n.) 配給量
allowance (n.) 分配額

When they travel, they always stay at budget hotels instead of luxury ones.
當他們去旅行時，他們總是住在青年旅館而不是豪華的旅館。

point instead of 意為「取而代之」。此句也可以改寫成 They don't stay at luxury hotels, but budget hotels instead.

The aim of the meeting is to decide the budget for the company trip.
這個會議的目標就是要決定員工旅遊的預算。

point company trip 意為「員工旅遊」。

---

24 **figure**
★
★
[`fɪgjɚ]
n 外型，人物，數字，圖表
v 計算，認為
同 number (n.) 數字
chart (n.) 圖表

I need to figure out when will be appropriate for the meeting.
我必須知道何時為會議合適的時間。

The figure didn't include temporary workers.
這個數據沒有包含臨時工。

Chapter 004

1 商務會議與溝通

25 convenience
★
★
★
[kən`vinjəns]

n 方便，舒適，便利設施
同 advantage 益處
反 inconvenience 不便，麻煩
衍 convenient
(a.) 方便的，合宜的

I hope to arrange a meeting with you at your convenience.
我希望能在你方便時跟你安排一個會議。

point at your convenience 意為「在你方便的時候」。

The online banking service brings convenience to those who cannot go to banks during the opening hours.
網路銀行服務帶給那些沒辦法在銀行營業時間辦理業務的人方便。

point opening hours 意指「營業時間」。

---

26 reschedule
★
★
★
[ri`skɛdʒul]

v 重新安排……的時間，
重新計畫
同 rearrange 重新安排
reorganize 重新制定

Because of the contingency, the secretary had no choice but to reschedule the date of the board meeting.
因為一樁偶發事件，祕書不得不重新安排董事會議的日期。

point have no choice but to 意指「不得不」。

Due to schedule conflicts, I have to reschedule my travel plan.
因為行程衝突，我必須重新安排我的旅遊計畫。

point schedule conflicts 意為「行程衝突」。

---

27 item
★
★
[`aɪtəm]

n 項目，條款，
一則（新聞等）
同 object 項目
unit 單元
衍 itemize (v.) 分條列述

Splurging on unnecessary items may be a waste of resources.
揮霍在不需要的東西上可能是一種浪費資源的作法。

point splurge on 意為「揮霍」。

There are only two items on the agenda, so the meeting might be ended within two hours.
議程上只有兩件事情要討論，因此會議可能會在兩小時內結束。

---

28 purpose
★
★
★
[`pɝpəs]

n 目的，意圖，效用
v 意圖，決意
同 motive (n.) 動機
motivation (n.) 刺激；推動

The assistant didn't forget to bring the key on purpose.
助理並非故意忘記帶鑰匙。

point on purpose = purposely 意為「故意地」。

The purpose of this meeting is to nominate the chief of the committee.
這個會議的目標是為了要提名委員會的主席。

29 above

★
★
★

[əˈbʌv]

prep 在……之上，超過
ad 在上面，（數目）更多
同 over (prep.) 在……之上
　　upon (prep.) 在……之上
反 below (prep.) 在……之下

As mentioned above, we will rearrange the date of the meeting at your convenience.
就如同我上述所說的，我們將會在你方便時重新跟你安排會議的日期。

This candidate is professional, outgoing, above all, passionate.
這個求職者很專業、外向，更重要的是，他很熱情。

point above all 意為「首先，特別重要的是」。

30 absent

★
★

[ˈæbsn̩t]

a 缺席的，不存在的，心不在焉的
同 vacant 空著的
反 present 出席的
衍 absence (n.) 缺席

I will be absent for tomorrow's campaign because I am going to take personal leave.
明天的行銷活動我會缺席，因為我要請事假。

point personal leave 事假、annual leave 年假、sick leave 病假。

She absent-mindedly left the contract on the desk.
她心不在焉地將合約留在了桌上。

point absent-mindedly 意為「心不在焉地」。

31 adhere

★

[ədˈhɪr]

v 黏附，遵守
同 stick to 堅持
　　abide by 遵守
反 give up 放棄

Both parties should adhere to the original agreement.
雙方都必須遵守原定的協議。

point party (n.) 一方，對方；政黨，黨派（活動）。

The new wallpaper didn't adhere to the walls so I called the store for help.
新的壁紙黏不住牆壁，因此我打給店家尋求幫助。

32 apparent

★

[əˈpærənt]

a 表面的，外觀的，明顯的
同 clear 明瞭的
　　noticeable 顯著的
　　obvious 明顯的
反 subtle 隱約的
衍 apparently (adv.) 顯然地

The judge said it was apparent that the first participant would win the talent show.
評審說第一位參賽者顯然會贏得這個選秀。

The meeting was cancelled for no apparent reason.
會議莫名其妙被取消了。

point for no apparent reason 意為「沒有什麼特別的原因」。

Chapter 005

1 商務會議與溝通

33 argument

★
★
★

[ˈɑrgjəmənt]

n 爭執，辯論，論點

同 disagreement 爭吵
  dispute 爭論
  quarrel 爭吵
  fight 打架

反 agreement 同意
  harmony 一致

衍 argue (v.) 爭論

The consultant tried his best to settle the argument between the couple.
顧問試著解決這對夫妻的爭吵。

point settle 意為「解決」。

During the annual meeting, he proposed several convincing arguments to back up his stand.
在年度會議中，他提出很多具說服力的論點來支持他的立場。

point back up 意為「支持」。

34 assert

★

[əˈsɝt]

V 斷言，聲稱，堅持

同 declare 宣告
  claim 主張
  maintain 主張
  affirm 斷言

The manager taught her subordinates how to assert themselves more in meetings.
經理教她的下屬如何在會議上立場更堅定一些。

The educational consultant suggested the mother assert her authority over the children sometime.
教育顧問建議媽媽有時還是要擺出大人的權威來管教孩子。

point suggest sb. (should) + V 意為「建議（某人）做……」。

35 attempt

★
★
★

[əˈtɛmpt]

n 企圖，嘗試

V 企圖，試圖

同 seek (v.) 企圖
  try (v.) 嘗試
  endeavor (v.) 力圖

The boy turned off the TV in an attempt to stay focused on his studies.
男孩關掉電視，試圖專注在他的學習。

point in an attempt to = try to 意為「試圖」。

None of our attempts at convincing the clients was successful.
我們多次試圖說服我們的客戶，但都未能成功。

36 breach

★

[britʃ]

n 破壞，違反，破裂

V 破壞，違反，傷害

同 violate 違背

反 follow 跟隨
  obey 服從

You will be fined if you breach the contract.
如果你違反合約的話將會被罰錢。

point fine (v.) 罰錢 (a.) 好的。

The accident caused a breach between the two companies.
這個意外在兩間公司之間造成了裂痕。

37 brief

★
★

[brif]

a 短暫的，簡略的
n 摘要，訴書
v 做……摘要，簡報
同 short (a.) 短的
反 long (a.) 長的

His presentation was brief but precise.
他的簡報很短卻很精要。

The manager briefed the newcomers on the job duties and the company benefits.
經理向新人們介紹工作職責及公司福利。

point brief sb. on sth. 意為「向……介紹情況」。

38 calm

★
★
★

[kɑm]

a 鎮靜的，沉著的
n 寧靜
v 使平靜，鎮定下來
同 peaceful (a.) 平靜的
　　pacific (a.) 溫和的
　　undisturbed (a.) 寧靜的
　　tranquil (a.) 平穩的

The consultant suggests his client stay calm and rethink the problem again.
顧問建議他的客戶保持冷靜並重新思考一下問題。

point suggest sb. (should) + V 表示「建議（某人）做……」。

He was chosen to work as a representative of customer service because he is rather calm and responsible compared with other candidates.
他被選作客服代表，因為他比其他候選者更冷靜且負責任。

point as 後面加職稱，意為「做為……」。

39 generation

★
★

[ˌdʒɛnəˈreʃən]

n 世代，一代人，產生
同 age group 同年齡層的人
衍 generate (v.) 產生

How to conquer and bridge the generation gap and conflicts in workplaces?
要如何對抗及縮小職場上的代溝及紛爭呢？

The colorful and approachable design aims at appealing to the young generation.
色彩豐富且平易近人的設計旨在吸引年輕世代。

40 forum

★

[ˈforəm]

n 論壇，公開討論的場所，討論會
同 meeting 會議
　　assembly 集會
　　gathering 集合
　　conference 會議
　　seminar 討論會
　　convention 大會

KIDI is the most widely used online forum in this nation.
KIDI 是在這個國家中最被廣泛使用的線上論壇。

Before we start today's Economic Forum, there is one addition to our schedule.
在我們開始今天的經濟論壇之前，有一項新增的行程要跟大家宣布。

point 多益聽力測驗情境中，研討會開場白常有「新增行程」的句子。

017

商務會議與溝通

41 **facilitate**
★★
[fə`sɪlə͵tet]
V 使容易，促進，幫助
同 accelerate 促進
advance 推進
promote 晉升
further 助長
encourage 促進
反 impede 妨礙

The updated system facilitates tracking and managing inventory.
這個更新系統有助於追蹤及管理存貨。

To facilitate discussion during the meeting, all attendees should submit questions to the assistant by this Friday.
為了協助會議中的討論，所有出席者應該要在週五前提交問題給助理。

42 **facilitator**
★
[fə`sɪlə͵tetɚ]
n 促進者，便利措施
同 helper 助手
衍 facilitate (v.) 促進

The facilitator skillfully used conversation skills to extend the discussion.
協助者熟練地使用對話策略來延長討論。

Generally speaking, the facilitator was appointed to arrange the project.
概括地說，這名促進者被指派來安排專案。

43 **compromise**
★★★
[`kamprə͵maɪz]
V 互讓解決（分歧），危及
n 妥協，和解，折衷
同 agreement (n.) 同意
settlement (n.) 解決
yield (v.) 屈服
concede (v.) 讓步

After hours of negotiations, they have no choice but to compromise.
在數小時的協商後，他們沒有選擇只好妥協。

point have no choice but to + V 意為「不得不……」。

Never compromise either your principles or dreams for the reality.
不要為了現實而放棄了你的原則及夢想。

point either... or... 意為「兩者之一」。

44 **collide**
★★★
[kə`laɪd]
V 碰撞，衝突，抵觸
同 conflict 衝突
clash 抵觸
differ 相異
diverge 偏離
disagree 不一致

Two cars collided together in the tunnel, which caused severe traffic congestion.
兩台車在隧道裡衝撞了，造成了嚴重的交通堵塞。

point which 代替前面的整句句子。

How will you respond when you collide with your supervisor over the matter?
當你和上司在某件事情上有所抵觸時，你會如何回應？

45 badge
★
[bædʒ]
ｎ 徽章，獎章，象徵
ｖ 授予徽章

Visitors are required to wear visitor badges when they enter the building.
訪客進入大樓時需要佩戴訪客證。

Attendees to the conference should carry badges for safety purposes.
為了安全目的，研討會出席者必須要帶識別證。

---

46 within
★
★
★
[wɪˋðɪn]
prep 在……之內

Please note that the meeting will start within five minutes.
請注意會議將在五分鐘內開始。

 延伸詞彙：conference（討論會）、seminar（研討會）、workshop（工作坊）、convention（大型會議）、luncheon（午餐會，lunch 的正式說法）、orientation（新生訓練）。

The residents complained the noise from the construction that would be finished within a couple of weeks.
居民抱怨將在兩週後完工的工地噪音。

 a couple of 意為「兩個」，a couple of days 意為「兩天」。

---

47 similar
★
★
[ˋsɪmələ]
ａ 相像的，類似的
同 identical 完全相同的
　　interchangeable 可互換的
反 dissimilar 相異的
　　different 不同的
　　unlike 不同的

Many patrons commented that the latest model was similar to the previous one.
很多老顧客評論最新的型號和之前的相似。

 latest = newest 意為「最新的」。

Surprisingly, my demanding supervisor and I have similar views on the new project.
令人意外地，我那個要求很高的上司和我在新專案上的觀點相似。

---

48 section
★
★
★
[ˋsɛkʃən]
ｎ 部分，地區，階層
同 segment 部門
　　part 部分
　　component 成分
　　division 區域
　　partition 部分

There are two sections for the interview, including group discussions and individual interviews.
面試有兩個階段，包含團體面試及個人面試。

The breakout meetings and workshop sections will be followed by the keynote speaker's speech.
分組的會議及工作坊將會在主題報告人的演講之前。

商務會議與溝通

49 reach
★
★
★
[ritʃ]

Ⓥ 抵達，達到，伸出手

同 achieve 達到
　 attain 獲得
　 gain 得到
　 accomplish 完成

You can **reach** me by calling my secretary.
你可以藉由打給我的祕書聯絡到我。

point reach 在此處表達「聯絡」，意同 contact。

After hours of negotiations, the design team finally reached an agreement and **finalized** the plan.
在數個小時的協商後，設計團隊終於達成協議並定案了計畫。

point 延伸詞彙：finalize (v.) 定案、final (n.) 決賽、finalist (n.) 參加決賽者。

---

50 main
★
★
★
[men]

ⓐ 主要的，最重要的

ⓝ 主要部分，管道

同 principal (a.) 主要的
　 leading (a.) 最重要的
　 foremost (a.) 最先的
　 major (a.) 重要的

反 subsidiary (a.) 次要的
　 minor (a.) 次要的

The marketing manager from the **main office** will hold a seminar next week.
總部的行銷經理將於下週舉辦研討會。

point main office = headquarters 意為「總部」，branch 意為「分部」。

While the main elevator is undergoing repair, people are suggested to use another one at the back of the building.
當主電梯時正在維修時，人們被建議使用另一個在大樓後方的電梯。

---

51 inconvenient
★
★
★
[ˌɪnkənˈvinjənt]

ⓐ 不方便的，打擾的，令人為難的

同 troublesome 令人煩惱的
　 bothersome 討厭的
　 problematic 造成困難的

反 convenient 方便的

It's inconvenient to bring so much redundant stuff while traveling.
旅行時帶太多累贅的東西很不方便。

The senior specialist's secretary said next Wednesday was an inconvenient day to have a sales meeting.
資深專員的祕書說下週三不便開業務會議。

---

52 illustrate
★
★
[ˈɪləstret]

Ⓥ 用圖表說明，加插圖，闡明

同 clarify 闡明

衍 illustration (n.) 圖示

Can you illustrate your idea with some concrete examples and diagrams?
你可以用具體的例子及圖表來說明你的想法嗎？

The picture book illustrated by the famous illustrator is a bestseller.
這位知名插畫家所畫的繪本是暢銷書。

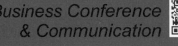
53 illustration

[ˌɪlʌsˋtreʃən]

★
★

n 說明，圖示，實例

同 picture 圖片
  drawing 圖畫
  sketch 素描
  figure 圖解
  graph 圖表

反 text 正文，本文

Ms. Tobin's colleagues were amazed by her clear illustrations.
托賓女士的同事對她清楚的圖例說明感到驚豔。

point be amazed by 意為「感到驚豔」。

The illustrations of the book have made it especially popular among children.
這本書的插畫已經讓它在小孩之中格外受歡迎。

point among 意為「在三者（以上）之中」，between 意為「在兩者之中」。

54 global

[ˋglobl]

★
★
★

a 球狀的，全世界的，總體的

同 worldwide 遍及全球的
  international 國際的

反 national 國家的
  local 當地的
  domestic 國內的

衍 globe (n.) 球，地球

Based on the revised schedule, the global financial meeting will be delayed.
根據這個修改後的行程，全球財務會議將會被延期。

point delay = put off = postpone 意為「延期」。

One of the most serious global problems is water shortage.
全球最嚴重的問題之一就是水資源短缺。

point one of Ns 意為「其中一個」，注意後面的是名詞複數。

55 finalize

[ˋfaɪnlˌaɪz]

★
★

V 完成，結束

同 complete 完成

衍 final (a.) 最後的，決定性的
  finalizing (a.) 最後的

We will finalize the schedule tomorrow.
我們明天會將行程定案。

Mr. Morales finalized the application for automatic payments.
莫拉斯先生完成了自動付款的申請。

56 develop

[dɪˋvɛləp]

★
★
★

V 發展，使成長，展開

同 grow 成長
  evolve 發展
  expand 擴展

衍 developer (n.) 開發者
  development (n.) 發展

Three years ago, the town was still under-developed but now it's a prosperous commercial area.
三年前，這個城鎮仍是一個尚未開發的地帶，但現在是一個繁榮的商業區。

point 延伸詞彙：industrial area 意為「工業區」。

The main focus of the meeting is to develop the budget for the new product line.
會議的主旨是要編制新產品線的預算。

Chapter 008

1 商務會議與溝通

57
★
★
★
enable
[ɪn`ebl̩]
V 使能夠，使可能
同 allow 允許
　 permit 許可
　 equip 使有能力
反 forbid 禁止
　 prohibit 禁止

The machine is equipped with a function that can enable users to record songs automatically.
這台機器有一個功能可以讓使用者自動錄下歌曲。
point be equipped with 意為「具備著」。

The video conference enabled overseas colleagues to discuss issues together.
視訊會議讓海外的同事能夠共同討論議題。

58
★
★
beside
[bɪ`saɪd]
prep 在⋯⋯旁邊，
　　　 與⋯⋯相比
同 alongside
　 (prep.) 在⋯⋯旁邊
　 neighboring (a.) 鄰近的
　 near (prep.) 在⋯⋯附近

The villa is beside the Gold Beach, which makes it attract many tourists around the world.
這棟別墅就在黃金海岸旁，這使它吸引許多世界各地的遊客。
point , which 代表了前面整件事情（The villa is beside the Gold Beach）。

The coordinator reminded members that the discussion was beside the point.
協調者提醒成員們討論離題了。
point beside the point 意為「離題」。

59
★
★
★
around
[ə`raʊnd]
ad 到處，周圍，大約
prep 圍繞，在附近，將近
同 throughout (prep.) 遍布
　 everywhere (adv.) 到處
　 about (prep.) 周圍
　 approximately (adv.) 大約

Mr. Pachulia will be in the office around ten. Do you want to call back later?
帕楚里亞大約十點時會進辦公室。你要不要晚點再打？
point be in the office 意為「在辦公室」。

Three architects sat around the table, discussing the blueprint.
三位設計師圍著桌子坐著，討論著藍圖。
point 此句為分詞構句，第二句原句為 and they discussed the blueprint。

60
★
★
★
agree
[ə`gri]
V 同意，贊同，相符
同 approve 贊成
反 disagree 不同意
　 differ 意見不同
衍 agreement (n.) 同意

I can't agree with you more.
我非常認同你。
point 「不能再認同你更多」也就是「非常認同你」。

The subcontractor agreed to start the construction in summer since the severe weather conditions in winter were likely to delay the construction.
承包商同意在夏天開始工程，因為冬天嚴重的天氣狀況可能會延誤工程。

61 **certain**
★
★ [ˋsɝtən]
★
a 有把握的，可靠的
pron 某些
同 definite 明確的
　confirmed 確定的
反 doubtful 懷疑的
　unreliable 不可靠的

Due to some technical problems, we are not certain when the meeting will start.
因為一些技術上的問題，我們還不確定何時會議會開始。

A qualified teacher should make certain that every student understands the contents.
一個合格的教師應該要確保每個學生都了解內容。

62 **agreement**
★
★ [əˋgrimənt]
★
n 協定，協議，一致
同 consensus 一致
　harmony 調和
　accordance 一致
　unity 一致性
反 disagreement 意見不合

The agreement was signed by both parties.
雙方都簽了合約。
point party (n.) 黨派；派對。

But for your help, I could not have reached an agreement with my client.
要不是有你的幫忙，我可能能無法與我的客戶達成協議。
point reach an agreement 意為「達成協議」。

63 **ago**
★
★ [əˋgo]
ad 在……以前
同 before 在……以前
　earlier 早先的
　formerly 以前
　previously 以前
反 after 在……之後

Two years ago, the prosperous business area was just a small town.
兩年前，這繁榮的商業區只是一個小鎮。
point area, district, community, neighborhood 皆可指「區域；鄰近地區」。

The manager rushed into the boardroom where the meeting just started five minutes ago.
經理衝去董事會會議室，而在那舉行的會議才剛開始五分鐘。
point boardroom, meeting room, conference room 皆可指「會議室」。

64 **widespread**
★
★ [ˋwaɪdˏsprɛd]
a 普遍的，廣泛的
同 general 普遍的
　extensive 廣大的
　common 普通的
反 local 當地的
　limited 有限的

After hours of negotiations, the proposal finally had gained widespread acceptance.
在好幾個小時的協商後，這個計畫終於得到廣泛的贊同。

The new policy regarding social welfare has attracted widespread criticism from different industries.
有關社會福利的新政策已經引來了不同行業廣泛的批評。
point regarding = about 意為「關於」。

65 **tense**
★
[tɛns]
a 拉緊的，緊張的
同 tight 緊的
rigid 堅硬的
反 loose 鬆的
relaxed 鬆懈的

The inexperienced speaker looked tense before the presentation.
這位沒經驗的講者在簡報前看起來很緊張。

The athlete's back was tense, so he took a bath to relax his tense muscles.
這名運動員的背非常緊繃，因此他洗個澡以放鬆緊繃的肌肉。

---

66 **tension**
★
[`tɛnʃən]
n 緊張狀況，繃緊
同 tightness (n.) 堅固
tenseness (n.) 緊張
rigidity (n.) 堅硬
反 looseness (n.) 鬆弛

The clerical worker takes yoga class once a week to remove her tension from her body.
這名文書工作者每週上一次瑜珈課以釋放身體的緊繃。

point twice a week 意為「一週兩次」，three times a week 意為「一週三次」。

Anyone who walked into the meeting room could feel the tension in this room.
任何走進這間會議室的人都能感受到房間裡的緊張氣氛。

---

67 **switch**
★
★
★
[swɪtʃ]
n 開關
v 打開（關掉）開關，轉換，改變
同 handle (v.) 操作
control (v.) 調節
change (v.) 改變
replace (v.) 代替
swap (v.) 交換

The assistant could not switch on the flat screen TV; therefore, he asked the technician to fix it.
助理沒辦法打開平板電視，所以他請技師來修。

Please switch your mobile phone to vibrate mode before you enter the meeting room.
在你進入會議室之前，請把你的手機轉成震動模式。

point vibrate mode 意為「震動模式」，silent mode 意為「靜音模式」。

---

68 **slot**
★
★
[slɑt]
n 狹長孔，硬幣投幣口，位置，時段
同 hole 洞
opening 空缺
spot 場所
time 時間
period 期間

Just put a coin in the slot, press the button, and then get the train tickets.
只要把錢投入投幣口，按按鈕，就可以拿到車票。

Friday afternoon is the only time slot available for staff meeting.
週五下午是唯一可以開員工會議的時間。

point staff meeting 意為「員工會議」。

69 vacancy
★
★
★
['vekənsɪ]

n 空位，空缺，空白

同 opening 空缺
emptiness 空白
space 空間
position 位置

There will be a job vacancy in this firm.
這間公司之後會有一個職缺。

point firm, company, business, concern, corporate 皆可指「公司」。

The board had a meeting to decide the best person to fill this vacancy.
委員會開會決定填補這職位的最佳人選。

point fill the vacancy 意為「填補空缺」。

70 remarkable
★
★
[rɪ'mɑrkəbl]

a 非凡的，卓越的

同 extraordinary 特別的
exceptional 例外的
outstanding 傑出的
distinctive 有特色的
distinguished 卓越的
prominent 突出的
反 ordinary 普通的

The critic is known for his remarkable power of observation.
評論家以他驚人的觀察能力而聞名。

point 延伸詞彙：impressive 給人深刻印象的、amazing 驚人的、marvelous 非凡的、wonderful 非同尋常的、notable 顯著的、incredible 驚人的、stunning 令人震驚的。

The newcomer has made remarkable progress in negotiating with clients.
新人在與客戶協商上有了顯著的進步。

point make progress in 意為「在……方面取得進步」。

71 relief
★
★
[rɪ'lif]

n 緩和，減輕，慰藉

同 reassurance 寬慰
comfort 舒適
calmness 平靜
relaxation 放鬆
ease 減輕

It was such a relief to find my passport and boarding pass.
找到我的護照和登機證，真是如釋重負。

point It is / was such a relief to + V 意為「……真是如釋重負」。

After the presentation, the sales felt a sense of relief.
在簡報過後，那名業務感到輕鬆無比。

point a sense of + N 意為「……感」。

72 precise
★
★
[prɪ'saɪs]

a 精確的，確切的，清晰的

同 exact 確切的
accurate 準確的
反 imprecise 不精確的
inaccurate 不正確的

Many officials were persuaded by the analyst's precise analysis.
很多官員都被這位分析師的精確分析給說服了。

point were persuaded 為過去被動式，意為「被說服」。

To be precise, there were only ten people attending the meeting due to schedule conflicts.
更精確一點地說，因為行程衝突導致只有十個人參加會議。

point To be precise 意為「精確地說，詳細地說」。

Chapter 010

1 商務會議與溝通

73 plain
★
[plen]
a 簡樸的，清楚的，平易的
同 comprehensible 可理解的
　　unambiguous 明白的
　　clear 清楚的
　　simple 簡易的
反 unclear 不清楚的
　　obscure 難解的

To present in that formal conference, she wore a plain black dress.
為了在那個正式的研討會中做簡報，她穿了一件樸素的黑色連身裙。

Plain food is the only thing that the patient can eat right now.
病人現在能吃的只有清淡簡單的食物。

point mild food 也可表示「清淡的食物」。

---

74 overview
★
★
★
[`ovɚ,vju]
n 概觀，綜述
同 outline 概述
　　summary 總結

Before I start today's meeting, I will give everyone a brief overview.
在我開始今天的會議之前，我會給大家一個簡短的摘要。

The director gave us an overview of the marketing plans.
主任為我們介紹了銷售計畫的概要。

---

75 outline
★
★
[`aut,lain]
n 外形，輪廓，素描
v 畫出輪廓，概述
同 figure (n.) 外形
　　shape (n.) 形狀
　　contour (n.) 輪廓

Please take a look at the outline of the presentation.
請看一下簡報的大綱。

point take a look at 意為「看一下」。

The CEO read the meeting minutes to know a broad outline of the discussion.
執行長看了會議記錄以得知討論的大致內容。

---

76 objection
★
[əb`dʒɛkʃən]
n 反對，異議，缺點
同 opposition 反對
　　argument 爭執
　　disapproval 不贊成
　　dissent 異議
　　disagreement 意見不合
反 approval 贊成
　　acceptance 接受

He has a strong objection to the proposal.
他強烈反對那個提案。

point have a strong objection to 意為「對……強烈反對」。

The editor indicated the chief objection to the article.
編輯指出這篇文章的主要缺點。

Question

以下題目完全擬真新制多益 Part 5，請選出最符合句意的選項。

1. The team leader ------- the work to his subordinates before he took leave.

   (A) had distributed
   (B) distributed
   (C) distributing
   (D) to distribute

2. I signed up for the conference at the ------- desk.

   (A) generation   (B) reception   (C) illustration   (D) agreement

3. The conference room that ------- computers and Internet access should be booked in advance.

   (A) were equipped with
   (B) was equipped with
   (C) equips
   (D) is equipped with

4. The ------- will have discussions about the emergent issue that happened last week.

   (A) permit   (B) figure   (C) panel   (D) badge

5. Having a good ------- record is crucial since it somehow reflects your attitude to work.

   (A) overview   (B) reach   (C) attendance   (D) develop

6. The online banking service brings convenience to those who cannot go to banks ------- the opening hours.

   (A) during   (B) when   (C) even   (D) if

>> 正確答案與解析請翻至下一頁查看

Answer

正確答案與解析

1. 組長在請假前就已經分配好工作給他的下屬。
   (A) 在 took leave（過去式）前就做完這件事，故用 had distributed（過去完成式）

   正確答案 (A)

2. 我在接待處報名了這場討論會。
   (A) 世代　　　　　(B) 接待　　　　　(C) 插圖　　　　　(D) 協議

   正確答案 (B)

3. 有電腦即可上網的那間會議室必須要事先預約。
   (D) 現在式（事實陳述）+ 被動（被裝備著）+ 單數（room）

   正確答案 (D)

4. 專家小組將會討論上週發生的緊急議題。
   (A) 許可證　　　　(B) 數字　　　　(C) 專家小組　　(D) 識別證

   正確答案 (C)

5. 有好的出缺席紀錄是重要的，因為這多少會反映出你對工作的態度。
   (A) 概要　　　　　(B) 到達　　　　(C) 出席　　　　(D) 發展

   正確答案 (C)

6. 網路銀行服務帶給那些沒辦法在銀行營業時間辦理業務的人方便。
   (A) 在……期間 (prep.) + N / Ving　　(B) 當 (conj.) + S + V
   (C) 甚至　　　　　　　　　　　　　(D) 如果

   正確答案 (A)

Chapter 2
行政文書作業

以下多益必考單字，你認識哪些？

☐ storage (p.032)	☐ document (p.039)	☐ diligent (p.048)
☐ senior (p.031)	☐ throughout (p.040)	☐ stable (p.041)
☐ involve (p.045)	☐ carton (p.037)	☐ immediate (p.046)
☐ inquire (p.030)	☐ amount (p.036)	☐ supply (p.031)
☐ response (p.033)	☐ internal (p.045)	☐ principle (p.043)
☐ inform (p.031)	☐ receive (p.042)	☐ unfortunately (p.038)

2 行政文書作業

01 inquire

★★★

[ɪn`kwaɪr]

V 訊問，查問，調查

同 ask 詢問
question 探問

反 answer 回答
reply 回覆
respond 回應

I am writing to inquire about the publication date.
我寫信來詢問你出版日期。

The police inquired into the background of the businessperson who just immigrated to Canada.
警方調查剛移民去加拿大的那位商人的背景。

point inquire into 意為「調查」。

02 inquiry

★★★

[ɪn`kwaɪrɪ]

n 詢問，打聽，質詢

同 investigation 調查
query 質問
interrogation 訊問

The sales responded to his customer's inquiry by email immediately.
這名業務立即以電子郵件來回覆顧客的問題。

The reporter kept making inquiry about the politician's schedule.
這名記者一直在打聽這個政治人物的行程。

03 informative

★★

[ɪn`fɔrmətɪv]

a 提供資訊的，見聞廣博的

同 instructive 增進知識的
instructional 教學的
illuminating 啟發的
enlightening 啟蒙的
educational 教育的

Undeniably, both his presentation and written report are informative.
不可否認地，他的簡報和書面報告都非常具有知識性。

point both... and（兩者皆是）／ either...or（兩者其一）／ neither... nor（兩者皆非）。

The questionnaire showed that most audiences were satisfied with the informative speech delivered by Dr. Morgan.
問卷顯示大部分的觀眾都很滿意摩根博士的演講。

point be satisfied with 意為「滿意」。

04 official

★★★

[ə`fɪʃəl]

a 官員的，官方的，正式的
n 官員，公務員

同 formal (a.) 正式的
authorized (a.) 公認的

反 unofficial (a.) 非正式的
unauthorized
(a.) 未被授權的

I only buy products from official websites so that I can make sure the quality of them.
我只在官網買東西，這樣我才能確保產品的品質。

point so that 意為「如此一來」。

Please submit the official documents to the immigration department.
請呈交官方文件到入境事務處。

point submit to 意為「提交」。

05 **inform**

★
★
★

[ɪn`fɔrm]

V 通知，告知，告密

同 tell 告訴
let someone know 告訴某人
notify 通知

衍 info (n.) 通知
information (n.) 消息
informative (a.) 提供資訊的

I'm writing to inform you of the extension of our business hours in December.
我寫信來通知你十二月營業時間的延長。

point I'm writing to 意為「我是寫信來……」，常為書信的開頭。

The senior specialist was informed that she would be transferred to the headquarters.
資深專員被告知她將會被調到總部。

point transfer to 意為「調到；轉學；轉讓財產」。

06 **senior**

★
★
★

[`sinjɚ]

a 年長的，地位較高的，年資較深的

同 higher-ranking 高階的
superior 較高的，上級的

反 junior 年紀較輕的
younger 年輕的

The senior specialist passed out the handouts for the workshop.
資深專員發下工作坊的講義。

point pass out 意為「發下」。

The senior politician demanded police protection.
這位高層政界人士需要警方的保護。

07 **supply**

★
★
★

[sə`plaɪ]

V 供給，供應，補充

n 供給，供應量，庫存

同 give (v.) 給予
provide (v.) 提供
furnish (v.) 提供
stock (n.) 庫存品

We order our office supplies from that company.
我們向那間公司訂辦公室用品。

You can ask Jane from the supply room.
你可以問儲藏室的珍。

point 多益聽力測驗 Part 2 中很容易聽到這類的句子，問句常是 who 開頭。

08 **supplier**

★
★
★

[sə`plaɪɚ]

n 供應商，供應者

同 provider (n.) 供應者

We are looking for a reliable office supplier to purchase office supplies.
我們正在尋找可信賴的供應商以購買辦公室用品。

point be looking for 意為「尋找」。

The supplier you contacted last week just sent us the latest pamphlets.
你上週聯絡的供應商才剛寄給我們最新的小冊子。

point contact 後面不能接 with。

Chapter 012

2 行政文書作業

09 ★ directory
[dəˈrɛktərɪ]

- **n** 姓名住址簿
- **同** index 索引
  - list 名冊
  - listing 列表
  - catalogue 目錄
- **衍** director 主管

We <u>used to</u> find stores' numbers in the telephone directory but now we tend to use the internet to find them.
我們過去在電話簿裡找店家電話，但現在我們傾向於用網路找。

(point) used to 意為「過去習慣」。

The assistant looked up the address and the <u>contact</u> number in the directory.
助理在電話簿中查地址跟聯絡電話。

(point) 易混淆字：contact (n.) 聯絡方式 (v.) 聯絡／contract (n.) 合約。

10 ★★ storage
[ˈstorɪdʒ]

- **n** 貯藏，貯藏庫，倉庫
- **同** storage 貯藏
  - warehouse 倉庫
  - storehouse 倉庫

The assistant went to the <u>supply room</u> to check the storage of the office supplies.
助理去供應室確認辦公室用品的存貨量。

(point) supply room 意為「供應室」。

The landlord customized a closet to give the apartment more storage space.
房東訂製了一個衣櫥，讓這間公寓有更多的儲藏空間。

11 ★★★ attach
[əˈtætʃ]

- **v** 裝上，貼上，依附，附屬
- **同** add 添加
  - connect 連接
  - affix 貼上
  - append 附加
- **反** detach 分開

I <u>had</u> my assistant attach a stamp to the envelope.
我請我的助理將郵票貼在信封上。

(point) have, let, make 為使役動詞，後面須加原形動詞。

I attached a copy of your bank statement.
茲附上您的銀行對帳單一份。

12 ★★★ attachment
[əˈtætʃmənt]

- **n** 連接，附件，愛慕
- **同** connection 連接
  - love 愛
  - affection 情愛
- **衍** attach (v.) 依附

The attachments are my resume and application form.
附檔是我的履歷及申請表。

(point) 「附檔」很容易在多益測驗的書信題目中提到。

This attachment allows you to listen to music while <u>charging</u> your mobile phone.
這個附加裝置讓你能夠邊聽音樂邊充電。

(point) charge (v.) 充電；收費 (n.) 收費。

13 **response**

★
★ [rɪˋspɑns]
★
🄝 回答，反應

🔄 answer 回答
reply 回答
acknowledgement
確認收到信的通知

🔄 question 質問

🔄 responsive (a.) 反應積極的
respond (v.) 回應

I am writing in response to the complaint letter you sent to the customer service department.
我寫信是要回應你寄給客服部的抱怨信。

point in response to 意為「回應」。

The researcher used the hidden cameras to record the participants' response when they saw different television images.
研究者使用隱藏相機來錄下受試者看到不同電視影像的反應。

point 延伸詞彙：security camera = surveillance camera，意為「監視器」。

---

14 **archive**

★ [ˋɑrkaɪv]

🄝 檔案館，文件，記錄
🅅 存檔，歸檔

🔄 file 文件夾
document 文件
documentation 文件

Files are stored in the archive room.
檔案被保存在檔案室。

This updated online database only allows administrator to archive and retrieve confidential files.
只有管理員能用這個更新的線上資料庫來儲存和檢索機密檔案。

point 此句的 archive 當作動詞使用。

---

15 **assignment**

★
★ [əˋsaɪnmənt]

🄝 任務，功課，分配

🔄 task 任務
mission 任務

🔄 assign 分配

Please submit your assignment by this Friday.
請在週五前交出作業。

point by 意為「在……之前」。

Who might be the best candidate for this assignment?
誰可能是這個任務的最佳人選呢？

---

16 **enclose**

★ [ɪnˋkloz]

🅅 圍住，圈起，封入

🔄 include 包括
put in 加進
contain 包含

🔄 exclude 不包括

It would be great if you can enclose your latest catalog with your letter.
如果你能隨信附上你們最新的目錄會很棒。

point latest = newest，意為「最新的」。

The candidate enclosed her resume and certificates with her application form.
求職者在申請表中附上履歷及證照。

point 多益閱讀測驗的求職廣告題目，有時會問「附檔為何？」常見答案為 resume（履歷）及 application form（申請表）。

033

行政文書作業

17 enclosure

★

[ɪnˈkloʒɚ]

n 圍住，封入，信函附件

同 attachment 附件

Please include your application form in the enclosure.
請在附件中附上你的申請表。

The old building was confined by a white enclosure.
這幢老建築用白色籬笆給圍了起來。

---

18 fill

★
★
★

[fɪl]

V 裝滿，充滿，任職

n 填滿的量，充足

同 occupy (v.) 占領
hold (v.) 握著
take up (ph.) 占據

反 empty (v.) 清空

Just fill out the application form before you leave the office.
離開辦公室之前，把申請表填好。

(point) form (n.) 表格；形式 (v.) 形成。

As soon as we receive your payment, we will fill out the order.
我們一收到你的款項，就會填寫訂單。

(point) as soon as = once 意為「一旦」，為連接詞。

---

19 folder

★
★
★

[ˈfoldɚ]

n 文件夾

同 file 文件夾
binder 紙夾
ring binder 資料夾
portfolio 文件夾
document case 公文包

衍 fold (v.) 摺疊

The folders are arranged according to the categories.
檔案夾是按照分類歸類。

(point) according to 意為「根據」。

The software automatically saves all the files in this folder.
這個軟體能自動複製檔案夾中的所有檔案。

---

20 file

★
★
★

[faɪl]

n 文件夾，檔案

V 歸檔，提出申請

同 folder (n.) 文件夾
portfolio (n.) 文件夾
binder (n.) 紙夾

All the files have been arranged in alphabetical order.
所有的檔案都已經按照字母順序排好了。

(point) in alphabetical order 意為「按照字母順序」。

The documents will be stored in the file cabinets.
這些文件將會被放在檔案櫃。

Administrative Paperwork

CH 2

行政文書作業

21 form
★
★
★
[fɔrm]
n 表格，形式，形狀
v 形成
同 shape (n.) 形狀
　formation (n.) 形成

Do you want the original form or the duplicate?
你要正本還是副本？

Please fill out the form and send it back.
請填寫表格再寄回來。

---

22 minute
★
★
★
[`mɪnɪt]
n 分鐘，片刻
同 moment (n.) 瞬間
衍 minutes (n.) 會議記錄

The banquet will start in 10 minutes.
宴席將會在十分鐘內開始。

Who will be in charge of taking meeting minutes this time?
這次誰負責做會議紀錄呢？

point take meeting minutes 意為「做會議紀錄」。

---

23 capable
★
★
[`kepəbl]
a 有能力的，有才華的
同 accomplished 熟練的
　adept 熟練的
反 incompetent 無能力的
　inept 笨拙的
衍 capability (n.) 能力

A secretary is expected to be capable of multitasking.
一個祕書被期待要能夠做很多事情。

point multitask 意為「多工化；多任務化」。

His boss thinks he is a very capable administrator.
他的老闆認為他是個十分能幹的行政人員。

point 相關詞彙：competent 有能力的、experienced 有經驗的、skilled 熟練的、qualified 勝任的、proficient 熟練的。

---

24 advocate
★
★
[`ædvəˌket]
v 擁護，提倡，主張
[`ædvəkɪt]
n 提倡者，擁護者
同 defend (v.) 答辯
　support (v.) 擁護
反 oppose (v.) 反對
　object to (ph.) 反對

The concept of adopting dogs instead of buying them is widely advocated in recent years.
領養狗代替購買狗，這個觀念近年來被廣泛推廣。

point in recent years = recently= lately，皆可表達「近年來；最近」。

The company advocates that employees can use used paper when they make copies for internal use.
公司倡導員工可以用印過的單面紙來印公司內部使用的文件。

point 「二手的」相關詞彙：used car 二手車／ second-hand store = thrift store 二手店／ flea market 跳蚤市場。

035

014

25 **amount**
★
★
[ə`maʊnt]
n 總數，數量
v 達到，總計
同 quantity (n.) 數量

The amount of office supplies is insufficient.
辦公室用品的數量不夠。
point office supplies 為多益聽力和閱讀測驗皆常見的詞彙。

The total cost of accommodation amounted to 80 dollars.
住宿總額為八十美元。
point 此處的 amount 當動詞使用。

---

26 **deadline**
★
★
★
[`dɛd.laɪn]
n 截止日期，截稿時間
同 time limit 期限

The deadline for the project is this afternoon!
I have to hurry!
專案的截止日期是這個下午！我必須快一點！

I am behind the schedule, which means I probably can't meet the deadline.
我的進度落後，意思是我有可能無法趕上截止日期。
point meet the deadline 意為「符合期限」。

---

27 **apology**
★
★
[ə`pɑlədʒɪ]
n 道歉，賠罪，辯解
衍 apologize (v.) 道歉

The main idea of the email is to offer an apology for the inconvenience caused by the employee's absence.
這封信的主旨是要為員工缺席所造成的不便道歉。

The customer service department sent the customer a written apology about the defective items.
有關瑕疵產品，顧客服務部對顧客做出了書面道歉。
point defect (n.) 缺陷／ defective (a.) 有缺陷的。

---

28 **concur**
★
[kən`kɝ]
v 同意，一致，同時發生
同 agree 同意
反 disagree 不同意

In terms of movie reviews, sometimes what critics feel does not necessarily concur with audiences.
就電影評論而言，有時候影評家的感受未必與觀眾一致。
point movie / food / book critic 意為「影評家／美食評論家／書籍評論家」。

I am writing to confirm whether the board of directors concurred in the merger.
我寫信來確認董事會是否同意合併。
point merge (v.) merger (n.) 合併／ acquire (v.) acquisition (n.) 收購。

29 **interruption**

★

[ˌɪntəˈrʌpʃən]

n 中止，阻礙，干擾

同 interference (n.) 阻礙
　　 intervention (n.) 干預
　　 disturbance (n.) 擾亂

衍 interrupt (v.) 打斷

Even a brief interruption will distract the office worker from his work.
即使是簡短的打斷，也會使上班族在工作上分心。

point distract sb. from + N / Ving 意為「使（某人）從……分心」。

Fortunately, the administrative assistant had worked for three hours without interruption.
很幸運地，這名行政助理已經工作了三小時而沒有被打斷。

30 **carton**

★
★

[ˈkɑrtn̩]

n 紙盒，紙板箱

同 box 箱子
　　 package 包裝盒
　　 cardboard box 紙箱
　　 container 容器
　　 case 箱子

These cartons have been piled up against the wall.
這些紙箱已經沿著牆面被疊起來。

point 若出現在圖片題，時態要有進行式，圖片才會有人。

The carton is full of the company's confidential correspondence with the client.
這個紙箱充滿了公司與那名客戶的機密信件往來。

point correspondence (n.) 通信聯繫；信件。

31 **amend**

★
★
★

[əˈmɛnd]

V 修訂，改進，改善

同 alter 改變
　　 change 改變
　　 qualify 使合格
　　 rework 修訂
　　 reform 改革

The clerical worker was employed to amend texts.
文書職員被僱用來修改文字。

point 相關詞彙：modify 更改／ adjust 調節／ reword 改寫／ adapt 改寫／ revise 修訂。

Before publication, some parts of the article needed amending.
在出版前，文章有些部分需要修改。

point need amending = need to be amended 意為「需要被修改」。

32 **amendment**

★
★

[əˈmɛndmənt]

n 改正，修正（案）

同 change 改變
　　 adjustment 調整
　　 enhancement 改善

The chief editor indicated that the book needed amendment.
總編輯指出這本書需要修改。

point 相關詞彙：revision 修訂／ alteration 改變／ modification 修改／ correction 訂正／ rewriting 重寫／ adaptation 改寫。

I am writing to inform you that the amendment will be effective next quarter.
我寫信來通知你修正案將於下一季生效。

point 新制多益閱讀測驗中，常考「新政策何時生效」。

行政文書作業

---

33 unfortunately

★
★
★

[ʌnˈfɔrtʃənɪtlɪ]

ad 不幸地，遺憾地

同 unluckily 不幸地
sadly 可惜

反 luckily 幸運地
fortunately 幸運地

Unfortunately, the construction will be delayed due to the severe weather.
很不幸地，工程將會因為惡劣的天氣所延誤。

point delay = put off = prolong，意為「延誤」。

Unfortunately, he was unable to submit the project which was due at the end of the week.
很不幸地，他沒辦法交出這週末到期的專案。

---

34 unable

★
★
★

[ʌnˈebl̩]

a 不能的，無能力的

同 inadequate 不夠格的
incompetent 無能力的
unfit 不勝任的
unqualified 不合格的

反 capable 有能力的

I am unable to go to Mrs. Wright's farewell party because I am so tied up with the financial report.
我沒辦法去萊特女士的歡送會，因為我忙於做財務報告。

point be tied up with = be busy，意為「忙碌」。

The clerk was dismissed from his job because he was unable to answer the customer's questions about the products properly.
店員因為無法妥善地回答顧客有關產品的問題而被解僱。

---

35 kickoff

★

[ˈkɪkˌɔf]

n （足球）開球，
（集會）開始

同 beginning 開始
start 開始
opening 開頭
starting point 出發點
initiation 創始

反 end 結束

The chairman made some opening remarks before the kickoff of the soccer game.
主席在足球比賽開賽前發表了一些開幕致詞。

point opening remark 意為「開幕致詞」。opening 在多益測驗中常見語意是「職缺」。

The assistant had to cancel his medical appointment because of the project kickoff meeting tomorrow.
助理必須要取消他的看診預約，因為明天的專案開始開會。

point 多益測驗中常見的取消預約的原因為「be on a business trip（出差）」。

---

36 blank

★
★

[blæŋk]

a 空白的，茫然的
n 空白處，空格

同 empty (a.) 空的

Please fill in the blank on the form.
請填寫表格的空白處。

point fill in the blank 意為「填空（題）」。

After the car accident, his memory was completely blank.
在車禍後，他的記憶一片空白。

37 **gradual**
★ [`grædʒuəl]
　a 逐漸的，逐步的，平緩的
　同 slow 慢的
　　　moderate 適度的
　反 sudden 迅速的
　　　abrupt 突然的
　衍 gradually (adv.) 逐步地
　　　graduate (v.) 畢業

The senior specialist has noticed the intern's gradual improvement in data processing.
資深專員已經注意到實習生在資料處理上的細微進步。

point 延伸詞彙：internship (n.) 實習。

The weather forecaster reported the gradual climate changes these years.
天氣預報員報導了這些年來氣候的細微變化。

point 延伸詞彙：weather forecast 意為「天氣預報」。

---

38 **document**
★
★ [`dɑkjəmənt]
★ **n** 公文，文件
　[`dɑkjəˌmɛnt]
　v 用文件證明
　同 certificate (n.) 證明書
　　　contract (n.) 合約書
　　　legal agreement
　　　(ph.) 法律協議

The assistant sent the documents out according to the date of last revision.
助理根據最後的修改日期來寄出文件。

point 相關詞彙：paper 文件，form 表格，report 報告書，record 記錄。

All the information you provided will be documented.
你提供的所有資訊都會被記錄下來。

point 多益聽力測驗 Part 3 電話留言情境會出現這樣的句子。

---

39 **documentation**
★ [ˌdɑkjəmənˋteʃən]
　n 證明文件，文件證據
　同 proof 證據
　　　certification 證明
　　　papers 文件

Please bring official documentation that can prove your identity.
請攜帶可以證明你身分的文件。

All attendees will be sent a documentation containing their personal information.
所有的出席者都會收到包含他們個人資料的憑證。

point containing 是由 that / which contains 簡化而來。

---

40 **database**
★ [`detəˌbes]
　n 資料庫
　衍 data (n.) 資料

Only managerial positions have access to the database.
只有管理職位人士有權限使用資料庫。

Those clerical workers are responsible for keeping the database up-to-date.
這些文書職員工負責更新資料庫。

point 要熟記各種職業的英文，多益測驗中很常出現。

Chapter 016

2 行政文書作業

41 confidential
★
★ [ˌkɑnfə`dɛnʃəl]
★ @ 機密的，表示信任的
同 private 祕密的
　　personal 私人的
　　secret 祕密的
反 public 公開的
衍 confident (a.) 自信的

Only the marketing manager is allowed to read the confidential document.
只有行銷經理能夠讀那份機密文件。

All confidential files should be sent by internal mail system.
所有機密文件都應該使用內部郵件系統傳送。

---

42 via
★
★ [`vaɪə]
★ **prep** 經由，透過，憑藉
衍 viable (a.) 可實行的

Employees can contact each other via internal mail system.
員工可以透過內部通信系統聯絡彼此。

point 延伸詞彙：for internal use 意為「供內部使用」。

The merchant will take the flight from London to Washington via New York.
商人將會搭乘從倫敦經過紐約到華盛頓的班機。

---

43 unacceptable
★
★ [ˌʌnək`sɛptəbl]
@ 不能接受的，不受歡迎的
同 intolerable 不能忍受的
　　unsatisfactory 不滿的
　　inappropriate 不適當的
　　unsuitable 不合適的
　　undesirable 不受歡迎的
反 acceptable 可接受的
　　satisfactory 滿意的

The proposal is not unacceptable but you have to explain the benefits that will bring to our company more specifically.
這提案不是不能被接受，但你必須要詳盡地解釋會帶給公司什麼利益。

Revealing confidential documents to other competitors is totally unacceptable under any circumstances.
無論在什麼情況下，洩露機密文件給我們的競爭者都是不能容忍的。

point under any circumstances 意為「無論在什麼情況下」。

---

44 throughout
★
★ [θru`aʊt]
prep 遍及，從頭到尾
同 everywhere (in) (adv.) 到處
　　round (prep.) 在周圍
　　through (prep. / adv.)
　　從頭到尾

Ms. Bogut had been checking her e-mail throughout Sunday morning.
波格特小姐週日上午期間一直在收信。

People throughout the country are waiting for the election results.
全國各地的人們都在等待選舉結果。

CH 2

行政文書作業

---

45 suspect
★
[sə`spɛkt]
V 察覺，懷疑，不信任
[`sʌspɛkt]
n 嫌疑犯
同 guess (v.) 猜測
suppose (v.) 料想

The security guard found the suspect by the security camera.
警衛透過監視器找到嫌疑犯。

point security camera 意為「監視器」。

The manager suspected his secretary's loyalty to work.
經理懷疑他祕書對工作的忠誠度。

point 求職廣告中常見的特質：loyalty (n.) 忠誠／ commitment (n.) 忠誠；奉獻／ dedication (n.) 專心致力。

---

46 supplementary
★
★
[ˌsʌplə`mɛntəri]
a 增補的，追加的
n 增補者，補充物
同 additional (a.) 添加的
extra (a.) 額外的
increased (a.) 增加的
further (a.) 另外的
supplement
(n.) 增補，副刊，補給品
(v.) 補充

All the supplementary materials will be uploaded to the website by the assistant.
所有補充教材都會被助理上傳到網頁上。

Enclosed please find the application form for supplementary grant.
附檔是申請追加補助金的申請表格。

point Enclosed please find + N 意為「附檔為……」，多益測驗常在書信中帶出附檔的內容。

---

47 stationery
★
★
★
[`steʃənˌɛri]
n 文具，信紙
衍 station (n.) 車站
secretary (n.) 祕書

We usually order stationery in bulk in order to get some discounts.
我們通常都大量訂購文具以獲得一些折扣。

point in bulk 意為「大量地」。

Office Supply King offers you the best quality of stationery.
辦公室供應王提供你最高品質的文具。

---

48 stable
★
★
★
[`stebl̩]
a 穩定的，牢固的，平穩的
同 firm 穩固的
steady 穩固的
反 unstable 不穩的

He prefers a stable lifestyle while his wife enjoys a more challenging life.
他較喜歡穩定的生活型態，然而他老婆享受更有挑戰性的生活。

The clerical worker longs for a peaceful and stable life.
這名文書工作者嚮往和平穩定的生活。

point long for 意為「渴望；嚮往」。

041

49 smoothly
★
[smuðlɪ]

ad 平滑地，流暢地，平穩地

同 evenly 平坦地

反 roughly 粗糙地

The assistant's clear and detailed rundown made the campaign run as smoothly as expected.
助理清楚且詳細的流程表讓這個活動執行得和預期一樣順利。

point as... as 意為「一樣」。

If all goes smoothly, the proposal of decreasing transportation costs will be submitted this Friday.
如果一切進展順利，降低交通成本的計畫書將會在這週五被提交。

---

50 sign
★
★
[saɪn]

n 記號，標誌，招牌

v 簽名

同 indication (n.) 指示
signal (n.) 信號
pointer (n.) 指示物，指標
mark (n.) 記號

Please come over to my office and sign this form.
請前來我的辦公室簽這個表格。

point 多益聽力測驗的電話留言中常有這類的簽收文件，或補交文件的用語。

You can sign up for the seminar at the reception desk.
你可以在接待處報名研習會。

point sign up 意為「報名參加」。

---

51 sequence
★
★
★
[ˈsikwəns]

n 順序，一連串

同 succession 一連串
order 順序
series 系列
chain 一連串

Files in the archive are arranged in chronological sequence.
檔案室裡的檔案以時間順序排列。

point 易混淆字：archive 意為「檔案室」，achieve 意為「到達」。

There was a sequence of meetings on the Financial Executive Officer's agenda last Friday.
上週五財務長的行程有一連串的會議。

point a sequence of 意為「一連串」。

---

52 receive
★
★
★
[rɪˈsiv]

v 收到，遭受，接待

同 collect 收集
obtain 得到

反 provide 提供
offer 提供

衍 receipt (n.) 收據

You're receiving this letter because of the overdue payment.
你因為逾期的付款而收到這封信。

point 類似字：outstanding bill 意為「未付清的帳單」。

The applicant just received the acceptance letter.
申請人才剛收到入學接受信。

CH 2

行政文書作業

53 refuse

[rɪ`fjuz]

V 拒絕，不願

同 decline 婉拒
reject 拒絕

反 accept 接受
grant 授予

衍 refusal (n.) 拒絕

The assistant was frustrated because his supervisor refused his proposal.
助理因為上司拒絕他的提案而感到挫折。

point 多益中常見的文件：report (n.) 報告，document (n.) 文件，file (n.) 檔案。

She had a very tight schedule; therefore, she had no choice but to refuse their invitation.
她的行程很緊湊，所以不得不拒絕他們的邀請。

point have no choice but to + V 意為「不得不做⋯⋯」。

---

54 random

[`rændəm]

a 隨機的

同 casual 隨便的

反 systematic 有系統的
planned 有計畫的

The assistant took a file folder from the archive at random.
助理從檔案室隨機拿出一個檔案夾。

point at random 意為「隨意地」。

The reporter asked a random sample of people which candidates they preferred.
記者隨機問了一些民眾比較偏好哪個候選人。

---

55 principle

[`prɪnsəpl]

n 原則，原理，信條

同 rule 規則
ethics 道德標準

All staff should follow the principles written in the book.
所有員工都該遵守書中所記載的原則。

He might not be a reliable lawyer because he doesn't have any principles.
他可能不是一個值得信賴的律師，因為他毫無原則可言。

---

56 pile

[paɪl]

n 一堆，大量

同 lot 多量
large quantity 大數量
plenty 大量
mass 大宗

反 little 少的

She put those dirty clothes in a pile.
她把髒衣物放成一堆。

After arranging the old documents, there was a pile of paper on the assistant's desk.
在整理舊文件後，助理桌上有一堆紙。

point after 可作為介係詞（+ N / Ving）或連接詞（+ S + V）。

行政文書作業

57 **outstanding**

★
★

['aut'stændɪŋ]

- a 凸出的，顯著的，未支付的
- 同 excellent 出色的
  marvelous 非凡的
  exceptional 卓越的
- 反 mediocre 中等的

I'm writing to remind you of your outstanding bill.
我寫信來提醒你未付清的帳單。

(point) 此句的 outstanding = overdue，意為「逾期的」。

She is definitely the most outstanding one among the 20 candidates.
她絕對是這二十位求職者中最出眾的一位。

58 **margin**

★

['mardʒɪn]

- n 邊緣，頁邊空白
- 同 edge 邊緣
  border 邊緣
- 反 center 中心

The sales took notes in the margin.
業務在邊緣的空白處抄筆記。

(point) take notes 意為「抄筆記」。

The couple live in the margin of the wood.
這對老夫妻住在樹林的邊緣。

59 **layout**

★
★
★

['le,aut]

- n 安排，布局，版面編排
- 同 arrangement 安排
  design 設計
  organization 編制

I like the layout of the building.
我喜歡這座房子的布局。

The assistant redesigned the layout of the application form.
助理重新設計申請表的格式。

(point) redesign = re-（再次）+ design（設計），意為「再次設計」。

60 **lack**

★
★
★

[læk]

- n 欠缺，不足
- v 缺乏，沒有
- 同 insufficiency (n.) 不充分
  deficiency (n.) 不足
  unavailability (n.) 不可用
- 反 abundance (n.) 豐富
  sufficiency (n.) 充足
- 衍 lacking (a.) 缺乏的

The clerical worker lacks patience.
這名文書職員缺乏耐性。

(point) 相關詞彙：absence (n.) 缺乏，shortage (n.) 短缺，shortfall (n.) 不足。

He lacks a sense of humor.
他沒有幽默感。

(point) a sense of humor 意為「幽默感」。

61 **involve**
★
★

Ⅴ 包含，使參與

同 include 包含
  contain 包含

反 exclude 排除在外

衍 involvement (n.) 參與

The interviewer said to the interviewee that the position would involve replying to clients' emails **in** English.
面試官和求職者說這個職位會需要以英文回覆顧客的信件。

(point) in + 語言，意為「以……（語言）」。

The team leader tried to involve every team member in the process of problem-solving.
組長試著讓所有人都參與問題解決的過程。

62 **internal**
★
★
★

ａ 內部的，國內的

同 inner 內部的
  interior 內部的

反 external 外部的

The files are for internal use only.
這些檔案只給內部使用。

The company conducted the internal investigation.
公司執行了內部調查。

63 **intelligence**
★
★

ｎ 智力，情報

同 brilliance 才華
  ability 才能
  giftedness 資優
  talent 天分

All the students must take the intelligence test when they enter the school.
所有的學生入學時都必須做智力測驗。

(point) student = pupil，意為「學生」。

The secretary handled the disagreement about the fee with great intelligence.
祕書有智慧地處理了這項費用爭議。

64 **recipient**
★
★
★

ｎ 接受者，收領者

反 sender (n.) 傳送者

衍 reception (n.) 接待，接待會
  receptionist (n.) 接待員

Please write down the name of the recipient and pay the delivery fee.
請寫下收件者的名字，並付運費。

(point) write down 意為「寫下來」。

As the last year's award recipient, I am honored to announce this year's winner.
身為去年的得獎人，我很榮幸能宣布今年的贏家。

(point) as 意為「身為」。

行政文書作業

65 **incoming**

★
★

['ɪnˌkʌmɪŋ]

a 進來的，接踵而來的
n 進來，收入
同 arriving (a.) 到來的
    approaching (a.) 接近的
反 outgoing (a.) 外出的

For the incoming president, financial problems will be the first priority.
對於新任總統而言，金融問題將是第一優先要處理的事。

(point) priority (n.) 優先考慮的事／prioritize (v.) 把事情按優先順序排好。

My assistant is responsible for the incoming orders.
我的助理負責處理新進的訂單。

(point) be responsible for = be in charge of + N / Ving，意為「負責」。

66 **immediate**

★
★
★

[ɪˈmidɪɪt]

a 立即的，即刻的，目前的
同 prompt 迅速的
    swift 快速的
    speedy 迅速的
    rapid 迅速的
    instant 立即的
反 gradual 逐漸的

I'm writing to thank you for your immediate assistance.
我寫信是來感謝您的即時援助。

(point) I'm writing to... + V，後面常加上「寫信的目的」。若出現在多益測驗閱讀題中，後面常是重點。

The secretary can make immediate responses according to different situations.
那名祕書能夠依照不同情況做出立即的反應。

(point) according to 意為「根據」。

67 **engage**

★
★

[ɪnˈgedʒ]

v 佔用（時間精力等），使忙於，訂婚
同 employ 僱用
    hire 僱用
    take into employment 僱用
反 dismiss 遣散

The couple just got engaged last Sunday.
那對新人上週日才剛訂婚。

The assistant was engaged in replying to customers' questions.
那名助理正忙著回覆客人問題。

(point) be engaged in 意為「從事於；忙於；埋頭致力於」。

68 **engagement**

★

[ɪnˈgedʒmənt]

n 訂婚，婚約，諾言
同 appointment 約會
    arrangement 安排
    commitment 承諾
    meeting 會面

I reschedule the engagement via email.
我透過電子郵件來更改邀約。

(point) via (prep.) 經由；透過。

I can't make it tonight because I have a previous engagement.
我今晚不能去，因為我已經有約了。

(point) previous engagement = prior engagement 意為「先前已經有約」。

69 even

★
★
★

[`ivən]

a 平坦的，一致的，相等的
ad 甚至，連
同 equal (a.) 相等的
   the same (ph.) 一樣的
   to the same degree
   (ph.) 一樣的
反 unequal (a.) 不相等的

Even experienced writers have experienced writer's block before.
即使是有經驗的作家都曾經歷過寫不出來的時候。

point writer's block 意為「作者心理阻滯；寫不出東西」。

Even if the chance was considerably challenging, the assistant was still determined to finish it.
即使這個冒險相當具有挑戰性，助理仍堅決要完成它。

point even if 意為「即使」。

---

70 habit

★
★
★

[`hæbɪt]

n 習慣，習性
同 inclination 趨向
   manner 方式
衍 habitual (a.) 習慣的

It takes time to cultivate a good habit.
養成一個好習慣需要花很多時間。

point It takes time to + V 意為「這需要時間做……」。

It's the assistant's habit to check spellings before sending emails.
寄信前檢查拼字是這名助理的習慣。

---

71 forward

★
★
★

[`fɔrwɚd]

a 前面的，早熟的
ad 向前，今後
v 轉交，發送
同 ahead (ad.) 事前
   forwards (ad.) 今後
   onwards (ad.) 向前
   further (ad.) 更遠地
反 backward (ad.) 向後

The secretary will forward your email to the manager as soon as she receives it.
一旦祕書收到信，她就會把你的信轉寄給經理。

point forward... to 意為「轉寄給」。

The apprentice was told to look forward.
這名學徒被告知要放眼未來。

---

72 format

★

[`fɔrmæt]

n 版式，形式，安排
v （電腦）格式化
同 design (n.) 設計
   arrangement (n.) 安排
   composition (n.) 構成

The format has been used for a long time because it is easy to follow.
這個格式已經被用了很久，因為很容易上手。

point has been used 為現在完成被動式，意為「已經被使用」。

The document should be saved in the right format.
檔案應該要存成正確的格式。

2 行政文書作業

---

73 elimination
★
[ɪˌlɪmə`neʃən]
🅝 排除，根除，淘汰
🔄 removal 移除
　　eradication 根除
　　disposal 處理
🔤 eliminate (v.) 排除

The administrator finally entered the right password by a process of elimination.
行政人員最終用排除法輸入了正確的密碼。

The potential player's elimination from the competition surprised many supporters.
那位有潛力的選手從比賽中被淘汰，震驚了很多支持者。

(point) supporter 的相反詞為 opponent，意為「反對者」。

---

74 duplicate
★
[`djupləkɪt]
🅐 完全一樣的，副本的
🅝 複製品，副本
[`djuplə͵ket]
🆅 複製，影印
🔄 copy (n.) 副本
　　carbon copy (ph.) 副本
　　carbon (n.) 複寫本
　　photocopy (n.) 影印件
🔁 original (n.) 原版

Can you duplicate the document for me?
你可以幫我複印這文件嗎？

I lost the original form, so they sent me a duplicate.
我把表格的原件弄丟了，所以他們又發給了我一份副本。

(point) 易混淆字：form (n.) 表格；形式 (v.) 形成／from (prep.) 來自。

---

75 dismiss
★
[dɪs`mɪs]
🆅 使離開，解散，開除
🔄 send away 趕走
　　let go 解僱
　　release 釋放
　　free 解放
🔁 form 形成
　　assemble 集合

He was dismissed because he sent the confidential documents to other companies.
他因為把機密文件寄給其他公司而被解僱。

After considering the budget, the director dismissed all thoughts of increasing employee welfare.
在考量預算後，主任屏除一切增加員工福利的想法。

(point) 相關字彙：social welfare 意為「社會福利」。

---

76 diligent
★
[`dɪlədʒnt]
🅐 勤勉的，費盡心血的
🔄 industrious 勤勉的
　　hard-working 努力工作的
🔁 lazy 懶惰的

The secretary was diligent in preparing the meeting materials.
祕書非常認真地準備會議資料。

The diligent student received a scholarship to study abroad.
那位勤奮的學生得到獎學金可以出國。

Test 1

一、請寫出下列單字的中文意思。

① capable _____　　⑥ confidential _____

② informative _____　　⑦ advocate _____

③ supply _____　　⑧ dismiss _____

④ engage _____　　⑨ assignment _____

⑤ inquiry _____　　⑩ random _____

二、請寫出符合下列句意的單字。

① The security guard found the _____ by the security camera.
警衛透過監視器找到嫌疑犯。

② Please include your application form in the _____.
請在附件中附上你的申請表。

③ The secretary can make _____ responses according to different situations.
那名祕書能夠依照不同情況做出立即的反應。

④ The company conducted the _____ investigation.
公司執行了內部調查。

解答

1. ① 能勝任的，有能力的　② 增長見聞的，提供資訊的　③ 供給，補充　④ 訂婚，使忙於
⑤ 質詢，調查，問題　⑥ 機密的，表示信任的　⑦ 擁護，擁護者　⑧ 解散，開除
⑨ 任務，分配，功課　⑩ 隨機的
2. ① suspect　② enclosure　③ immediate　④ internal

Test 2

一、請選擇符合下列文意的單字。

Ⓐ habit   Ⓑ smoothly   Ⓒ supplementary
Ⓓ principle   Ⓔ outstanding   Ⓕ duplicate

① If all goes _____, the proposal of decreasing transportation costs will be submitted this Friday.

② I lost the original form, so they sent me a _____.

③ He might not be a reliable lawyer because he doesn't have any _____.

④ She is definitely the most _____ one among the 20 candidates.

⑤ It's the assistant's _____ to check spellings before sending emails.

二、請寫出下列片語的中文意思。

① meet the deadline _____   ⑤ according to _____

② long for _____   ⑥ be tied up with _____

③ in bulk _____   ⑦ inquire into _____

④ pass out _____   ⑧ put off _____

解答

1. ①B ②F ③D ④E ⑤A
2. ① 符合期限 ② 渴望，嚮往 ③ 大量地 ④ 發下 ⑤ 根據 ⑥ 忙碌於 ⑦ 調查 ⑧ 延誤

Chapter 3
調查研究

以下多益必考單字，你認識哪些？

- [ ] distinguish (p.057)
- [ ] analyze (p.056)
- [ ] research (p.053)
- [ ] feedback (p.056)
- [ ] variable (p.059)
- [ ] examine (p.060)
- [ ] suggestion (p.052)
- [ ] interpret (p.063)
- [ ] secure (p.069)
- [ ] approach (p.067)
- [ ] graph (p.061)
- [ ] relevant (p.062)
- [ ] survey (p.053)
- [ ] alternative (p.066)
- [ ] essential (p.065)
- [ ] compose (p.066)
- [ ] source (p.068)
- [ ] evaluation (p.055)

3 調查研究

01 suggestion
★
★
★
[sə`dʒɛstʃən]

ｎ 建議，暗示，啟發

同 recommendation 推薦
advice 忠告
hint 暗示
tip 提示
clue 提示
idea 意見

衍 suggest (v.) 建議

Regarding this problem, he didn't have **any** suggestions.
有關這個問題，他沒有任何建議。

point any 後可加上可數名詞和不可數名詞。

The **panel** provided many constructive suggestions that our organization could use to modify the existing system.
專家小組提供了我們組織許多可以用來修改現行系統的有建設性的建議。

point panel (n.) 專家小組；儀表板；操縱台。

02 baseline
★
[`beslaɪn]

ｎ 基線，底線

同 reference point 參照標準

衍 base (n.) 基礎
basement (n.) 地下室

The manager indicated that the baseline should be modified.
經理指出底線應該要被修改。

The baseline of the badminton court **will be repainted** next week.
羽球場的底線下週將會被重新油漆。

point will be repainted 是未來式加被動式，表示「將會被重新油漆」。

03 indication
★
[ˌɪndə`keʃən]

ｎ 指示，徵兆，暗示

同 signal 信號
demonstration 證明
proof 證據

衍 indicate (v.) 指出

The market survey might be an **indication** of the sales result.
市場調查或許會是銷售結果的一個指示。

point 相關詞彙：sign 徵象，hint 暗示，pointer 指示物，guide 指南。

It would be great if you could give me an indication of the price.
如果你能提供一個參考價格，那就太棒了。

04 support
★
★
★
[sə`port]

ｖ 支撐，支持，擁護

ｎ 支撐物，支柱，支持者

同 aid (v.) 幫助
assist (v.) 協助

反 oppose (v.) 反對

衍 supportive (a.) 支援的

The scientist supported his arguments by citing the research.
科學家引用研究來支持他的論點。

But for the government's financial support, the project would have failed.
要不是有政府的金錢援助，這計畫會失敗。

point but for 意為「要不是有」。

05 extend

★
★

[ɪk`stɛnd]

Ⓥ 延長，延伸，擴展

同 expand 擴展
 enlarge 擴大

反 contract 縮小

衍 extension (n.) 伸展
 extensive (a.) 廣大的
 extent (n.) 範圍，程度

To extend your conversation, try to read more.
為了延長你的對話，試著多讀點東西。

point to + V 表示「為了做……」。

After a series of negotiations, the client has agreed to extend the deadline.
在一連串協商後，客戶已經同意延長期限。

06 reliable

★
★

[rɪ`laɪəbl]

ⓐ 可靠的，可信賴的

同 dependable 可靠的
 sound 忠實可信的

反 unreliable 不可靠的
 untrustworthy 不可信賴的

We are looking for a reliable senior designer to lead the whole design team.
我們在找一位可信賴的資深設計師來領導整個設計團隊。

point be looking for 意為「尋找」。

The experiment has proved that the quality of the laptop was rather reliable.
實驗證明了這台筆電的品質相當可靠。

07 research

★
★
★

[`rɪsɜtʃ]

Ⓝ 研究，調查

[rɪ`sɜtʃ]

Ⓥ 探究，調查

同 investigation (n.) 調查
 experimentation (n.) 實驗
 testing (n.) 試驗
 analysis (n.) 分析
 examination (n.) 檢查

The research was conducted to find out the pattern of consumer buying behavior.
這項研究被執行來找出消費者的購買行為。

point buy, purchase, procure, acquire 皆可表達「購買」。

The research assistant is responsible for collecting and analyzing data.
研究助理負責收集及分析資料。

point research assistant = RA，意為「研究助理」；teaching assistant = TA，意為「教學助理」。

08 survey

★
★
★

[sɚ`ve]

Ⓥ 考察，測量，檢視

[`sɚve]

Ⓝ 調查，民意調查，概論

同 research (v.) 研究
 observe (v.) 觀測
 examine (v.) 檢查

The firefighters closely surveyed the damage of the building.
消防員仔細地檢查房子受損的情況。

The survey about people's spending habits was conducted both in the downtown and suburbs.
有關人們消費習慣的研究在城市和郊區都有執行。

09 **expert**

★
★
★

['ɛkspɚt]

n 專家，能手
a 熟練的，專門的
同 specialist (n.) 專家
　　authority (n.) 權威人士
　　master (n.) 大師
　　professional (n.) 專業人士
反 inexpert (a.) 不熟練的
　　amateur (a.) 業餘的

A panel of experts was appointed to solve the problem.
一個專家小組被指定去解決問題。

The statistical expert analyzed the data she received from the online database.
統計專家分析她從線上資料庫得到的資料。

10 **advisor**

★
★

[əd'vaɪzɚ]

n 顧問
同 consultant 顧問
衍 advice (n.) 忠告
　　advisable (a.) 明智的
　　advise (v.) 勸告

I have meetings with my advisor to discuss my thesis once every two weeks.
我和我的指導老師兩週開一次會，討論我的論文。
point discuss 後面不會接 about，直接加上要討論的事物。

He is one of the financial advisers to the CEO.
他是執行長的財務顧問之一。

11 **appropriate**

★
★
★

[ə'proprɪet]

a 適當的，相稱的
v 撥出（款項），挪用
同 applicable (a.) 適當的
　　proper (a.) 適合的
　　right (a.) 正當的
反 inappropriate (a.) 不適當的
　　inapt (a.) 不適當的

The team leader tried to come up with appropriate methods to address this difficult issue.
團隊領導者試著想出適當的方法來處理這個困難的問題。
point come up with 意為「想出」。

Sales might not be an appropriate position for those who are not proficient in socializing and communicating with people.
對於那些不擅長交際及溝通的人們來說，業務可能不是一個合適的職位。

12 **strengthen**

★

['strɛŋθən]

v 加強，鞏固，變強大
同 reinforce 加強
　　make stronger 增強
反 weaken 減弱
　　decrease 減少
衍 strength (n.) 力量

The marketing manager's proposal was strengthened by the result of the market survey.
市場調查結果鞏固了行銷經理的提案。

The head of the personnel department proposed that the connection between employees and employers should be strengthened.
人事部主任提出員工和雇主間的關係應該要被強化。
point between A and B 意為「在兩者之中」，among 意為「在三者之中」。

13 evaluation
★
★ [ˌɪˌvæljuˋeʃən]
★
n 評估，評價，估算
同 assessment 估價
appraisal 評價
judgment 評價
estimation 評價
ranking 等級
衍 evaluate (v.) 評估

The reliability of the evaluation result was questioned by many researchers.
評估結果的信度被很多研究員質疑。

Regular job evaluations are necessary to improve employees' performance.
定期的工作評估對於增進員工表現是必須的。

14 acceptance
★
★ [əkˋsɛptəns]
★
n 接受，贊同，承認
同 agreement 同意
approval 贊同
acknowledgment 承認
反 rejection 拒絕
refusal 拒絕
衍 accept (v.) 接受
acceptable (a.) 可接受的

I was surprised that the plan won a wide acceptance among my colleagues.
我很驚訝這項計畫贏得我同事的廣泛歡迎。

(point) 易混淆字：colleague 同事／college 大學。

After I submitted the article for the conference, I received an acceptance letter.
在我提交文章給研討會後，我收到了接受信。

15 assemble
★
★ [əˋsɛmbl̩]
v 集合，收集，裝配
同 congregate 聚集
converge 會合
gather 收集
反 dismiss 使離開

People assembled in the lobby, waiting to check in.
人們聚在大廳，等著辦理住宿登記。

(point) 多益聽力測驗 Part 1 圖片題中，若有人們聚在一起常用 assemble 或 gather 來形容。

Research found that children who are fond of assembling model cars or model robots are more likely to develop abstract thinking.
研究顯示，喜歡組裝模型車或模型機器人的小孩比較容易發展抽象思考。

(point) be fond of + N / Ving 意為「喜歡」。

16 scale
★
★ [skel]
★
n 刻度，比率，等級，規模
同 degree 等級
proportion 比例

The digital scale is inconsistent.
這個電子秤不穩定。

Large-scale studies should be conducted to test the effectiveness of the products.
為了測試產品的有效度，大規模的研究必須被執行。

17 feedback

★ [ˈfidˌbæk]

🄝 回饋，回饋的訊息

🄟 response 回答
reaction 反應
advice 消息
comment 評論

All the feedback will be included in the questionnaires.
所有的回饋都會被包含在問卷中。

We are constantly improving our services based on our customers' feedback.
我們根據顧客的回饋來持續改進我們的服務。

---

18 analyze

★
★
★ 🄥 分析，解析

🄟 examine 檢查
study 研究
inspect 檢閱
evaluate 估價
probe 探查

The analyst analyzed and interpreted the statistical data to his supervisor so that they could adjust the sales goal.
分析師向他的主管分析並詮釋統計數據，如此一來他們才能調整銷售目標。

point so that 意為「如此一來」。

Some architects analyzed the structure of the building and tried to figure out the reasons for the collapse.
一些建築師分析了這棟建築的結構，試著找出崩塌的原因。

point figure out 意為「弄明白；了解」。

---

19 structure

★
★
★ 🄝 結構，構造，建築物
🄥 構造，組織

🄟 construction (n.) 建造
formation (n.) 形成
composition (n.) 構成
organization (n.) 組織

The researcher submitted his well-structured paper to the journal.
研究者將他結構嚴謹的研究投稿到期刊。

point submit to 意為「提交」。

The structure of the building is quite confusing, so there is a sign on the wall to show the direction to the lecture hall.
這棟建築的結構相當複雜，所以牆上有個牌子指引演講廳的方向。

---

20 statistics

★ [stəˈtɪstɪks]

🄝 統計資料，統計學
🄟 data 資料

Professor Fultz teaches Statistics in a community college.
富爾茲教授在社區大學教統計。

Statistics suggest that electronic devices distract children from their learning.
統計資料顯示，電子裝置會使小孩在學習上分心。

point distract... from 意為「使……分心」。

21 **obtain**

★
★
★

[əb`ten]

v 得到，通用

同 get 得到
procure 取得
derive 取得
earn 賺得
achieve 達到

He **is good at** obtaining information.
他很擅於取得資訊。

(point) be good at 意為「擅長」。

The scientist **obtained** the research results by conducting an experiment.
科學家透過做實驗來取得研究結果。

(point) 相關詞彙：attain 獲得，acquire 取得，gain 得到。

---

22 **distinguish**

★
★
★

[dɪ`stɪŋgwɪʃ]

v 區別，識別，辨認

同 differentiate 區別
set apart 撥出
tell apart 分辨
separate 分隔

衍 distinctive (a.) 特殊的

The experienced **appraiser** can distinguish the real jewelry from the fake one easily.
這個有經驗的鑑定師能夠輕鬆地辨別珠寶的真假。

(point) appraiser (n.) 鑑定師，appraise (v.) 鑑定。

What are the common ways to distinguish American accents from British accents?
什麼是辨別美腔及英腔的常見方法？

---

23 **adversary**

★

[`ædvɚ͵sɛrɪ]

n 敵人，對手

同 opponent 對手
foe 敵人
enemy 敵人
rival 競爭者

反 ally 同盟者

衍 adverse (a.) 逆向的

Adam always **views** Roy **as** the main adversary in his field.
亞當總是視羅伊為他的領域的主要競爭對手。

(point) view... as... 意為「視……為……」。

After conducting the marketing survey, we know that FAC Company is our **principal** adversary.
在做完市場調查後，我們發現 FAC 公司是我們主要的競爭對手。

(point) 易混淆字：principal (a.) 主要的 (n.) 資本；校長／ principle (n.) 原則。

---

24 **abstract**

★

[`æbstrækt]

a 抽象的，難懂的
n 摘要，抽象概念

[æb`strækt]

v 提取，做摘要

同 imaginary (a.) 虛構的

反 actual (a.) 實際的
concrete (a.) 實在的
real (a.) 真實的

Some people mentioned that his poems were **too** abstract **to** understand.
有些人提到他的詩太抽象，以至於不能理解。

(point) too... to... 意為「太……以致於不能」。

If you don't have sufficient time to read, you can just read the abstract of the study to know the general idea.
如果你沒有足夠的時間，你可以只讀研究摘要來知道整篇大意。

調查研究

25 barely
★

[`bɛrlɪ]

ad 僅僅，幾乎沒有，貧乏地

同 hardly 幾乎不
rarely 很少

衍 bare (a.) 光禿禿的
bareness (n.) 赤裸

He had barely enough money to pay the tuition fee.
他的錢勉強能夠支付學費。

The researcher found that those who live shorter lifes barely exercise on a regular basis.
研究者發現那些壽命較短的人較少規律運動。

point on a regular basis = regularly = frequently，表示「經常地」。

26 commodity
★
★

[kə`mɑdətɪ]

n 商品，日用品

同 item 品目
material 材料
product 產品
article 商品
object 物體

The item is a rare commodity in this inland country and thus it's particularly pricy.
這項產品在這個內陸國家來說相當稀有，因此特別貴。

The powerful system can automatically analyze the international commodity markets.
這個強大的系統可以自動分析國際商品市場。

27 surely
★

[`ʃurlɪ]

ad 確實，一定

同 certainly 無疑地
definitely 肯定地
undoubtedly 無疑地
unquestionably 毫無疑問地
undeniably 不可否認地
inevitably 必然地

One of the employee benefits is that employees can surely receive at least one-month year-end bonuses.
其中一項員工福利就是員工可以確定至少領到一個月的年終獎金。

point one-month 意為「一個月的」，當作形容詞。

Due to time constraints, we will surely adopt the panel's suggestions without further discussion.
因為時間限制，我們無疑地會直接採用專家小組的建議，而不用進一步的討論。

point 易混淆詞彙：adopt (v.) 採納／ adept (a.) 擅長的／ adjust (v.) 調整。

28 appraise
★
★

[ə`prez]

V 估計，估價

同 assess 估定價值
evaluate 估價
estimate 估計

The appraiser appraised the authenticity of the jewelry.
鑑定師鑑定珠寶的真偽。

According to the survey results, our service is highly appraised by our customers.
根據調查結果，顧客對我們的服務有很高的評價。

CH 3

調查研究

29 behavioral
★
[brˋhevjərəl]
a 行為的
衍 behave (v.) 表現
behavior (n.) 行為

He analyzed children's language structures by behavioral approach.
他以行為主義來分析孩子的語言結構。

The researcher summarized the behavioral responses from the participants.
研究人員總結出受試者的行為反應。

point 相關詞彙：participate (v.) 參加，participant (n.) 參加者，受試者。

---

30 approximate
★
★
[əˋprɑksəmɪt]
a 近似的，大約的
V 接近
同 close (a.) 接近的
反 exact (a.) 確切的
precise (a.) 精確的

The approximate travel expenditure was 500 dollars.
旅遊支出大約為五百美金。

The participant indicated that the flavor of the new soda approximated to its opponent's product.
受試者指出新的蘇打飲料味道和其競爭者的產品一樣。

---

31 variable
★
★
[ˋvɛrɪəbḷ]
a 易變的，可變的
n 可變物，可變因素
同 changeable (a.) 易變的
shifting (a.) 轉變的
fluctuating (a.) 變動的
irregular (a.) 不穩定的
反 constant (a.) 不變的
uniform (a.) 始終如一的

The research assistant indicated that those variables would directly influence the results.
研究助理指出這些變因會直接影響結果。

You had better bring rain gear since the weather in that district is rather variable.
你最好帶雨具，因為那區的天氣很多變。

point had better + V 意為「最好⋯⋯」。

---

32 opportunity
★
★
★
[ˌɑpəˋtjunətɪ]
n 機會，良機
同 chance 機會

Usually, job opportunities in big cities are more.
大城市的工作機會通常比較多。

The only advice that the principal gave to the students was to seize every opportunity.
校長給學生的唯一建議就是抓住每個機會。

point 易混淆字：principle 意為「規則」。

3 調查研究

33 ★ **nationwide**
[ˋneʃənˌwaɪd]

a 全國性的，全國範圍的
同 national 全國性的
countrywide 全國性的
state 國家的
general 公眾的

Some politicians had doubts about the accuracy of the nationwide survey.
有些政治人物對全國性調查的正確性有疑問。

(point) have doubts about 意為「對……有疑問」。

There was nationwide opposition to the new policy about tariffs.
對於關稅的新政策，發生了全國性的反對。

---

34 ★ **legal**
[ˋligl]

a 法律上的，合法的
同 judicial 司法的
反 illegal 違法的
criminal 犯罪的
衍 legalize (v.) 使合法化
legitimate (a.) 合法的

Before implementing the new policy, the specialist checked whether it was legal.
在執行新政策前，專員確認新政策是否合法。

(point) before 為連接詞（+ S + V）及介係詞（+ N / Ving）。

The consultant was employed to provide legal advice to the firm.
顧問被僱用來提供公司法律建議。

---

35 ★ ★ ★ **journal**
[ˋdʒɝnl]

n 日報，雜誌，期刊
同 diary 日記
log 記錄
daily record 日誌

The teenager has cultivated a habit of writing a journal.
這名年輕人已經建立了寫日記的習慣。

(point) cultivate a habit 意為「建立一個習慣」。

The researcher had successfully submitted his article to the journal before the deadline.
研究員已經成功在期限前將他的文章提交給期刊。

(point) submit to 意為「提交；使服從，使屈服」。

---

36 ★ ★ ★ **examine**
[ɪgˋzæmɪn]

V 檢查，細查，審問
同 inspect 檢查
survey 考察
scrutinize 細查
investigate 調查
衍 examination (n.) 檢查
examiner (n.) 審查員

The certified inspector will examine the safety standards of the factory.
合格的稽查員將會檢視工廠的安全標準。

(point) 延伸詞彙：safety inspection 意為「安全檢查」。

Interviewees should examine employment contracts carefully before they sign them.
求職者必須在簽僱用合約前仔細地檢視內容。

37 **graph**

★ [græf]

n 圖表，曲線

v 用圖表表示

同 chart (n.) 圖表
diagram (n.) 圖表

The graph included in the brochure is used to explain the improvement in sales volume.
包含在小冊子裡的圖表被用來解釋公司的業績成長。

The graph shows the progress of the project which should be completed within one month.
圖表顯現了應該要在一個月完成的專案進度。

---

38 **glove**

★ [glʌv]

n 手套，拳擊手套

Wearing leather gloves keeps you warm in winter.
在冬天戴皮手套能讓你保持溫暖。

point Ving 當主詞（wearing gloves），動詞使用單數。

The research assistant wore rubber gloves to protect himself from chemicals.
研究助理戴橡皮手套以保護自己不碰到化學物品。

point protect... from 意為「保護某人或某物之安全」。

---

39 **substantial**

★
★ [səbˋstænʃəl]

a 真實的，堅固的，
重要的，大量的

同 sizeable 相當大的
significant 重大的
large 大的

There have been some substantial changes in my hometown, ever since I left there.
自從我搬離我的家鄉以來，那裡有了很多重大的改變。

point ever since 意為「自從」。

The research shows a substantial difference between the languages used by men and women in workplace.
研究顯示男性和女性在職場上使用的語言有重大的差異。

point 相關詞彙：considerable 相當大的。

---

40 **spot**

★ [spɑt]

n 污漬，地點，職位

v 發現

同 mark (n.) 汙點
patch (n.) 補釘
dot (n.) 點狀物

衍 spotted (a.) 有斑點的

The inspector spotted one problem in the plant.
稽查員發現了工廠的一個問題。

point plant = factory，意指「工廠」。

This looks like a perfect spot for running a cafeteria.
看起來這裡是個開食堂的好地方。

Chapter 026

3

調查研究

41 violation
★
[ˌvaɪəˈleʃən]

n 違犯，違背，違反行為

同 breach 破壞
breaking 破壞

衍 violator (n.) 違犯者

Drivers will be fined for violation of the traffic regulations.
駕駛會因為違反交通規則而被罰款。

The inspector indicated some violations of safety regulations in the factory.
稽查員指出一些違反工廠安全規章的事項。

---

42 setback
★
★
[ˈsɛtˌbæk]

n 挫折，失敗，倒退

同 disappointment 挫折
misfortune 不幸
reversal 翻轉
reverse 相反

反 breakthrough 突破
step forward 向前邁步

The failure of entering the final was one of the biggest setbacks in the participant's life.
未能進入決賽是那名參加者人生最大的挫折之一。

point final (n.) 決賽，finalist (n.) 參加決賽者，finalize (v.) 最終確定。

The temporary setback in experiment frustrated the scientist.
實驗上的暫時挫敗讓科學家很受挫。

point 相關詞彙：difficulty 困難，impediment 妨礙，obstruction 阻礙，complication 障礙。

---

43 relevant
★
★
★
[ˈrɛləvənt]

a 有關的，恰當的，關係重大的

同 related 有關的
suitable 適當的

反 irrelevant 無關的
inappropriate 不適當的

Candidates should have at least five years of relevant work experience.
申請人至少要有五年的相關工作經驗。

point 多益測驗中的求職信件常提到求職者的必要條件（requirement）：degree 學位／work experience 工作經驗／personality 個性。

The chief editor deleted some unnecessary and unimportant details and only left the relevant information.
總編輯刪掉一些不必要且不重要的細節，只留下相關的訊息。

point editor-in-chief = chief editor，意為「總編輯」。

---

44 randomly
★
★
★
[ˈrændəmlɪ]

ad 任意地，隨機地

同 casually 隨意地
by chance 偶然

反 deliberately 故意地

These questionnaires were randomly distributed.
這些問卷是隨機發下的。

The reporters randomly chose a few passengers to ask their opinions about the accident.
記者隨意挑選了幾名乘客，詢問他們對於那個事故的意見。

45 **opposite**

★
★
★

[ˋɑpəzɪt]

a 相反的，對立的，對面的

同 conflicting 矛盾的
　　 contradictory 矛盾的

反 same 一樣地
　　 identical 同樣的
　　 like 相像的

On the opposite, he was laid off.
相反地，他被裁員了。

point on the opposite 意為「相反地」。

The analyst held the opposite view to the critic.
分析師抱持著和這名評論家不同的意見。

---

46 **large-scale**

★
★

[ˋlɑrdʒˋskel]

a 大規模的，大範圍的

同 extensive 廣大的
　　 wide-reaching 廣泛的
　　 wide-ranging 廣泛的
　　 global 全世界的
　　 universal 全球的

反 small-scale 小規模的
　　 minor 較小的

The research team will conduct a large-scale survey to collect data.
研究團隊會執行一項大規模的調查來收集資料。

point conduct = implement 意為「執行」。

The government is trying to improve the response to large-scale natural disasters.
政府正在試著加強對大規模自然災害的對應方式。

point 延伸用語：on a large scale 意為「大規模地」。

---

47 **interpret**

★
★

[ɪnˋtɜprɪt]

v 解釋，說明，理解

同 explain 解釋

衍 interpreter (n.) 口譯員

It's difficult to interpret the hidden meaning of the poem.
很難解讀詩的背後含義。

The researcher interpreted these statistics and wrote the results in the report.
研究員解讀了這些統計數字，並將結果寫在報告裡。

---

48 **insignificant**

★

[ˌɪnsɪgˋnɪfəkənt]

a 不重要的，無意義的

同 unimportant 不重要的
　　 pointless 無意義的
　　 worthless 不重要的

反 important 重要的
　　 significant 有意義的
　　 noteworthy 顯著的

Compared to other issues, this problem is insignificant and can be solved in a short time.
跟其他的問題相比，這個問題根本不算什麼，且可以短時間就被解決。

point compared to 意為「與……相比」。

The research showed that the difference between two groups was insignificant.
研究顯示這兩個群組間的差異不顯著。

point 相關詞彙：of minor importance 次要，of no importance 不重要，
of little importance 次要。

49 inference

★
★
★

[ˋɪnfərəns]

n 推論，推斷的結果

同 conclusion 結論
  speculation 推測
  assumption 假定

衍 infer (v.) 推斷

The lawyer made an inference from my statement.
律師從我的聲明中做出了推斷。

point make an inference 意為「做出了推斷」。

His inference seemed logical and reasonable.
他的推論似乎很有邏輯且有道理。

point seem + (to be) + a. 意為「似乎」。

50 habitual

★

[həˋbɪtʃʊəl]

a 習慣的，習以為常的

同 constant 不變的
  persistent 持續的
  repeated 反覆的
  frequent 慣常的

反 occasional 偶爾的

The researchers observed the participants' habitual actions and analyzed them.
研究者觀察受試者的習慣性行為，並分析之。

point habitual action 意為「習慣性行為」。

The designer always dresses in his habitual black.
設計師總是身穿他慣常的黑色衣服。

51 foreign

★
★
★

[ˋfɔrɪn]

a 外國的，陌生的，不適合的

同 overseas 海外的
  distant 久遠的
  remote 遙遠的
  non-native 非本地的

反 domestic 國內的

She would be the one to pick up the foreign clients from the airport, so she took a three-day language crash course.
她將會是那個要去機場迎接外國賓客的人，所以她上了三天的語言速成課程。

point crash course 意為「速成課程」。

The latest research methodology was completely foreign to the old scientist.
最新的研究方法對這名老科學家來說是非常陌生的。

52 incline

★

[ɪnˋklaɪn]

v 傾斜，傾向，有意

同 intend 想要
  tend 趨向

衍 inclination (n.) 傾向

Nowadays, most health professionals incline towards this theory.
現在，大多數的醫療專業人士傾向這個理論。

The coach asked the athlete to incline his upper body forward.
教練請這名運動員將上半身往前傾斜一點。

point coach = trainer 意為「訓練者；教練」。

53 **feasibility**

★
★

[ˌfizəˈbɪlətɪ]

n 可行性，可能性

同 practicality 可行性
workability 可使用性
achievability 可達成性
reasonableness 合理
possibility 可能性
chance 可能性

反 infeasibility 不可行性

The team members were considering the feasibility of the alternate plan.
團員們正在想替代性計畫的可行性。

Experts in this field held different opinions on the feasibility of building a casino.
該領域的專家對於建賭場的可行性抱持著不同的看法。

point hold different opinions 意為「抱持著不同的看法」。

54 **essential**

★
★
★

[ɪˈsɛnʃəl]

a 必要的，本質的，基本的

n 要素，本質

同 crucial (a.) 重要的
vital (a.) 極重要的

反 secondary (a.) 次要的
inessential (a.) 非必要的

Taking the initiative at work is essential.
在工作上，自動自發是重要的。

point take the initiative 意為「自動自發」。

It is essential for reporters to report the truth.
對記者而言，報導事實是重要的。

point It is essential for sb. to V 意為「對某人……是重要的」。

55 **enforce**

★

[ɪnˈfors]

V 實施，執行，強制

同 force 強迫
compel 強迫
exact 強要
demand 要求

The company strictly enforces the rule.
該公司嚴格實施此規定。

We will enforce the contract between the client and the subcontractor.
我們會履行該名客戶和外包廠商的契約。

56 **consistent**

★
★
★

[kənˈsɪstənt]

a 始終如一的，符合的

同 steady 不變的
constant 不變的
unchanging 不變的
unvarying 不變的

反 inconsistent 不一致的
irregular 不規則的

We found the product descriptions are not consistent with the product itself.
我們發現產品敘述並不符合產品本身。

point 相關詞彙：even 一致的，uniform 相同的。

There has been a consistent increase in the sales volume since the last campaign.
自從上次行銷活動以來，銷售量一直持續增加。

point in + 方面，意為「在……（方面）」。

57 **concrete**

★
★

['kɑnkrit]

a 有形的，具體的，實在的
n 混凝土
同 material (a.) 有形的
　　real (a.) 實際的
反 abstract (a.) 抽象的
　　vague (a.) 含糊的

Can you provide some concrete examples?
你可以提供具體的例證嗎？

(point) 相關詞彙：solid 充實的，tangible 實際的。

The concrete path is being repaved.
這條混凝土道路正被重鋪。

(point) 若在多益聽力測驗圖片題中聽到此敘述，圖片要有「人」才可選，因為有「進行式」。

58 **compose**

★

[kəm'poz]

v 作（詩曲），構圖，使平靜
同 write 編寫
　　create 創造
　　devise 設計
　　make up 編造
　　formulate 規劃

The prestigious musician is known for composing songs in a short time.
這名傑出的音樂家以短時間內創作歌曲而聞名。

(point) be known for 意為「以……而聞名」。

The survey shows that the consumers of this product are composed largely of middle-aged people.
研究顯示這項產品的消費者大部分都是中年人。

59 **complicate**

★

['kɑmplə‚ket]

v 使複雜化，使惡化
同 mix up 弄混
　　confuse 混淆
反 simplify 簡化
衍 complicated (a.) 複雜的

Please try to explain the thing in a simple way but not complicate it.
請試著以簡單的方式解釋這件事情，不要把它弄得更複雜。

It will only complicate the situation if we fail to follow the schedule.
如果我們沒有跟上進度的話，只會使狀況更加複雜。

60 **alternative**

★
★
★

[ɔl'tɜnətɪv]

a 兩者擇一的，替代的，供選擇的
n 選擇，供選擇的東西
同 choice (n.) 選擇
　　option (n.) 選項
　　possibility (n.) 可能的事

Do you have any alternative plan?
你有任何其他的替代性計畫嗎？

(point) 此句的 alternative 當形容詞。

I have no alternative but to reschedule the deadline.
我別無選擇，只能重新安排截止日。

(point) 此句的 alternative 為名詞。

61 **search**

★
★
★

[sɝtʃ]

Ⓥ 搜查,細看,探究

同 hunt 搜索
   look 看
   explore 探測
   seek 尋找

The job seeker is searching for better work opportunities overseas.
求職者找尋更好的海外工作機會。

This is the most widely used search engine around the world.
這是全世界最被廣泛使用的搜尋引擎。

---

62 **refer**

★
★
★

[rɪˋfɝ]

Ⓥ 歸因於,起源於,提及,查閱

同 mention 提到
   cite 引用
   name 列舉

衍 reference (n.) 提及

Brad referred to the task as a mission impossible.
布萊德把這任務稱為是不可能的任務。

point refer to O as + N 意為「視……為……」。

The professor suggested his readers refer to another book to know the background of The Great Recession.
教授建議讀者參考另一本書,以知道經濟大蕭條的背景。

point The Great Recession 意為「經濟大衰退」。

---

63 **segment**

★

[ˋsɛgmənt]

Ⓝ 部分,部門,切片

Ⓥ 分割,切片

同 section (n.) 部分
   division (n.) 分割
   portion (n.) 部分
   fragment (n.) 斷片
   component (n.) 成分

反 whole (n.) 整體

The food critic especially enjoyed the orange segments in the salad.
美食評論家尤其喜歡沙拉裡的橘子瓣。

point 相關詞彙:piece 部分,part 一部分。

With the updated database, we can figure out what is the fastest-growing segment of the market.
有了這個更新的資料庫,我們可以找出什麼是市場中發展最快的部分。

point figure out = realize,意為「了解」。

---

64 **approach**

★
★
★

[əˋprotʃ]

Ⓥ 接近,著手處理

Ⓝ 接近,通道,入口

同 way (n.) 通路
   method (n.) 方法

Several approaches can be adopted to change the situation.
很多方法都可以用來改變這個情況。

After 45 minutes, the train finally approached the station.
在四十五分鐘後,火車終於抵達車站。

point approach 當「接近」時不加 to,approach to 為「高達」。

65 comprise

★
★

[kəm`praɪz]

V 組成，構成，包括

同 consist of 由……組成
　　 be made up of 由……組成
　　 be composed of 由……組成
　　 contain 包含
　　 include 包括
　　 involve 包含

The sales team is comprised of five experienced employees.
業務團隊由五位經驗豐富的員工所組成。

According to the market survey, females comprises 40 percent of our consumers.
根據市場調查，女性占我們顧客人數的百分之四十。

66 conclude

★
★
★

[kən`klud]

V 結束，斷定，做出決定

同 finish 結束
　　 come to an end 終結
　　 draw to a close 結束

反 start 開始
　　 begin 開始
　　 commence 開始

衍 conclusion (n.) 結論

The broadcast host concluded what the guests said and then provided feedback.
廣播主持人總結來賓說的話並提供回饋。

point 相關詞彙：close 結束，cease 終止。

To conclude, his addition will bring great benefits to our team.
總之，他的加入會帶給我們團隊很大的利益。

point 多益測驗相關常見情境：研討會開始前說「There is an addition to our schedule.」，意思是有新增一項行程。

67 source

★
★
★

[sors]

n 源頭，來源，原始資料

同 origin 起源
　　 cause 原因
　　 beginning 開始

Some residents questioned the source of the news.
有些居民質疑新聞消息的來源。

point question = doubt 意為「質疑」。

The source of contamination in the river was finally found by a group of experts.
河裡汙染物的來源終於被一群專家找到了。

68 breadth

★

[brɛdθ]

n 寬度，寬容，廣泛性

同 width 寬度
　　 wideness 廣闊

反 narrowness 狹窄

The worker measured the length and the breadth of the table.
工人丈量桌子的長度及寬度。

The host of the talk show is famous for her breadth of knowledge.
脫口秀主持人以她的知識淵博聞名。

point be famous for 意為「以……聞名」。

69 secure

★
★

[sɪˋkjur]

a 安全的，有把握的，牢固的

v 使安全，保證，獲得

同 tight (a.) 牢固的
firm (a.) 穩固的
fixed (a.) 固定的

反 loose (a.) 鬆的
unlocked (a.) 沒有鎖的

The janitor fell off the ladder because it was not secure at all.
管理員從梯子摔了下來，因為它一點都不牢固。

point ladder（梯子）和 letter（信）的發音相似，在多益測驗 Part 1 圖片題裡很容易混淆，要注意。

The survey shows that 85% of the users felt secure to use our online storage.
調查顯示百分之八十五的使用者在使用我們的線上儲存空間時感到安心。

70 sink

★

[sɪŋk]

v 下沉，降低，滲透

n 水槽

同 fall (v.) 落下
descend (v.) 下降
disappear (v.) 消失
vanish (v.) 消逝
drop (v.) 落下

反 rise (v.) 升起

The kitchen sink has been leaking for three days.
廚房水槽已經漏水三天了。

point for + 一段時間，代表「已經……」。

According to the latest report, the number of unemployment has sunk significantly this year.
根據最新的報告，今年失業人口大幅減少。

point latest = newest，意為「最新的」。

71 explore

★
★
★

[ɪkˋsplor]

v 探測，探險，考察

同 survey 勘測
inspect 審查
investigate 調查
search 搜查

The education expert indicated that reading is beneficial for children to explore the world.
教育專家指出閱讀對於小孩探索世界是有益的。

The teacher took her students to explore the botanical garden.
老師帶她的學生們去探索植物園。

72 exception

★
★
★

[ɪkˋsɛpʃən]

n 例外，除外

同 special case 例外

He is making an exception on that special case.
他對那特別的案例破了例。

point make an exception 意為「破例」。

All of Tim's family members are quite good at logical thinking but he is the exception.
提姆的家人都很擅長邏輯思考，但他卻是個例外。

3 調查研究

---

73 election

★
★
★

[ɪˈlɛkʃən]

n 選舉，當選

同 ballot 投票
vote 投票
poll 投票
general election 大選
popular vote 投票

The result of the election will be announced in 8 hours.
選舉的結果在八小時內就會被宣布。

point will be announced 意為「將會被宣布」，結合了未來式和被動式。

The election for the legislators will take place next month.
立法委員選舉下個月會舉行。

point take place 意為「發生；舉行」。

---

74 compare

★
★
★

[kəmˈpɛr]

v 比較，比喻為
n 比較

同 contrast (n.) 對比
differentiate (v.) 區分

The inspector compared two safety procedures.
稽查員比較了兩套安全步驟。

Compared with the cafeteria in my company, the sanitary condition of this restaurant is not that satisfying.
和我公司的自助餐比，這家餐廳的衛生條件不是那麼令人滿意。

point sanitary condition 意為「衛生條件」。

---

75 flawed

★

[flɔd]

a 有缺點的，錯誤的

同 defective (a.) 有缺陷的
faulty (a.) 有缺點的
imperfect (a.) 不完美的
damaged (a.) 毀壞的
反 perfect (a.) 完美的

The professor indicated that Tom's study was probably flawed.
教授指出湯姆的研究可能有疏漏。

The article teaches people how to sell flawed products without deceiving your customers.
這篇文章教人如何在不欺騙顧客的情況下賣出有缺陷的商品。

---

76 know

★
★
★

[no]

v 知道，了解，認識

同 realize 了解
figure out 理解
perceive 理解
understand 理解

The assistant didn't know whether he could arrive there on time since he was stuck in traffic.
助理不知道他能不能準時到，因為他困在車陣之中。

point be stuck in traffic 意為「困在車陣之中」。

The marketing team knew customers' needs by conducting the market survey.
行銷團隊藉由執行市場調查以知道顧客的需求。

point 延伸詞彙：questionnaire 問卷，comment 評論，feedback 回饋。

Question

以下題目完全擬真新制多益 Part 5，請選出最符合句意的選項。

1. The panel provided many constructive ------- that our organization could use to modify the existing system.
   (A) commodity   (B) violation
   (C) suggestions   (D) consistent

2. Regular job ------- are necessary to improve employees' performance.
   (A) evaluations   (B) assembles
   (C) experts   (D) spots

3. The digital ------- is inconsistent.
   (A) advisor   (B) acceptance   (C) segment   (D) scale

4. Candidates should have at least five years of ------- work experience.
   (A) complicate   (B) relevant   (C) approach   (D) exception

5. The certified inspector will ------- the safety standards of the factory.
   (A) examine   (B) obtain   (C) variable   (D) abstract

6. Do you have any ------- plan?
   (A) explore   (B) inference   (C) randomly   (D) alternative

>> 正確答案與解析請翻至下一頁查看

Answer

正確答案與解析

1. 專家小組提供了我們組織許多可以用來修改現行系統的有建設性的建議。

   (A) 商品　　　　(B) 違反　　　　(C) 建議　　　　(D) 一致的

   正確答案 (C)

2. 定期的工作評估對於增進員工表現是必須的。

   (A) 評估（名詞複數）　　　　(B) 聚集；組裝（動詞現在式單數）

   (C) 專家（名詞複數）　　　　(D) 地點（名詞複數）

   正確答案 (A)

3. 這個電子秤不穩定。

   (A) 顧問　　　　(B) 接受　　　　(C) 部分　　　　(D) 秤

   正確答案 (D)

4. 申請人至少要有五年相關工作經驗。

   (A) 複雜的　　　　(B) 相關的　　　　(C) 方法　　　　(D) 例外

   正確答案 (B)

5. 合格的稽查員將會檢視工廠的安全標準。

   (A) 檢查　　　　(B) 得到　　　　(C) 變異的　　　　(D) 提取

   正確答案 (A)

6. 你有任何其他的替代性計畫嗎？

   (A) 探索　　　　(B) 推斷結果　　　　(C) 隨機地　　　　(D) 替代性的

   正確答案 (D)

Chapter 4
投資與設備

以下多益必考單字，你認識哪些？

☐ consultant (p.074)   ☐ situation (p.086)   ☐ equipment (p.079)

☐ investor (p.075)   ☐ possibility (p.087)   ☐ operate (p.078)

☐ maintain (p.076)   ☐ particularly (p.090)   ☐ install (p.082)

☐ inspection (p.080)   ☐ trial (p.082)   ☐ encounter (p.085)

☐ software (p.082)   ☐ sensitive (p.089)   ☐ system (p.080)

☐ abundance (p.083)   ☐ function (p.085)   ☐ utilize (p.088)

Chapter 031

4 投資與設備

01 routine
★
★
★
[ru`tin]
n 例行公事，日常工作，慣例
a 日常的，平凡的
同 procedure (n.) 常規
反 unusual (a.) 非凡的

Exercising has been his daily routine for 10 years.
這十年來，運動已經是他的每天例行公事。

Routine maintenance on the equipment takes place every month.
例行性的設備維修每個月都會舉行一次。

point 維修類的情境在多益測驗中很容易出現，請留意。

02 basement
★
[`besmənt]
n 地下室
衍 base (n.) 基礎
baseline (n.) 底線
baseless (a.) 無基礎的

The ventilation of the basement is not satisfying.
地下室的通風系統令人不滿意。

point sb. be satisfied with sth. 意為「人對⋯⋯感到滿意」。sth. be satisfying 意為「某事物令人滿意」。

The conference venue is on the basement of this hotel, not the second floor.
研討會地點在飯店的地下室，不是二樓。

point venue 意為「地點」。

03 consultancy
★
[kən`sʌltənsɪ]
n 顧問公司，諮詢意見
同 consulting firm 諮詢公司

There is a job opening in that financial consultancy right now.
金融諮詢公司現在有一個職缺。

point opening = vacancy，意為「職缺」。

The business hours of RTC Management Consultancy are from 8 a.m. to 5 p.m.
RTC 管理顧問公司的營業時間是早上八點到下午五點。

04 consultant
★
★
★
[kən`sʌltənt]
n 顧問，會診醫生，諮詢者
同 adviser 顧問
guide 嚮導
counselor 顧問
expert 專家
specialist 專家

He was employed as the CEO's personal consultant.
他被僱用為執行長的個人顧問。

The financial consultant explained the investment options to his clients.
財務顧問向他的顧客解釋投資選擇。

point explain sth. to sb. 意為「向某人解釋某事」。

05 invest
★
★ [ɪn`vɛst]
★
Ⓥ 投資，耗費，投入
圓 venture 冒險

He invests in stocks for his retirement.
他投資股票，為了他的退休做準備。

The government will invest three million in the domestic project.
政府將在這個國內的專案上投資三百萬。

06 investment
★
★ [ɪn`vɛstmənt]
★
Ⓝ 投資（額），
   投入（時間、精力）
圓 venture 冒險事業

The reliable investment advisor gave me some suggestions.
這名可靠的投資顧問給我一些建議。

The speaker highlighted the importance of making investment in education.
這名講者強調投資教育的重要性。

point make investment 意為「投資」。

07 investor
★
★ [ɪn`vɛstɚ]
★
Ⓝ 投資者，出資者
圓 shareholder 股東

The investor would like to know the information about the updated project plan.
投資者想要知道最新計畫案的資訊。

point would like to + V 意為「想要做⋯⋯」。

The investor has always been looking for other opportunities to invest.
這名投資者一直在找其他機會來投資。

08 defect
★
★ [dɪ`fɛkt]
Ⓝ 缺點，缺陷
圓 weakness (n.) 缺點
   weak spot (ph.) 弱點
   limitation (n.) 限制
反 strength (n.) 力量
   advantage (n.) 優點
衍 defective (a.) 有缺陷的

The mechanic was sent to fix some defects in the machine.
技師被派去修理機器中的一些問題。

point 相關詞彙：flaw 瑕疵，fault 缺陷，deficiency 缺點，imperfection 瑕疵，inadequacy 不適當，shortcoming 短處。

The disabled child tried to overcome his speech defect by learning sign language.
這名有身心障礙的孩子藉由學習手語來克服他的語言障礙。

point sign language 意為「手語」。

4 投資與設備

09 efficient
★
★
★
[ɪˋfɪʃənt]

a 效率高的，有能力的，能勝任的

同 productive 生產的
反 inefficient 無效率的
   disorganized 混亂的
衍 effective (a.) 有效的
   efficiency (n.) 效率

The researcher has developed a more efficient method of improving productivity.
研究人員已經研發出一種更有效率的方法來提升生產力。

He tried to figure out a more efficient way to simplify the task.
他試著想出一個更有效率的方法來簡化工作。

point figure out 意為「想出；理解；明白」。

10 additionally
★
★
★
[əˋdɪʃənl̩ɪ]

ad 附加地，同時，此外

同 in addition 此外
   furthermore 再者
   moreover 並且
   besides 此外
   also 並且
衍 addition (n.) 附加
   additional (a.) 額外的

Investing in stocks requires knowledge about the market; additionally, it's also crucial to have luck.
投資股票需要有關市場的知識，此外，有運氣也是相當重要。

point additionally 為副詞，不能當連接詞。用分號「;」連結有連接詞的作用。

Additionally, our company also provides employees with gift certificates to the malls on their birthdays.
此外，我們公司也在員工生日時提供給他們商場的禮券。

11 stock
★
★
[stɑk]

n 貯存，存貨，股份，原料
v 進貨，貯存

同 capital (n.) 資本
   fund (n.) 資金
   asset (n.) 資產
   property (n.) 財產

The new Gasol toys are out of stock.
這個新的蓋索玩具已經沒貨了。

point out of stock 意為「無庫存」。

The stock broker introduced the benefits and the risk of investments.
股票經紀人介紹了投資的好處及風險。

point stock broker 意為「股票經紀人」。

12 maintain
★
★
★
[menˋten]

v 維持，維修，堅持

同 continue 繼續
   keep 保持
   sustain 維持
反 neglect 忽視

Compared with the normal elevators, it's harder to maintain transparent elevators.
和普通的電梯相比，要維修透明電梯是比較困難的。

point 延伸詞彙：lift（英式）電梯。

One of the duties of police officers is to maintain social order.
警察的責任之一就是維持社會秩序。

13 **handle**
★
★
★
['hændl]

Ⅴ 操作，處理，經營

ⓝ 把手，把柄

同 deal with (ph.) 處理
cope with (ph.) 處理
manage (v.) 經營

衍 handling (n.) 操作

The mechanic is excellent in handling this complicated machine.
這名技師很擅長操作這台複雜的機器。

point be excellent in 意為「傑出的」。

I have no doubt that you can handle the problem on your own.
我相信你能夠自己解決這個問題。

point on you own = by yourself，意為「靠你自己」。

---

14 **maintenance**
★
★
★
['mentənəns]

ⓝ 維持，維修

同 preservation 維護
conservation 保存
repair 修理

反 neglect 疏忽

Please note that the west elevator will be closed for regular maintenance next Monday.
請注意下週一西側的電梯將會關閉，進行例行性維修。

point Please note that 意為「請注意」，後面常接重要訊息，常出現在多益測驗考題中，要注意。

The clerk apologized that the machine was currently not in service due to routine maintenance.
店員為了機器目前無法提供使用而道歉，因為例行性維修。

point be not in service 意為「不提供使用」。

---

15 **replace**
★
★
[rɪ'ples]

Ⅴ 把……放回原處，取代，歸還

同 substitute 代替
exchange 交換
change 改變
return 歸還
restore 恢復

The photocopier has been used for more than 20 years and it's high time to replace it.
這台影印機已經使用超過二十年，是時候換掉它了。

point it's high time to + V 意為「是時候做……」。

The coach replaced the rookie player with the more experienced one.
教練讓比較有經驗的球員替換掉那位菜鳥球員。

point replace A with B 意為「用 B 換掉 A」。

---

16 **replacement**
★
★
[rɪ'plesmənt]

ⓝ 代替，更換，歸還

同 renewal 更新
replacing 替換
substitution 代替

The wooden chair is in need of replacement.
這木椅需要更換。

Please send the defective items back, so that you can receive the replacements.
請寄回有缺陷的項目，這樣你才能收到換貨。

Chapter 033

4 投資與設備

17 operate
★
★
★
[ˋɑpəˏret]
Ⅴ 經營，操作，動手術
同 work 運作
　use 使用
　utilize 使用
　employ 利用
　handle 處理
　control 控制

The newest model is easier to operate than the previous one.
最新的型號比之前的還好操作。

The manual includes the detailed information about how to operate the forklift.
手冊包含了如何操作堆高機的詳細訊息。

18 operation
★
★
★
[ˏɑpəˋreʃən]
ⁿ 操作，運轉，經營，手術
同 functioning 運轉
　working 運轉
　running 運轉

Operation systems should be upgraded regularly to improve work efficiency.
營運系統應該要定期更新，以增強工作效率。

point regularly = on a regular basis，意為「規律地」。

Only some business operations were entitled to receive financial funding from the government.
只有一些企業夠資格得到政府的財政資助。

point be entitled to + V 意為「夠資格做……」。

19 operational
★
★
[ˏɑpəˋreʃənl]
ª 操作的，經營的，運轉的
同 operative 操作的
　workable 可使用的
　serviceable 可使用的
　functional 起作用的
　feasible 可實行的
反 broken 損壞的

Unfortunately, the equipment in the laboratory is not yet operational.
很不幸地，實驗室的儀器尚未能正常運轉。

The system is out of service due to some unexpected operational difficulties.
系統因為一些不可預期的營運問題而暫時提供服務。

point out of service 意為「暫停服務」。

20 operator
★
[ˋɑpəˏretɚ]
ⁿ 操作者，接線生，經營者
同 worker 工作者

The computer operator took a three-day vacation.
這名電腦操作員休假三天。

point take a vacation 意為「度假」。

By the time you transfer the deposit, the tour operator will send you the itinerary.
等到你匯完訂金，旅行社會寄給你行程。

point tour operator 意為「旅行社」。

21 shareholder
★
[`ʃɛr͵holdɚ]
n 股東
同 owner 所有人
investor 投資者
shareowner 股份持有人

The shareholders have meetings every year to discuss the development of the company.
股東每年都會開會討論公司的發展。

The shareholders required that the manager modify the contract.
股東要求經理修改合約。

point S + require + that + S + (should) + V 意為「某人要求某人該做……」。本句因為 modify 前面省了 should，所以用原形動詞。

---

22 gear
★
★
[gɪr]
n 齒輪，工具，設備
v 使適應，開動機器，準備好
同 gearwheel (n.) 大齒輪
facility (n.) 設備
equipment (n.) 配備

Remember to bring the camping gear.
記得帶露營用具。

point 多益聽力測驗的 Part 1 圖片題常出現 gear 這個詞，要多注意。

They geared up for the new campaign.
他們為新活動做好準備。

---

23 equipment
★
★
★
[ɪ`kwɪpmənt]
n 配備，裝備，用具
同 tool 工具
utensil 用具
instrument 器具
hardware 裝備
gadget 器具
stuff 材料

Researchers at this lab are familiar with operating all kinds of equipment.
這個實驗室裡的研究者很熟悉操作所有設備。

point all kinds of 意為「各式各樣的，所有種類的」。

The old and outdated equipment will be labeled and disposed of.
這台老舊過時的儀器將會被貼上標籤且丟掉。

point dispose of sb. / sth. 意為「處理某人／清除某物」。

---

24 monitor
★
★
★
[`manətɚ]
n 顯示器，螢幕，班長
v 監控，監測，監視
同 detector (n.) 發現者
scanner (n.) 掃描器
recorder (n.) 記錄器

The security guard stared at the monitor to find out who broke the window.
警衛盯著螢幕，試著要找出誰打破玻璃。

The employee from the IT department is fixing the problems about the assistant's computer monitor.
該名資訊科技部門的員工正在修理助理的電腦螢幕問題。

point IT 為 Information Technology 的縮寫，意為「資訊科技」。

Chapter 034

4

投資與設備

25 inspection

★
★

[ɪnˋspɛkʃən]

n 視察，檢查

同 exploration 探測
observation 觀測
review 再檢查
evaluation 評估

衍 inspect (v.) 檢查
inspector (n.) 視察員

The company will conduct the safety inspection next week.
下週公司會進行安全檢查。

(point) 相關詞彙：examination 檢查，check 檢查，investigation 調查，survey 調查。

The vase looked perfect, but on closer inspection, it was defective on its bottom.
這花瓶看似完美，但仔細檢查後，底部有缺陷。

(point) on closer inspection 意為「仔細檢查」。

26 laboratory

★

[ˋlæbrəˌtorɪ]

n 實驗室，研究室

同 lab 實驗室

All the equipment  is available for the laboratory workers to use.
實驗室員工都能使用所有設備。

(point) be available for 意為「可供使用」。

The defective product is still being examined in the laboratory.
這個有缺陷的產品仍然還在實驗室被檢驗中。

27 repair

★
★
★

[rɪˋpɛr]

v 修理，補救，糾正

n 修理，修補，恢復

同 cure (v.) 治癒
remedy (v.) 糾正

反 worsen (v.) 使惡化
destroy (v.) 破壞

The mechanic was sent to repair the machine.
技師被派去修機器。

(point) 相關詞彙：fix 修理，improve 改善，right 糾正（錯誤）。

The road is temporarily closed because it's under repair.
這條路暫時被封閉，因為正在維修中。

(point) be under repair 意為「在修理；正在維修中」。

28 system

★
★
★

[ˋsɪstəm]

n 體系，制度，秩序

同 structure 結構
organization 組織
order 秩序
arrangement 安排
administration 管理

The customers found the new system more user-friendly.
顧客覺得新系統更容易使用。

The technician was troubleshooting the air conditioning system.
技師正在解決空調系統的問題。

(point) troubleshoot (v.) 排解問題。

29 systematically
★
[ˌsɪstə`mætɪk̟lɪ]

ad 有系統地，有組織地
同 methodically 有條理地
thoroughly 徹底地
analytically 分析地
scientifically 有系統地
反 unsystematically
雜亂無章地

The experienced lecturer is confident that his students can learn software design systematically.
這名資深講師深具信心，認為他的學生可以很有系統地學習軟體設計。

The updated system allows workers to record production cost systematically.
這個更新的系統能使員工系統性地記錄生產成本。

30 technician
★
★
[tɛk`nɪʃən]

n 技術人員，技巧純熟的人
同 specialist 專家
expert 專家
skilled worker 熟練的技工
衍 technique (n.) 技巧

The electrical technician repaired the machine in no time.
那位電工技師馬上去修理機器。

point in no time = immediately，意為「立即地」。

Only technicians with that certificate are qualified to apply for this position.
只有擁有那個證照的技師才有資格申請這職位。

point be qualified to 意為「具有……的資格」。

31 electrician
★
★
[ˌilɛk`trɪʃən]

n 電工，電氣技師
衍 electric (a.) 電的
electronic (a.) 電子的

The website introduces 10 tips on how to become a licensed electrician.
網站介紹了十個成為有證照的電工的訣竅。

point licensed (a.) 有證照的，由 license (n.) 變化而來。

Working as an electrician is sometimes hazardous.
當電工有時是非常危險的。

point work as + 職稱，表示「做……（職務）」。

32 electricity
★
★
★
[ˌilɛk`trɪsətɪ]

n 電，電流，電力
同 electrical energy 電能
衍 electric (a.) 電的
electronic (a.) 電子的

My electricity bill is overdue.
我的電費帳單逾期了。

Due to construction, the electricity supply will be temporarily cut off in this small town the day after tomorrow.
因為施工，這個小鎮後天的電力供給將會被暫時中斷。

point the day after tomorrow 表示「後天」，the day before yesterday 表示「前天」。

4 投資與設備

33 software
★
★
★
[ˋsɔftˌwɛr]
n 軟體，程式材料
反 hardware 硬體

Many users found the face recognition software useful.
很多使用者覺得面部識別軟體很好用。

point find + O + a. 意為「覺得（事／物）……」。

The rumor that the senior software engineer is going to resign has become so widespread.
那名資深軟體工程師即將退休的謠言已經廣為流傳。

point 延伸詞彙及易混淆字：scandal (n.) 醜聞／ sandal (n.) 涼鞋。

34 trial
★
★
★
[ˋtraɪəl]
n 試驗，考驗，磨煉
a 試驗的，審訊的
同 test (n.) 試驗
try out (ph.) 試驗
experiment (n.) 實驗
examination (n.) 檢驗
assessment (n.) 估計
evaluation (n.) 評估

The trial version of the software has limited functions.
試用版軟體的功能有限。

point trial version 意為「試用版」。

It's a trial-and-error process, so just learn from your mistakes.
這就是一個不斷試驗與犯錯的過程，所以就從你的錯誤中學習吧。

point trial-and-error 意為「反覆試驗的」。

35 install
★
★
★
[ɪnˋstɔl]
V 任命，安裝，安頓
同 place 安置
put in place 安置
set in place 安置
locate 設置
situate 使處於
反 remove 移動

In this firm, the computers installed with online service are available to certain officials.
在這間公司，有安裝線上服務的電腦只供特定官員使用。

point installed 前面省略了 which / that are。

The head of the community patrol mentioned the benefits of installing smart street lighting.
社區巡邏隊隊長提到安裝智慧街燈的好處。

point community patrol 意為「社區巡邏隊」，security guard 意為「保全」。

36 plumber
★
[ˋplʌmɚ]
n 水管工，堵漏人員

The plumber checked the sink carefully.
水管工仔細地檢查了水槽。

It took 2 hours for the plumber to fix the leakage in the kitchen.
水管工花了兩小時修理廚房的漏水。

point It takes 時間 for sb. to + V 意為「花某人（時間）去做某事」。

37 caution

★
★
★

['kɔʃən]

n 小心，謹慎，警告

V 警告，使小心

同 advise (v.) 勸告
　　warn (v.) 警告
　　admonish (v.) 告誡

反 carelessness (n.) 粗心大意

衍 cautious (a.) 謹慎的

Before implementing the new policy, you should think it through with caution.
在執行新政策前，你應該要謹慎地想清楚。

point with caution 意為「謹慎地」。

The factory foreman cautioned his workers to wear helmets while going to the construction sites.
工廠工頭提醒他的工人去工地時要戴安全帽。

point construction site 意為「工地」。

---

38 panel

★

['pæn!]

n 嵌板，儀表盤，小組

同 group 小組

We need to rearrange the date for the panel discussion.
我們必須重新安排座談會的時間。

point panel discussion 指「小組討論會」。

The technician removed the instrument panel in the factory.
技工移除了工廠裡的儀表板。

point instrument 意為「儀器」，musical instrument 意為「樂器」。

---

39 abundance

★
★

[ə`bʌndəns]

n 豐富，充足，大量

同 affluence 豐富
　　plenty 大量

反 lack 缺少
　　scarcity 缺乏

衍 abundant (a.) 豐富的

The abundance of capital enables the company to develop new products.
充足的資金讓這間公司能發展新產品。

point capital 意為「首都；資本；大寫字母」。

The rainy season provides an abundance of water.
雨季提供充足的水資源。

point rainy season 意為「雨季」，dry season 意為「乾季」。

---

40 acquisition

★
★
★

[͵ækwə`zɪʃən]

n 獲得，取得，獲得物

同 acquirement 取得
　　attainment 獲得

反 loss 喪失

衍 acquire (v.) 取得

This heavy machine is my company's latest acquisition.
這台重型機器是我們公司最新的購置。

Are you familiar with the land acquisition process?
你熟悉土地收購的過程嗎？

point 在多益測驗中，acquisition 常表示為企業的收購。

41 activate

★

['æktə,vet]

ⓥ 使活動,使活化

同 trigger 觸發
begin 開始

反 inactivate 使不活躍

衍 action (n.) 行動
active (a.) 活躍的
activity (n.) 活動

Just push the button and you can activate the machine.

只要按這個按鈕就可以開啟這個機器。

point 延伸詞彙:set off 觸發,start 開啟。

The burglar alarm was activated accidently by my nephew.

防盜鈴不小心被我的姪子啟動了。

point nephew 意為「姪子」,niece 意為「姪女」。

---

42 automatic

★
★

[,ɔtə'mætɪk]

ⓐ 自動的,習慣性的,必然的

同 automated 自動化的
habitual 習慣的

反 controlled 被控制的
deliberate 故意的
intentional 有意的

One of the features of the air conditioner is that it has an automatic temperature control.

這台冷氣的其中一個特色就是有自動化的溫度調節系統。

For advanced learners, speaking a foreign language becomes automatic.

對於高階語言學習者而言,講外語也就成了一個自動化的過程。

point 意思是隨著程度越好,要擔心的細節(像是文法單字)就越少,也就像是一種自動化的過程。

---

43 cable

★
★

['kebl]

ⓝ 電纜,電報

ⓥ 發電報,裝有線電視

同 wire (n.) 電線
cord (n.) 電線
power line (ph.) 電源線

The factory worker dealt with the exposed cables.

工廠工人處理了暴露的電纜。

The form is for the termination of the cable TV service.

這個表格是用來停止有線電視的服務。

---

44 bent

★

[bɛnt]

ⓐ 彎曲的,決心的

ⓝ 愛好,天分

同 twisted (a.) 彎曲的
crooked (a.) 扭曲的
curved (a.) 彎曲的

反 straight (a.) 直的

Ken is bent on investing in real estate.

肯一心想投資不動產。

point be bent on 意為「下決心,決定做某事」。

The senior specialist got bent out of shape because she failed to be promoted to the managerial position this year.

這位資深專員因為今年沒有辦法升到管理職位而非常沮喪。

point get bent out of shape 意為「非常生氣或沮喪」。

CH 4

投資與設備

45 **lucrative**
★

['lukrətɪv]

a 賺錢的，有利可圖的

同 profitable 有利的
gainful 有利益的
moneymaking 賺錢的

反 unprofitable 無利益的

It's said that property investment is lucrative.
據說投資房地產是相當有賺頭的。

point It's said that 意為「據說」。

The cooperation between two brands is lucrative since it expands the potential customer base.
兩個品牌間的合作是十分有利可圖的，因為這擴大了潛在的顧客群。

point 延伸詞彙：co-branding strategy 意為「合作品牌策略」。

---

46 **function**
★
★
★

['fʌŋkʃən]

n 功能，作用，職責，盛大集會

v 運行，起作用

同 purpose (n.) 目的
use (v.) 使用
role (n.) 作用

You can refer to the brochure to know the functions of the new mixer.
你可以參閱小冊子以知道新的攪拌器的功能。

point pamphlet、brochure 也可指「小冊子」，這些字的發音都要記得，因為常在多益聽力測驗中出現。

Mr. Dragic's farewell party will be held in the function room.
卓吉奇先生的派對會在宴會廳舉辦。

point corporate function 意為「公司聚餐」，要注意 function 不只有「功能」的意思，多益測驗中都有出過這類考題。

---

47 **filter**
★

['fɪltɚ]

n 濾器，濾光鏡

v 過濾，滲透

The water is filtered by the advanced water filter.
這種水是用先進的濾水器所過濾。

point 延伸詞彙：water filter 意為「濾水器」。

The tutorial video will teach you how to customize spam filter setting.
這支教學影片會教您如何客製化過濾垃圾郵件的設定。

point customize (v.) 客製化，customer (n.) 顧客。

---

48 **encounter**
★
★

[ɪn'kauntɚ]

v 遭遇，偶然遇見

n 衝突，偶遇

同 experience (v.) 經歷
face (v.) 面臨
confront (v.) 遭遇

If you encounter problems using this copier, please call Mr. Gao.
如果你在使用這台影印機上有問題，請打給高先生。

The interviewer asked the candidate when he encountered these difficulties and how he reacted to them.
面試官問求職者何時遇到這些困難及如何反應。

49 unique
★
[juˋnik]

a 唯一的，獨特的

同 individual 單獨的
especial 特別的
single 單一的
sole 唯一的
only 僅有的

反 common 普通的
ordinary 平凡的

Remember to prepare some unique gifts from your own country for the host family.
記得從你的國家帶一些特別的禮物給寄宿家庭。

(point) 延伸詞彙：hotel 飯店，hostel 青年旅館，inn 小旅館，B&B 民宿，villa 別墅。

Seize this unique opportunity, and invest in property in that district!
抓住這個難得的機會，投資那區的房地產吧！

(point) 相關詞彙：special 特別的，unrepeatable 不能重複的，exclusive 獨有的，distinctive 特殊的，uncommon 罕見的，unusual 稀有的。

50 tool
★
★
★
[tul]

n 工具，器具，方法

同 instrument 器具
utensil 用具
machine 機器
equipment 裝備

The certified mechanic used the tool to fix the tour bus.
合格認證的技師使用這個工具來修理遊覽車。

(point) 多益測驗中常見形容職位的形容詞：certified 合資格的，skilled 技術高超的，experienced 經驗豐富的。

The small tool is designed to open jars more effortlessly.
這個小工具是設計用來更不費力地開罐子。

(point) 相關詞彙：device 設備，gadget 小器具，gear 工具。

51 situation
★
★
[ˌsɪtʃuˋeʃən]

n 處境，形勢，情況

同 circumstance 情況
state 狀況
condition 情況
case 實情

Whether the merchant will invest in the property totally depends on the market situation.
那個商人是否會投資房地產，完全要看市場狀況。

The analyst analyzed the current economic situation and reported the analysis in the board meeting.
分析師分析目前的經濟狀況並在董事會會議上報告此項分析。

52 reasonable
★
★
[ˋriznəbl̩]

a 合理的，正當的，適當的

同 logical 合邏輯的
fair-minded 公正的

反 unreasonable 不合理的

Given safety precaution, the officer's demands seemed reasonable.
有鑑於安全預防，長官的要求似乎很合理。

(point) 相關詞彙：fair 公正的，sensible 明智的。

If you purchase the cartridges in bulk, the price is relatively reasonable.
如果你大量購買墨水匣，價格會相對划算。

53 **possibility**

★
★
★

[ˌpɑsə`bɪlətɪ]

n 可能性，可能發生的事

同 chance 可能性
likelihood 可能性
probability 可能性

衍 possible (a.) 可能的

The possibility of winning the competition is relatively low.
贏得比賽的可能性相對地低。

point The possibility of winning the competition 為主詞。

The safety inspector wouldn't rule out the possibility that the machine was defective.
安全稽查員不排除機器有缺陷的可能性。

point 延伸詞彙：safety inspection 意為「安全檢查」。

54 **narrowly**

★
★

[`nærolɪ]

ad 狹窄地，勉強地，
仔細地

同 just 僅僅
barely 僅僅
scarcely 勉強地
hardly 勉強地

衍 narrow (a.) 狹窄的

The pedestrian narrowly escaped the accident.
路人驚險地逃過那場意外。

The accountant narrowly looked at the annual finance summary.
會計嚴密地檢查年度財務摘要。

55 **fortune**

★

[`fɔrtʃən]

n 財富，幸運，命運

同 luck 幸運
fate 命運
destiny 命運

衍 fortunate (a.) 幸運的
fortunately (ad.) 幸運地

The merchant made a fortune by buying and selling stocks.
商人藉由買賣股票來賺大錢。

Considering the waterproof materials, the coat must cost the shopper a fortune.
若考量到這個防水材質，這件大衣一定花了這名買家很多錢。

point cost a fortune 意為「花大錢」。

56 **control**

★
★
★

[kən`trol]

v 控制，管理，抑制
n 支配，控制，調節

同 regulate (v.) 管理
adjust (v.) 調整
determine (v.) 決定
govern (v.) 管理

衍 controlling (a.) 控制的

Automatic climate control systems will be installed to improve the quality of our products.
自動控溫系統將會被安裝，以提升我們產品的品質。

The process of quality control should be modified to meet our demanding clients' needs.
品質管理的過程必須要修改，以符合我們高標準顧客的需求。

point needs (n.) 需求（恆為複數）。

---

57 central

★
★
★

[`sɛntrəl]

@ 中心的，主要的，重要的

同 primary (a.) 主要的
leading (a.) 主要的
middle (a.) 中間的

反 side (a.) 旁邊的
extreme (a.) 極端的
outer (a.) 外面的

The **central** authority made an official announcement.
中央當局發出了一則官方宣布。

point 相關詞彙：main 主要的，chief 最重要的，principal 首要的。

The headquarters will be relocated to Central London.
總部將會被遷移到倫敦中部。

---

58 warn

★
★

[wɔrn]

V 警告，提醒，通知

同 notify 通知
alert 警告
inform 通知
give notice 通知

衍 warning (n.) 警告

The client was warned **not to put all the eggs into one basket** when it comes to investment.
當論及投資時，客戶被警告不要把所有雞蛋都放在同一個籃子裡。

point Don't put all your eggs in one basket. 意為「不要把所有雞蛋都放在同一個籃子裡」，即「分散風險」。

The warning sign **attached** to the bottle of the chemical warns people about the danger of it.
化學瓶底部的警告標語警告人們這個東西的危險。

point attached 前面省略了 which / that is。

---

59 utilize

★
★

[`jutḷˌaɪz]

V 利用

同 use 使用
employ 利用
apply 應用

衍 utilization (n.) 利用

In order to fully utilize the barren farmland, the company decided to turn it into a parking lot.
為了要充分運用這貧瘠的農地，公司決定要把它變成停車場。

point utilize = utilise（英式拼法）。

The candidate expects himself to find a job that can totally utilize his ability and experience.
面試者期待自己能找到一個可以完全運用他的能力及經驗的工作。

---

60 label

★
★

[`lebḷ]

n 貼紙，標籤，商標

V 貼標籤於，把……稱為

同 tag (n.) 標籤
brand (n.) 商標

The label is attached under the table.
標籤被貼在桌子下。

We labeled the malfunctioning machine with red labels.
我們用紅色標籤來標示有問題的機器。

61 term
★
★
[tɝm]

n 學期，條款，關係，名稱，限期

同 semester 一學期
expression 表現

Switching to energy-efficient lighting is beneficial in the long term.

換成使用節能省電的燈具長期來看是有益處的。

point in the long / medium / short term 意為「長期／中期／短期來看」。

 In terms of academic resources, the university will definitely be the first choice in this area.

就學術資源來說，這所大學絕對會是這區域的第一首選。

point in terms of... 意為「就……而言」。

---

62 suspend
★
[sə`spɛnd]

v 懸掛，使漂浮，使中止，使停職

同 exclude 排除在外
eliminate 排除

反 continue 繼續
resume 繼續

The project was suspended due to the lack of funds.

這個計畫被中止了，因為缺少資金。

point lack of sth. 意為「缺少某物」。

Because of the severe weather, the flights to Bangkok were suspended.

因為惡劣的天氣，往曼谷的班機停飛了。

---

63 stability
★
★
[stə`bɪlətɪ]

n 穩定（性），堅定，恆心

同 solidity 堅硬

反 unreliability 不可靠
uncertainty 不確定
unpredictability 不可預測

The engineer has tested the stability of the machine under different situations.

工程師已經在不同情況下測試了機器的穩定度。

The safety inspector examined the stability of the manufacturing processes.

安全稽查員檢測製程的穩定性。

---

64 sensitive
★
★
★
[`sɛnsətɪv]

a 敏感的，易受傷害的，機密的

同 delicate 纖弱的
tender 敏感的

反 unresponsive 反應遲鈍的
insensitive 感覺遲鈍的

The toothpaste is made especially for those who are highly sensitive to cold.

這種牙膏是特別給那些對冰冷極為敏感的人使用的。

Please cover these sensitive electronic devices.

請覆蓋住這些靈敏的電子裝置。

point sensitive 在此句意為「（儀器）靈敏的；敏感度高的」。

65 **persuade**

★
★
★

[pɚˈswed]

V 說服，使某人相信

同 convince 說服

反 dissuade 勸阻
　discourage 勸阻

衍 persuasion (n.) 勸說
　persuading (a.) 具說服力的

The sales tried to persuade him that it was the right time for having a meeting with the shareholders.

業務試著說服他是時候和股東開會了。

(point) it is the right time for + Ving 意為「是時候做……」。

The doctors persuaded the smoker to quit smoking but in vain.

醫生試著說服這名吸菸者戒菸，但徒勞無功。

(point) in vain 意為「徒勞無功」。

66 **particularly**

★
★
★

[pɚˈtɪkjələˑlɪ]

ad 特別，詳細地，具體地

同 peculiarly 特別地
　distinctly 確實地
　unusually 非常地
　extraordinarily 非常地

The rookie driver found driving in the narrow streets particularly difficult.

菜鳥駕駛覺得開在窄路尤其困難。

(point) find + O + a. 意為「覺得……」。

The client liked the overall design of the building, particularly the lighting fixtures.

客戶喜歡這棟建築的整體設計，尤其是燈具設備。

(point) 相關詞彙：especially 特別，specially 特別地，exceptionally 特殊地。

67 **overhead**

★

[ˈovɚˈhɛd]

a 在頭頂上的，高架的

ad 在上頭，高高地

同 above (adv.) 在上面

反 underground (a.) 地下的

The overhead projector seems to be broken.

懸掛式的投影機好像壞了。

You can put your carry-on bag in the overhead compartments.

你可以把隨身行李放到頭上的置物櫃。

(point) carry-on bag 意為「可帶上飛機的隨身行李」。

68 **outgoing**

★
★

[ˈautˌgoɪŋ]

a 外出的，直率的

同 extroverted 性格外向的
　uninhibited 不受約束的

反 introverted 內向的

We expect our candidates for this position to be outgoing.

我們期待這職位的求職者能夠很外向。

Only this telephone can be used for outgoing calls.

只有這台電話可以用來打外線。

(point) incoming call 則為「內線（打進來的電話）」。

CH 4

投資與設備

---

69 leak
★
[lik]

n 裂縫，漏出
v 滲漏，洩漏
同 disclose (v.) 揭發
reveal (v.) 揭露
反 seal (v.) 密封

The ceiling is leaking.
天花板正在漏水。

Unfortunately, the design of the new tablet leaked out.
很不幸地，新的平板電腦的設計被洩漏出去了。

---

70 leakage
★
★
[ˋlikɪdʒ]

n 洩漏，漏損物，漏損量
衍 nuclear leakage (ph.) 核洩漏

The leakage is too serious to be fixed.
漏水太嚴重了，以至於沒辦法修理。

The utility bill this month was high because a lot of water was wasted through leakage.
這個月的水電雜費很高，因為大量的水因漏掉而被浪費了。

---

71 possession
★
★
[pəˋzɛʃən]

n 擁有，所有物，領地
同 ownership 所有權
衍 possess (v.) 擁有
possessor (n.) 擁有人
possessory (a.) 所有者的

The lesson provides some tips of decreasing the desire for material possessions.
這個課程提供一些降低物質欲望的訣竅。

For the interior designer, the painting that once belonged to his grandfather is one of the most treasured possessions.
對這名室內設計師來說，這幅曾經屬於他爺爺的畫是他最珍貴的擁有物之一。

point belonged to 為過去式，因為是過去的事實，is 為現在式，代表此句 the painting is one of the most treasured possessions 為事實。

---

72 inactive
★
[ɪnˋæktɪv]

a 不活動的，怠惰的，失效的
同 motionless 不活動的
sluggish 懶散的
calm 沉著的
lazy 懶散的
passive 消極的
反 active 活躍的

Some teenagers are politically inactive.
有些年輕人對政治不熱衷。

The engineers at CMS Corporation decided to dispose of the inactive machine.
CMS 公司的工程師決定處置這台閒置的機器。

point dispose of 意為「清除；處理」。

Chapter 040

4 投資與設備

73 hazard
★
['hæzɚd]
- **n** 危險，危害物，機會
- **v** 冒險做出，嘗試
- **同** danger (n.) 危險
  risk (n.) 風險
  threat (n.) 威脅
  difficulty (n.) 困難
- **反** safety (n.) 安全
  security (n.) 安全

The old overhead cables might be a hazard to the workers.
舊的高架電纜可能對工人造成危險。

point a hazard to sb. 意為「對某人是個危險」。

Photographers who take pictures of some breathtaking natural views sometimes hazard their lives.
拍攝驚人自然景觀的攝影師有時要冒生命危險。

74 hardware
★
★
['hɑrd͵wɛr]
- **n** 金屬器件，硬體，武器
- **反** software 軟體

The new computer hardware will be installed next month.
下個月會安裝新的電腦硬體設備。

The hardware engineer's colleague didn't notice that he was laid off.
那名硬體工程師的同事不知道自己被裁員了。

point lay off 意為「解僱」。

75 fix
★
★
★
[fɪks]
- **v** 使固定，決定，修理，安排，操縱
- **n** 困境，窘境
- **同** fasten (v.) 釘牢
  attach (v.) 繫上
  affix (v.) 附上
  secure (v.) 弄牢

We sent a mechanic to fix the unexpected technical problem.
我們派一位技師來修理不可預測的技術性問題。

point mechanic, technician 皆可表示「技師」。

The elevator was temporarily out of service because it needed fixing.
電梯暫時停止服務，因為需要修理。

point it needed fixing = it needed to be fixed，意為「需要被修理」。

76 fixture
★
★
['fɪkstʃɚ]
- **n** 固定裝置
- **同** fixed appliance 固定裝置
  attachment 附加裝置
  installation 設置

The mall is famous for its light fixtures.
這個商城以燈具設備聞名。

point be famous for 意為「以……聞名」。

The bathroom fixtures are all included in the house.
浴室裝置都有被包含在房子中。

Test 1

一、請寫出下列單字的中文意思。

① replace _____   ⑥ technician _____

② central _____   ⑦ handle _____

③ equipment _____   ⑧ unique _____

④ investment _____   ⑨ routine _____

⑤ install _____   ⑩ activate _____

二、請寫出符合下列句意的單字。

① The old overhead cables might be a _____ to the workers.
舊的高架電纜可能對工人造成危險。

② Investing in stocks requires knowledge about the market;
_____, it's also crucial to have luck.
投資股票需要有關市場的知識,此外,有運氣也是相當重要。

③ Unfortunately, the equipment in the laboratory is not yet _____.
很不幸地,實驗室的儀器還未能正常運轉。

④ The pedestrian _____ escaped the accident.
路人驚險地逃過那場意外。

解答

1. ① 替換,歸還 ② 中央的,主要的;總局 ③ 設備,裝備 ④ 投資,投入 ⑤ 安裝,任命
   ⑥ 技師,技巧成熟的人 ⑦ 處理,操作;把手 ⑧ 唯一的,獨特的 ⑨ 常規,例行程式;日常的
   ⑩ 使活動
2. ① hazard ② additionally ③ operational ④ narrowly

Test 2

一、請選擇符合下列文意的單字。

- Ⓐ invest
- Ⓑ trial
- Ⓒ maintenance
- Ⓓ defects
- Ⓔ investor
- Ⓕ efficient

① Please note that the west elevator will be closed for regular _____ next Monday.

② The government will _____ three million in the project.

③ The _____ version of the software has limited functions.

④ The mechanic was sent to fix some _____ in the machine.

⑤ He tried to figure out a more _____ way to simplify the task.

二、請寫出下列片語的中文意思。

① in terms of _____   ⑤ with caution _____

② in no time _____   ⑥ cost a fortune _____

③ not in service _____   ⑦ figure out _____

④ on a regular basis _____   ⑧ all kinds of _____

解答

1. ①C ②A ③B ④D ⑤F
2. ① 就……而言 ② 立即地 ③ 不提供使用 ④ 規律地 ⑤ 謹慎地 ⑥ 花大錢 ⑦ 想出；明白；理解
   ⑧ 各式各樣的

Chapter 5
科技研發

以下多益必考單字，你認識哪些？

- [ ] adjust (p.096)
- [ ] portable (p.106)
- [ ] invent (p.099)
- [ ] mission (p.104)
- [ ] collaboration (p.111)
- [ ] measurable (p.112)
- [ ] experiment (p.108)
- [ ] retrieve (p.105)
- [ ] consist (p.110)
- [ ] abundant (p.101)
- [ ] innovation (p.103)
- [ ] economical (p.109)
- [ ] occur (p.106)
- [ ] recall (p.100)
- [ ] devise (p.110)
- [ ] embrace (p.098)
- [ ] reduce (p.097)
- [ ] expect (p.113)

Chapter 041

5 科技研發

01 advance
★★★
[əd`væns]
n 前進，發展
a 先行的，預先的
v 推進，提前，提高
同 improvement (n.) 增進
progress (n.) 前進
反 decline (n.) 下降
recession (n.) 後退
衍 advanced (a.) 先進的

Book the coach tickets in advance to get the better fares.
預先訂客運票，以取得更棒的票價。

Thanks to the advance of the technology, we can contact people from different countries through social media apps.
因為科技的進步，我們能透過社交軟體手機應用程式來跟不同國家的人聯絡。

(point) thanks to 意為「幸虧；因為」。

02 manually
★★
[`mænjuəlɪ]
ad 用手地，手工地
反 automatically 自動地
衍 manual (a.) 手工的
manually operated
(ph.) 手工操作的

The cellphone application allows users to manually input some personal information.
這個手機應用軟體讓使用者可以手動輸入一些個人訊息。

(point) allow sb. to + V 意為「允許某人做……」。

The customer service representative will teach you how to manually and automatically update new songs to your own playlists.
客服代表會教你如何手動及自動更新新歌到你自己的歌單。

03 adjust
★★★
[ə`dʒʌst]
v 調節，校正，解決
同 modify 修改
rearrange 重新整理
change 改變
transform 轉變
correct 改正

Before we finalize the itinerary, you can adjust your schedule.
在我們定案日程前，你可以調整你的行程。

The senior human resources manager shared how to adjust himself to working in the headquarters.
資深人力資源經理分享如何調適自己在總部工作。

(point) adjust to Ving 意指「適應做……」。

04 adjustment
★★★
[ə`dʒʌstmənt]
n 調節，調整，調解
同 alteration 改變
correction 改正
modification 修改

It takes time to get used to the adjustments in the operating system.
適應作業系統的調整是需要時間的。

(point) operating system 常簡稱為「OS 系統」，意為「作業系統」。

The renowned photographer asked his assistant to make some slight adjustments of the lens.
這位知名的攝影師請他的助理稍微調節一下鏡頭。

(point) professional / amateur photographer 意為「專業／業餘攝影師」。

05 reduce
★
★
★

[rɪ`djus]

v 減少，使處於，歸納為

同 decrease 減少
　　diminish 減小
　　minimize 使縮到最小

反 increase 增加
　　enlarge 擴大

The main purpose of this new policy is to reduce cost.

新政策的主要目的是要降低成本。

point 相關詞彙：lessen 變小，lower 減低。

Using solar panels can reduce your electricity bills and protect our Earth at the same time.

使用太陽能面板可以降低你的電費帳單並同時保護我們的地球。

point at the same time 意為「同時地」。

06 committed
★

[kə`mɪtɪd]

a 忠誠的，堅定的

同 devoted 忠實的
　　loyal 忠心的
　　faithful 忠實的

衍 commit (v.) 犯錯
　　commitment (n.) 承諾

The company is committed to developing environment-friendly products.

這間公司致力於發展對環境友善的產品。

point environment-friendly 意為「對環境友善的」。

No one will deny that he is a committed associate.

沒有人會否認他是一個很忠誠的同事。

point no one will deny 意為「沒人會否認」。

07 comparison
★
★

[kəm`pærəsn̩]

n 比較，對照

同 contrast 對比

反 resemblance 相似
　　likeness 相像
　　similarity 類似

The reporter made a comparison between the two flagship mobile phones.

記者做了兩隻旗艦手機的比較。

point cell phone = mobile phone = cell，意為「手機」。

The feature article included a comparison chart of the difference between traveling with groups and alone.

這個專欄包含了一個跟團旅遊和獨自旅遊差異比較的表格。

point feature article 意為「專欄」。

08 facility
★
★
★

[fə`sɪlətɪ]

n 能力，設備，場所，便利

同 equipment 裝備
　　ability 能力
　　skill 技能

All the newly updated facilities are available for tourists to use.

所有最新的更新設施都能讓遊客使用。

Only those who have permits can enter research facility.

只有那些有許可證的人才能進入研究中心。

point 此處的 facility 指「（尤指包含多個建築物，有特定用途的）場所」。

Chapter 042

5 科技研發

09 digital
★
[`dɪdʒɪtḷ]
a 數位的
衍 digital camera
(ph.) 數位相機

He went to the store to change the battery of his digital watch.
他去店裡換他電子錶的電池。

A majority of people use smartphones to take pictures but not digital cameras.
大部分的人使用智慧型手機來拍照而不是用數位相機。

---

10 engineer
★
★
★
[ˌɛndʒə`nɪr]
n 工程師
衍 engine (n.) 引擎
engineering (n.) 工程學

The engineers of this department are responsible for designing cellphone applications.
這個部門的工程師負責設計手機的應用程式。

point be responsible for = in charge of，意為「負責」。

The company plans to recruit more software engineers to work on the new project.
公司計劃招募更多的軟體工程師來做這份新計畫。

point recruit 可當動詞「招募」，也可當名詞「新進人員」。

---

11 technique
★
★
★
[tɛk`nik]
n 技巧，技術，方法
同 expertise 專門技術
衍 technician (n.) 技術人員

With advanced techniques, the garage mechanic always can satisfy his demanding clients.
因為有先進的技術，這名汽車技師總是能讓高要求的客戶滿意。

point 相關詞彙：skill 技能，ability 能力，capability 性能。

The technique used to be widely used in the field of marine biology.
這個科技曾在海洋生物學的領域中被廣泛運用。

point used to + V 意為「過去的習慣（現在沒有了）」。

---

12 embrace
★
★
[ɪm`bres]
v 擁抱，包含，欣然接受
n 擁抱
同 hug (v.) 擁抱
include (v.) 包含
comprise (v.) 包括

She embraced the idea of taking annual leave and traveling to Thailand.
她欣然接受放年假去泰國玩的提議。

point 延伸詞彙：personal leave 事假，sick leave 病假，official leave 公假，marriage leave 婚假，funeral leave 喪假，maternity leave 產假，compensatory leave 補休。

As an engineer in Research and Development Department, I always embrace the latest technology.
身為一個研發部門的工程師，我總是欣然接受最新的科技。

point as + 職稱，意為「身為……（職務）」。

13 **technological**
★
★
[tɛknəˋlɑdʒɪkl]]
ⓐ 技術的，工藝的
同 technical 技術的
衍 high technological crime
(ph.) 高科技犯罪

The article introduces the top ten technological changes in the twentieth century.
這篇文章介紹了二十世紀的前十大技術改變。

Technological advances in telecommunications enable the business to cooperate with other companies in other countries.
通訊技術進步讓企業可以和其他國家的公司合作。

14 **invent**
★
★
★
[ɪnˋvɛnt]
Ⓥ 發明，創造，虛構
同 create 創造
innovate 創新
反 copy 複製
imitate 模仿
mimic 模仿

The firm inventing a new kind of waterproof fabric made a fortune.
發明新種類的防水纖維的公司賺了大錢。
point make a fortune 意為「賺大錢」。

The foreman just invented a more efficient approach to cut down the production time.
監工才剛發明一個更有效率的方法來縮短製程。
point approach (n.) 方法 (v.) 接近，做為「接近」使用時，不加 to，例如：approach the station（進站）。

15 **suit**
★
★
★
[sut]
Ⓥ 適合，相稱，使適應
ⓝ 西裝，套，訴訟
同 be suitable for 與……相稱
衍 suitable (a.) 適合的

I bet the suit will suit you well since it was tailor-made.
我相信這西裝一定很適合你，因為是訂製的。
point tailor-made = customized，意為「訂製的」。

Pratt Electronics will bring a suit against Easylife Ltd.
Pratt 電子公司將對 Easylife 公司提起告訴。
point bring a suit against 意為「對……提起告訴」。

16 **inventor**
★
[ɪnˋvɛntɚ]
ⓝ 發明家，創造者
同 originator 創作者
creator 創作人
innovator 革新者
designer 設計者
developer 開發者

The inventor showed his gratitude to the sponsors in the award ceremony.
發明家在頒獎典禮上對贊助商表示感激。
point show one's gratitude to 意為「對……表示感激」。

The inventor shared where his inspiration came from in the latest publication.
發明家在他最新的出版品中分享他靈感的來源。

5 科技研發

17 convenient

★
★ [kən`vinjənt]
★ **a** 方便的，合宜的
反 inconvenient 不方便的
衍 convenience (n.) 便利

The advance of the Internet makes communication between people from different countries more convenient than before.
網路的先進讓不同國家的人溝通比以前更方便。

(point) more convenient than 意為「更加方便」，為比較級。

E-commerce is convenient to those residents who live far from the city center.
電子商務對於那些住得離市中心很遠的居民來說很方便。

(point) E-commerce 意為「電子商務」，在線上進行買賣交易。

18 technology

★
★ [tɛk`nɑlədʒɪ]
★ **n** 工藝，技術，科技
同 skill 技術
technique 科技

The advancement of technology has brought people convenience.
科技的進步帶給人們方便。

The host of the show *Tech-Now* introduced the current trends in technology.
《現今科技》的節目主持人介紹了科技的當前趨勢。

19 recharge

★ [ri`tʃɑrdʒ]
v 再充電，再裝填彈藥
同 refresh 使振作精神

My tablet is running out of battery. I'm going to recharge it.
我的平板電腦快沒電了。我要來充電。

(point) run out of + N 意為「用盡……」。

Once you fully recharge the mobile phone, you can use it all day because it has great durability.
一旦你完全充好電，這支手機可以用一整天，因為它有很好的續航力。

(point) 此句的 once 為連接詞，表達「一旦」。

20 recall

★ [rɪ`kɔl]
★ **v** 回想，回憶
同 call back 收回
bring back 帶回

All the electronic devices had been recalled because of some serious faults in their design.
所有電子裝置都因為設計上的一些嚴重缺失被召回。

(point) because of = due to = owing to + N / Ving 意為「因為……」。

The accountant has incredible memory that she can recall every detail that her supervisor asked.
這名會計有驚人的記憶力，她可以記得她上司問的每件事情的細節。

21 **abundant**

★
★
★

[əˋbʌndənt]

a 大量，豐富的，充足的

同 more than enough
　　相當足夠的
　　rich 豐富的

反 infrequent 罕見的
　　insufficient 不足的
　　rare 稀有的
　　uncommon 罕見的

The teacher provided abundant learning resources for his students.
該名老師提供給他的學生大量的學習資源。

(point) 相關詞彙：ample 大量的，plentiful 豐富的，sufficient 充分的。

Although our country has abundant supplies of oil now, we still need to develop biofuel.
雖然現在我們國家有足夠的石油，我們仍然需要發展生質能源。

(point) 生質能源為利用構成生物體的有機質做為燃料的再生能源，像是木屑或是稻殼。biofuel = biology（生物）+ fuel（燃料）。

22 **battery**

★

[ˋbætərɪ]

n 電池

Remember to charge the cellphone battery before you go on a business trip so that your client can reach you.
記得在出差前要充好手機的電，這樣你的客戶才能聯絡到你。

(point) reach 意為「到達；連絡上」。

I bought the batteries because they last about 10 hours.
我買這些電池是因為它們可以維持十小時。

23 **groundbreaking**

★

[ˋgraʊnd͵brekɪŋ]

a 開創性的

同 innovative 革新的
　　revolutionary 革命的
　　leading-edge 尖端的
　　original 獨創性的

反 old 老的

The groundbreaking innovation won the international design award.
這個創新發明贏了國際設計大獎。

The groundbreaking update of the cellphones has appealed to many engineers.
手機創新的更新已經吸引了許多工程師。

(point) appeal to 意為「吸引」。

24 **fulfill**

★
★
★

[fʊlˋfɪl]

V 執行，實現，達到

同 realize 實現
　　manage 設法做到
　　deliver 履行

反 neglect 疏漏

The restaurant menu is upgraded frequently in order to fulfill patrons' needs.
這份餐廳目錄經常更新，以便滿足老顧客的需求。

It seems that the candidate fulfills all the requirements and is kind of overqualified.
這名求職者似乎符合所有的條件，而且還有點大材小用。

(point) overqualified (a.) 資歷過高的，大材小用的。

Chapter 044

5

科技研發

---

25 dynamic
★
[daɪˈnæmɪk]

a 動力的，有活力的

同 energetic 精力旺盛的
spirited 活潑的
lively 精力充沛的
vital 充滿活力的
vigorous 精力充沛的
powerful 強有力的

One of the special requirements is that candidates must have the ability to work in a dynamic situation.
其中一個特別的必要條件，就是求職者必須要有能在多變的環境下工作的能力。

Technology development is a dynamic process; therefore, engineers should always keep themselves updated.
科技發展是一個不斷變化發展的過程，因此，工程師應該要不斷讓自己保持更新。

---

26 invention
★
★
★
[ɪnˈvɛnʃən]

n 發明（物），創造，捏造

同 origination 創作
creation 創作
innovation 革新

Up to now, people still benefit from the invention of the light bulb.
直到現在，人們仍然受惠於燈泡的發明。

point benefit from 意為「受益於」。

The invention is a huge success in this field.
這個發明是這領域很大的成功。

---

27 maximum
★
★
[ˈmæksəməm]

a 最大的，最多的，最高的
n 最大量，最大限度

同 greatest (a.) 最大的
highest (a.) 最高的
utmost (a.) 最大的
supreme (a.) 最高的
反 minimum (n.) 最小量

The mechanic is testing the vehicle's maximum speed.
技師正在測試這台車的最高速度。

point 多益測驗中可以概括很多字的詞彙：vehicle（交通工具）、device（裝置）、equipment（設備）、instrument（儀器）。

The weather forecaster reported the maximum temperature today.
天氣預報員播報今天最高溫度。

---

28 innovate
★
★
★
[ˈɪnəˌvet]

v 改變，革新

同 change 改變
renovate 更新
remodel 重新塑造
renew 更新
invent 創造

The firm has hired more promising recruits to innovate the old system in order to make progress.
公司僱用更多有潛力的員工來改革舊系統，以便取得進步。

point in order to + V = in order that + S + V 意為「為了做……」。

The pop-up store keeps innovating to provide different customer experiences.
這間限定快閃店不斷地創新，以提供不同的消費者感受。

point keep + Ving 意為「保持／不斷做……」。

CH 5

科技研發

29 innovation
★
★
★
[ˌɪnə`veʃən]

n 創新，新方法，新事物

同 change 改變
　　alteration 變更
　　revolution 革命

The new innovation is designed to respond to plenty of customers' needs.
這個新的發明被設計用來回應很多顧客的需求。

point respond to 意為「回應」。

The manager asked his staff to attend conferences to keep updating the latest innovations in the area.
經理要求他的員工參加研討會以持續更新該領域的最新發展。

30 innovator
★
★
[`ɪnəˌvetɚ]

n 改革者，創新者

同 pioneer 先驅者
　　developer 開發者

As an innovator in this field of contemporary art, Mrs. Morgan will deliver a speech after the reception.
身為當代藝術這領域的先驅，摩根女士將在招待會會後演講。

point 延伸詞彙：receptionist (n.) 接待人員，reception desk (ph.) 接待台。

Mr. McCaw is regarded as one of the major innovators of change.
麥考先生被認為是變革的主要改革者之一。

point be regarded as 意為「被認為是……」。

31 gradually
★
★
[`grædʒuəlɪ]

ad 逐步地，漸漸地

同 steadily 不斷地
　　evenly 均勻地
　　constantly 不斷地
　　consistently 一貫地

反 suddenly 意外地
　　abruptly 突然地

Recently, the demand for robot vacuums has gradually increased.
近來，掃地機器人的需求逐漸增加。

Green buildings have gradually become common in this nation.
綠建築在這國家逐漸變得普遍。

32 developer
★
★
★
[dɪ`vɛləpɚ]

n 開發者，顯影劑

衍 property developer (ph.) 房地產商

The software developer is addressing the problems that the users mentioned.
軟體研發者正在處理使用者提及的問題。

point address (n.) 地址 (v.) 演講；應付，處理。

Due to insufficient funds, the developer was forced to terminate the project.
因為資金不足，開發者被迫中止計畫。

point 延伸詞彙：terminal (a.) 晚期的 (n.) 航廈。

---

33 development
- ★
- ★ [dɪ`vɛləpmənt]
- ★
- n 發展，新情況，已開發土地
- 同 evolution 發展
  growth 成長
  expansion 擴展

Having a balanced diet is beneficial to the development of children.
均衡飲食有益於兒童的成長。

(point) be beneficial to 意為「有益於」。

The research and development department has worked overtime for the launch of the new product for one month.
研發部門已經為了新產品上市而加班一個月了

(point) research and development 縮寫為 R&D，意為「研發部門」。

---

34 besides
- ★
- ★ [bɪ`saɪdz]
- adj 此外，而且
- prep 此外
- 同 excluding
  (prep.) 除……之外
  except (prep.) 除……之外
  beyond (prep.) 越過

Besides Mr. Renner, you are also nominated as the best employee of the year.
除了雷納以外，你也被提名為年度最佳員工。

(point) nominee (n.) 參選人；被提名者／ nomination (n.) 提名；任命。

Besides being a highly renowned novelist, he is a popular columnist as well.
他除了是個有名的小說家，也是個受歡迎的專欄作家。

(point) as well = too，意為「也是」。

---

35 mission
- ★
- ★ [`mɪʃən]
- ★
- n 使節團，使命，任務
- 同 commission 委任
  task 任務
  job 工作
  business 日常工作
  duty 責任

The executive is a man with a mission and he has led his team to accomplish many projects.
這位高級行政主管是個有使命感的人，他已經領導他的團隊完成了許多專案。

The housewife felt that her mission in life was to take care of her children.
這名家庭主婦認為照顧她的小孩是她的天職。

(point) sb's mission in life 意為「某人的天職」。

---

36 setup
- ★
- ★ [`sɛt‚ʌp]
- ★
- n 組織，計畫，姿勢，設定
- 同 structure 結構
  framework 架構
  composition 構成

The engineer was checking the specialist's network setup page.
工程師正在確認這個專員的網路設定頁面。

The instructor explained the setup procedures in detail.
講師仔細地介紹設置步驟。

(point) in detail 意為「仔細地；詳細地」。

37 retrieve
★ [rɪ`triv]
Ⅴ 收回，使恢復，挽回
同 recover 復原
　 regain 取回

These dogs were trained to retrieve balls.
這些狗被訓練如何撿球。

The system allows users to retrieve data in a short time.
這個系統能讓使用者快速讀取資料。

38 venture
★
★ [`vɛntʃɚ]
Ⅴ 冒險，以……做賭注
ⁿ 冒險，企業，投機活動
同 adventure (n.) 冒險
　 risk (n.) 風險

The joint venture was subsidized by the government so it had enough funds to develop a new product line.
這家合資公司被政府資助，所以有資金去研發新的產品線。

 joint 意指「共同的」。

After being worn out by the daily routines, he made up his mind to have a venture by applying for a working holiday visa next year.
在被每天的例行公事給消磨殆盡後，他下定決心明年要申請打工度假簽證來場冒險。

point wear sb. out 意為「使（某人）筋疲力盡」。

39 rank
★
★ [ræŋk]
★
ⁿ 等級，行列
Ⅴ 排列，評級，列隊
同 position (n.) 位置
　 grade (n.) 等級
　 level (n.) 等級
　 class (n.) 階級
　 status (n.) 地位

Please rank your top five travel destinations.
請排出你的前五名旅遊景點。

point travel destination = tourist attraction 意為「旅遊景點；觀光勝地」。

The senior engineer ranks above the assistant.
資深工程師的職位比助理高。

40 radical
★ [`rædɪkl̩]
a 根本的，徹底的，激進的
同 revolutionary 革命的
反 conservative 保守的
　 moderate 適度的
　 progressive 漸進的

The company has gone through a radical reform.
這公司已經歷了根本的革新。

point go through 意為「經歷」。

The scientist used this radical approach to analyze the research results.
科學家使用這個激進的方法來分析研究結果。

---

41 ★ **profound**
[prəˋfaʊnd]
ⓐ 深刻的，深奧的，完全的
同 intense 強烈的
extreme 極度的
sincere 真摯的
反 superficial 表面的
mild 溫和的

I learned a lot from my mentor's profound thinking.
我從我導師的深奧想法中學到了很多。

The invention of smartphones has brought about profound changes in modern people's lives.
智慧型手機的發明帶給現代人的生活重大變化。

point bring about 意為「導致；促成」。

---

42 ★ ★ **portable**
[ˋpɔrtəbl]
ⓐ 便於攜帶的，手提式的
同 transportable 可運輸的
movable 可移動的
反 fixed 固定的
immovable 不可移動的

The electronic device is completely portable, durable and approachable.
這個電子裝置完全是可攜帶式、耐用且好操作。

Portable cellphones make communication a lot easier than before.
與以前相比，攜帶式電話使溝通更加便利。

point a lot 修飾 easier 的程度。

---

43 ★ ★ ★ **element**
[ˋɛləmənt]
ⓝ 元素，要素，成分
同 component 成分
constituent 成分
segment 部分
detail 細節
point 要點
衍 elemental (a.) 基本的

I only learned the elements of geography in my freshman year.
我在新生第一年時只學到地理的基礎元素。

point 延伸詞彙：freshman 大一／ sophomore 大二／ junior 大三／ senior 大四。

They tried to include all the important elements in their discussions.
他們試著在討論中包含所有重要的元素。

point 相關詞彙：part 一部份，section 部分，portion 部分，piece 片段。

---

44 ★ **occur**
[əˋkɝ]
ⓥ 發生，出現，浮現
同 happen 發生
exist 存在
衍 occurrence (n.) 發生

The reporter reported that two large earthquakes occurred almost one after another.
記者報導兩個大規模的地震幾乎一個接著一個發生。

The new system can precisely analyze how errors occurred.
新系統能精確分析錯誤如何發生。

45 **visible**

★ [`vɪzəbl]

🅰 可看見的，顯而易見的，明白的

🔁 perceptible 可感知的
perceivable 可感知的

🔄 invisible 看不見的
hidden 隱藏的

衍 visibility (n.) 能見度

The landmark is visible from the balcony.
從陽台可以看到這個地標。

point 延伸詞彙：seeable 可看見的，observable 看得見的。

The sample is not visible to the naked eye, so you should use this microscope.
這個樣本無法以肉眼看見，所以你要使用這個顯微鏡。

point naked eye 意為「肉眼」。

46 **invisible**

★ [ɪn`vɪzəbl]

🅰 看不見的，無形的，不顯眼的

🔁 unseeable 看不見的
undetectable 探測不到的
indistinguishable
不易察覺的

🔄 visible 可看見的

The scientist used a microscope to observe these bacteria because they were invisible to the naked eye.
科學家用顯微鏡來觀察這些細菌，因為有些用肉眼是看不見的。

point microscope 有時會出現在多益聽力測驗 Part 1 圖片題，相關詞彙：laboratory (n.) 實驗室。

The differences between the real and the fake paintings are almost invisible.
真畫與假畫之間的差別簡直難以辨認。

47 **institute**

★
★
★ [`ɪnstətjut]

🅝 學院，原則，摘要

🅥 創立，制定，著手

🔁 establishment (n.) 建立
foundation (n.) 建立
academy (n.) 學院
university (n.) 大學

衍 institution (n.) 機構

I have heard that the new institute will invest 5 million in developing the new product.
我聽說這間新機構會花五百萬在開發新產品上。

point 相關詞彙：organization 組織。

After graduating from college, the young man found a job in a research institute.
在大學畢業後，這名年輕人在一個研究機構找了一份工作。

48 **immature**

★ [ˌɪmə`tjʊr]

🅰 未成熟的，粗糙的，幼稚的

🔁 childish 幼稚的
babyish 孩子氣的
inexperienced 經驗不足的

🔄 mature 成熟的

The technique is still immature.
這項技術仍然不成熟。

After cooperating with the freelance photographer, we found that he was immature and irresponsible.
和這名自由攝影師合作後，我們發現他不成熟且不負責任。

point 易混淆字：cooperate (v.) 合作／ corporate (a.) 公司的。

Chapter 047

5 科技研發

49 honest
★
['anɪst]
a 誠實的，正直的，坦率的
同 truthful 誠實的
　　sincere 真摯的
　　frank 坦白的
反 devious 不坦率的
　　dishonest 不誠實的
　　untruthful 不誠實的

To be honest, I don't think we can finish the project on time.
說實話，我認為我們不可能準時完成計畫。
(point) to be honest 意為「說實話」。

It would be great if you could give me your honest opinion on the book.
如果你能給我關於這本書的誠實意見，將會非常棒。

50 counter
★
★
['kaʊntɚ]
n 對立物，還擊，櫃檯
ad 反方向地，相反地
v 反對，反駁，抵銷
同 dispute (v.) 爭論
　　refute (v.) 駁斥
　　contradict (v.) 反駁

Hannah chose a white kitchen counter to fit the overall interior design of her apartment.
漢娜選擇一個白色的廚房檯面來搭配她公寓的整體室內設計。
(point)「選擇」的動詞三態：choose / chose / chosen。

The company's plan for next season ran counter to their original proposal.
公司下一季的計畫跟原本的提案完全不同。
(point) run counter 表示「背道而馳」；此處的 counter 是副詞，表示「相反地」。

51 framework
★
★
['frem,wɝk]
n 架構，骨架，機構
同 structure 結構
　　body 組織
　　foundation 基礎
衍 frame (n.) 架構

The company established a basic framework for their organization.
公司建立了組織的基本架構。

The framework for classification is widely used by scientists.
這個分類的架構被科學家們廣泛使用。

52 experiment
★
★
★
[ɪk'spɛrəmənt]
v 進行實驗，試驗
n 實驗，試驗
同 test (n.) 試驗
　　investigation (n.) 調查
　　examination (n.) 檢查
　　observation (n.) 觀察

The success of the experiment has brought the technology to the next level.
實驗的成功將科技帶到下一個階段。

The passionate teacher is experimenting the new teaching approach in order to improve the students' learning motivation.
這名熱情的老師正在嘗試新的教學法以增強學生的學習動機。

53 **evident**
★ [ˋɛvədənt]
a 明顯的，明白的
同 obvious 明顯的
apparent 明顯的
noticeable 顯著的
visible 可看見的
observable 顯著的
反 unnoticeable 不易察覺的

It's evident that **neither** he **nor** she is competent for that position.
很明顯地，他和她都不適任那個職位。

(point) neither... nor 意為「兩者皆非」。

The data analyst reported his great findings with evident enjoyment.
資料分析師喜形於色地發表他重大的發現。

---

54 **pioneer**
★ [͵paɪəˋnɪr]
n 拓荒者，先驅者
v 開闢，倡導
同 explorer (n.) 探險者
discoverer (n.) 發現者
反 follower (n.) 追隨者

He is absolutely the pioneer in this industry.
他絕對是這個行業的先驅。

The pop singer pioneered the new fashion trend.
這名流行歌手開創了新的流行趨勢。

---

55 **education**
★
★
★ [͵ɛdʒuˋkeʃən]
n 教育，教育學
同 teaching 教學
schooling 學校教育
instruction 教學

Early childhood education will be the government's focus this year.
早期兒童教育將會是政府今年的焦點。

For this job **opening**, a master degree in Education is necessary.
對這個職缺來說，教育學碩士學位是必須的。

(point) opening = vacancy，意為「職缺」。

---

56 **economical**
★
★ [͵ikəˋnɑmɪkl]
a 經濟的，節儉的，節約的
同 cheap 便宜的
inexpensive 不貴的
discounted 折扣的
cost-effective 划算的
反 expensive 昂貴的
衍 economize (v.) 節約

It's more economical to **take** a bus than a taxi.
搭公車比搭計程車還經濟實惠。

(point) 搭交通工具使用 take 這個動詞。

The research and development department is developing new cars that are more economical **on fuel** than the last generation.
研發部門正在研發比上一代更省燃料的新車。

(point) energy-efficient, fuel-efficient, energy-saving, fuel-saving 皆可表達「省燃料的」。

57 **devise**

★ [dɪ`vaɪz]

V 設計，發明，策劃

同 form 形成
formulate 規劃
frame 構築
compose 構成
construct 建造
produce 製造

The engineer devised a new machine that can make the production **much** more effective.
工程師設計了一台新機器，可以讓生產更加有效率。

> **point** much 修飾形容詞比較級。

The thermometer was **devised** to measure the water temperature.
這個溫度計是設計來測量水溫的。

> **point** 相關詞彙：design 設計，develop 發展，create 創造，invent 創造。

58 **defend**

★ [dɪ`fɛnd]

V 防禦，保衛，辯護

同 protect 保護
shield 保衛

反 attack 攻擊

She learns **martial arts** to defend herself.
她學習武術來防禦自己。

> **point** martial arts 意為「武術」。

The scientist defended the theory by writing a **journal paper**.
這名科學家透過寫期刊來捍衛該理論。

> **point** 相關字彙：research (n.) 研究，survey (n. / v.) 調查，questionnaire (n.) 問卷。

59 **consist**

★ [kən`sɪst]

V 組成，存在於

同 be made up 由……組成
comprise 包含
contain 包含
include 包括
involve 包含

Our team **consists of** six senior engineers.
我們團隊由六個資深工程師所組成。

> **point** consist of... 表示「由……組成」。

60 **comparatively**

★ [kəm`pærətɪvlɪ]
★

ad 對比地，比較地，稍微

同 relatively 相對地

衍 compare (v.) 比較
comparison (n.) 比較

This new fabric is comparatively **durable**.
這種新的布料比較耐用。

> **point** durable (a.) 耐用的。很常在多益測驗中出現，用來形容衣服或材質。

According to the marketing manager, the campaign was comparatively successful.
根據行銷經理表示，這次的行銷活動比較成功。

61 **come across**
★
★ [kʌm] [əˈkrɔs]

ph 偶然碰見，被理解，出現

同 meet / find by chance 偶然遇見
run into 偶然碰到
bump into 偶遇
run across 偶然遇見

I came across an old friend at the conference.
我在研討會上遇到一位老朋友。

Tina asked her coworker whether they had **come across** this problem.
提娜問她的同事是否曾遇過這個問題。

point 相關詞彙：discover 找到，encounter 遭遇。

---

62 **collaboration**
★
★ [kəˌlæbəˈreʃən]
★

n 合作，共同研究，勾結

同 cooperation 合作
alliance 結盟
partnership 合夥
衍 collaborate (v.) 合作

The collaboration between two technology companies has become one of the popular topics recently.
兩家科技公司的合作已經變成最近其中一個熱門話題。

The two well-known singers are working in close collaboration with each other on the new **single**.
這兩位有名的歌手於這首新單曲有密切合作。

point single (n.) 單曲 (a) 單身的。

---

63 **appoint**
★
★ [əˈpɔɪnt]
★

v 任命，委派，約定

同 assign 指派
designate 委任

Mr. Tucker was appointed to become his coworker's **deputy**.
塔克先生被指派為他同事的副手。

point deputy 意為「副手；代理人」。

From June, we've appointed three new consultants this year.
從六月開始，我們今年已經任用了三名新顧問。

---

64 **decisive**
★ [dɪˈsaɪsɪv]

a 決定性的，果斷的

同 deciding 決定性的
conclusive 決定性的
determining 決定的
反 indecisive 無決斷力的
insignificant 無足輕重的

He was promoted to the senior specialist **in that** he was decisive and responsible.
他因為很果斷且負責而被升為資深專員。

point in that = because 意為「因為」。

The team had a decisive victory, which got a big round of applause.
隊伍獲得決定性的勝利，這讓他們贏得了一陣熱烈的掌聲。

5 科技研發

65 rarely
★
★
['rɛrlɪ]

ad 很少，極度，出色地

同 hardly 幾乎不
scarcely 幾乎不
seldom 很少
infrequently 稀少地

反 often 常常
frequently 經常地

The executive assistant rarely forgets what he is required to do.
行政助理很少忘記他被要求做什麼。

The industrial designer rarely had time to attend the training course, so he chose online tutorials instead.
這名工業設計師沒有時間參加訓練課程，所以取而代之他選擇線上課程。

66 disposal
★
[dɪ'spozl]

n 處理，配置，控制

同 throwing away 丟棄
getting rid of 擺脫
discarding 丟棄

衍 dispose (v.) 處理

The disposal of chemical substances is a problem for the government.
對政府來說，化學物品的處理是個難題。

The fee is charged for the disposal of sewage.
這個費用是收來作為汙水處理費的。

(point) 相關字彙：utility bill 意為「水電雜費」。

67 describe
★
★
★
[dɪ'skraɪb]

v 描寫，形容，畫（圖形）

同 report 記述
express 表達

衍 description (n.) 形容

The witness described the whole car accident in detail.
目擊者仔細地描述整個車禍狀況。

The product manager described the conditions of the defective product to the engineer.
產品經理跟工程師描述瑕疵產品狀況。

(point) product manager 簡稱為 PM，意為「產品經理」。

68 measurable
★
★
['mɛʒərəbl]

a 可測量的，重要的

反 immeasurable 不可計量的
measureless 不可量的

衍 measure (v.) 測量
measurement (n.) 測量

Some regulars noticed that there was a measurable improvement in the food quality and service.
一些常客發現食物品質及服務有很顯著的進步。

(point) regular (a.) 經常的 (n.) 常客，regularly (adv.) 經常地，on a regular basis (ph.) 規律地。

According to the scientist's presentation, no measurable change in this experiment was being observed.
根據科學家的簡報，這個實驗中沒有發現任何顯著的改變。

69 admiration
★
[͵ædmə`reʃən]
n 欽佩，讚美，
受到讚美的人（物）
同 respect 敬重
反 disdain 輕蔑
scorn 藐視
衍 admire (v.) 欽配
admirable (a.) 值得讚揚的

He was the admiration of his whole team.
他受到整個團隊的敬重。

The journalist showed admiration for the police who saved an old lady.
記者對那名救了老奶奶的警察展現出欽佩之意。

---

70 admirable
★
[`ædmərəbl̩]
a 值得讚揚的，令人欽佩的
同 respectable 值得尊敬的
adorable 值得崇拜的

The manager did an admirable job in solving the problems.
經理在解決問題方面表現可嘉。

point in + 方面，表示「在……方面」。

You will know why Madame Curie is admirable once you read her autobiography.
一旦你讀過居禮夫人的自傳，你就會知道為什麼她那麼值得尊敬。

point 居里夫人是首位獲得諾貝爾獎的女性，也是第一名兩度榮獲諾貝爾獎的科學家。她發現兩種新元素釙（Po）和鐳（Ra）。在她的指導下，人們第一次將放射性同位素用於治療腫瘤。

---

71 expect
★
★
★
[ɪk`spɛkt]
v 預料，期待，指望
同 anticipate 期望
衍 expectation (n.) 期待

The flagship cellphone is considerably better than what people expected.
這台旗艦款的手機比人們期待的還要更好。

point 延伸詞彙：flagship store 旗艦店，flagship product 旗艦商品。

The movie director expected his latest movie could be nominated as the best movie of the year.
電影導演預期他的最新電影能夠被提名為年度最佳電影。

point be nominated as 意為「被提名為……」。

---

72 hourly
★
★
★
[`aʊrlɪ]
a 每小時的，頻繁的，隨時
衍 hourly employee 時薪人員

Thanks for listening to the hourly traffic update.
感謝收聽每小時的交通報導更新。

point 此句常為多益聽力測驗中廣播題型的第一句話，有時考題會問「報導多久更新一次」，如果說到 hourly，那就是一小時一次。

The intelligent sports bracelet is set to vibrate hourly to remind users to take a short break.
智能運動手環被設定一小時震動一次來提醒使用者稍稍休息。

Chapter 050

5 科技研發

73 achievement

[əˋtʃivmənt]
★★★

n 達成，成就

同 accomplishment 成就
attainment 成就
fulfillment 完成
realization 體現

反 failure 失敗
defeat 失敗

Winning the best employee of the year gave him **a great sense of** achievement.
贏得年度最佳員工獎給他很大的成就感。

 point a sense of + N 意為「……感」。

The professor evaluated the achievements of his students by the reports and group presentation.
教授透過報告和小組簡報來評估學生的學習成效。

---

74 available

[əˋveləbḷ]
★★★

a 可利用的，可得到的，有空的

同 accessible 可得到的
free 空閒的
handy 便於使用的
at hand 即將到來

反 inaccessible 達不到的
unusable 不能用的
occupied 已佔用的

Are you available next Monday? We are going to throw a retirement party for Jim.
你下週一有空嗎？我們會幫金辦一個退休餐會。

point retirement party = farewell party，意為「退休餐會；歡送會」，為多益測驗中常見的活動類型。

The executive is thinking when driverless cars will be available on the market.
行政主管在想無人駕駛汽車何時會在市面上發行。

---

75 giant

[ˋdʒaɪənt]
★★

n 巨人，偉人
a 巨大的，巨人般的

反 dwarf (n.) 矮子

The firm is the electronics giant.
這間公司是電子業界巨頭。

The biotechnology company's invention is one giant leap for mankind.
生物科技公司的發明對於全人類來說是一次巨大的飛躍。

---

76 compatible

[kəmˋpætəbḷ]
★★★

a 能共處的，適合的，相容的

同 well matched 相配的
反 incompatible 不相容的

Unfortunately, the newest operating system is not compatible with your electronic device.
很不幸地，最新的作業系統與你的電子裝置不相符。

The new policy that was announced yesterday is not compatible with the company culture.
昨天頒布的新政策與公司文化不相容。

point that was announced yesterday 修飾前面的 policy。

以下題目完全擬真新制多益 Part 5，請選出最符合句意的選項。

1. It takes time to get used to the ------- in the operating system.

    (A) adjustments   (B) missions

    (C) education   (D) collaboration

2. The company is committed to ------- environment-friendly products.

    (A) develop   (B) be developed

    (C) developed   (D) developing

3. Only those who have permits can enter research -------.

    (A) rate   (B) device   (C) element   (D) facility

4. The joint ------- was subsidized by the government so it had enough funds to develop a new product line.

    (A) comparison   (B) visible   (C) venture   (D) device

5. The firm has hired more promising recruits to ------- the old system in order to make progress.

    (A) be innovated   (B) innovate

    (C) innovation   (D) innovating

6. ------- being a highly renowned novelist, he is a popular columnist as well.

    (A) Besides   (B) However   (C) Whenever   (D) Whether

>> 正確答案與解析請翻至下一頁查看

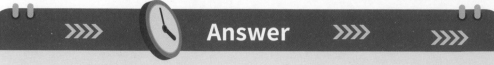

● 正確答案與解析

1. 適應作業系統的調整是需要時間的。

   (A) 調整　　　　(B) 任務　　　　(C) 教育　　　　(D) 合作

   正確答案 (A)

2. 這公司致力於發展對環境友善的產品。

   (D) 發展（動詞進行式）。be committed to（致力於）後面須加 Ving

   正確答案 (D)

3. 只有那些有許可證的人才能進入研究中心。

   (A) 速率　　　　(B) 裝置　　　　(C) 元素　　　　(D) 中心；設施

   正確答案 (D)

4. 這家合資公司被政府資助，所以有資金去研發新的產品線。

   (A) 比較　　　　(B) 顯而易見的　　(C) 企業　　　　(D) 裝置

   正確答案 (C)

5. 公司僱用更多有潛力的員工來改革舊系統，以便取得進步。

   (B) 創新（動詞原形）。to 後面須加原形動詞

   正確答案 (B)

6. 他除了是個有名的小說家，也是個受歡迎的專欄作家。

   (A) 此外　　　　(B) 然而　　　　(C) 不論何時　　(D) 是否

   正確答案 (A)

Chapter 6
金融財務

以下多益必考單字，你認識哪些？

☐ record (p.135)　　☐ financial (p.124)　　☐ incorrect (p.133)

☐ reimburse (p.121)　☐ rental (p.126)　　　☐ calculation (p.133)

☐ indicate (p.119)　　☐ occupied (p.127)　　☐ bankrupt (p.130)

☐ verify (p.119)　　　☐ absolute (p.129)　　☐ insurance (p.127)

☐ mortgage (p.125)　☐ legitimate (p.132)　☐ dependent (p.131)

☐ account (p.122)　　☐ arise (p.129)　　　☐ value (p.134)

01 anniversary
★
★
★
[͵ænə`vɝsərɪ]

n 週年紀念日，週年紀念

a 週年的，週年紀念的

The couple dressed up and reserved a fancy French restaurant to celebrate their wedding anniversary.
這對夫妻盛裝打扮並訂了奢華的法國餐廳來慶祝他們的結婚週年紀念日。

point dress up 意為「盛裝打扮」。

The dinner is to celebrate the 30th anniversary of the founding of the company.
晚宴的目的是要慶祝公司成立三十週年。

02 appear
★
★
★
[ə`pɪr]

V 出現，似乎，露面

同 arrive 到達
　 emerge 出現
　 turn up 出現
　 occur 發生

反 disappear 消失

衍 appearance (n.) 出現

By the time he appeared, his assistant had been there for 20 minutes.
等到他抵達時，他的助理已經到那裡二十分鐘了。

point 比較早發生的事情用過去完成式，比較晚發生的事情用過去式。

It appeared that the financial analyst's prediction was correct.
這位金融分析師的預測似乎是正確的。

point 相關詞彙：seem (v.) 似乎。

03 option
★
★
★
[`ɑpʃən]

n 選擇，可選擇的東西

同 choice 選擇
　 alternative 選擇

How many delivery options do they offer?
他們提供多少運送的選擇？

point 延伸詞彙：package（美式）包裹，parcel（英式）包裹。

The car rental agency provides a variety of options for customers to choose based on their needs and budgets.
租車公司提供很多選項給顧客，可根據他們的需求及預算來選。

point a variety of 意為「多樣的」。

04 revenue
★
★
[`rɛvə͵nju]

n 稅收，收入，收益

同 return 收益
　 gain 獲利

反 expenditure 支出

The revenue this quarter is significantly higher than what we expected.
這一季的收入比我們預期的還要高。

point 相關詞彙：income 收入，taking 進款，proceeds 收益，earnings 收入，profit 收益。

The government's new policy is to raise revenue without increasing taxes.
政府的新政策是要在不增加稅的狀況下提升收入。

05 forecast

★
★

[`forˏkæst]

v 預測，預言

n 預測，預料

同 predict (v.) 預言
foresee (v.) 預見

I checked the weather forecast to know the weather in my travel destination.
我確認天氣預報以得知我的旅行目的地的天氣。

The financial analyst forecasted that the unemployment rate would rise.
財政分析師預測失業率會上升。

point unemployment rate 意為「失業率」。

---

06 indicate

★
★
★

[`ɪndəˏket]

v 指出，表明，暗示

同 demonstrate 顯示
imply 暗示

衍 indication (n.) 指示
indicator (n.) 指示者

The accountant indicated that the financial problem was temporary and could be solved immediately.
會計指出這個財政問題是暫時的，可以馬上解決。

point temporary (a.) 暫時的／permanent (a.) 永久的。

The survey indicated that the population of the city is increasing.
調查顯示這個城市的人口正在上升中。

point 相關詞彙：show 顯示，suggest 暗示。

CH 6

金融財務

---

07 quarterly

★
★
★

[`kwɔrtɚli]

a 季度的

n 季刊

衍 quarter (n.) 季度，四分之一

The reader subscribed to the quarterly magazine.
讀者訂閱了季刊雜誌。

point 延伸詞彙：subscribe (v.) 訂閱，subscriber (n.) 訂閱者，subscription (n.) 訂閱。

The manager will report the quarterly budget and sales performance.
經理將會報告每一季度的預算及銷售表現。

---

08 verify

★
★
★

[`vɛrəˏfaɪ]

v 證明，核對，查清

同 confirm 證實
prove 證明
validate 證實
certify 證明
justify 證明

反 refute 駁斥

The assistant had verified the figures and the tables in this financial summary several times before the meeting.
助理在會議前已經查證過財務報表的數字和表格很多次。

point financial summary = financial report，意為「財務報表」。

The market survey verified that the manager's prediction to the customers' meal preference was inaccurate.
市場調查證明了經理對顧客的用餐偏好預測是不正確的。

point meal preference 意為「用餐偏好」。

Chapter 052

金融財務

09 bonus
★
★ [`bonəs]

n 獎金，紅利，意外的好處

同 extra payment 額外獎金
reward 獎賞
benefit 津貼
advantage 利益

We receive a bonus every quarter.
我們每季都會收到獎金。

I am appointed to have a business trip to Hong Kong next week, and it's a real bonus that I can visit my friends there.
我被指派下週去香港出差，意外的好處是我可以拜訪我在那邊的朋友。

10 temporary
★
★ [`tɛmpəˌrɛrɪ]
★

a 暫時的，臨時的

反 permanent (a.) 永久的
lasting (a.) 持久的
everlasting (a.) 永遠的

The financial problem is temporary and can be solved in a short time.
這個金融問題是暫時的，可以很快被解決。

Dragic Corporation hired more temporary staff to help with the increased work demands.
卓吉奇公司僱用了更多臨時工以協助增加的工作需求。

11 credit
★
★ [`krɛdɪt]

n 賒帳，信譽，讚揚

v 把……歸於

同 financial status
(ph.) 財務狀況

衍 creditor (n.) 債權人
credible (a.) 可信的
credential (n.) 證書

I asked my assistant to call the bank to increase my credit limit temporarily.
我請助理打給銀行暫時提高我的信用卡額度。

point credit limit 意為「信用卡額度」。

The producer gave his team credit for the hard work.
製作人對團隊的努力加以表揚。

point give sb. credit for... 意為「為……讚揚某人」。

12 exchange
★
★ [ɪks`tʃendʒ]

n 交換，交易，交戰

v 交換，調換

同 trade (n.) 交易
change (v.) 改變

I asked the banker the exchange rate right now.
我問銀行行員現在的匯率多少。

point exchange rate 意為「匯率」。

The workshop is held every month so that our members can exchange opinions on the ongoing projects.
工作坊每個月都會舉辦一次，這樣成員之間就可以互相交流對於正在著手的專案的看法。

point so that 意為「如此一來」。

13 reimburse
★
★
★
[ˌriɪmˈbɝs]

Ⅴ 償還，歸還，賠償

同 compensate 補償
recompense 賠償
refund 償還
repay 償還

The company will reimburse your travel expenses after you submit the receipts.
在你送出收據後，公司會補償你的差旅費。

The airline will reimburse passengers for any loss or damage.
航空公司將會補償乘客所受到的一切損失和損害。

---

14 reimbursement
★
★
[ˌriɪmˈbɝsmənt]

n 償還，退款，賠償

同 compensation 賠償
repayment 償還
recompense 賠償
refund 償還

金融財務

Please sign this reimbursement application form and return it to my associate.
請簽回這份核銷申請表格給我的同事。

The reimbursement request should be sent to the Accounting Department by the end of this month.
請款單要在這個月底前送到會計部。

---

15 approval
★
★
★
[əˈpruvl̩]

n 批准，認可，贊成，同意

同 agreement 同意
反 disagreement 不同意
衍 approve (v.) 贊成

With his supervisor's approval, he felt relieved to take a week off.
有了他上司的批准，他便安心地放了一週假。

point take... off = take a leave，意為「請假」。

---

16 necessary
★
★
★
[ˈnɛsəˌsɛrɪ]

a 必要的，必需的

n 必需品

同 compulsory (a.) 必須做的
mandatory (a.) 義務的
imperative (a.) 必要的
反 unnecessary (a.) 不需要的
dispensable (a.) 非必要的

It's necessary for interviewees applying for this position to prepare both a resume and portfolio.
對這個職位的求職者而言，準備履歷和作品集是必要的。

point applying for this position 由 who apply for this position 簡化而來。

Due to budget constraints, we are only allowed to purchase what is necessary.
因為預算限制，我們只被允許買必要的東西。

point 相關詞彙：required 需要的，obligatory 必須的。相反詞彙：non-essential 非必要的。

Chapter 053

6 金融財務

17 improvement

★
★
★
[ɪmˋpruvmənt]

n 改進，改善，改善的事物

同 advance 進展
development 發展
upgrade 改進
change for the better
變得更好

反 deterioration 惡化

I have noticed the newcomer's gradual improvement **in** dealing with problems on his own.
我發現那個新人在自己解決問題上有逐漸進步。

(point) in + 方面，意為「在……方面」。

The chart showed that there is a slight **improvement** in the economy.
這個圖表顯示經濟上稍有起色。

(point) 相關詞彙：refinement 細微改進，enhancement 提高，advancement 進展。

18 regulate

★
★
[ˋrɛɡjəˏlet]

v 管理，調整，使規則化

同 control 控制
adjust 調整
manage 管理

衍 regular (a.) 規則的
regulation (n.) 規則

The Finance department regulates the budget and expenditure.
財務部門管理預算和支出。

The new central heating system can regulate the temperature automatically.
新的中央暖氣系統可以自動調節溫度。

19 statement

★
★
★
[ˋstetmənt]

n 陳述，聲明，結算單

同 declaration 宣布
pronouncement 聲明
explanation 說明

The politician's statements were inconsistent.
這個政治人物的聲明前後不一致。

Bank statements list clients' monthly financial transactions.
銀行對帳單列出客戶每月的金融交易。

20 account

★
★
[əˋkaunt]

n 帳單，帳戶，描述，解釋

v 把……視為，解釋，導致

同 financial statement
(ph.) 財務狀況

How do you **account for** the unsatisfying marketing campaign?
你要怎麼解釋這個不令人滿意的行銷活動？

(point) account for 意為「解釋」。

I guess **opening a** joint **account** with my wife would be a great idea so that we can manage money together.
我認為開一個和我老婆的共同帳戶會是個很不錯的點子，這樣我們就可以一起管理錢。

(point) open an account 意為「開戶」。

21 **accountable**

★
★ [ə`kauntəbl]
★ a 有解釋義務的，應負責的
同 responsible 需負責的
反 irresponsible 不負責任的

The newcomer is only accountable to his supervisor who is on a business trip now.
這個新人只對他那名正在出差的上司負責。

point business trip 在多益聽力測驗中很常見，出差時常會去研討會（conference / seminar）或工作坊（workshop）。

Since he is required to record his expenses by his mother, he becomes more accountable for his spending.
因為被媽媽要求要記帳，他變得對他的開支負責任了。

22 **accountant**

★
★ [ə`kauntənt]
n 會計師，會計人員
同 auditor 審計員

With the implementation of the policy, the accountant is required to change her way to record the expenses and revenues.
隨著新政策的實施，這名會計必須改變記錄支出和收入的方式。

The applicants for the position of accountant, require 10 years of work experience.
這個會計職位的求職者需要十年的工作經驗。

point 多益測驗中的求職廣告常考求職者的「requirement（必要條件）」。

23 **accounting**

★ [ə`kauntɪŋ]
n 會計，會計學
衍 tax accounting 稅務會計

Accountants are required to be familiar with the accounting software.
會計被要求熟悉會計軟體。

The accounting assistant is rather responsible and enthusiastic.
這名會計助理相當負責任且有熱誠。

point 此句中的形容詞皆為求職廣告中常見的正向個性詞彙。

24 **deposit**

★ [dɪ`pazɪt]
v 放置，使沉澱，存錢
n 存款，押金，堆積
同 advance payment (ph.) 預付款
　 prepayment (n.) 預付

Please pay a two-month deposit to rent the house.
請付兩個月的租金來租房子。

point 多益閱讀測驗中若提到租屋，常會提到租金。

I deposit 23,000 dollars in my account every month.
我每個月都存兩萬三千元到我的帳戶。

054

金融財務

25 banking
★
[ˋbæŋkɪŋ]

ⓝ 銀行業

衍 network banking
網路銀行業
online banking 網路銀行

Many users showed positive feedback toward
online banking services.
很多使用者對線上銀行服務有正向回饋。

point online banking service 意思是可以在網路上檢視帳戶、匯款等等
交易。

Nowadays, more and more people can accept
electronic banking services.
現在，有越來越多人能夠接受電子銀行業務。

---

26 fee
★
★
[fi]

ⓝ 酬金，費用，賞金

ⓥ 付費，給小費

同 payment (n.) 付款
wage (n.) 報酬
salary (n.) 薪資
allowance (n.) 津貼
price (n.) 價錢
amount (n.) 總額

Since you are our regular customer, I will waive
the processing fee.
因為你是我們的常客，我將會取消手續費。

You can either pay the registration fee by cash or
credit card.
你可以用現金或刷卡來支付註冊費。

point 相關詞彙：toll 使用費，cost 花費，charge 費用。

---

27 financial
★
★
★
[faɪˋnænʃəl]

ⓐ 財政的，金融的

同 economic 經濟上的
commercial 商業的
fiscal 財政的

The company is facing the financial crisis.
這家公司正在面臨金融危機。

The financial issue has been discussed by many
politicians and analysts.
許多政治人物及分析家已經討論過這個金融議題。

---

28 finance
★
★
★
[faɪˋnæns]

ⓝ 財政，金融，資金

ⓥ 提供資金，融資

同 money (n.) 錢
commerce (n.) 交易
business (n.) 交易
investment (n.) 投資

A college degree in Finance is necessary for this
position.
擁有大學財金系學歷對於這個職位而言是必須的。

point sth. is required / necessary 意為「……是必須的」。

The director in the finance department can
anticipate budget with precision.
財務部門主任能夠精確地預測預算。

29 constraint ★

[kənˋstrent]

🄝 約束，限制，拘束

🄘 restriction 限制
limitation 限制
restraint 抑制

Due to the financial constraints, our company will not recruit new employees this year.
因為財政吃緊，我們公司今年不會僱用新員工。

(point) constraint 的其他用法：under constraint 表示「被強迫地；迫於壓力；在強制下」。

To protect local companies, the government is going to increase the constraints on foreign imports and tariffs at the end of this year.
為了保護本土公司，政府在今年年底要增加外國進口商品的限制及關稅。

(point) import 可當動詞「進口」，也可當名詞「進口商品」，相反詞為 export「出口（商品）」。

CH6

金融財務

30 loan ★

[lon]

🄥 借出

🄝 借出的東西，貸款

🄘 mortgage (n.) 抵押借款

We applied for a loan to buy a house.
我們申請貸款去買房子。

(point) apply for a loan 意為「申請貸款」。

This book is on loan from another library.
這本書是從另一家圖書館借來的。

31 transaction ★ ★

[trænˋzækʃən]

🄝 辦理，交易，業務

🄘 deal 交易
business 交易

🄹 transact (v.) 處理

Clients can login to the online banking system to track their transaction records.
客戶可以登入網路銀行系統，追蹤他們的交易紀錄。

The agency charges a 10% processing fee for each transaction.
代辦機構每項業務都會收百分之十的手續費。

(point) processing fee 意為「手續費」。

32 mortgage ★ ★

[ˋmɔrgɪdʒ]

🄝 貸款

🄥 抵押貸款

🄘 loan (n.) 貸款

He had an extra part-time job to pay his mortgage.
他有額外的兼職工作來支付他的貸款。

(point) part-time job 意為「兼職工作」，full-time job 意為「全職工作」。

He could hardly afford his mortgage, so he asked his family for help.
他幾乎沒辦法支付他的貸款，所以他向家人尋求協助。

(point) ask sb. for help 意為「尋求某人幫忙」。

6

金融財務

33
★
★

installment
[ɪnˈstɔlmənt]

n 就任，安置，安裝，
分期付款

衍 partial payment 部分付款

The worker came to the office for the installment of air conditioners.
工人為了冷氣的安裝去了辦公室。

The bank provides a 0% **interest** installment plan.
銀行提供零利率的分期付款方式。

point interest (n.) 興趣；利息。

34
★
★
★

property
[ˈprɑpɚtɪ]

n 財產，房產，所有權

同 building 建築物
premise 場所
house 房屋
land 地產
estate 地產
real estate 不動產

The **real estate agent** showed us some properties downtown.
房屋仲介帶我們去看市中心的幾處房產。

point real estate agent 意為「房屋仲介」。

The retired hotel manager **invested** part of his pension **in** property.
那名退休的飯店經理投資他部分的退休金到房地產。

point invest in 意為「投資」。

35
★
★
★

rent
[rɛnt]

v 租用，出租
n 租金，出租的財產

同 hire (v.) 租借
lease (v.) 出租

The landlord will **raise** the tenant's rent due to the rise of the utility bills.
因為水電雜費的上漲，房東將會漲房客的租金。

point raise 直接加受詞，rise 後面不加受詞。

The surgeon still couldn't afford to buy his own apartment in the city center, so he rented one instead.
這名外科醫生沒辦法在市中心買自己的公寓，所以取而代之他租了一間。

36
★
★
★

rental
[ˈrɛntl̩]

n 租金，租賃，出租
a 租賃的，供出租的

The monthly rental is 500 dollars, and you need to pay a deposit before you move in.
每月租金是五百美金，你搬進來前要先付租金。

He **works as** a receptionist in the car rental company.
他在汽車租賃公司擔任招待人員。

point work as 意為「擔任……」。

37 report
★
★
★
[rɪˋport]
v 報告，記述，告發
n 報告，報導，傳聞
同 account (v.) 報導
review (v.) 檢閱
record (v.) 記錄
description (n.) 敘述

The financial report has been sent to the CFO.
財務報表已經寄給財務長了。
(point) CFO = Chief Financial Officer，意為「財務長」。

It was reported that she was one of the most influential politicians of that period.
據報導，她是那個時期最具影響力的政治家之一。
(point) it is reported that 意為「據報導……」。

---

38 annual
★
★
★
[ˋænjʊəl]
a 一年的，每年的
n 年刊
同 every year (ph.) 每年
yearly (a.) 每年地
once a year (ph.) 一年一次
衍 annually (adv.) 每年地

The annual bonus is dependent on your work performance.
年終獎金是看你的工作表現而定。
(point) be dependent on 意為「依靠，依賴」。

Thank you for joining the annual financial meeting.
感謝您參加年度財務會議。
(point) 表示活動的時間詞彙常在多益聽力測驗一開始就會提到，題目會問「多久辦一次會議」，如果聽到「annual」就要回答每年一次。

---

39 insurance
★
[ɪnˋʃʊrəns]
n 保險，保險金額，安全保證
同 assurance 保證
policy 政策
security 保證

My car insurance is going to expire at the end of this month, so I will renew the contract this week.
我車子的保險在這個月底就要到期，所以我這週會更新合約。
(point) contract「合約」和 contact「聯絡」常在多益聽力測驗中出現，考生容易混淆，請特別注意。

Can your insurance cover your expenditures on medical treatment?
你的保險可以支付你的醫療開銷嗎？
(point) cover (n.) 封面；表面 (v.) 覆蓋；包含；掩護；給……保險。

---

40 occupied
★
[ˋɑkjʊpaɪd]
a 已佔用的，在使用的，無空間的
同 engaged 被佔用的
busy 忙碌的
反 unoccupied 空著的
衍 occupancy (n.) 佔有
occupation (n.) 職業

The tellers were occupied in handling bank transactions.
銀行行員們忙著處理銀行交易。
(point) be occupied in + 動作 / be occupied with + N 表示「忙著做某事」。

After he examined the procedures of the safety inspection, several questions occupied his mind.
在他檢視安全檢查的步驟後，心中充滿了疑問。
(point) procedure, process 皆表示「步驟」。

127

Chapter 056

6 金融財務

41 emerge

★

[ɪ`mɝdʒ]

v 浮現，顯露，擺脫

同 appear 出現
come out 出現

反 submerge 淹沒

The financial analyst predicted that there will be some emerging industries next year.
金融分析師預測明年會有一些新興產業的出現。

point emerging 在此為「新興的」。

When I read the books that relate to my fields, some ideas just suddenly emerged in my mind.
當我閱讀有關自身領域的書籍時，一些點子突然在我腦袋中出現。

point relate to 意為「與……相關」。

42 accurate

★
★
★

[`ækjərɪt]

a 精確的，準確的

同 correct 正確的
right 準確的
truthful 真實的

反 defective 有缺陷的
imperfect 不完美的
inaccurate 不精準的

衍 accuracy (n.) 正確（性）

It is essential for accountants to be accurate when they make financial reports.
對於會計來說，做財務報告時要很精確這件事情是很重要的。

point it's a. for sb. 意為「對於某人來說，……是很……」。

The witness gave the police an accurate description of the robbery.
目擊證人給了警察精確的搶案描述。

point 相關詞彙：precise 精確的，exact 確切的，perfect 完美的。相反詞彙：incorrect 不正確的，wrong 錯誤的。

43 adoption

★

[ə`dɑpʃən]

n 採用，收養

衍 adopt (v.) 採取，收養
adoption agency
(ph.) 收養機構

She put a child up for adoption because she was laid off and couldn't afford to raise the kid by herself.
她將孩子給人收養，因為她被裁員，沒有能力獨立撫養小孩。

point put a child up for adoption 意為「將孩子給人收養」。

The Finance Department expected the adoption of this policy would cut the expenses on office supplies.
財務部門期望藉由採取這個政策能夠減少辦公室用品的開銷。

point 「開銷」的其他講法：expenditure、cost。

44 bank

★
★
★

[bæŋk]

n 堤岸，銀行

v 築堤，堆積，存入銀行

How can I open a bank account with you?
我要如何向你們開戶呢？

People walked along the river banks.
人們沿著河岸散步。

point river bank 為多益聽力測驗圖片題可能會出現的詞彙，要注意。

45 absolute
★
★
★

[`æbsə͵lut]

ⓐ 完全的，絕對的，確實的

🔄 complete 完全的
entire 完全的

🔄 incomplete 不完全的

衍 absolutely (ad.) 完全地

The director of the Finance Department is a man of absolute integrity.

財務部門的主任是位公正不阿的人。

The secretary was an absolute life-saver because she found the file for the meeting was wrong just 5 minutes before the meeting started.

這位祕書根本就是救星，因為她在會議開始的五分鐘前發現會議的文件是錯誤的。

ⓟ life-saver 意為「救星」。

46 actual
★
★
★

[`æktʃuəl]

ⓐ 實際的，事實上的

🔄 factual 事實的
genuine 真的
true 真實的
real 真正的

🔄 fake 假的

The director of the Finance Department examined the financial report to know the actual sales volume.

財務部主任檢視財務報表以知道真實的銷售量。

ⓟ sales volume 意為「銷售量，業績」。

The reporter went to the war zone to report on the actual situation.

記者到戰區報導真實的情況。

ⓟ zone 意為「區域」，time zone 為「時區」。

47 arise
★
★

[ə`raɪz]

ⓥ 升起，產生，形成

🔄 appear 出現
occur 發生

🔄 disappear 消失

Should any disagreements arise, let me know and I'll help.

如果有任何歧異發生，隨時告訴我，我會幫你。

ⓟ should = if，意為「如果」。

Several finance-related problems arose once the company was acquired by another big firm.

這公司一被另一間大公司收購，很多財政相關的問題就產生了。

ⓟ acquire (v.) 收購，acquisition (n.) 收購／merge (v.) 合併，merger (n.) 合併。

48 audit
★

[`ɔdɪt]

ⓝ 審計，查帳，決算

ⓥ 審核，查帳，旁聽

🔄 inspect (v.) 審查
review (v.) 檢閱
examine (v.) 檢查

The retired manager plans to audit university classes next year.

退休的經理計劃明年去大學旁聽課程。

ⓟ 此處的 audit 是「旁聽」的意思。

The accountant is busy during the yearly audit.

會計在年度審計時非常忙碌。

Chapter 057

6 金融財務

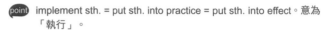

---

49 assess

★
★
★

[əˈsɛs]

V 估價，徵稅，罰款

同 estimate 估計
　　evaluate 估價

衍 access (v.) 讀取
　　　　 (n.) 通道，途徑

The head of the Financial Department assessed whether the company could afford to **implement** this project.
財務部主任評估公司是否能負擔執行這項計畫。

(point) implement sth. = put sth. into practice = put sth. into effect。意為「執行」。

The school provides several **means** to assess students' learning performance.
該所學校提供許多評估學生學習成果的方法。

(point) 此處的 means 為名詞，意為「方法」。

---

50 banker

★

[ˈbæŋkɚ]

n 銀行家，莊家

衍 merchant banker
　　 (ph.) 工商銀行家

The news reported the banker's **latest** investment.
新聞報導了這名銀行家的最新投資。

(point) late (a. / adv.) 晚的（地）；latest 最新的（最晚出來的事情也就是最新的）。

The distinguished banker is going to retire this year.
那位出眾的銀行家即將在今年退休。

---

51 basic

★
★
★

[ˈbesɪk]

a 基礎的，初步的，起點的
n 基礎，基本原理

同 primary (a.) 初級的
　　 prime (a.) 基本的

反 unessential (a.) 非必要的
　　 supplementary (a.) 追加的

We hope to hire people with **basic** accounting knowledge.
我們希望僱用有基本會計知識的人。

(point) 相關詞彙：elementary 基本的，essential 基本的，fundamental 基礎的。

Good customer service is the basic but important requirement to **run** a business.
好的顧客服務是很基本但卻重要的經營商家的必要條件。

(point) run 意為「經營；跑步」。

---

52 bankrupt

★
★

[ˈbæŋkrʌpt]

a 破產的，完全失敗的
V 使破產，使枯竭

同 broke (a.) 破產的
反 wealthy (a.) 富裕的

Splurging on luxury goods will eventually bankrupt us.
揮霍於奢侈品上終究會使我們破產。

(point) 此句 bankrupt 為及物動詞，意為「使破產」。

The bankrupt company couldn't afford to pay the rent.
這間破產的公司沒辦法負擔房租。

53 **bankruptcy**

★
★
★

[`bæŋkrəptsɪ]

🄝 破產，倒閉，徹底失敗

衍 declare bankruptcy
(ph.) 宣告破產
bankruptcy order
(n.) 破產令

The bankruptcy of the big company hit the headlines.
那家大公司破產的消息上了頭條新聞。

point hit the headlines 意為「登上頭條」。

The retailers are at risk of bankruptcy due to the economic recession.
因為經濟蕭條，零售商們正處於破產的危機中。

point be at risk of 意為「處於危險之中」。

CH6

金融財務

54 **bill**

★
★
★

[bɪl]

🄝 帳單，目錄，議案，傳單
🅥 開帳單，貼海報

同 charge (v.) 索價
statement (n.) 結算單

You're receiving this letter due to the outstanding bill.
你因為有沒付清的帳單而收到這封信。

point 延伸詞彙：outstanding (a.) 傑出的；未付清的，overdue (a.) 逾期的。

Some couples apply for joint accounts to pay bills directly.
有些夫妻申請共同帳戶來直接付帳單。

point 延伸詞彙：joint account 共同帳戶／ saving account 存款戶／ check account 支票戶。

55 **independent**

★

[͵ɪndɪ`pɛndənt]

🄐 獨立的，單獨的，
無黨派的

同 individualistic
(a.) 個人主義的
free-spirited
(a.) 自由自在的人
反 dependent (a.) 依賴的

The teenager's goal is to become financially independent.
這名青少年的願望是能夠在財務上變得自由。

Independent thinking is highly regarded in this institute.
獨立思考在這個機構被高度推崇。

56 **dependent**

★

[dɪ`pɛndənt]

🄐 依靠的，取決於，隸屬的

同 relying on 依賴
counting on 依靠
反 independent 獨立的

The newcomer remained dependent on his senior.
新進員工很依賴他的前輩。

The branch is dependent on the financial support from the parent company.
分公司仰賴母公司的財政支助。

point 延伸詞彙：headquarters = main office，意為「總部」。

57 tackle

★
★

[`tæk!]

V 處理，交涉，抓住
n 裝備，釣具
同 solve (v.) 解決
　　deal with (ph.) 處理
　　cope with (ph.) 處理
　　manage (v.) 處理

The customer service department will tackle the matter as soon as possible.
客服部門會盡快處理這個問題。

(point) as soon as possible = ASAP 意為「盡可能地快」。

The program is designed to tackle global financial crisis.
這個計畫是設計用來處理全球財務危機。

---

58 discipline

★

[`dɪsəplɪn]

n 紀律，訓練，懲罰
V 訓練，使有紀律，懲戒
同 direction (n.) 指導
　　order (n.) 指揮
　　routine (n.) 程序
　　training (n.) 訓練
　　teaching (n.) 教導

One of the school disciplines is that students are required to wear uniforms.
校規的其中一條規定就是學生需要穿制服。

(point) 相關詞彙：regulation 規則，rule 規則，instruction 指示。

The CFO is in charge of maintaining strict financial discipline.
財務長負責維持嚴謹的財政紀律。

(point) be charge of 意為「負責」。

---

59 total

★
★
★

[`tot!]

a 總計的，完全的
n 合計
同 complete (a.) 完全的
　　whole (a.) 全部的
　　comprehensive (a.) 全面的
反 partial (a.) 部分的

The system can count your total spending automatically.
這個系統可以自動幫你計算支出。

The manager concluded the campaign was a total failure.
經理總結這個行銷活動完全是一個失敗。

---

60 legitimate

★

[lɪ`dʒɪtəmɪt]

a 合法的，合理的
V 使合法
同 legal (a.) 合法的
　　lawful (a.) 法定的
反 illegal (a.) 違法的
　　illegitimate (a.) 非法的
衍 legalize (a.) 使合法化

Undeniably, the protester's argument was quite legitimate.
不可否認地，抗議者的言論很合理。

The accounting department didn't regard the bill as a legitimate business expense.
會計部門不認為這張帳單是一筆合理的業務開支。

(point) regard A as B 意為「將 A 視為 B」。

61 calculation

★
★

[ˌkælkjəˈleʃən]

n 計算，推測，深思熟慮

同 computation 計算結果
estimation 估計
estimate 估計

The accountant made a calculation of other employees' travel allowances.
這名會計計算了其他員工的出差津貼。

point travel allowance 意為「出差津貼」。

According to my calculations, we still need to hire more temporary workers to finish the task before the deadline.
根據我的計算，我們仍然要僱用更多的臨時工才能在期限前完成任務。

62 incorrect

★
★
★

[ˌɪnkəˈrɛkt]

a 錯誤的，不真實的，不適當的

同 wrong 錯誤的
反 correct 正確的

The secretary found the figures incorrect before the financial meeting.
祕書在財務會議開始前發現數字有誤。

point find + O + a. 意為「覺得……；發現……」。

The market trend has proved that the director's prediction was incorrect.
市場趨勢已經證明了主任的預測不正確。

63 examiner

★
★

[ɪgˈzæmɪnɚ]

n 主考人，審查員

同 interviewer 面試官
inspector 檢查員
auditor 審計員
appraiser 鑑定人
reviewer 檢閱人

The examiner used the newest rubric to assess the test-takers' performance in speaking.
主考官用最新的量表來評量受試者的口說能力。

The bank examiner is responsible for auditing bank accounts.
銀行查帳員負責審計銀行帳戶 。

point be responsible for = be in charge of + N / Ving 意為「負責某事」。

64 diverse

★
★
★

[daɪˈvɝs]

a 不同的，多變化的

同 various 不同的
multiple 多樣的
反 similar 相似的
uniform 相同的
衍 diversity (n.) 多樣性

The tourists were amazed by the diverse cultures in this area.
遊客對這個區域的多元文化感到驚豔。

point be amazed by 意為「因……感到驚豔」。

The retired couple had diverse views on cable charges.
這對退休夫妻在有線電視費上有迥然不同的看法。

65 despite
★
★ [dɪ`spaɪt]
　prep 不管，儘管
　同 in spite of 不管
　　notwithstanding 儘管
　　regardless of 不管

Despite the limited budget, employees who work overtime can receive overtime pay.
儘管預算限制，加班的員工還是可以拿到加班費。

The new vacuum's overall performance is satisfactory despite a few minor problems.
除了一些小問題以外，新型的吸塵器整體表現令人滿意。

point 延伸詞彙：sales performance 銷售表現，sales volume 銷售量。

---

66 wage
★ [wedʒ]
　n 薪水，報酬
　v 進行，從事
　同 pay (n.) 薪俸
　　payment (n.) 付款
　　salary (n.) 薪資
　　income (n.) 收入

Unfortunately, his wages are insufficient to support his family.
很不幸地，他的工資沒有辦法支持他的家庭。

Some workers advocated raising their wages.
一些工人主張提高他們的工資。

point advocate + Ving 意為「主張某事」。

---

67 value
★
★ [`vælju]
★
　n 價值，重要性
　v 評價，重視
　同 worth (n.) 價值
　　benefit (n.) 好處
　　efficacy (n.) 功效
　　importance (n.) 重要性
　　significance (n.) 重要性

The insurance company valued my used car at $3,000.
保險公司給我的二手車估價美金三千元。

What are the core values that the candidate possesses?
這名求職者擁有的核心價值為何？

point core value 意為「核心價值」。

---

68 urgent
★
★ [`ɝdʒənt]
★
　a 緊急的，急迫的
　同 emergent 緊急的
　　hurried 匆促的
　　rushed 匆忙的
　　hasty 匆忙的

Due to the urgent personal matter, I need to take one day off.
因為緊急的個人因素，我需要請一天假。

The board all agreed the financial problem required urgent attention.
委員會都同意這財務問題需要立即的處理。

point board (n.) 板子；委員會 (v.) 登上（船、火車或飛機）；寄宿。

69 unnecessary
★

[ʌnˈnɛsəˌsɛrɪ]

a 不需要的，多餘的

同 optional 非必須的
not required 不需要的

反 necessary 需要的

It will be a kind of waste if you buy things that are unnecessary.
如果你買不必要的東西，那將會是種浪費。

(point) a kind of 意為「一種」。

While reviewing budget for next year, the financial department cut out all unnecessary expenses.
當審查明年的預算時，財務部門刪去了所有不必要的開支。

---

70 separate
★
★
★

[ˈsɛpəˌret]

v 分隔，區分，使分居

[ˈsɛprɪt]

a 個別的，單獨的

同 discrete (a.) 分離的
distinct (a.) 有區別的
disparate (a.) 迥然不同的
individual (a.) 個別的

反 same (a.) 一樣的

衍 separation (a.) 分開

Whenever he receives his paycheck, he separates his earnings into two bank accounts.
不論什麼時候他收到薪資，他都會把收入分到兩個銀行帳戶。

(point) whenever 意為「不論什麼時候」，搭配的動詞為現在式。

The two companies are located in two separate buildings.
這兩家公司坐落於兩座獨立的大樓。

(point) be located in 意為「坐落於」。

---

71 retirement
★
★
★

[rɪˈtaɪrmənt]

n 退休，退役，退休生活

衍 retire (v.) 退休
retirement age
(ph.) 退休年齡

Owen is going to retire and we will hold a retirement reception for him.
歐文要退休了，我們會為他辦一個退休餐會。

The financial consultant suggested his client start to plan for his retirement as soon as possible.
財金顧問建議他的客戶盡快開始為退休做打算。

(point) suggest that sb. (should) + V 意為「建議某人該做……」，should 被省略，但後面的動詞要是原形動詞。

---

72 record
★
★
★

[ˈrɛkɚd]

n 記錄，經歷，唱片

[rɪˈkɔrd]

v 記錄，錄下，標明

同 documentation (n.) 文件
data (n.) 資料

You can keep a record of your spending.
你可以記錄你所花的費用。

(point) spending 意為「花費」，earnings 意為「收入」。

Sam's performance evaluation record showed that he is a diligent and responsible employee.
山姆的表現評估記錄顯示他是一個勤奮且負責任的員工。

060

6 金融財務

---

73 prediction

★

[prɪ`dɪkʃən]

n 預報，預言

同 forecast 預報
prophecy 預言

衍 predictable (a.) 可預料的

The sport announcer made a prediction about the result of the soccer game.
體育主播對足球比賽的結果做了預測。

point make a prediction about 意為「對……做了預測」。

The prediction of the revenue this year was based on last year's sales volume.
今年營收的預測是根據去年的業績而來的。

---

74 predict

★

[prɪ`dɪkt]

V 預言，預料

同 forecast 預報
foresee 預見
tell in advance 預報

The fortune teller claimed that he could predict his future.
算命師聲稱可以預測他的未來。

The financial consultant predicted the sales performance next quarter.
財金顧問預測下一季的銷售表現。

---

75 layoff

★
★
★

[`le͵ɔf]

n 臨時解僱，停止活動

同 unemployment 解僱
firing 開除

反 recruitment 徵募
hiring 僱用

The reason for the company's massive layoffs remained unknown.
這間公司大量解僱的原因依然不明。

After a layoff, Jerome made a lot of life-changing decisions, such as learning something that was totally different from his major.
在被解僱後，傑洛姆做了很多會改變生涯的決定，例如學一些和本科完全不同的事物。

point such as + N / Ving 意為「例如……」。

---

76 insist

★
★

[ɪn`sɪst]

V 堅持，堅決主張

同 persist 堅持
maintain 維持

反 give up 放棄

The manager insisted on finishing the job before leaving the office.
經理堅持在離開辦公室之前完成工作。

point insist on = persist in，意為「堅持」。

His supervisor insisted that expanding the project budget was not practical.
他的上司主張擴大專案預算很不切實際。

point insist that + S + V 意為「堅持……」。

Test 1

一、請寫出下列單字的中文意思。

① legitimate _____   ⑥ assess _____

② unnecessary _____   ⑦ temporary _____

③ predict _____   ⑧ transaction _____

④ appear _____   ⑨ reimburse _____

⑤ deposit _____   ⑩ discipline _____

二、請寫出符合下列句意的單字。

① Can your _____ cover your expenditures on medical treatment?

你的保險可以支付你的醫療開銷嗎？

② Since he is required to record his expenses by his mother, he becomes more _____ for his spending.

因為被媽媽要求要記帳，他變得對他的開支負責任了。

③ Bank _____ list clients' monthly financial transactions.

銀行對帳單列出客戶每月的金融交易。

解答

1. ① 合法的，合理的；使合法　② 不必要的，多餘的　③ 預報，預言　④ 出現，似乎　⑤ 存錢；押金　⑥ 評定，估計　⑦ 暫時的，臨時的　⑧ 交易，業務　⑨ 償還，賠償　⑩ 訓練，紀律；懲罰
2. ① insurance　② accountable　③ statements

Test 2

一、請選擇符合下列文意的單字。

Ⓐ dependent	Ⓑ insisted	Ⓒ accurate
Ⓓ separates	Ⓔ arose	Ⓕ urgent

① It is essential for accountants to be _____ when they make financial reports.

② Several finance-related problems _____ once the company was acquired by another big firm.

③ The branch is _____ on the financial support from the parent company.

④ The financial director _____ that expanding the project budget was not practical.

⑤ Whenever he receives his paycheck, he _____ his earnings into two bank accounts.

二、請寫出下列片語的中文意思。

① dress up _____   ⑤ be known for _____

② be located in _____   ⑥ hit the headlines _____

③ try one's best _____   ⑦ so that _____

④ a variety of _____   ⑧ be charge of _____

解答

1. ①C ②E ③A ④B ⑤D
2. ① 盛裝打扮 ② 坐落於 ③ 盡全力 ④ 多樣的 ⑤ 以……聞名 ⑥ 登上頭條 ⑦ 如此一來 ⑧ 負責

Chapter 7
經營管理

以下多益必考單字，你認識哪些？

☐ competitive (p.140)　　☐ strength (p.144)　　☐ observe (p.141)

☐ administrate (p.142)　☐ cooperation (p.147)　☐ skillful (p.151)

☐ executive (p.143)　　　☐ necessarily (p.147)　☐ enlargement (p.148)

☐ propose (p.142)　　　 ☐ belief (p.150)　　　　☐ supervise (p.145)

☐ establish (p.141)　　　☐ president (p.152)　　 ☐ attribute (p.148)

☐ manage (p.144)　　　　☐ relationship (p.146)　☐ offer (p.153)

Chapter 061

7 經營管理

01 council
★
★
['kaʊnsl̩]

n 會議，協調會，商討

同 committee 委員會
commission 委員會
assembly 集會

The city council is responsible for building local infrastructure.
市議會負責建設地方公共建設。

(point) be responsible for + Ving / N 意為「為某事負責」。

The council finally approved the proposal.
理事會終於批准了提案。

---

02 competition
★
★
★
[ˌkɑmpə'tɪʃən]

n 競賽，比賽，競爭者

同 contest 競爭
game 競賽
match 比賽
race 比賽

反 cooperation 合作

He was suspended from the competition for one month for his violation of rules.
他因為違反規則而被停賽一個月。

(point) for + 原因，意為「因為……（原因）」。

---

03 competitive
★
★
★
[kəm'pɛtətɪv]

a 競爭的，競爭性的，好競爭的

同 aggressive 好鬥的
ambitious 有雄心的
keen 激烈的

反 uncompetitive 無競爭力的

Working in big cities is far more competitive than working in small towns.
在大城市工作比在小城鎮工作還要競爭。

(point) far 修飾形容詞，強調程度。

You need to pass a competitive examination to become a public servant.
你必須要通過具競爭力的考試才能成為公務人員。

---

04 competitor
★
★
★
[kəm'pɛtətɚ]

n 競爭者，對手，敵手

同 opponent 對手
rival 競爭者
challenger 挑戰者
participant 參與者
enemy 敵人

反 ally 同盟者

Once the competitors come up with similar products, our company will start to develop new products.
一旦我們的競爭者想出類似的產品，我們公司就會開始研發新產品。

(point) come up with 意為「想出」。

The department store provided a better discount than its competitors did during the semi-annual sale.
這家百貨公司在年中慶時提供比它的競爭者更好的折扣。

(point) semi 意為「一半」。

05 **guideline**

★
★
['gaɪd‚laɪn]

n 指導方針

同 instruction 指示
direction 方向
rule 規則

衍 guide (n.) 指南
guidance (n.) 指導
guidebook (n.) 旅行指南

What's your guideline in choosing the clothes for different occasions?
你為不同場合選衣服的準則是什麼？
point 「in + 方面」表示「在……方面」。

This common guideline is followed by every company in this business complex.
這棟商業大樓裡的每間公司都遵守這個通則。
point complex (a.) 複雜的 (n.) 建築群；情節。

06 **observe**

★
★
★
[əb`zɝv]

V 注意到，觀察，遵守

同 watch 觀察
see 看到
spot 認出
detect 察覺
discover 發現

Usually, the senior will observe whether the newcomers are reliable and responsible.
通常較資深的人員都會觀察新人是否可靠且負責任。

It is widely believed that children learn by observing people who surround them.
人們普遍相信兒童透過觀察身旁的人來學習。
point It is widely believed that 意為「人們普遍相信……」。

07 **establish**

★
★
★
[ə`stæblɪʃ]

V 建立，使立足，證實

同 set up 開創
create 創設
organize 組成
construct 建造

反 demolish 毀壞

The plant was established in 1898.
這工廠建於一八九八年。
point plant = factory，意為「工廠」。

The design staff established a new business model.
設計團隊建立了一個新的商業模式。

08 **establishment**

★
★
★
[ɪs`tæblɪʃmənt]

n 建立，企業，機關

同 business 企業
firm 公司
company 公司
enterprise 企業
organization 機構
industry 企業

Since the company's establishment in 1989, it has developed many innovative products.
自從公司在一九八九年創立以來，已經發展了許多有創意的產品。
point 完成式常與 since 一起連用。

There are two vacancies in that well-run establishment now.
現在那間經營完善的企業有兩個職缺。
point vacancy = opening，意為「職缺」。

---

09 ★★★ **proposal**

[prə`pozl]

n 建議，計畫，提案，求婚

同 scheme 計畫
plan 計畫
project 計畫
suggestion 建議
recommendation 建議

反 withdrawal 撤回

Unfortunately, his proposal was not accepted.
很不幸地，他的提案沒有被接受。

(point) 多益聽力測驗或閱讀測驗中，unfortunately 後面接的通常都是重要的訊息。

The team finally finalized the proposal for the tower restoration.
團隊最終定案了塔台的整修提案。

---

10 ★★★ **propose**

[prə`poz]

V 提議，提出，打算，求婚

同 suggest 建議
advance 提出
offer 提供
present 提出
advocate 提倡

反 withdraw 撤回

The manager proposed opening up the overseas branch office in Bangkok.
經理提議在曼谷設立海外分公司。

(point) propose + Ving 意為「提議某事」。

I propose that we expand the company's product line.
我建議我們擴展公司的產品線。

(point) propose that + S + V 意為「提議……」。

---

11 ★★ **administrate**

[əd`mɪnə,stret]

V 管理，支配

同 control 支配
manage 管理
oversee 管理
govern 管理
supervise 監督
be in charge of 負責

My supervisor asked us to administrate and update customers' documents in a timely manner.
我的上司要求我們要及時管理及更新客戶的文件。

(point) in a timely manner 意為「及時地」。

The training course taught us some useful tools to administrate and control budget.
這個訓練課程教我們一些管理控制預算的好用工具。

---

12 ★★ **administration**

[əd,mɪnə`streʃən]

n 管理，行政，執行

同 execution 執行
management 管理

Do you charge an administration fee?
你們收行政費用嗎？

(point) 常見的其他費用：admission fee = entrance fee 入場費／registration fee 登記費／service fee 服務費。

We expect that the candidates major in Business Administration and can finish jobs independently.
我們希望求職者是主修商業管理系，而且能夠獨自完成工作。

(point) major in + 科系，意為「主修……系」。

Business Management

13 administrator
★★
[əd`mɪnə͵stretɚ]

🔟 管理人，行政官員
🔘 manager 管理者
　 overseer 管理人
　 governor 管理者
　 supervisor 監督者

He has been working as an administrator in a school for 10 years.
他已經在學校擔任行政人員十年了。

Only the administrator can access the online database.
只有管理員能夠讀取線上資料庫。

(point) access (n.) 使用；門路；接近 (v.) 取出（資料）；進入；使用。

14 execute
★★★
[`ɛksɪ͵kjut]

🅥 實施，履行，處死，演奏
🔘 carry out 執行
　 accomplish 實現
　 perform 表演
　 implement 履行

The plan was badly executed.
計劃執行得很糟。

Despite the serious shortage of supplies, we will still execute our original plan.
儘管嚴重的供給短缺，我們仍然會執行我們原本的計畫。

(point) despite + N / Ving = in spite of + N / Ving = although + S + V = though + S + V，意為「儘管……」。

CH7
經營管理

15 executive
★★★
[ɪg`zɛkjutɪv]

🔟 執行者，行政官，經理
🅐 執行的，行政的，經營的
🔘 chief (n.) 長官
　 head (n.) 首長
　 principal (n.) 首長
　 senior official (ph.) 資深官員
　 senior manager (ph.) 資深經理
　 senior administrator (ph.) 資深行政官員
🔄 subordinate (n.) 下屬

The executive introduced the newcomers in the training session.
行政主管在訓練課程中介紹了新人。

The Chief Executive Officer's executive skills will be very useful to the company.
執行長的管理能力對公司將會非常有用。

(point) Chief Executive Officer 縮寫為 CEO，意為「執行長」。

16 management
★★★
[`mænɪdʒmənt]

🔟 管理，管理部門
🔘 administration 管理

The topic of the workshop is stress management.
工作坊的主題是壓力管理。

The experienced management consultant's advice has greatly improved employee productivity.
經驗豐富的管理諮詢師的建議大大地增加員工生產力。

143

Chapter 063

7 經營管理

17 manage
★
★
★
['mænɪdʒ]
V 管理，控制，使用
同 be in charge of 負責
run 管理
direct 管理
control 控制
lead 領導
govern 管理
反 ignore 忽視

The general manager managed a team of 50 people on his own.
總經理獨自管理五十個人的團隊。

(point) on his own = by himself，意為「他獨自」。

The CEO believed that the experienced manager had an ability to manage to finish this urgent project while doing other tasks at the same time.
執行長相信這名經驗豐富的經理有能力同時做很多任務並完成這個緊急專案。

(point) manage to 意為「設法做到」，manage 意為「管理」。

18 manager
★
★
★
['mænɪdʒɚ]
n 經理，主任
同 executive 經理
supervisor 管理人
administrator 管理者
head 經理
boss 老闆
director 主任

All the managers should attend the meeting at 10 a.m. sharp.
所有經理都要在十點整準時出席。

(point) sharp 意為「準時地」。

The plan of purchasing protective gear is still under discussion and will be announced by the sales manager.
這個購買防護裝置的計畫仍在討論中，將會被業務經理宣布。

19 managerial
★
[ˌmænə'dʒɪrɪəl]
a 經理的，管理方面的

The senior specialist was promoted to the managerial position.
資深專員被升為管理職。

After the CEO's opening remarks, the senior manager will share some useful managerial skills.
在執行長的開幕致詞後，資深經理將會分享一些有用的管理技巧。

20 strength
★
★
[strɛŋθ]
n 力量，實力，長處
同 power 力量
energy 能量
force 力量
反 weakness 軟弱
衍 strengthen (v.) 加強

The trainer shared some tips for developing strength at work.
訓練人員分享發展工作上長處的訣竅。

The country's growing economic strength has attracted many businesses worldwide to extend their operations there.
這個國家日漸上升的經濟實力已經吸引了許多世界各地的企業到該國擴大經營。

(point) extend operation = extend business，意為「擴大經營」。

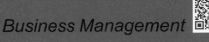

21 **supervise**
★
★
★
['supɚˌvaɪz]

v 監督，管理，指導

同 oversee 管理

He was assigned to supervise the construction that will be completed next year.
他被指派監督明年要完工的工程。

point be assigned to 意為「被指派」。

Mr. Korver's reference letter was written by Ms. Ginobili because she used to supervise him at City Library.
柯佛先生的推薦信是吉諾比利女士寫的，因為她過去在市立圖書館指導過他。

point reference letter = recommendation letter，意為「推薦信」。

---

22 **supervisor**
★
★
★
[ˌsupɚˈvaɪzɚ]

n 監督人，管理者，指導者

同 director 主管
chief 主任
head 首領
superior 上司
organizer 組織者
conductor 管理人

The supervisor has been working overtime for one week to meet the deadline of the project.
主管已經加班一週來趕計畫的期限。

point work overtime 意為「加班」。

Mr. Brown's supervisor checked his performance review to decide the amount of his annual bonus.
布朗先生的上司看了他的績效報告來決定他年終獎金的數目。

point performance review 意為「績效報告」。

---

23 **comprehend**
★
★
[ˌkɑmprɪˈhɛnd]

v 理解，領會，包括

同 apprehend 理解
perceive 理解
interpret 理解

衍 comprehensive (a.) 廣泛的

The assistant couldn't comprehend the officer's standard.
那名助理沒有辦法了解該長官的標準。

The legislator said not many people comprehended the scale of the problem.
立法委員說不是所有人都了解問題的嚴重程度。

---

24 **tenure**
★
['tɛnjur]

n 佔有權，任期，終身職位

衍 tenancy (n.) 租賃

The CEO remained popular throughout his tenure.
執行長在整個任期內都相當受到歡迎。

Professor Saric has tenure at Chicago University.
芝加哥大學的薩利奇教授有終身職位。

Chapter 064

7 經營管理

25 bargain
★
[`bɑrgɪn]
n 協議，買賣，特價商品
v 討價還價，達成協議
同 arrange (v.) 洽商
　　deal (v.) 交易
　　haggle (v.) 討價還價
　　negotiate (v.) 協商

The manager made a bargain with his subordinates that if they reached the sales goal, they could receive a bonus.
經理和他的下屬達成協議，如果他們能夠達到銷售目標，他們就能拿到獎金。

point make a bargain with sb. 意為「和某人達成協議」。

You should keep your own word since a bargain is a bargain.
你應該要信守承諾，因為協議就是協議，應當遵守。

point keep one's word 意為「信守承諾」。

26 allow
★
★
★
[ə`laʊ]
v 允許，使成為可能，認可
同 grant 承認
　　permit 允許
反 ban 禁止
　　forbid 禁止
　　prohibit 禁止
衍 allowance (n.) 津貼

I am sorry that I am currently not allowed to give the new administrative employees overtime pay.
很抱歉我目前沒辦法給行政部新進員工加班費。

Normally, my employees are required to wear uniforms, but they are allowed to dress casually on Fridays.
一般來說，我的員工被要求穿制服，但他們可以在週五穿休閒的衣服。

point be required to 被要求／be allowed to 被允許。這兩個字的被動式在多益測驗中都很常見。

27 dispose
★
★
[dɪ`spoz]
v 配置，處理，使傾向於
同 get rid of 擺脫
　　discard 丟棄
反 retain 保留

Man proposes, but God disposes.
謀事在人，成事在天。

The merchant is disposed to listen to any suggestions.
這商人樂於傾聽任何建議。

point be disposed to 意為「樂於……」。

28 relationship
★
★
[rɪ`leʃən`ʃɪp]
n 關係，人際／戀愛／親屬關係
同 relation 關係

The relationship between the two companies has been strengthened through the cooperation.
透過合作，這兩家公司之間的關係被強化了。

The assistant has a good interpersonal relationship with the technical crews.
這名助理和技術人員們有良好的人際關係。

29 cooperation
★
★
★
[koˌɑpəˋreʃən]

n 合作，協力

同 collaboration 合作
working together 搭檔
teamwork 協力
partnership 合夥

反 competition 競爭

This project was completed by the cooperation of the sales team and marketing team.
這專案是由業務和行銷團隊合作所完成。

The company produced a limited edition cookie in cooperation with a well-known chef.
這間公司和一名知名廚師合作生產限定版餅乾。

point in cooperation with 意為「與……合作」。

---

30 necessarily
★
★
★
[ˋnɛsəsɛrɪlɪ]

ad 必定，必然地

同 certainly 必定
surely 確實
definitely 明確地
undoubtedly 肯定地

反 possibly 也許

Just a reminder, the plan doesn't necessarily go as how we planned.
只是想提醒一下，計畫並不一定會照著我們預計的進行。

point just a reminder 意為「提醒一下」。

The information obtained from the internet is not necessarily accurate.
網路上取得的資訊不一定正確。

---

31 revise
★
★
[rɪˋvaɪz]

v 校訂，修改，複習功課

同 review 再檢查
re-examine 重新檢查
re-evaluate 重新評價
change 改變

反 retain 保留
confirm 證實

Please revise your article to meet the word limit.
請修改你的文章以符合字數限制。

Our client was not satisfied with one term in the contract; therefore, we were required to revise it.
我們客戶不滿意合約中的一項條款，因此我們必須要修改它。

point 相關詞彙：modify 修改，alter 改變，reconsider 重新考慮，rethink 重新考慮。

---

32 profit
★
★
★
[ˋprɑfɪt]

n 利潤，盈利，益處
v 有益於，得益

同 payback (n.) 償付
interest (n.) 利益
yield (n.) 收益
advantage (n.) 利益

反 loss (n.) 喪失
disadvantage (n.) 不利條件

The salesperson made a huge profit by selling camping gear.
這商人藉由賣露營器具來賺大錢。

point make a profit 意為「賺錢」。

I profited enormously from reading the biography of the successful entrepreneur.
閱讀那位成功創業家的自傳，我獲益匪淺。

point profit from 意為「從……獲利；得益」。

7 經營管理

---

33 profitable
★
★ ['prɑfɪtəbl]
★
🅐 有利的，營利的，有益的
🔵 profit-making 營利的
commercial 營利本位的
successful 成功的
commercially successful
商業成功的
🔴 unprofitable 無利益的
loss-making 老是虧損的

Selling china plates is profitable in that country.
在那個國家賣瓷盤是有利可圖的。
(point) china 小寫為「瓷製品」，China 大寫為「中國」。

The consultant is proficient in making profitable use of her time.
顧問擅長充分利用她的時間。
(point) make use of one's time 意為「善用某人的時間」。

---

34 enlargement
★
★ [ɪn'lɑrdʒmənt]
🅝 擴大，增建，放大
🔵 extension 擴大
expansion 擴展
amplification 擴大
🟢 enlarge (v.) 擴大

The enlargements of your wedding photos have been sent to your address that was provided by you.
你婚禮的放大照片已經寄到你提供的地址了。
(point) that was provided by you 為形容詞子句，修飾前面的 address。

The enlargement of the business has brought them profit and great reputation.
這間企業的擴展已經帶給他們利益及好的名聲。

---

35 eager
★
★ ['igɚ]
🅐 熱切的，渴望的
🔵 enthusiastic 熱烈的
zealous 熱心的
🔴 unenthusiastic 冷淡的

He is eager to change the safety inspection procedures to ensure the safety of his employees.
他急於改變安全檢查步驟，以確保他的員工的安全。
(point) inspection (n.) 檢查，inspector (n.) 稽查員。

She was eager to get back to work right after she just gave birth.
在生產完後她就急著想回去工作。
(point) 此句的情況可用 workaholic（工作狂）來形容。

---

36 attribute
★
★ [ə'trɪbjut]
★
🅥 把……歸因於
['ætrəˌbjut]
🅝 屬性，特性，象徵
🔵 ascribe (v.) 把……歸因於
assign (v.) 把……歸於

The lecturer attributed his success to hard work and dedication.
這名講師將他的成功歸因於努力工作和奉獻。

Creativity is a crucial attribute for an excellent designer.
創意力是一個出色的設計師必備的素質。
(point) important, essential, crucial, critical, key, major 皆可表達「重要的」。

37 **ability**
★
★ [ə`bɪlətɪ]
★
n 能力，才能，能耐
同 intelligence 理解力
know-how 技能
反 inability 無能
incapability 無能力
incapacity 無能
incompetence 無能力
weakness 弱點

The ability to be well-organized is required for this position.
這個職位需要良好統整能力。
point is required 為被動式，表示「被需要」。

His supervisor shows exceptional ability in leading people.
他的上司展現了出眾的領導能力。
point 相關詞彙：capability 能力，competence 能力，proficiency 精通，talent 天資。

38 **accumulation**
★
★ [əˌkjumjə`leʃən]
n 積累，積聚，累積物
同 collection 收集
mass 堆，群
amassment 累積
衍 accumulate (v.) 累積

The steady accumulation of money enables him to do whatever he wants.
不斷累積的金錢讓他能做他想做的任何事情。
point whatever = no matter what 意為「不論什麼」。

The accumulation of your work experience will be a great asset that no one can take away from you.
你累積的工作經驗將會成為別人帶不走的最棒的資產。

39 **allocate**
★ [`æləˌket]
v 分配，分派
同 distribute 分發
assign 分派
allot 分配

The secret of his success is that he allocates himself some time to learn new things every day.
他成功的祕訣就是每天分配給自己一些時間學習新東西。

The director allocated the bonus to his subordinates according to their job performance.
主任根據下屬的工作表現來分配獎金。
point subordinate, staff, employee 皆可表達「員工」。

40 **altogether**
★ [ˌɔltə`gɛðɚ]
ad 完全，合計，總而言之
同 entirely 完全地
totally 完全
wholly 全部
反 partially 部分地

The CEO was altogether for this project that would be implemented soon.
執行長完全支持這個即將實施的計畫。
point be for... 意為「支持……」。

I only spent 5,000 dollars altogether on the plane ticket because I flew on the budget airline.
因為我搭廉價航空，在機票上總共只花了五千元。
point spend... on... 意為「花在……」。

Chapter 066

7 經營管理

41 ambition
★

[æmˈbɪʃən]

n 雄心，野心，追求的目標

同 goal 目標
objective 目的
aspiration 抱負
yearning 渴望

The company's ambition is to expand their business to Europe.
公司的目標是要擴展生意到歐洲。

He attained his ambition by constant learning and seizing opportunities.
他透過不斷的學習及抓住機會來達成他的抱負。

42 battle
★

[ˈbætl̩]

n 戰鬥，交戰

v 與……作戰，鬥爭

同 combat (v.) 戰鬥
fight (v.) 奮鬥
war (n.) 戰爭

The battle between the firm and its opponent never stops.
這家公司和它的對手之間的戰鬥永遠不會停止。

> **point** firm = company = business，意為「公司」。

The soldier showed his courage and wisdom in that battle.
那位軍人在那場戰役中展現出他的勇氣和智慧。

43 belief
★
★
★

[bɪˈlif]

n 信任，信念，信仰

同 opinion 見解
viewpoint 觀點
point of view 看法
attitude 看法
stance 立場
standpoint 觀點
position 立場

He is firmly of the belief that the construction of the new subway line will attract people from other cities to come to this town.
他深深相信新地鐵線的建造將會吸引其他城市的人們來這個城鎮。

> **point** be of the belief that + S + V 意為「相信；認為……」。

It's beyond belief that the manager appointed a newcomer to be responsible for this crucial project.
經理指派一個新人來負責這個重要的專案是很令人難以置信的。

> **point** beyond belief 意為「令人難以置信的」。

44 trivial
★

[ˈtrɪvɪəl]

a 瑣細的，不重要的，
淺薄的

同 unimportant 不重要的
insignificant 不重要的
inessential 非必要的

反 important 重要的
significant 重要的

The counselor suggested the manager not be angry over such trivial matters.
顧問建議經理不要為這些瑣事生氣。

> **point** 相關詞彙：meaningless 無意義的，pointless 無意義的，worthless 無價值的。

For some citizens, sticking to traffic regulations is often not a trivial task.
對一些市民來說，遵守交通規則不是一件簡單的任務。

> **point** stick to 意為「堅持；遵守；黏在」。

45 **blame**

★

[blem]

V 責備，歸咎於

n 責備，責任

同 criticize (v.) 批評

The manager should take all the blame for the high employee turnover rate.
經理應該要為員工的高流動率負全責。

(point) take the blame for 意為「為⋯⋯負責」。

The director blamed the bad sales performance for the failure of the campaign.
主任把不好的銷售表現歸咎於行銷活動的失敗。

46 **extent**

★
★

[ɪkˋstɛnt]

n 寬度，程度，範圍

同 degree 程度
　　scale 規模
　　level 等級
　　scope 範圍

The radio host reported the extent of the driver's injuries.
廣播主持人報告駕駛的傷勢程度。

To what extent did you believe your employees when they explained why they failed to reach the sales goals?
當你的員工跟你解釋他們為何沒有辦法達成銷售目標時，你有多相信他們呢？

(point) employee = staff = subordinate，意為「員工；下屬」。

47 **skillful**

★
★
★

[ˋskɪlfəl]

a 有技術的，熟練的

同 accomplished 熟練的
　　skilled 熟練的

反 incompetent 無能力的

衍 skill (n.) 技術

The skillful and experienced technician was appointed to teach other new recruits.
這名熟練、有經驗的技師被指派教導其他新進員工。

Those skillful workers' requests to increase their wages were refused by the supervisor.
這些技術精練的工人提高薪資的要求被上司拒絕了。

48 **seek**

★
★

[sik]

V 尋求，企圖，徵求

同 pursue 追求
　　request 要求
　　look for 尋找
　　explore 探索

Considering the sales volume last year, the company started seeking business opportunities abroad.
考量到去年的業績，公司開始找尋海外的商業機會。

(point) start to + V = start + Ving，意為「開始做⋯⋯」。

The specialist is seeking to figure out the difference between the two models.
專員試著找出兩個型號的差別。

(point) seek to = try to，意為「試著」。

49 rather
★
★
★

[ˋræðɚ]

ad 相當，寧願

同 quite 相當
very 非常
extremely 非常
fairly 頗為
relatively 相當

The backpacker would rather invest money in traveling not luxury goods.
這名背包客寧願把錢投資在旅遊而非奢侈品。

(point) invest in 意為「投資」。

The company chose to expand its operations to Asia rather than other countries.
這間公司寧願選擇擴張營運到亞洲而非其他國家。

(point) rather than = instead of，意為「而不是」。

50 president
★
★
★

[ˋprɛzədənt]

n 總統，主席，董事長

同 director 董事
leader 領導人
governor 管理者
principal 首長
master 院長
captain 首領

The president was determined to expand the company's product line.
總裁決定擴大公司的產品線。

(point) be determined to = decide = make up one's mind，意為「決定」。

51 press
★
★

[prɛs]

v 按壓，催促，強迫

n 報刊，新聞界，出版社

同 push (v.) 促使
force (v.) 強迫
compress (v.) 壓緊

The entrepreneur tried to get press coverage for his business.
這名創業家試著讓媒體報導他的企業。

The journalist works for the national press, instead of the local press.
這名記者是為這個全國性報刊工作，而不是地方性報刊。

52 narrow
★
★

[ˋnæro]

a 狹窄的，勉強的，精細的

v 限制，使變窄

同 small (a.) 小的
narrowing (a.) 縮小的

反 wide (a.) 寬闊的
broad (a.) 寬的
spacious (a.) 寬敞的

衍 narrowly (adv.) 狹窄地

The narrow-minded businessman refused to cooperate with the corporates he barely knew.
這個心胸狹窄的商人拒絕和他幾乎沒聽過的企業合作。

(point) 易混淆字：cooperate (v.) 合作。co（一起）+ operate（營運）。記憶訣竅是有兩個 oo 就是合作，corporate (n.) 公司。

The young candidate won a narrow victory, which surprised many voters.
這名年輕的候選人險勝，讓很多投票者都很驚訝。

(point) which 代替前面那句 The young candidate won a narrow victory。

53 **own**

★
★★ [on]
★
 Ⓥ 擁有，承認
 ⓐ 自己的，特有的
 Ⓢ possess (v.) 擁有
　 personal (a.) 個人的
　 individual (a.) 個人的

The retired lady has her own grocery store which is just near the public library.
這名退休的女士有一間自己的雜貨店，就在公立圖書館附近。
(point) 延伸詞彙；grocery shopping 意為「買菜；買雜貨」。

The assistant finished all the challenging tasks within three days on her own.
助理在三天內獨立完成所有艱難的任務。
(point) on her own = by herself 意為「靠她自己」。

54 **owner**

★
★★ [ˋonɚ]
★
 Ⓝ 所有人，物主
 Ⓢ possessor 擁有人
　 holder 持有人
　 keeper 保管人

The owner of the RV forgot where he parked the car.
休旅車的車主忘記他把車停在哪。
(point) RV = recreational（休閒的）vehicle（車輛），意為「休旅車」。

The owner of the corporation led the meeting about merger and acquisition.
公司的所有者引導有關合併及收購的會議。

55 **offer**

★
★★ [ˋɔfɚ]
★
 Ⓥ 提供，提議，出價
 Ⓝ 提議，報價
 Ⓢ provide (v.) 提供
　 give (v.) 給予
 Ⓐ withdraw (v.) 撤回

The graduate had already received three job offers before he graduated.
這名畢業生在畢業之前，已經收到三個工作邀約。
(point) graduate (n.) 畢業生 (v.) 畢業。

The consultant offers free advice to people in need.
顧問提供免費諮詢給需要的人。

56 **individual**

★
★★ [ˌɪndəˋvɪdʒʊəl]
★
 ⓐ 個人的，單獨的，特有的
 Ⓝ 個人，個體
 Ⓢ single (a.) 單一的
　 separate (a.) 個別的
　 independent (a.) 獨立的
　 sole (a.) 單獨的
 Ⓐ ordinary (a.) 通常的
　 collective (a.) 集體的

Every individual is valuable to our team.
每個人對我們團隊來說都很寶貴。
(point) every 和 each 後面的名詞及動詞都是單數。

Joseph's individual writing style has made him one of the most famous contemporary writers.
喬瑟夫與眾不同的寫作風格使他成為最有名的當代作家之一。
(point) one of the Ns 意為「其中一個」，要記得後面的名詞都是複數，才能表達眾多中的一個。

CH 7

經營管理

Chapter 068

7 經營管理

57 export
★
★ [ɪks`port]
★
★ **V** 輸出，出口
[`ɛksport]
n 輸出，出口，輸出物資
反 import (v. / n.) 進口

All staff received a extra bonus this quarter due to the **considerable** increase in export sales.
因為外銷的大幅增加，所有員工在這一季收到額外的獎金。

(point) 易混淆詞彙：considerable (a.) 大量的／considerate (a.) 體貼的。

The managerial officers will finalize when to develop the export market.
管理人員將會定案何時拓展出口市場。

58 almost
★
★ [`ɔɹˌmost]
★
★ **ad** 幾乎，差不多
同 nearly 幾乎
about 大約
practically 幾乎
roughly 大體上
approximately 大概

The entrepreneur started his business when he was almost 40.
這名企業家在他差不多快四十歲時才開啟他的事業。

Almost all the participants preferred products that are not artificially flavored.
幾乎所有受試者偏好不添加人工香料的產品。

59 willingness
★
[`wɪlɪŋnɪs]

n 自願，樂意
同 eagerness 渴望
keenness 熱心
enthusiasm 熱忱
反 reluctance 不情願
unwillingness 不願意

The manager shows a willingness **to lead** other team members and **to share** methods that increase efficiency.
經理展現出願意領導其他團隊成員以及分享增加效率的方法。

(point) to lead... 和 to share... 為對等的平行結構。

The applicant was hired **as** he possessed these qualities: creativity, willingness, and enthusiasm.
這名求職者因為有創意力、自願性及熱誠這些特質而被僱用。

(point) as = since = because = in that，意為「因為」。

60 unify
★
[`junəˌfaɪ]

V 統一，聯合，使一致
同 blend 混合
mix 混合
consolidate 聯合
integrate 使結合
反 separate 分開
split 分割

The excellent leader unified different **divisions**.
優秀的領導者統籌結合了不同部門。

(point) department, sector, division 皆可指「部門」。

Traffic regulations that differ among different states were **unified** by the new president.
不同州的不同交通規則被新總統統一了。

(point) 相關詞彙：unite 統一，join 使結合，merge 合併，bind 使結合，combine 結合。

61 ultimately

★

['ʌltəmɪtlɪ]

ad 最後，最終，根本上

同 in the end 最終
in the long run 最後
at length 終於

反 immediately 立即地

The committee ultimately adopted the manager's proposal.
委員會最終採用了經理的提案。

(point) 相關詞彙：eventually 最後，finally 終於。

The client ultimately secured a three-year lease with the agent.
客戶最終與顧問簽下三年的合約。

---

62 tremendous

★
★

[trɪ`mɛndəs]

a 巨大的，極大的，驚人的

同 huge 巨大的
enormous 龐大的
immense 巨大的
massive 巨大的

反 tiny 極小的
small 小的
slight 微小的

Those lawmakers made tremendous efforts to change the policy.
這些立法委員做了很大的努力以改變政策。

(point) make tremendous efforts to + V 意為「做了很大的努力去……」。

Undeniably, the company's merger with another firm has made a tremendous impact on its staff.
不可否認地，這家公司與另一家公司的合併對它的員工帶來很大的影響。

(point) 延伸詞彙：acquisition and merger 意為「收購與合併」。

---

63 takeover

★

[`tek.ovɚ]

n 收購，接管

同 purchase 購買
acquisition 收購
buying 購買

Rondo Materials made a takeover bid for another company.
朗多材料公司出價收購另一家公司。

(point) make a bid for 意為「出價買」。

The board discussed the pros and cons of takeovers and mergers.
委員會討論收購及合併的利與弊。

(point) pros and cons = advantages and disadvantages，意為「優缺點」。

---

64 rely

★
★
★

[rɪ`laɪ]

v 依靠，信賴，倚仗

同 depend 依靠
count on 依靠
confide 託付

反 distrust 不相信

The responsible foreman is a person you can rely on.
這名負責任的監工是你可以依賴的人。

(point) rely on = depend on = count on，意為「依賴」。

The completion of the challenging project relied on every employee's effort.
這個具有挑戰性的專案的完成要靠每個人的努力。

CH 7

經營管理

經營管理

65 **subordinate**
★
★ [sə`bɔrdṇɪt]
★
a 下級的，次要的
n 部屬
[sə`bɔrdṇ‚et]
v 列入下級，使服從
同 lower (a.) 較低的
minor (a.) 次要的
反 superior (a.) 上級的
senior (a.) 較資深的

The manager is kind to his subordinates and that's why they are willing to work for him.
經理對他的下屬很好，這就是為什麼他們願意替他工作。

point be willing to 意為「願意」。

Delegating tasks to subordinates fairly is rather challenging.
把任務公平地委託給下屬很具有挑戰性。

---

66 **standard**
★
★ [`stændəd]
★
n 標準，水準，規格
同 quality 品質
level 等級
grade 等級
degree 程度
worth 價值

It's rather difficult to meet the vice president's standards.
很難達到副總裁的標準。

point meet one's standards 意為「達到某人的標準」。

The shareholders set a high standard for the company.
股東們給公司定下了高標準。

---

67 **significant**
★
★ [sɪg`nɪfəkənt]
★
a 有意義的，重要的，顯著的
同 notable 顯著的
noteworthy 顯著的
remarkable 值得注意的
outstanding 傑出的
反 insignificant 不重要的
minor 次要的

It's significant to prepare enough funds before you run your company.
在你經營自己的公司前，準備足夠的資金是重要的。

point 相關詞彙：important 重要的, of importance 重要的, crucial 決定性的, exceptional 卓越的。

There has been a significant increase in the sales of LED light bulbs in recent years.
近年來，LED 燈泡的銷售有了顯著增加。

---

68 **pretend**
★
[prɪ`tɛnd]
v 假裝，自稱，假扮
同 fake 偽造
衍 pretense (n.) 假裝
pretentious (a.) 自負的

The assistant pretended that he understood what his supervisor said.
助理假裝他懂上司說的話。

After the accident, it was hard to pretend that nothing had happened.
在那個意外之後，很難去假裝沒什麼事發生過。

69 reward
★
★
★
[rɪ`wɔrd]

n 報償，酬金，報應
v 報答，酬謝，報應
同 pay (n.) 報償
　　tip (n.) 小費
　　honor (n.) 榮譽
反 punish (v.) 懲罰

The company has a well-organized reward system to encourage employees' good performance.
公司有完整的獎勵制度來鼓勵員工的好表現。

When the construction of the building was finished, the architect felt all his hard work was rewarded.
當建築工程完成時，這建築師感到一切的艱辛都得到了回報。

---

70 relocate
★
★
★
[ri`loket]

v 重新安置

The shareholders decided to relocate the main plant to the suburbs.
股東們決定將主要工廠遷至郊區。

 suburbs, outskirts 皆表示「郊區」。city, city center, downtown 皆表示「城市；市區」。

The director asked 15 staff members to relocate to Mexico.
主任讓十五名員工調到墨西哥。

 relocate to + 地方，意為「調到某處」。

---

71 refusal
★
★
★
[rɪ`fjuzl̩]

n 拒絕
同 denial 拒絕
反 acceptance 接受
衍 refuse (v.) 拒絕

The startup was disappointed at the company's refusal to cooperate.
新創企業對於那家公司拒絕跟它們合作感到失望。

 be disappointed at 意為「對……感到失望」。

The client's refusal to make payment on time caused us great trouble.
客戶拒絕準時付款造成我們很大的麻煩。

 make payment 意為「付款」。

---

72 rational
★
★
[`ræʃənl̩]

a 理性的，合理的
同 logical 合理的
　　sensible 明智的
　　reasonable 合理的
　　enlightened 開明的
反 irrational 無理性的
　　illogical 不合邏輯的

His rational thinking is beneficial to his work.
他很有邏輯的思考對他的工作很有幫助。

point be beneficial to 意為「有益於」。

An excellent team leader should be able to make rational decisions in emergent situations.
一個優秀團隊領導者應該要能夠在緊急的情況下做出合理的決定。

point be able to + V = be capable of + Ving 意為「能夠做……」。

CH 7
經營管理

157

73 policy

★
★
★

['palǝsɪ]

n 政策，策略，手段
同 strategy 策略
衍 privacy policy
(ph.) 隱私政策

The new policy that was agreed to by all the members will be effective next Monday.
所有成員都贊同的新政策將會在下週一實施。

 will be effective = will be implemented = will be carried out 意為「將會被執行」。

Many residents were against this policy because it will inevitably raise the cost of living.
很多居民反對這個政策，因為這將不可避免地提高生活開支。

 cost of living 意為「生活開支」。

74 mentor

★

['mɛntɚ]

n 導師
v 指導
同 adviser (n.) 顧問
guide (n.) 指導者
consultant (n.) 顧問
master (n.) 大師
trainer (n.) 訓練者
instructor (n.) 指導者

The senior engineer is responsible for mentoring and training less experienced engineers.
該名資深工程師負責指導及訓練較資淺的工程師。

75 incorporation

★
★
★

[ɪnˌkɔrpǝ'reʃǝn]

n 團結，合併，公司
同 union 合併
merger 合併
反 division 分開
separation 分開

The CEO is considering the pros and cons of incorporation.
執行者正在考量合併的優缺點。

point pros and cons = advantage and disadvantage，意為「優缺點」。

76 important

★
★
★

[ɪm'pɔrtn̩t]

a 重要的，有權力的
同 principal 最重要的
vital 極重要的
反 unimportant 不重要的
inessential 非必要的

When you are making travel plans, it's important to make sure your passport is valid.
當你在制定旅遊計畫時，確保你的護照是有效的很重要。

point valid (a.) 有效的／invalid (a.) 無效的。

It is important for the company to expand its business to other countries.
對於這間公司而言，擴展業務到不同國家是很重要的。

point It is important for sb. to V 意為「對於某人，……是重要的」。

Question

👁 以下題目完全擬真新制多益 Part 5，請選出最符合句意的選項。

1. He was suspended from ------- for one month for his violation of rules.

   (A) compete
   (B) competitive
   (C) competition
   (D) competitor

2. The team finally ------- the proposal for the tower restoration.

   (A) finally
   (B) finalists
   (C) final
   (D) finalized

3. He has been working ------- an administrator in a school for 10 years.

   (A) for
   (B) as
   (C) in
   (D) on

4. The ------- introduced the newcomers in the training session.

   (A) execute
   (B) executive
   (C) administrate
   (D) administration

5. The senior specialist was promoted to the ------- position.

   (A) manage
   (B) management
   (C) manager
   (D) managerial

6. The shareholders decided to ------- the main plant to the suburbs.

   (A) relocate
   (B) relocating
   (C) be relocated
   (D) relocated

>> 正確答案與解析請翻至下一頁查看

Answer

● **正確答案與解析**

1. 他因為違反規則而被停賽一個月。

   (A) 競爭 (v.)　　　(B) 競爭的　　　(C) 競賽 (n.)　　　(D) 競爭者

   正確答案 (C)

2. 團隊最終定案了塔台的整修提案。

   (A) 最終地　　　(B) 參加決賽者　　　(C) 最終的　　　(D) 最終確定 (v.)

   正確答案 (D)

3. 他已經在學校擔任行政人員十年了。

   (B) work as 意為「做為」的意思

   正確答案 (B)

4. 行政主管在訓練課程中介紹了新人。

   (A) 執行 (v.)　　　(B) 行政主管　　　(C) 管理 (v.)　　　(D) 管理 (n.)

   正確答案 (B)

5. 資深專員被升為管理職。

   (A) 管理 (v.)　　　(B) 管理 (n.)　　　(C) 經理　　　(D) 管理的

   正確答案 (D)

6. 股東們決定要將主要工廠遷至郊區。

   (A) 遷移（原形動詞），to 後面須加原形動詞

   正確答案 (A)

Chapter 8
生產製造與品管

以下多益必考單字，你認識哪些？

☐ evaluate (p.164) ☐ cautious (p.170) ☐ expose (p.178)

☐ product (p.165) ☐ generate (p.171) ☐ complicated (p.180)

☐ manufacture (p.166) ☐ measure (p.173) ☐ remain (p.174)

☐ component (p.163) ☐ threat (p.175) ☐ downsize (p.178)

☐ advantage (p.166) ☐ ordinarily (p.176) ☐ admit (p.171)

☐ inspector (p.168) ☐ factory (p.175) ☐ improve (p.167)

Chapter 071

8 生產製造與品管

01 postpone
★
★
★
[post`pon]

☑ 使延期，延緩，推遲

同 put off 延遲
　 delay 延緩

反 advance 前進
　 bring forward 提前

The assistant was informed that the meeting was postponed.
助理被告知會議被延期了

Owing to the shortage of raw materials, we had no choice but postpone the production schedule.
因為原物料的短缺，我們不得不延遲生產行程。

point have no choice but + V 意為「不得不……」。

---

02 validate
★
[`væləˌdet]

☑ 使有效，確認，證實

同 support 支持
　 justify 證明
　 demonstrate 證明

反 invalidate 使無效
　 disprove 反駁

The equipment can validate the effectiveness of the skincare products.
這個儀器可以用來驗證護膚產品的有效性。

point 易混淆字：efficiency 意為「效率」。

The actual sales volumes validate the finance director's forecasts.
實際的銷售量驗證了財務長的預測。

point 相關詞彙：prove 證明，verify 證實，confirm 證實。

---

03 procedure
★
★
★
[prə`sidʒɚ]

ⓝ 程式，步驟，手續

同 step 步驟
　 method 方法
　 series of steps 步驟

The procedures are clearly printed in the manuals.
步驟清楚地印在手冊上。

point brochure (n.) 小冊子，leaflet (n.) 傳單。此為多益測驗中會提到的紙本文件類型。

The company changed the manufacturing procedures to make production more efficient.
公司改變了製造過程，以讓製程更有效率。

---

04 process
★
★
★
[`prɑsɛs]

ⓝ 過程，步驟，程序

☑ 加工，處理，起訴

同 procedure (n.) 程序
　 processing (n.) 處理

Overcoming challenges is also a process of learning.
克服困難也是種學習的過程。

point Overcoming challenges 為 Ving 當主詞，動詞用單數。

There are some changes in the manufacturing processes and it will take the workers a while to adjust.
生產過程有些改變，這將會花工人一些時間去適應。

point a while 意為「一陣子」。

05 **efficiency**
★
★
★
[ɪˋfɪʃənsɪ]

n 效率，效能

同 cost-effectiveness
成本高效益

反 inefficiency 無效率
incompetence 無能力

衍 efficient (a.) 效率高的

Efficiency is highly regarded in the assembly line.
效率在生產線被高度推崇。

point assembly line 意為「生產線」。

The foreman expected his workers to achieve the maximum of efficiency.
工頭期待他的工人能達成最大效率。

point 相關詞彙：productivity 生產力，effectiveness 有效。

06 **specification**
★
★
★
[ˌspɛsəfəˋkeʃən]

n 詳述，規格，說明書

同 statement 陳述
description 敘述

衍 specify (v.) 詳細指明

The product specifications are clearly written in the report.
產品規格在報告中清楚地列出來。

The catalogues include the price and detailed specifications for every product.
產品目錄包含了每個產品的價格和詳細規格。

07 **contract**
★
★
★
[ˋkɑntrækt]

n 契約，契約書

[kənˋtrækt]

v 簽約，承辦，使收縮

同 agreement (n.) 協定
settlement (n.) 解決
commitment (n.) 承諾

Both parties will sign the contract tomorrow.
明天兩方都會簽合約。

point party (n.) 黨派；派對。

Our pupils contract in bright light and expand in dim light.
我們的瞳孔在光亮時收縮，在黑暗時擴大。

point pupil (n.) 瞳孔；學生。

08 **component**
★
★
[kəmˋponənt]

n 構成要素，零件

a 組成的，構成的

同 part (n.) 部分
piece (n.) 部分
unit (n.) 單位
section (n.) 部分

All the components had already been sent to the factory.
所有的零件都已經寄給工廠了。

point 相關詞彙：ingredient 原料，element 要素，item 品目，portion 部分。

The speaker highlighted that good communication is an important component to raise employee productivity.
講者強調良好的溝通是提高員工生產力的重要元素。

point employee productivity 意為「員工生產力」，為多益測驗中演講者常提到的主題。

163

8 生產製造與品管

09 contractor
★
[`kɑntræktɚ]

🔲 立契約者，承包商

衍 building contractor
(ph.) 建築承包商

The company is the contractor of this construction project.
公司是這個工程計畫的承包商。

Due to the inclement weather, the contractor could not meet the deadline.
因為天候不佳，承包商沒辦法在期限內完成。

point meet the deadline 意為「在期限內完成」。

---

10 evaluate
★
★
★
[ɪ`væljuˌet]

🔲 估價，鑑定

同 rate 估價
estimate 估計
appraise 估計

衍 evaluation (n.) 評估

Most of the factories evaluate the performance of assemble line workers by efficiency and productivity.
大部分的工廠以效率和生產力來評估生產線工人的表現。

point 相關詞彙：assess 估計，judge 評定。

---

11 initially
★
★
[ɪ`nɪʃəlɪ]

🔲 最初，開頭

同 originally 起初

反 finally 最終
in the end 最後

衍 initiate (v.) 開始
initiative (n.) 主動行動

The new recruit's performance was considerably worse than initially expected.
這名新進員工的表現比一開始預期的還要糟糕很多。

point 延伸詞彙：be superior to 意為「優於」，be inferior to 意為「劣於」。

The company started out as a manufacturer of furniture initially, but now it produces plastic.
公司一開始是家具製造商，但現在生產塑膠。

point 延伸詞彙：manufacture (v. / n.) 製造。

---

12 labor
★
★
★
[`lebɚ]

🔲 勞動，勞工，工作

同 work 工作
laborer 勞動者

反 capitalist 資本家

The labor welfare program is the focus of the strike.
勞工福利制度是這次罷工的焦點。

The new system will definitely increase the labor productivity.
新的系統絕對會增加勞動生產力。

13 **product**
★
★
★
[`prɑdəkt]
n 產品，結果，作品
回 commodity 商品
   goods 商品
   wares 貨物
   merchandise 商品
   produce 產品

The product has been modernized according to the customers' feedback.
這個產品已經根據客人的回饋現代化了。
point has been modernized 為完成式加被動式。

Despite the budget constraints, the marketing department still tried to promote the products by social media.
儘管預算限制，行銷部門依然試著用社交媒體推廣產品。

14 **production**
★
★
★
[prə`dʌkʃən]
n 生產，製作，產量
回 manufacturing 製造業
   making 製造
   producing 生產
   creation 創造

The additional assembly line will greatly reduce the production time.
額外的生產線將會大大地減少生產時間。

The company finally decided to temporarily terminate production.
公司終於決定要暫時停止生產。
point temporarily (ad.) 暫時地，permanently (ad.) 永遠地。

CH 8

生產製造與品管

15 **productivity**
★
★
★
[ˌprodʌk`tɪvətɪ]
n 生產力，生產率，多產
回 efficiency 效率
   output 出產
   yield 出產
   capacity 生產力

The specialist specializes in increasing employee productivity.
這名專員專精於增加員工生產力。
point 延伸詞彙：speciality (n.) 專長；招牌菜。

Employees who work hard are entitled to receive a productivity bonus.
認真工作的員工有資格得到生產效率獎金。
point be entitled to 意為「給予權利；使符合資格」。

16 **manual**
★
★
★
[`mænjuəl]
a 手工的，體力的
n 手冊，簡介
回 handbook (n.) 手冊
   guidebook (n.) 手冊
   reference book
   (ph.) 工具書
衍 manually (ad.) 手工地

The manual provides tips on how to set up chairs without any tools.
手冊介紹了如何不用工具組裝椅子的訣竅。
point set up (ph.) 擺放，組裝，建立。

Nowadays, automatic production lines have replaced manual labor.
現今，自動化生產線已經取代了手工勞作。

17 **considering**

★
★
[kən`sɪdərɪŋ]

prep 就……而言

conj 考慮到

同 given that (ph.) 考慮到

衍 consider (v.) 考慮
consideration (n.) 考慮

Considering he is new here, his performance is rather satisfactory.
考量到他才剛來，他的表現相當令人滿意。

point newcomer = new staff = new employee，意為「新員工」。

I am impressed by the quality of the protocols, considering the budget constraints.
考量到預算限制，我對這個協議的品質感到印象深刻。

---

18 **advantage**

★
★
★
[əd`væntɪdʒ]

n 有利條件，優點，好處

同 benefit 利益
superiority 優勢

反 disadvantage 不利條件

The advantages of this product outweigh its disadvantages.
這項產品的優點勝過它的缺點。

When I decided which houses to buy, I listed the advantages and the disadvantages of every property.
當我在決定要買哪間房子時，我列出了所有房子的優缺點。

point property, site, venue, premises, location 皆可表達「房屋；地點；場所」。

---

19 **artificial**

★
★
[͵ɑrtə`fɪʃəl]

a 人工的，人造的，假的

同 fake 假的
unnatural 不自然的

反 genuine 真的
real 真的

The restaurant is decorated with artificial flowers.
這間餐廳用人造花來布置。

point 相關詞彙：man-made 人造的。

One of the advantages of this product is that it's not made of artificial ingredients.
這個產品的其中一個優點是，它不是由人工成分製成的。

point One of the Ns 表示「其中一個」，of 後面是名詞複數。

---

20 **manufacture**

★
★
★
[͵mænjə`fæktʃɚ]

n 製造

v （大量）製造，捏造

同 produce (v.) 生產
mass produce (ph.) 大量生產
construct (v.) 建造
assemble (v.) 配裝

The automobile manufactured in the factory is quite unsatisfactory.
這家工廠製造的這台汽車相當令人不滿意。

The firm that manufactures furniture decided to expand its business by building another plant.
製造家具的公司決定藉由建造另一個工廠來擴展它的生意。

21 manufacturer
★
★
★
[͵mænjəˋfæktʃɚ]

n 製造業者，廠商
同 maker 製作者
　　producer 生產者
　　builder 建造者
　　constructor 建造者
　　processor 製造者

The company is the biggest tire manufacturer in the nation.
這間公司是這個國家中最大的輪胎製造商。

(point) big（形容詞原級）／ bigger（形容詞比較級）／ biggest（形容詞最高級）。

The manufacturer and his clients still remain in contact.
製造商和他的客戶仍然保持聯絡。

(point) remain in contact = keep in touch，意為「保持聯絡」。

---

22 improve
★
★
★
[ɪmˋpruv]

v 改進，提高價值，利用
同 refine 提煉
　　boost 提高
反 decline 下降
　　diminish 減少
衍 improvement (n.) 改善

Even since she changed to another teacher, her English speaking skills have improved a lot.
自從她更換了另一位老師，她的英文口說技巧增強很多。

(point) ever since 意為「自從」。

The manager offered a suggestion to improve the production efficiency.
經理提出一個建議，以改進生產效率。

(point) 相關詞彙：upgrade 提高，enhance 提高。

CH 8
生產製造與品管

---

23 quantity
★
★
[ˋkwɑntətɪ]

n 數量，大量
同 amount 數量
　　number 數量
　　quota 定額
　　mass 大量
　　bulk 大量
　　load 大量

The backpacker was challenged to travel abroad with a small quantity of money.
這名背包客要挑戰帶少量的錢出國旅遊。

(point) a small / large quantity of 意為「少量／大量……」。

In terms of the production of luxury goods, quality is far more crucial than quantity.
就生產奢侈品而言，質量遠比數量還來得重要。

(point) far 修飾 more crucial，強調「更加」重要。

---

24 plant
★
★
★
[plænt]

n 植物，工廠
v 栽種，放置
同 factory (n.) 工廠
　　equipment (n.) 裝備

There are some huge potted plants in the lobby.
大廳裡有一些大型盆栽。

(point) potted plant 意為「盆栽」，有時會出現在多益測驗 Part 1 圖片題。

The plant will be temporarily closed due to safety inspection.
工廠因為安全檢查會暫時被關閉。

Chapter 074

8 生產製造與品管

25 upgrade
★★★
['ʌp'gred]

Ⓥ 升級，提高
Ⓝ 上坡，升級
同 improve (v.) 提高
enhance (v.) 提高
update (v.) 更新
反 degrade (v.) 降低
downgrade (v.) 降級

The software upgrade has successfully improved the service quality.
軟體更新成功地改進服務品質。

The online questionnaires show that 70% of our users are satisfied with our upgraded system.
線上問卷指出我們百分之七十的使用者滿意我們更新的系統。

point be satisfied with 意為「滿意」。

26 sample
★★★
['sæmpl]

Ⓝ 樣品，樣本，例子
Ⓥ 取樣，抽樣檢查，體驗
同 specimen (n.) 樣品
example (n.) 例子
illustration (n.) 實例
demonstration (n.) 示範

The labeled samples were defective.
有做標記的樣本是有缺陷的。

point defective 意為「有缺陷的」，在多益測驗中很常用來形容有問題的產品或機器。

Before the products leave the plant, those workers will sample products for defects.
在產品離開工廠前，那些工人會抽樣檢查產品的瑕疵。

point plant = factory，意為「工廠」。

27 inspector
★★
[ɪn'spɛktɚ]

Ⓝ 檢查員，視察員
同 reviewer 檢閱人
analyst 分析者
observer 觀察者
supervisor 監督者
衍 inspection (n.) 檢查

The inspector mentioned several things that could be improved in the safety standards.
稽查員提及了好幾個在安全標準中可以精進的部分。

point 相關詞彙：examiner 審查員，investigator 調查員，surveyor 調查員。

The ticket inspector asked to see the passenger's train ticket.
查票員要求查看這名乘客的火車票。

28 electronic
★★★
[ɪlɛk'trɑnɪk]

ⓐ 電子的
衍 electronic cigarette
(ph.) 電子香菸

Workers on the assembly line are not allowed to use any electronic devices while working.
生產線的工人在工作時不能使用任何電子裝置。

point electronic device 意為「電子裝置」，也可以指「手機」，是多益測驗 Part 1 圖片題中常用來代替手機的講法。

Many books nowadays are available in electronic version.
現在很多書都有電子版。

29 **durable**

★
★
['djurəbl]
a 耐用的，持久的
同 long-lasting 持久的
　　 hard-wearing 耐穿的
反 delicate 脆弱的
　　 short-lived 短暫的

The sneakers are made of durable materials.
這雙球鞋由耐用的材料製造而成。
point be made of 意為「由……所製成」。

The material is light and durable, which makes it popular among many bag designers.
這材質很輕且耐用，這讓它在很多包包設計師之間很受歡迎。
point among 意為「在……之間」。

---

30 **appliance**

★
★
[ə'plaɪəns]
n 器具，用具，裝置
同 instrument 器具
　　 utensil 用具
　　 device 設備

When people move to new places, some people prefer to buy new household appliances instead of keeping using old ones.
當人們搬到新地方時，有些人偏好買新的家電，而不繼續用舊的。
point of 介係詞，後面加 Ving，Keep 後面動詞也要加 Ving，因此變成 keeping using。

The company's electrical appliance is considerably more durable than its competitors'.
這間公司的家電比其競爭者的家電還要更加耐用。
point considerably 修飾形容詞比較級 more durable。

CH8
生產製造與品管

---

31 **premises**

★
★
['prɛmɪsɪz]
n 住宅或辦公室的建築及地基，生產場所
同 building 建築物
　　 site 地點
　　 office 辦公室

No smoking in this premises.
這個地方禁止吸菸。

Our company will relocate to the new premises; therefore, we have to inform our clients of the new address.
我們的公司要搬到新廠址去，因此我們要通知客戶新地址。

---

32 **basically**

★
★
★
['besɪklɪ]
ad 根本地，在根本上
同 principally 主要地
衍 basic (a.) 基本的
　　 basis (n.) 基礎

Basically, the problems come from the process of quality control.
基本上，問題是來自品質控管的過程。
point come from 意為「來自於」。

So we will basically launch the product by the end of this month.
所以我們基本上會在本月底前上架產品。

Chapter 075

8 生產製造與品管

33 cautious
★
★
★
[ˈkɔʃəs]
ⓐ 十分小心的，謹慎的
⑩ careful 仔細的
　 attentive 注意的
　 prudent 審慎的
衍 caution (n.) 小心

The director expected his secretary could tackle this problem in a cautious way.
主任期望他的祕書能夠謹慎地處理這個問題。
(point) tackle = deal with = cope with，意為「處理」。

After receiving several customer complaints about the defective products, the company is more cautious of quality control.
在收到許多有關瑕疵產品的顧客抱怨後，這家公司在品質控管上更加小心。
(point) defective 意為「有缺陷的」，是多益測驗裡常常用來描述產品有問題的形容詞。

34 accelerate
★
★
[ækˈsɛləˌret]
ⓥ 使增速，促進，加快
⑩ hurry 加快
　 hasten 加速
反 delay 延遲
　 decelerate 減速

My company decided to accelerate the output of the products for the upcoming peak season.
為了即將到來的旺季，我們公司決定加速產品的產量。
(point) output 為產出，相反字為 input（輸入）。

Several passengers fell down as soon as the driver accidentally accelerated the bus.
公車司機不小心加速後，許多乘客馬上就跌倒了。

35 adept
★
★
★
[əˈdɛpt]
ⓐ 熟練的，內行的
[ˈædɛpt]
ⓝ 內行
⑩ proficient (a.) 精通的
　 skilled (a.) 熟練的
　 expert (a.) 老練的
反 inept (a.) 無能的

The foreman of the assembly line is adept at operating heavy machinery.
生產線的工頭在操作重型機器上相當熟練。
(point) 延伸詞彙：foreman 工頭，supervisor 上司，director 主任。

The designer is an adept in designing timeless clothes.
這名設計師是位設計經典款衣服的專家。
(point) expert 也可指「專家」。

36 blur
★
[blɝ]
ⓝ 模糊，汙點
ⓥ 使模糊不清，弄髒
⑩ make indistinct (ph.) 使模糊
　 make vague (ph.) 使模糊

The distinctions between the two flagship products began to blur.
這兩個旗艦產品的界線開始模糊。

The witness said the accident was just a blur to him.
目擊者說已經記不清楚那個意外了。

37 **admit**

★ [əd`mɪt]

Ⅴ 承認，准許進入，容納

同 allow 允許

反 reject 拒絕
　 refuse 拒絕

衍 admittance (n.) 入場許可

The suspect admitted his crime after being caught by the police.

嫌疑犯在被警察逮捕後承認了自己的罪。

point be caught 為被動式，after 在此句為介系詞，後面加 Ving，因此 be 變成 being。

The company admitted they cut corners in building the house.

這家公司承認他們蓋房子偷工減料。

point cut corners 意為「偷工減料」。

38 **affirm**

★ [ə`fɝm]

Ⅴ 斷言，堅稱，證實

同 assert 斷言
　 confirm 證實
　 maintain 維持

反 deny 否認

衍 affirmative (a.) 肯定的

In the board meeting, He kept affirming himself to be right.

在委員大會上，他一直堅持自己是正確的。

point keep + Ving 表示「一直；持續」。

It can be affirmed that the new materials will be more durable than ordinary ones.

可以斷言，新的材質比一般的還要耐用。

point one 代替 material，於此句的意思是指「一般的材質」。

39 **apparently**

★ [ə`pærəntlɪ]
★

ad 顯然地，表面上，似乎

同 obviously 明顯地
　 evidently 明顯地
　 visibly 明顯地

反 subtly 不易察覺地

衍 apparent (a.) 顯然的

Apparently, the manufacturing procedures still can be improved.

很明顯地，製造過程仍然可以被改進。

Apparently, the landlord is going to raise the rent.

很明顯地，房東要提高房租。

point 延伸詞彙：tenant 意為「房客」。

40 **generate**

★ [`dʒɛnəˌret]
★
★

Ⅴ 產生，發生，造成

同 cause 造成
　 give rise to 導致
　 lead to 導致
　 result in 導致
　 bring about 引起

The profit generated this year is twice as much as last year.

今年產生的利益是去年的兩倍。

point The profit generated this year 為主詞，後接單數動詞。

Compared with the previous model, the new solar power panels generate electricity more efficiently.

與先前的型號相比，新型太陽能面板能更有效率地發電。

point compare with 意為「與……相比」。

171

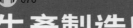

Chapter 076

8 生產製造與品管

---

41 vary
★
[`vɛrɪ]

V 使不同，變更，使多樣化
同 differ 不同
反 agree 相符
衍 variation (n.) 變化
variety (n.) 多樣化
various (a.) 多樣化的

The dealers complained that the products he received varied in quality.
經銷商抱怨他收到的產品品質有差異。

point in quality 意為「在品質上」。

The lifelong learning courses provided by this institute vary greatly in level.
這間機構提供的終生學習課程在程度上差異相當大。

---

42 site
★
★
★
[saɪt]

n 地點，舊址，部位
同 location 地點
place 地點
position 位置
situation 位置
venue 發生地

The skyscraper has an on-site nursery and a cafeteria.
這棟摩天大樓裡有一個內部托兒所及食堂。

point on-site 意為「在（工廠、辦公樓等的）內部」。

Workers are required to wear protective gear, like a helmet before entering the construction site.
工人被要求進入工地前要戴保護裝備，像是安全帽。

point 此句 before 為介係詞，後接 N / Ving。

---

43 output
★
★
[`aʊtˌpʊt]

n 出產，產量，輸出
同 production 生產
product 產品
yield 產出
harvest 產量
反 input 輸入

The factory employed more contract workers to increase the output of cement.
工廠僱用更多的契約工人來增加水泥的產量。

point factory = plant，意為「工廠」。

The senior executives were concerned about the quality of the output.
高階主管擔心產量的品質。

point be concerned about 意為「擔心」。

---

44 opinion
★
★
★
[ə`pɪnjən]

n 意見，評價，輿論
同 belief 看法
thought 想法
thinking 思想
way of thinking 思考方式
mind 想法
point of view 觀點

Feel free to share your opinion on the products.
儘管放心分享你對產品的意見。

point feel free to + V 意為「放心做……」。

In my opinion, the new policy can successfully react to economic fluctuations.
對我而言，新政策能夠成功地順應經濟波動。

point in my opinion = to me，意為「對我而言」。

45 **measure**

★
★
★

['mɛʒɚ]

ⓥ 測量，衡量

ⓝ 分量，措施，程度

同 calculate (v.) 計算
compute (v.) 計算
count (v.) 計算
quantify (v.) 使量化
assess (v.) 估價

The company has taken measures to cut down the time of application.
公司已經採取縮減申請時間的措施。

point take measures to 意為「採取措施」。

The worker will measure the size, and customize the cabinet for demanding clients.
工人測量尺寸並客製化衣櫥給那名高要求的顧客。

point 相關詞彙：estimate 估計，evaluate 估價，appraise 估計。

46 **major**

★
★
★

['medʒɚ]

ⓐ 較多的，重要的，主修的

ⓝ 成年人，重要人物，主修科目

同 utmost (a.) 最大的
prime (a.) 主要的

反 unimportant (a.) 不重要的
minor (a.) 次要的

Only candidates who major in Business Management can apply for this position.
只有主修商業管理的求職者才可以申請這個職位。

point major in + 科系，意為「主修某科系」。

The major difference between the new and previous models is their weight.
新型號與前一個型號的主要差異為它們的重量。

point 相關詞彙：crucial 重要的，vital 極重要的。

CH 8

生產製造與品管

47 **cope**

★
★

[kop]

ⓥ 競爭，對付，妥善處理

同 deal with 處理
handle 處理
tackle 交涉
solve 解決
manage 設法做到

Several mechanics are coping with the errors in the manufacturing process.
很多技師正在處理生產過程的錯誤。

point manufacture (v.) 製造，manufacturer (n.) 製造者。

Obviously, he was barely able to cope with the situation on his own.
很明顯地，他沒辦法自行處理這個狀況。

point 多益測驗情境常常都是在討論問題處理，因此要熟記「處理、解決」類的詞彙。

48 **overtime**

★
★

['ovɚ‚taɪm]

ⓐ 加班的，超時的

ⓝ 加班，延長賽

[‚ovɚ'taɪm]

ⓥ 使超過時間

The company provides overtime pay to the workers.
公司提供加班費給工人們。

The manufacturing workers have worked overtime for one month to meet the increasing demand for the products.
製造業工人為了要達到日漸上升的商品需求已經加班一個月了。

Chapter 077

8 生產製造與品管

49 booklet
★
★
★
[`buklɪt]

n 小冊子

同 pamphlet 小冊子
brochure 小冊子
leaflet 傳單
handout 傳單

The tour guide sent out the booklets **containing** the members' cellphone numbers.
導遊發下包含成員電話的小冊子。

(point) containing 是由 that contain 簡化而來。

Every employee will receive a booklet that includes detailed information on the climate control system.
每一位員工都會收到一本包含溫控系統詳細資訊的小手冊。

50 uniform
★
[`junə͵fɔrm]

a 相同的，一致的
n 制服，軍服
v 使成一樣

同 consistent (a.) 一致的
steady (a.) 不變的

反 changeable (a.) 易變的
variable (a.) 可變的
different (a.) 不同的

The products in the assembly line were **uniform** in appearance.
在生產線上的產品外表都是一樣的。

(point) 相關詞彙：invariable 不變的，unvarying 不變的，unvaried 不變的，unchanging 不變的。

All customers, **no matter what** they purchase, receive uniform service from the store.
所有的客人，無論他們買了什麼，都會得到一樣的服務。

(point) no matter what = whatever，意為「無論什麼」。

51 underline
★
[͵ʌndəˋlaɪn]

v 強調，在……下面劃線

[ˋʌndə͵laɪn]

n 劃在下面的線

同 mark (v.) 做記號
emphasize (v.) 強調
highlight (v.) 強調

The professor **asked** his students **to** underline the important points of this lesson.
教授請學生把這課的重點劃底線。

(point) ask sb. to 意為「要求某人去做……」。

The serious accident that happened in the factory **underlined** the need for updated security measures.
工廠裡發生的嚴重意外強調了更新安全措施的必要性。

52 remain
★
★
★
[rɪˋmen]

v 剩下，繼續存在，保持

同 stay 剩下

反 go 離去
depart 離去
leave 離開

The quantity of the items remains the same.
項目的數量保持一樣。

Even after the earthquake, the old wooden building still remained **intact**.
即使是在地震之後，這老舊的木製建築仍然保持完整。

(point) intact (a.) 完整無缺的。

53 **trade**

★
★
★

[tred]

n 貿易，行業，交換

同 commerce 貿易
buying and selling 交易
dealing 交易
business 生意

The sales is currently out of town to attend the trade show.
該業務目前出城參加商展。

 out of town 意為「出城」。多益測驗中出城的常見原因為參加展覽（exhibition, expo）、工作坊（workshop）、研討會（conference, seminar）或會議（meeting）。

If you buy products in bulk from the factory directly, you might get the trade price.
如果你直接從工廠大量購買產品，你可能可以拿到批發價。

 trade price 意為「批發價」，list price 意為「定價」。

---

54 **threat**

★

[θrɛt]

n 威脅，構成威脅的人（事物）

同 warning 警告
intimidation 恐嚇

The politician viewed the anonymous letter as a threat and he reported it to the police right after he received it.
政治人物把這封匿名信看作是一個威脅，並在收到後馬上就通報警方。

 view A as B 意為「把 A 看作是 B」。

For many assembly line workers, automation is a threat to their jobs.
對於很多生產線的工人而言，自動化對他們的工作是一種威脅。

---

55 **sincerely**

★

[sɪn`sɪrlɪ]

ad 真誠地，誠懇地

同 genuinely 真誠地
truly 真實地
truthfully 誠實地

反 insincerely 不誠實地

You are sincerely invited to the farewell party.
誠摯地邀請您參加歡送餐會。

I sincerely appreciate the way you dealt with the problems in the production line.
我很感謝你處理生產線問題的方式。

 deal with = cope with = tackle = handle = address = solve，意為「解決；處理」。

---

56 **factory**

★
★
★

[`fæktərɪ]

n 工廠，製造廠

同 plant 工廠

On today's factory tour, we will know the manufacturing process of tires.
在今天的工廠導覽中，我們會了解到輪胎的生產過程。

 多益聽力測驗 Part 4 的觀光導覽也會有參觀工廠的情境。

Factory workers are required to wear protective clothing and goggles.
工廠工人被要求穿戴防護衣和護目鏡。

Chapter 078

8 生產製造與品管

57 oversee
★
★
[`ovɚ`si]
V 監督，眺望，無意中看到
同 supervise 監督
keep an eye on 仔細看守
inspect 檢閱

The manager is responsible for overseeing the budget and its implementation.
經理負責監督預算及執行狀況。

(point) be responsible for = be in charge of，意為「負責」。

The construction foreman knows how to coordinate operations and oversee workers properly.
該名工程監工知道如何適當地協調運作及監督工人。

---

58 ordinarily
★
★
★
[`ɔrdn̩ˌɛrɪlɪ]
ad 通常地，一般地
同 usually 通常地
normally 一般地
generally 通常
反 exceptionally 例外地
unusually 不尋常地

Ordinarily, Ms. Juti takes business class but not economy class.
朱堤女士通常搭商務艙，而非經濟艙。

(point) 延伸詞彙：first class 意為「頭等艙」。

Access to the control room is ordinarily prohibited to all except staff.
控制室通常禁止進入，除了員工以外。

---

59 obligation
★
[ˌɑbləˋgeʃən]
n 義務，責任，債務
同 duty 責任
commitment 承諾
responsibility 責任
衍 obligatory (a.) 有義務的

Tour guides have an obligation to take care of every team member.
導遊有責任要照顧每位團員。

(point) every 或 each 後面都加單數名詞。

The subcontractor is under obligation to finish the construction project on time.
承包商有義務準時完成工程。

(point) be under obligation to + V 意為「有責任去做……」。

---

60 insecurity
★
[ˌɪnsɪˋkjʊrətɪ]
n 不安全，不穩定，
無把握，心神不定
同 lack of confidence 沒自信
uncertainty 不確定
反 security 安全

Many workers quit because of the insecurity of the work environment.
很多工人因為不安全的工作環境而辭掉工作。

Her family background made her have a deep sense of insecurity.
她的家庭背景讓她有很深的不安全感。

(point) a sense of insecurity 意為「不安全感」。

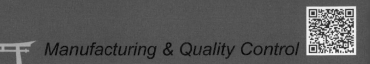

61 inferior

★
★
[ɪnˈfɪrɪɚ]

a 低等的，下級的，較差的

n 部下，次品

同 subordinate (n.) 下屬
junior (n.) 較年少者
secondary (n.) 副手

反 superior (n.) 上司
senior (n.) 前輩

We noticed that the quality of the new bag was inferior to the old one.

我們注意到新包包的品質比舊的還差。

point be inferior to 意為「劣於」。

Unfortunately, they could only afford to buy inferior materials.

很不幸地，他們只能負擔得起較低價的原料。

---

62 inevitable

★
[ɪnˈɛvətəbl]

a 不可避免的，必然發生的

同 unavoidable 不可避免的

反 avoidable 能避免的
uncertain 不確定的

衍 inevitably (ad.) 不可避免地

It's inevitable for construction workers to have career injuries.

對於建築工人而言，職業傷害是很難避免的。

point career injury 意為「職業傷害」。

In this situation, changes are inevitable.

在這種情況下，改變是不可避免的。

CH 8

生產製造與品管

---

63 inconsistent

★
★
[ˌɪnkənˈsɪstənt]

a 不一致的，前後矛盾的，
反覆無常的

同 changeable 易變的
contradictory 矛盾的

反 consistent 一致的
predictable 可預測的

The quality of the photocopier was very inconsistent.

這台影印機的品質時好時壞。

point 相關詞彙：unpredictable 不可預測的，unstable 不穩定的，irregular 不規律的。

The information he mentioned in his oral presentation was inconsistent with the one printed in his written report.

他在口頭報告提到的資訊跟他書面報告的內容不一樣。

---

64 incomplete

★
★
[ˌɪnkəmˈplit]

a 不完全的，未完成的

同 deficient 不足的
insufficient 不充足的
imperfect 不完美的

反 full 充滿的
complete 完整的
finished 完成的

The construction is still incomplete.

工程尚未完工。

The author's daughter continued to finish the incomplete novel.

作家的女兒持續完成那部未完成的小說。

point continue to + V 意為「持續做⋯⋯」。

177

Chapter 079

8

生產製造與品管

---

65 faith
★
[feθ]

n 信念，信仰，誠實

同 trust 信任
belief 信仰
confidence 信心
conviction 信念

Keep your word if you want to restore people's faith in you.
如果你想恢復人們對你的信任，你必須信守承諾。

The manager had faith in the new products that had already attracted people's attention before they were launched.
經理對未上市但已造成轟動的新產品非常有信心。

 have faith in = believe，意為「相信」。

---

66 expose
★
★
[ɪkˋspoz]

v 使暴露，揭露，使看見

同 reveal 揭發
反 conceal 隱藏
衍 exposure (n.) 暴露

The article exposed many political scandals.
那篇文章揭露了許多政治醜聞。

Do not expose the panel to direct sunlight.
不要把鑲板放在直射的陽光下。

---

67 emphasize
★
★
★
[ˋɛmfəˌsaɪz]

v 強調，使突出

同 focus 使聚焦
highlight 強調
stress 著重
put / lay stress on 著重於
反 understate 低估

The presenter emphasized the key points by different colors.
報告者藉由不同顏色來強調重點。

The factory foreman emphasized how important security inspection was to the workers.
工廠領班強調安全檢查對於工人的重要性。

 bring / call / draw attention to = give an emphasis to = give prominence to，皆可表示「強調」。

---

68 downsize
★
★
★
[ˋdaʊnˋsaɪz]

v 縮小規模，裁員

同 reduce 減少
trim 修剪
economize 節約
反 expand 擴張
衍 downsizing 縮減開支

The corporation had no choice but to downsize its contract workers.
公司不得不減少約聘工人的數量。

相關字彙：full-time worker 意為「全職工人」，part-time worker 意為「兼職工人」。

With the installation of the automatic system and the use of the new machine, the firm decided to downsize the workforce.
隨著自動化系統的安裝及新機器的使用，公司決定要減少一些員工。

69 content
★
[kən`tɛnt]
a 滿足的，甘願的
n 滿足
v 滿意
[`kɑntɛnt]
n 內容，要旨
同 satisfied 滿意的
反 discontented 不滿的

The sales was required to modify the contents of the contract.
這名業務被要求修改合約內容。

Go check the contents page for the contents you want to read.
去看目錄頁找你要讀的內容。

point contents page 意為「目錄頁」。

70 confuse
★
★
[kən`f juz]
v 使困惑，混淆，搞亂
同 puzzle 使迷惑
反 enlighten 啟發
clear 使乾淨
distinguish 區別
衍 confusion (n.) 困惑

Instructions should be clear, or consumers will get confused.
指示要夠清楚，不然消費者會很困惑。

point or 意為「或者；否則」。

Due to our unique product packaging designs, not many customers confuse our products with our opponents'.
因為我們特別的產品包裝設計，沒有太多顧客把我們的產品誤看成對手的產品。

71 comply
★
[kəm`plaɪ]
v 依從，順從，服從
同 abide by 遵從
obey 服從
adhere to 忠於
conform to 符合
反 ignore 忽視
disobey 違抗

After discussion, his coworker was still reluctant to comply with his suggestion.
經過討論之後，他的同事仍然不願意順從他的建議。

point be reluctant to 意為「不願意」。

You will be laid off if you don't comply with the factory regulations.
如果你不遵守工廠規矩的話，你將會被解僱。

point be laid off 意為「被解僱」。

72 instruction
★
★
★
[ɪn`strʌkʃən]
n 教學，指示，用法說明
衍 instruct (v.) 指示
instructor (n.) 指導者

The instruction manual explained every step clearly.
說明手冊清楚說明了每個步驟。

The course provides students with basic instruction in baking.
這門課提供學生烘焙方面的基本知識。

point in + N 意為「在……方面」。

CH 8

生產製造與品管

8 生產製造與品管

---

73 ★ ★

complicated

[`kɑmpləˌketɪd]

a 複雜的，難懂的

同 involved 複雜的
elaborate 複雜的

反 easy 簡易的
simple 簡單的
straightforward 直接的

The process of returning merchandise is **too** complicated **to** explain.
產品退貨的步驟太複雜了，以至於很難解釋。

point too... to... 意為「太……以至於不能……」。

The application form is rather **complicated** for the candidate.
這份申請表格對那名求職者來說非常複雜。

point 相關詞彙：complex 複雜的，intricate 難理解的，tangled 紊亂的。

---

74 ★ ★ ★

generally

[`dʒɛnərəlɪ]

ad 通常，普遍地，大體而言

同 in general 通常
by and large 一般而論
mostly 一般地
usually 通常

反 occasionally 偶爾

Generally, employees **have** no **access** to the database unless they are authorized.
通常，員工沒有管道進入資料庫，除非他們被授權。

point have access to 意為「使用；接近；可以利用」。

Generally speaking, 70% of our customers **are satisfied with** the new user interface.
普遍來說，我們百分之七十的顧客對新的使用者介面感到滿意。

point be satisfied with 意為「滿意」。

---

75 ★ ★ ★

regarding

[rɪ`gɑrdɪŋ]

prep 關於，就……而論

同 concerning 關於
as regards 至於
with regard to 關於
in regard to 關於

衍 regard (n.) 關心

Thank you for the recent inquiry regarding the new catalog.
感謝您最近有關新目錄的問題詢問。

The interviewer asked the applicant **several** questions regarding his former work experience.
面試者問求職者許多有關他之前工作經驗的問題。

point several = many = a lot of，意為「許多的」。

---

76 ★

waive

[wev]

v 放棄，撤回，擱置

同 abandon 放棄
cancel 取消

反 follow 追隨
pursue 追求

Since you are our regular, we will waive the **processing fee**.
因為你是我們的常客，我們會取消手續費。

point processing fee 意為「手續費」，admission fee 意為「入場費」。

Many clients complained about the time pressure; therefore, the company waived the time limit.
許多客戶抱怨時間壓力，因此公司取消了時間限制。

point therefore 為副詞，無法連接兩個句子，因此前面使用分號「;」來連接。

Test 1

◉ 一、請寫出下列單字的中文意思。

① specification _____　⑥ accelerate _____

② advantage _____　⑦ expose _____

③ improve _____　⑧ inspector _____

④ obligation _____　⑨ productivity _____

⑤ procedure _____　⑩ affirm _____

◉ 二、請寫出符合下列句意的單字。

① The factory foreman _____ how important security inspection was to the workers.
工廠領班強調安全檢查對於工人的重要性。

② _____, employees have no access to the database unless they are authorized.
通常，員工沒有管道進入資料庫，除非他們被授權。

③ The sales was required to modify the _____ of the contract.
這名業務被要求修改合約內容。

解答

1. ① 規格，說明書　② 優點，好處　③ 改進，提高　④ 職責，義務　⑤ 程式，手續，步驟
　　⑥ 加快，促進，加速　⑦ 揭露，曝光　⑧ 檢查員，巡視員　⑨ 生產力，生產率　⑩ 斷言，肯定
2. ① emphasized　② generally　③ contents

Test 2

一、請選擇符合下列文意的單字。

Ⓐ process	Ⓑ boost	Ⓒ contractor
Ⓓ remains	Ⓔ initially	Ⓕ upgrade

① The quality of the items _____ the same.

② The company started out as a manufacturer of furniture _____, but now it produces plastic.

③ The company is the _____ of this construction project.

④ The software _____ has successfully improved the service quality.

⑤ The increase of the part-time workers will _____ the production.

二、請寫出下列片語的中文意思。

① in short supply	_____	⑤ be inferior to	_____
② lay off	_____	⑥ have access to	_____
③ have faith in	_____	⑦ full-time	_____
④ as soon as	_____	⑧ in my opinion	_____

解答

1. ①D ②E ③C ④F ⑤B
2. ① 短缺 ② 解僱 ③ 相信 ④ 一……就…… ⑤ 劣於 ⑥ 使用，接近 ⑦ 全職的 ⑧ 對我而言

Chapter 9
人事組織

以下多益必考單字，你認識哪些？

- [ ] extensive (p.184)
- [ ] department (p.185)
- [ ] arrange (p.184)
- [ ] interview (p.189)
- [ ] require (p.192)
- [ ] employee (p.193)
- [ ] association (p.187)
- [ ] contact (p.196)
- [ ] energetic (p.198)
- [ ] accomplish (p.199)
- [ ] general (p.186)
- [ ] organize (p.196)
- [ ] field (p.189)
- [ ] select (p.190)
- [ ] certificate (p.188)
- [ ] reference (p.188)
- [ ] qualify (p.191)
- [ ] recognition (p.192)

01 **arrange**

★
★
★

[əˋrendʒ]

Ⓥ 整理，安排，改編

同 plan 計畫
　　organize 安排

Ever since the proposal, the couple has spent one year arranging their wedding ceremony.
自從求婚以來，這對新人已經花了一年準備他們的婚禮儀式。

point ever since 後面加名詞，表示時間的起點，與完成式 has spent 連用。

It has been arranged that the applicants for this position will have an interview this Friday.
已經安排好這個職位的面試者於本週五進行面試。

---

02 **international**

★
★
★

[ˌɪntɚˋnæʃənl̩]

ⓐ 國際性的

同 global 全球的
　　worldwide 全世界的

反 national 國家的
　　domestic 國內的
　　local 當地的

衍 internationalize (v.) 國際化

The candidate was hired because she had worked in international corporations.
這位求職者因為曾經在跨國公司裡工作而被僱用。

point was hired 為過去被動式（時間發生較晚），had worked 為過去完成式（時間發生較早）。

Excellence Telecommunication Company provides the cheapest rate for international calls.
Excellence 電信公司提供最低的國際電話費率。

---

03 **extensive**

★

[ɪkˋstɛnsɪv]

ⓐ 廣大的，廣泛的，大量的

同 large-scale 大規模的
　　substantial 大量的
　　vast 廣闊的
　　boundless 無窮的

反 small 小的
　　limited 有限的

The applicant's extensive knowledge of international trade convinced the interviewer.
那位求職者以廣泛的國際貿易知識說服了面試官。

point 相關詞彙：sizeable 相當多的，ample 豐富的，considerable 相當多的，immense 無邊際的。

Extensive reading is beneficial to children's cognitive development.
廣泛閱讀有益於小孩的認知發展。

point be beneficial to 意為「對……有益」。

---

04 **impress**

★
★
★

[ɪmˋprɛs]

Ⓥ 給……深刻印象，使銘記

[ˋɪmprɛs]

ⓝ 印象，影響

同 make an impression on (ph.) 給……深刻的印象

His outstanding performance impressed all the judges and the audiences.
他傑出的表演使評審和觀眾印象深刻。

The interviewer was clearly impressed by the candidate's attitude.
面試官顯然對那名求職者的態度感到印象深刻。

point be impressed by 意為「對……感到印象深刻」。

05 impression

[ɪmˈprɛʃən]

★
★
★

n 印象，感想，影響

同 feeling 感覺
　　sense 感覺
　　notion 想法
　　thought 想法

Leaving a good first impression is important at your job interview.
在面試時留下好的第一印象是很重要的。

point Leaving a good first impression 為 Ving 當主詞，動詞使用單數。

What was your impression of the newcomer?
你對那新人的印象如何？

06 potential

[pəˈtɛnʃəl]

★
★
★

a 潛在的，可能的
n 潛力，可能性

同 possibility (n.) 可能性
　　capacity (n.) 能力

According to the reference letter, he is a potential researcher.
根據他的推薦信，他是一位有潛力的研究員。

The coach can tell whether his students have potential to be excellent basketball players.
教練能夠分辨他的學生是否有潛力成為一位優秀的籃球員。

point 相關詞彙：capability 能力，ability 能力，talent 天資。

07 quarter

[ˈkwɔrtɚ]

★
★

n 四分之一，一刻鐘，區域

同 district 地區
　　area 區域
　　region 地區
　　section 地區
　　zone 地帶
　　territory 領域

The firm hired three executive assistants last quarter.
公司在上一季僱用了三個行政助理。

point firm = company = business，意為「公司」。

The clerk cut the pastry into quarters for the customer.
店員幫顧客將糕點切成四塊。

08 department

[dɪˈpɑrtmənt]

★
★
★

n 部門，系所

同 division 部門
　　section 部門
　　sector 部門
　　subdivision 分支
　　segment 部門

衍 departmental (a.) 部門的

You should provide the model number of the defective items to the customer service department.
你要提供有瑕疵的項目的型號給客戶服務部。

point 換貨必備：serial number 序號，receipt 收據，invoice 發票。

The new mayor is considering merging two different departments of city hall.
新市長正考量合併市政廳的兩個部門。

point 延伸詞彙：merger (n.) 合併，acquire (v.) 收購，acquisition (n.) 收購。

CH 9

人事組織

Chapter 082

9 人事組織

09 general

★
★
★

['dʒɛnərəl]

a 一般的，普遍的，全體的
n 將軍，一般
同 usual (a.) 通常的
customary (a.) 慣常的
normal (a.) 正常的
conventional (a.) 普通的
regular (a.) 正常的
反 exceptional (a.) 例外的

The general manager was concerned that he was not able to lead the discussion this time.
總經理擔心他這次沒辦法引導討論。

point concern (v.) 擔心，concerned (a.) 憂心的。很容易出現在多益測驗題目裡問說話者或作者在擔心什麼。

The candidate applying for the position of secretary can handle general office duties.
這名應徵祕書的面試者可以應付一般的辦公室工作。

point apply for the position of 意為「申請……的職位」。

10 raise

★
★
★

[rez]

v 舉起，增加，提升
同 promote 晉升
advance 提高
upgrade 提升
反 lower 降低
reduce 減少

The landlord will raise the tenant's monthly rent.
房東將會提高房客的每月租金。

point 相關詞彙：increase 增加，elevate 提高。

Personnel and benefits office tried to raise employee morale by planning incentive programs.
人事與福利部門藉由籌劃獎勵計劃來提高員工的士氣。

11 associate

★
★

[ə'soʃɪɪt]

n 夥伴，同事，合夥人
a 夥伴的，副的，聯合的
[ə'soʃˌɪet]
v 聯想，使聯合，結交
同 partner (n.) 夥伴
反 rival (v.) 敵手

My associate is rather reliable because he always finishes projects on time.
我的夥伴相當可靠，因為他總是會在時間內完成專案。

Smart businessmen associate their products with holidays to raise consumers' shopping desires.
聰明的商人會使他們的產品和假期產生連結，以引起消費者的購買欲望。

12 headquarters

★
★
★

['hɛd'kwɔrtɚz]

n 總部，總公司
同 main office 總公司
反 branch 分支

The company is moving its headquarters to the capital city.
公司要把總部遷到首都。

point move to 意為「遷到」。

The mechanical engineer had a video conference with the headquarters yesterday.
該名機械工程師昨天和總部進行視訊會議。

13 merger
★
★
★
[mɝdʒɚ]

🔲（公司等的）合併

🟰 combination 結合
affiliation 入會
alliance 聯盟
association 聯盟
connection 連結

🔄 split 分開

<u>Have you ever heard of</u> a merger between the two technology companies?
你聽說那兩家科技公司的合併了嗎？

point have you ever heard of 意為「你聽說了嗎？」

The CEO announced a merger in the annual staff meeting.
執行長在年度員工會議中宣布公司合併。

---

14 merge
★
★
★
[mɝdʒ]

🔲 合併，同化

🟰 unite 聯合
unify 統一
affiliate 使緊密聯繫

🔄 separate 分隔
split 分開

Does <u>merging</u> two departments improve efficiency?
合併兩個部門會增加效率嗎？

point 相關詞彙：integrate 整合，combine 結合，join 連結。

Two lanes merge into one.
兩條車道會合併成一條車道。

---

15 association
★
★
★
[ə,sosɪ'eʃəl]

🔲 協會，社團，聯盟

🟰 alliance 結盟
league 聯盟
union 聯盟

Korea Tourist Association invites the most famous actor in their nation to promote tourism.
韓國觀光協會請他們國內最有名的演員來推廣觀光。

Welcome to the 42ⁿᵈ Dental Association Conference.
歡迎來到第四十二屆牙醫協會研討會。

point 多益聽力測驗 Part 4 的第一句話常會介紹活動的地點。

---

16 applicant
★
★
★
[`æpləkənt]

🔲 申請人

🟰 candidate 候選人
job hunter 求職者
interviewee 面試者

🔗 apply (v.) 申請

The applicants <u>attached</u> the application form <u>to</u> their resumes.
申請者把申請表格黏到他們的履歷上。

point attach... to... 意為「把……黏到……」。

Applicants with creativity <u>are</u> more <u>preferred</u>.
有創意力的面試者會更有優勢。

point sth. is required / necessary 意為「某能力是必須的」。sth. is a plus / sth. is preferred 意為「某能力是加分的」（這個條件是讓面試者加分，而非必要的）。

Chapter 083

9 人事組織

---

17 certificate
★
★
★
[sɚˋtɪfəkɪt]

n 證明書，執照

同 guarantee 保證書
　proof 證明
　certification 證明
　document 證件
　authorization 授權

Candidates are required to provide valid language certificates.
求職者被要求提供有效的語言證照。

(point) be required to 意為「被要求」。

His driver's certificate was temporarily suspended.
他的駕照暫時被吊銷。

(point) 延伸詞彙：permanently 意為「永久地」。

---

18 anxious
★
★
★
[ˋæŋkʃəs]

a 焦慮的，掛念的，渴望的

同 disturbed 心亂的
　edgy 急躁的
　tense 緊張的
　stressed 緊張的
反 carefree 無憂無慮的
　unconcerned 不擔心的

The applicant was anxious about the interview result.
應徵者對面試結果感到很緊張。

(point) 相關詞彙：nervous 緊張的，worried 擔心的，concerned 擔心的，fearful 害怕的，uneasy 不安的。

Many parents feel anxious that TV programs might distract children from their assignments.
很多家長焦慮於電視節目可能會使小孩做功課時分心。

(point) distract sb. from sth. 意為「使某人在某事上分心」。

---

19 reference
★
★
★
[ˋrɛfərəns]

n 提及，參考，推薦

同 source 來源
　information source
　資料來源
　citation 引用
衍 refer (v.) 歸因於

These are the tips for writing reference letters.
這些是寫推薦信的訣竅。

(point) reference letter = recommendation letter，意為「推薦信」。

The reference book which is widely recommended by a lot of professors is useful to my research.
這本被很多教授推薦的參考書對我的研究很有用。

(point) be useful to 意為「有用」。

---

20 prioritize
★
★
★
[praɪˋɔrəˌtaɪz]

V 按優先順序處理，給予優先權

衍 prior (a.) 在先的
　priority (n.) 優先

The main focus of the workshop is to teach new recruits how to prioritize their work.
工作坊的重點在於教導新進員工區分他們工作的輕重緩急。

(point) new recruit = newcomer = new staff = new employee，意為「新進員工」。

The top tip for working more efficiently and effectively is to prioritize your tasks.
要更有效率且有效的工作，最重要的訣竅就是要區分任務的優先順序。

21 **encourage**
★
★
★
[ɪnˋkɝɪdʒ]

Ⅴ 鼓勵，慫恿，促進，助長

同 inspire 啟發
motivate 刺激

反 discourage 勸阻

衍 encouragement (n.) 鼓勵

Some companies encourage their staff to work harder by giving bonuses.
有些公司用獎金來鼓勵員工認真工作。

The government encourages the elderly to learn new things by providing a variety of complimentary courses.
政府提供多樣化的免費課程以鼓勵年長者學習新事物。

 a variety of = various，意為「多樣化的」。

22 **field**
★
★
★
[fild]

ｎ 原野，田地，領域

同 area 區域
industry 產業，領域

Candidates who have worked in related fields for five years should submit the application form before this Friday.
在相關領域有工作五年經驗的求職者要在本週五前交申請表。

 who have worked in related fields for five years 為形容詞子句，用來修飾前面的名詞 candidates。

I read books on different fields to broaden my horizons.
我讀不同領域的書來擴大我的視野。

23 **interview**
★
★
★
[ˋɪntɚˏvju]

Ⅴ 接見，訪問，面試
ｎ 會見，採訪，面談

衍 exclusive interview
(ph.) 專訪

The interview will be conducted in English.
面試會以英文進行。

point in + 語言，意為「以……語言」。

There are two stages to the interview, a group interview and an individual interview.
面試有兩個階段，團體面試及一對一面試。

24 **payroll**
★
[ˋpeˏrol]

ｎ 薪資單，薪水總額

同 paysheet 薪資單

衍 pay (v.) 支付
payable (a.) 應支付的
payment (n.) 付款

Should you have any questions regarding the new payroll policy, please contact Kent.
如果你有任何有關薪資政策的問題，請聯絡肯特。

point 此句的 should = if，意為「如果」。

Please stop by the payroll department and submit the travel expenses application form.
請順道來薪資部門呈交你的差旅費申請表。

point 延伸詞彙：reimburse (v.) 報銷，reimbursement (n.) 報銷。

CH 9

人事組織

Chapter 084

9 人事組織

---

25 interviewee
★
★
★
[ˌɪntɚvjuˋi]

n 被會見者，被面試者
同 applicant 求職者
　　individual 個人
反 interviewer 面試官

The interviewee prepared his portfolio to show his work as well.
這名求職者也準備作品集以展現他的作品。
point as well = too，意為「也」。

It is suggested that interviewees prepare questions that might be asked.
求職者被建議要事先準備可能會被問的問題。

---

26 interviewer
★
★
★
[ˋɪntɚvjuɚ]

n 接見者，採訪者，面試官
同 questioner 發問者
　　examiner 主考人
　　assessor 估價人
　　appraiser 鑑定人

The interviewer asked the candidate some problem-solving scenarios.
面試官問求職者一些問題解決的情境。

The interviewee tried to impress the interviewer with his fluent English speaking ability.
面試者試著要用他流利的英文能力來使面試官印象深刻。
point 延伸詞彙：impressive (a.) 令人印象深刻的。

---

27 candidate
★
★
★
[ˋkændədet]

n 候選人，候補者，應試者
同 applicant 申請人
　　interviewee 面試者
　　individual 個人

One of the presidential candidates visited the capital city of this nation.
總統候選人之一拜訪這國家的首都。
point capital 意為「首都；資本；大寫字母」。

The candidates for the position will receive both the oral test and physical fitness test.
這個職位的求職者將會有口試及體能測試。

---

28 select
★
★
★
[səˋlɛkt]

v 選擇，挑選
同 choose 選擇
　　pick 挑選
衍 selection (n.) 選擇
　　selective (a.) 有選擇的

The selected participants would be interviewed in another meeting room.
被挑選的受試者會在另一間會議室進行面談。

The purchase department carefully selected products for next quarter.
採購部門仔細地挑選下一季的產品。
point 多益測驗中常見的公司部門：sales department 業務部門，marketing department 行銷部門，human resources department 人力資源部門。

29 portfolio

★
★

[port`folɪo]

n 文件夾，公事包，
投資組合

同 case 手提箱
folder 文件夾
file 公文箱

Attached is my portfolio.
附檔是我的作品集。

point 多益閱讀測驗裡，求職信件中的夾帶檔案常見為：portfolio (n.) 作品集、resume (n.) 履歷 、application form (ph.) 申請表。

Creating a career portfolio is beneficial to your interview.
製作工作作品集對面試很有益。

point be beneficial to 意為「有益」。

30 qualification

★
★
★

[ˌkwɑləfəˈkeʃən]

n 資格，能力，限制

同 diploma 文憑
degree 學位
license 證照
eligibility 資格

What are the qualifications for this position?
這個職位的條件是什麼？

Please send the assistant your application form and academic qualifications.
請將你的申請表和學術資格證明寄給助理。

point form (n.) 表格；形式 (v.) 形成。

31 qualify

★
★
★

[ˈkwɑləˌfaɪ]

v 使具有資格，限制，
證明合格

同 certify 證明
licence 給……發許可證

This license qualifies you to apply for jobs in any public hospitals.
這個證照可以讓你有資格申請任何公立醫院。

The student hopes to qualify as a lifeguard before he goes abroad to study.
這名學生希望在出國讀書前取得救生員資格。

32 recruit

★
★
★

[rɪˈkrut]

v 徵募，僱用，補充

同 hire 僱用

反 dismiss 遣散
lay off 解僱

All the recruits are required to attend the orientation.
所有新人都必須出席新進員工訓練。

point be required to + V 意為「被要求做……」。

The company will recruit more temporary part-time workers who have a master's degree in marketing management.
公司將會僱用更多有行銷管理碩士學位的臨時兼職工。

CH 9

人事組織

191

33 staff

★
★
★

[stæf]

n 全體職員，工作人員，支柱

同 employee 員工
worker 勞工
workforce 勞工
personnel 人員

All staff should attend the annual employee meeting.

所有員工都該參加年度員工大會。

(point) annual employee meeting 意為「年度員工大會」。

Unfortunately, we do not have enough staff to cope with their service needs.

很不幸地，我們沒有足夠的員工來處理他們的服務需求。

---

34 require

★
★
★

[rɪ`kwaɪr]

V 需要，要求，命令

同 need 需要
necessitate 需要
demand 要求
command 命令

The bankers in this bank are required to wear a uniform.

這間銀行的行員必須要穿制服。

These newcomers required training.

這些新人需要訓練。

(point) required training = require to be trained，意為「需要被訓練」。

---

35 requirement

★
★
★

[rɪ`kwaɪrmənt]

n 需要，要求，必要條件

同 want 想要
necessity 需要
essential 必需品
prerequisite 必要條件
requisite 必要條件

The minimum requirement for this job is to have at least 2 years of related work experience.

這個工作的最低要求是至少要有兩年的相關工作經驗。

(point) at least 意為「至少」。

The company management did not think the candidate fulfilled the requirements for this position.

公司管理階層不覺得這名求職者符合這個職位的需求。

(point) company management, managerial position 皆可表達「管理階層」。

---

36 recognition

★
★
★

[ˌrɛkəg`nɪʃən]

n 認出，承認，賞識

同 identification 認出

衍 recognizable (a.) 可辨認的
recognize (v.) 識別

The judge's recognition meant a lot to the player.

評審的認可對這名球員的意義很大。

(point) sth. means a lot to sb. 意為「某事對某人意義很大」。

In recognition of Jenny's efforts for the campaign, she will be promoted to the position of project manager.

為了認可珍妮對活動的努力，她將會被升為專案經理。

37 recruitment

★
★

[rɪˋkrutmənt]

n 徵募，補充

衍 campus recruitment fair
(ph.) 校園招聘會

The information of recruitment has been posted on the company's website.
招募的資訊已經被放到公司的網站上。

The trainer introduced the recruitment process to the cabin crew in detail.
訓練員向空服員詳細地介紹招募過程。

38 initial

★

[ɪˋnɪʃəl]

a 開始的，字首的
n 首字母
v 簽名（姓名的首字母）
同 beginning (n.) 開始
opening (n.) 開頭
反 final (a.) 最終的
衍 initiate (a.) 新加入的
initiative (a.) 開始的

The initial agreement was not accepted by some new members.
有些新的成員不接受一開始的協議。

Ms. Statham asked the experienced carpenter whether he could carve her initials into the customized table.
史塔森小姐詢問這名經驗豐富的木匠，是否可以把她名字的首字母刻在這張客製化的桌子上。

point customized = tailor-made，意為「客製化的」。

CH 9

人事組織

39 employ

★
★
★

[ɪmˋplɔɪ]

v 僱用，使用，利用
n 僱用，使用
同 hire (v.) 僱用
recruit (v.) 招募
反 dismiss (v.) 遣散
unemployed (a.) 未被僱用的

The marketing department decided to employ more contract employees.
行銷部門決定要僱用更多約聘人員。

The painter employed different painting techniques in his latest work.
畫家在他最新作品中使用了不同的繪畫技巧。

point use, utilize 也可指「使用」。

40 employee

★
★
★

[ˌɛmplɔɪˋi]

n 雇員，受雇者
同 worker 勞動者
staff 職員
反 employer 雇主

All new employees need training.
所有的新進員工都需要被訓練。

point need training = need to be trained，意為「需要被訓練」。

D&K Limited is going to relocate one of its branches to another city, and hire 20 employees.
D&K 有限公司將要遷移其中一個分部到另一個城市，並且要僱用二十位員工。

Chapter 086

9 人事組織

41 employer
★
★
★
[ɪm`plɔɪɚ]

n 雇主，雇用者

同 boss 老闆
owner 所有者
manager 負責人

The employer went over the employment contract with the newcomer.
雇主和新人一起檢視一次僱用契約。
point go over 意為「察看」。

The employer asked Tina to cover Jack's morning and afternoon shifts while he was away on business.
雇主請緹娜在傑克出差時幫他代早上及下午的班。
point cover one's shift 意為「代班」。

---

42 employment
★
★
★
[ɪm`plɔɪmənt]

n 僱用，職業，使用

同 engagement 僱用
hiring 僱用

The interviewee was asked whether he was in employment.
面試者被問他是否在職中。
point be in employment 意為「有工作，在職」。

He was out of employment, which means he is between jobs.
他失業了，也就是說現在在待業中。
point be between jobs 意為「待業中」。

---

43 session
★
★
[`sɛʃən]

n（議會）開會，集會，學期

同 period 期間

The training session will be held after lunch.
訓練課程會在午餐後舉行。
point will be held 為未來被動式，意為「將會被舉行」。

Every new recruit is required to attend the training session before they start to work.
每位新人在開始工作前都必須要參加訓練課程。

---

44 intensive
★
[ɪn`tɛnsɪv]

a 加強的，精深的，集約的

同 comprehensive 廣泛的

衍 intense (a.) 強烈的
intensify (v.) 加強

After intensive negotiations, the two companies finally reached an agreement.
在密集的談判後，兩家公司終於達成協議。
point reach an agreement 意為「達成協議」。

The intensive training program provided all the interns the knowledge they required to accomplish the job.
這個密集的培訓課程提供所有實習生完成工作所需的知識。

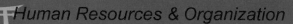

45 comprehensive
★
★
[ˌkɑmprɪˈhɛnsɪv]
ⓐ 廣泛的，綜合的
同 inclusive 包含的
thorough 徹底的
extensive 廣泛的
反 partial 部分的
limited 有限的
衍 comprehend (v.) 理解

The company offers a comprehensive employee training on a regular basis.
公司規律地提供全方位的員工訓練。

(point) employee training 意為「員工訓練」。

The guidebook is a bestseller because it provides comprehensive and detailed information about New York.
這本旅遊書是暢銷書，因為它提供了關於紐約全面性且詳細的資訊。

(point) bestseller 意為「暢銷書；暢銷商品；暢銷作者」。

46 placement
★
[ˈplɛsmənt]
ⓝ 布置，人員配置
同 positioning 位置
placing 位置
arrangement 安排
deployment 部署
location 位置

Every student is required to take a placement test in order to know their English levels.
每個學生都必須要考分班測驗，以知道他們的英文程度。

(point) placement test 意為「分班測驗；水平測試」。

The assistant director will find a placement for the new intern.
專員將會為新的實習生安排一個職位。

47 track
★
★
[træk]
ⓝ 行蹤，軌道，小徑
同 trace 痕跡
path 小徑
road 街道
route 路線

Anna uses office software, like Excel, to track her expenditures.
安娜使用辦公室軟體，像是試算表，來追蹤她的開銷。

(point) expenditure, expense 皆指「支出」。

He was on the track of a potential candidate who could maintain good community relations.
他正在尋找一個能維持良好公共關係的有潛力的求職者。

(point) on the track of 意為「尋找」。

48 branch
★
★
[bræntʃ]
ⓝ 樹枝，支線，分店
ⓥ 分岔，分支
同 division (n.) 分割
反 headquarters (n.) 總部

The sales manager of each branch will bring their assistants to the annual sales meeting.
每個分部的業務經理將會帶他們的助理來年度業務大會。

Lisa will be relocated to the new branch in Toronto.
麗莎將會被調到多倫多新的分部。

(point) relocate 也可以用在公司的搬遷。

195

49 **expansion**

★

[ɪk`spænʃən]

n 擴展，膨脹

同 growth 成長
enlargement 擴大
extension 擴張
development 發展

反 contraction 收縮

衍 expand (v.) 擴展

The company hired several temporary workers at a phase of rapid expansion.
公司在迅速發展的階段僱用了好幾個臨時工。

point 延伸詞彙：temporary (a.) 暫時的，permanent (a.) 永久的。

The professor illustrated this business model by mentioning the company's business expansion.
教授透過提及這公司的商業擴張米說明這個商業模式。

50 **organize**

★
★
★

[`ɔrgə‚naɪz]

v 組織，安排

同 arrange 安排

反 disorganize 擾亂

My company organized a car to pick up the foreign clients.
我的公司安排了一輛車去接外國客戶。

point pick up 意為「接；撿起來；搭訕」。

The ability to organize is highly required for the position of research assistant.
統整能力對於研究助理這個職位而言相當必要。

point The ability to organize 為主詞，後接單數動詞。

51 **capacity**

★
★

[kə`pæsətɪ]

n 容量，能量，生產力

同 ability 能力
power 力量
potential 潛力
competence 能力
volume 容積

反 inability 無能

She is the only one who is in a capacity to speak English fluently in her department.
她是唯一一個在她的部門中有能力把英文講得很流暢的人。

point be in a capacity to 意為「有這樣的能力做……」。

The customer asked the clerk the capacity of the bottle.
客人問店員水壺的容積多大。

52 **contact**

★
★
★

[`kɑntækt]

n 接觸，交往，聯繫

[kən`tækt]

v 接觸，聯繫

同 connection (n.) 連結
touch (v.) 接觸

The candidate included his contact information in his resume.
那位面試者的履歷中包括了他的連絡資訊。

He has a contact in the fashion industry.
他在時尚界有個熟人。

53 due
★
★ [dju]
★
ⓐ 應支付的，合適的，到期的
ⓝ 應得權益，應付款
圓 proper (a.) 合適的
衍 due to (ph.) 由於

The project is due tomorrow, so all the team members will work overtime tonight.
這個專案明天到期，所以所有的團隊成員今晚都會加班。

Due to the traffic collision, the road was temporarily closed.
因為車禍，道路暫時被封閉。

point traffic collision = car crash = car accident，意為「車禍」。

---

54 annually
★
★ [ˈænjʊəlɪ]

ⓐⓓ 每年，每年一次
圓 each year 每年
  every year 每年
衍 annual (a.) 每年的

It is a tradition that the flea market is held annually.
跳蚤市場每年都會舉辦，這是一個傳統。

point be held 意為活動「被舉辦」。

One of the employee benefits is that employees receive a pay rise annually.
其中一個員工福利就是員工每年都會被加薪。

---

55 unless
★
★ [ʌnˈlɛs]
★
ⓒⓞⓝⓙ 如果不，除非

I might not be able to attend the training session unless I finish the task by Friday.
我可能無法參加訓練課程，除非我在週五前完成這個任務。

point be not able to = be unable to + V，意為「不可能做……」。

All sophomores are required to take Elementary English unless they can provide language certificates to prove their English levels.
所有大二生都該修初階英文，除非他們可以提供語言證照證明他們的英文程度。

---

56 enthusiasm
★
★ [ɪnˈθjuzɪˌæzəm]
★
ⓝ 熱心，熱情，熱忱
圓 eagerness 熱切
  excitement 激動
  interest 關注
反 coldness 冷淡
  indifference 冷漠
  unconcern 不關心

An experienced interviewer can tell whether a candidate has enthusiasm for the position right away.
一個有經驗的面試官可以馬上看出一個面試者是否對於工作有熱誠。

point have enthusiasm for 表示「對……有熱誠」。

We were greeted with enthusiasm when we visited our headquarters.
當我們參訪總部時，我們被熱烈地招待。

point headquarters（總部）恆為複數。

CH 9

人事組織

197

9

人事組織

---

57 energetic
★
[ˌɛnɚˈdʒɛtɪk]

a 精力旺盛的，有力的，
積極的
同 active 活躍的
反 inactive 不活躍的
衍 energy (n.) 活力

The candidate was hired because he was energetic.
這名求職者因為他很有活力而被錄取了。

She is an energetic supporter of the teaching community.
她是教師社群的熱心支持者。

---

58 pleased
★
★
[plizd]

a 高興的，喜歡的，滿意的
同 contented 滿意的
satisfied 滿意的
cheerful 興高采烈的
delighted 高興的
反 displeased 不高興的

Obviously, the vice president was pleased with the results of the campaign.
很明顯地，副總裁很滿意這次活動的成效。

(point) campaign 指行銷廣告的活動。

I am very pleased to hear that you got promoted.
我非常開心聽到你升遷了。

(point) I am promoted. = I have had a promotion. = I have got a promotion. 皆可表達「我升遷了」。

---

59 alarm
★
★
[əˈlɑrm]

n 警報，驚慌，擔憂
v 報警，告急，使驚慌
同 alert (n.) 警戒

The audition was interrupted by the fire alarm.
試鏡被火警警報器給打斷了。

The rumors of company downsizing turned out to be a false alarm.
公司裁員的謠傳原來是虛驚一場。

(point) downsizing (n.) 意為「縮小規模」，在商業上為「減少員工數量」的意思。

---

60 comfort
★
[ˈkʌmfɚt]

n 安逸，舒適
v 安慰，慰問
同 ease (v.) 緩和
console (v.) 安慰
soothe (v.) 撫慰
relieve (v.) 減輕
relief (n.) 緩和

My mentor always encourages me to take challenges and get out of my comfort zone.
我的指導老師一直鼓勵我接受挑戰並離開我的舒適圈。

(point) comfort zone 為一個人所習慣的工作或生活圈。zone 意為「區域」。

His colleagues tried to comfort him after he failed to be promoted as the project manager.
他的同事試圖安慰他，因為他沒有被升為專案經理。

(point) fail to + V 意為「做……失敗了」。

61 **absence**
★ [`æbsn̩s]
🅝 不在，缺席，缺乏
🔄 nonappearance 不參加
   not being present 不在場
🔄 appearance 出現
   attendance 出席
   presence 在場

I apologize for any inconvenience caused due to my absence.
我很抱歉因為我的缺席造成您的不便。
(point) cause 前面省略了 that is。

The reason why they failed to get job offers was because they were in the absence of experience.
他們沒有得到這份工作的原因是因為他們缺乏經驗。
(point) job offer 意為「工作機會」。

---

62 **accomplish**
★
★
★ [ə`kɑmplɪʃ]
🆅 完成，實現，達到
🔄 achieve 完成
   attain 達到
   complete 完成
   finish 完成
🔄 fail 失敗
   give up 放棄

He worked overtime to accomplish the expense report that was due tomorrow.
他加班以完成明天到期的支出報告。
(point) 延伸詞彙：overtime pay 意為「加班費」。

The contractor tried to accomplish the task at any cost.
這名承包商無論如何都要完成任務。
(point) at any cost 意為「不惜任何代價；無論如何」。

---

63 **accustom**
★ [ə`kʌstəm]
🆅 使習慣於
   （+ (oneself) to V）
🔄 familiarize 使熟悉
   adapt 適應
   adjust 適應
   habituate 使習慣於

You will get accustomed to the culture, food, and environment there eventually.
你終究會習慣那裡的文化、食物及環境。

Compared with other new members, she accustomed herself to the new company quickly.
和其他的新成員比，她很快就習慣這家新公司了。
(point) compare with = compare to，意為「和……相比」。

---

64 **admire**
★ [əd`maɪr]
🆅 欽佩，欣賞，誇獎
🔄 appreciate 欣賞
   praise 讚賞
   respect 敬重
🔄 despise 鄙視
衍 admirable (a.) 令人欽佩的

The director of the Personnel Department admired his assistant's responsibility, dedication and loyalty.
人事部的主任欣賞他助理的負責、盡心盡力及忠誠。
(point) Personnel Department = Human Resources (HR)，意為「人事資源部」。

I admire the male character's bravery and creativity.
我欣賞男主角的勇氣及創意力。

Chapter 089

9 人事組織

65
★
★

aim
[em]

Ⓥ 瞄準，針對，致力
Ⓝ 瞄準，目標
圓 point (v.) 瞄準
　 strive for (ph.) 爭取
　 try (v.) 努力

The aim of the new policy is to reduce the amount of electricity used in our office.
新政策的主要目標是要減少我們辦公室的電使用量。

Since we aim for higher employee productivity, we send our employees to attend training courses regularly.
因為我們的目標是更高的員工生產力，所以經常送員工去參加員工訓練。

 「employee productivity（員工生產力）」常是多益聽力測驗 Part 4 演講者的主題之一，要注意。

66
★

alternate
[`ɔltənɪt]

Ⓐ 交替的，輪流的，間隔的
[`ɔltənet]
Ⓥ 交替，輪流
Ⓝ 替代者

They meet up on alternate Fridays.
他們每隔一個週五就會見一次面。

He is a perfect alternate since he has covered my shifts many times.
他是個完美的替代者，因為他曾經代過我的班很多次。

point 延伸詞彙：cover one's shift 代班／ morning shift 早班／ afternoon shift 午班／ night shift 晚班。

67
★

assume
[ə`sjum]

Ⓥ 以為，承擔，呈現，假裝
圓 presume 假設
　 suppose 猜想

We assumed that Susan would go back to work after her maternity leave but she applied for another job instead.
我們以為蘇珊在產假後會回來工作，但取而代之的是她直接申請另一份工作。

point 常見請假說法：sick leave 病假／ personal leave 事假。

They assumed the construction would be finished on schedule.
他們認為工程會如期完成。

68
★

programmer
[`progræmə]

Ⓝ 程式設計師，節目編排人
衍 program (n.) 節目

The programmer became a well-known journalist.
這名程式設計師成為了一位知名記者。

The programmer is looking for a more challenging job.
這名程式設計師在尋找一個更具挑戰性的工作。

69 **whether**

★
★ [ˋhwɛðɚ]
★ **conj** 是否，不論

Some passengers kept asking whether they could board the plane as scheduled.
有些乘客不斷在問他們是否能如期登機。

I wonder whether my company will employ extra contract workers to do seasonal jobs.
我好奇我的公司是否會僱用額外的約聘員工來做這個季節性工作。

(point) whether 在多益測驗中的選項出現時，要確認空格後是否為句子，是句子且符合語意時才能選。

70 **hire**

★
★ [haɪr]
★ **v** 租借，僱用
n 僱用，租金
同 rent (v.) 租借
   lease (v.) 出租
反 buy (v.) 購買

Seth Clothing, Inc., hired Mrs. Tanaka because she was much more qualified than other candidates.
賽斯服飾公司僱用了田中女士，因為她比其他面試者還要更符合資格。

(point) much 修飾形容詞比較級 more qualified。

If you cannot afford to buy a RV, you can hire one from Easylife Corporation.
如果你負擔不起休旅車，你可以從 Easylife 公司租一台。

CH 9

人事組織

71 **frequency**

★
★ [ˋfrikwənsɪ]
★ **n** 頻繁，頻率
同 recurrence 復發
   repetition 重複
   regularity 規律性
衍 frequent (a.) 頻繁的

The interviewee asked the frequency of business trips that the position required.
面試者詢問職務所需要的出差頻率。

(point) that the position required 修飾前面的 trips。

The machine is used to predict the frequency of earthquakes worldwide.
這台機器是用來預測全球地震的頻率。

(point) 延伸用語：used to + V 意為「過去常常做……」。

72 **resume**

★
★ [rɪˋzjum]
★ **v** 重新開始，繼續，恢復
[ˌrɛzjuˋme]
n 摘要，履歷
同 restart (v.) 重啟
反 suspend (v.) 中止

The engineer keeps updating his resume.
工程師不斷更新他的履歷。

(point) keep + Ving 意為「持續做……」。

The notice informed the residents of the date when the services would be resumed.
這個通知告知居民恢復正常服務的日期。

(point) inform sb. of sth. 意為「通知某人某事」。

73 **leaflet**
★
★ [ˋliflɪt]
★ n 傳單，單張印刷品
V 發傳單
同 pamphlet (n.) 小冊子
booklet (n.) 小冊子
brochure (n.) 小冊子
flyer (n.) 傳單
handout (n.) 傳單

The part-time worker handed out the leaflets about the new telecommunication service.
兼職工發送有關新的電信服務的傳單。

During the training session, each employee will be given a small printed leaflet containing the operation instructions of the new machine.
在訓練課程中，每個員工都會拿到一張小的有關新機器操作說明的印刷傳單。

point containing 由 that / which contains 簡化而來。

74 **incompetent**
★ [ɪnˋkɑmpətənt]
a 不能勝任的，不合適的
同 unskillful 不靈巧的
unskilled 拙劣的
inexpert 不熟練的
反 competent 有能力的
skillful 熟練的

After the probation period, the incompetent employee was dismissed.
在試用期後，這名不適任的員工被解僱了。

point probation period 意為「試用期」。

The incompetent executive was unable to decide the proposal of cutback on public expenditure by himself.
這個不適任的執行官員沒辦法自行決定減少公共開支的計畫。

point 相關詞彙：inept 不適當的，unprofessional 不專業的，inadequate 不夠格的。

75 **contest**
★ [ˋkɑntɛst]
★ n 競爭，比賽
[kənˋtɛst]
V 爭奪，競賽
同 competition (n.) 比賽
match (n.) 競賽

They are contesting for the position of general manager.
他們在爭總經理一職。

point general manager 意為「總經理」。

I am considering attending the singing contest.
我在考慮參加歌唱比賽。

point consider + Ving 意為「認為；考慮……」。

76 **certify**
★ [ˋsɝtə͵faɪ]
★ V 證明，擔保，發證書
同 verify 證明
guarantee 保證
confirm 證實

I certify all the personal information I provided is correct.
我證實我提供的所有個人訊息都是正確的。

I showed my employee badge to the security guard of the building to certify my identity.
我給那棟樓的警衛看我的員工證來證明我的身分。

Question

1. ------- the traffic collision, the road was temporarily closed.

   (A) Due to   (B) Because   (C) Since   (D) What's more

2. He worked overtime to ------- the expense report that was due tomorrow.

   (A) encourage   (B) accomplish

   (C) recruit   (D) subsidize

3. The part-time worker handed out the ------- about the new telecommunication service.

   (A) recognition   (B) impression

   (C) headquarters   (D) leaflets

4. I wonder ------- my company will employ extra contract workers to do seasonal jobs.

   (A) when   (B) which   (C) who   (D) whether

5. The notice informed the residents ------- the date when the services would be resumed.

   (A) for   (B) of   (C) in   (D) at

6. The last interviewee is the perfect candidate for this demanding -------.

   (A) position   (B) absence

   (C) enthusiasm   (D) expansion

>> 正確答案與解析請翻至下一頁查看

Answer

正確答案與解析

1. 因為車禍，道路暫時被封閉。
   (A) 因為 (prep.) + N / Ving　　　(B) 因為 (conj.)
   (C) 因為 (conj.) + S + V　　　(D) 再者

   正確答案 (A)

2. 他加班以完成明天到期的支出報告。
   (A) 鼓勵　　　(B) 完成　　　(C) 招募　　　(D) 資助

   正確答案 (B)

3. 兼職工發送有關新的電信服務的傳單。
   (A) 識別　　　(B) 印象　　　(C) 總部　　　(D) 傳單

   正確答案 (D)

4. 我好奇我的公司是否會僱用額外的約聘員工來做這個季節性工作。
   (A) 何時　　　(B) 哪一個　　　(C) 誰　　　(D) 是否

   正確答案 (D)

5. 這個通知告知居民恢復正常服務的日期。
   (B) 「inform 人 of 事」為固定用法

   正確答案 (B)

6. 最後一個面試者是這個高要求職位的最佳人選。
   (A) 職位　　　(B) 缺席　　　(C) 熱誠　　　(D) 擴張

   正確答案 (A)

Chapter 10
物流運輸與貿易

以下多益必考單字，你認識哪些？

☐ cargo (p.211)

☐ assure (p.212)

☐ enterprise (p.212)

☐ advise (p.206)

☐ shipment (p.210)

☐ logistics (p.211)

☐ surplus (p.213)

☐ behavior (p.219)

☐ accessible (p.221)

☐ delivery (p.209)

☐ currency (p.218)

☐ inventory (p.208)

☐ deliver (p.209)

☐ negotiate (p.213)

☐ overseas (p.210)

☐ payment (p.208)

☐ receipt (p.207)

☐ courier (p.214)

Chapter 091

10 物流運輸與貿易

01 status
★
★
★
['stetəs]

n 地位，身分，狀況
回 ranking 地位
　　position 位置
　　place 位置

The assistant called the delivery company to track the shipment status.
助理打給貨運公司以追蹤運送狀況。

(point) shipment status = delivery status，意為「運送狀況」。

Wearing designer clothing is a kind of status symbol to some people.
對於某些人來說，穿名牌服裝是一種身分象徵。

(point) status symbol 意為「地位的象徵；身分的象徵」。

---

02 chain
★
[tʃen]

n 鏈條，連鎖店
v 用鏈子拴住，拘禁
回 series (n.) 連續
　　succession (n.) 連續
　　sequence (n.) 連續

All the goods were locked with a long chain.
所有的貨物都被一條長鎖鏈給鎖住了。

(point) good (a.) 好的，goods (n.) 貨物。

One of the most popular fast food chains is McDonald's.
最受歡迎的速食連鎖店之一是麥當勞。

---

03 ensure
★
★
★
[ɪn'ʃur]

v 保證，擔保，保護
回 secure 保衛
　　certify 擔保
　　confirm 證實
　　check 核對
　　verify 查實

The new policy will be effective next Monday to ensure the safety of passengers.
新政策下週一會生效以確保乘客的安全。

(point) The new policy will be effective / The new policy will be adopted，意為「新政策將會生效／被採用」。

We can ensure that the goods will be delivered on time.
我們能擔保貨物會準時送達。

(point) 相關詞彙：make sure 確保，make certain 確定，guarantee 保證。

---

04 advise
★
★
[əd'vaɪz]

v 勸告，告知，建議
回 recommend 建議
　　suggest 建議
衍 advice (n.) 建議
　　adviser (n.) 顧問

I always advise my subordinates to check the spelling of the mail again before sending them to our clients.
我總是建議我的下屬在寄信給我們的客戶前，要重複確認信件的拼字。

(point) subordinate, employee, staff 皆可表達「員工；下屬」。

Please advise us when the goods will arrive.
請通知我們貨物何時會到。

05 **specify**
★
★ [`spɛsə,faɪ]
★
Ⅴ 具體指定，詳細指明
同 state 陳述
　　identify 確定
　　define 使明確
　　detail 詳述
衍 specification (n.) 詳述

Please specify the delivery time and date.
請具體說明運送時間及日期。

The down payment must be paid within a specified period.
頭期款必須在指定期限內償還。

point　down payment 意為「頭期款」。

---

06 **receipt**
★
★ [rɪ`sit]
★
ｎ 收據
同 proof of purchase 購買證明
　　sales slip 銷貨單
衍 receive (v.) 收到
　　recipient (n.) 接收者

Please include your receipt if you would like to get the refund.
如果你想要退款的話，請附上你的收據。

Your receipt will be sent along with your parcel.
收據會和你的包裹一起寄出。

point　parcel = package，意為「包裹」。

---

07 **itemize**
★
★ [`aɪtəm,aɪz]
★
Ⅴ 分條列述，詳細列舉
同 list 列出
衍 item (n.) 項目

The itemized list includes all the contact information of our dealers.
詳細表單包含了我們所有經銷商的連絡資訊。

point　延伸詞彙：retailer 意為「零售商」。

The responsible housekeeper itemized the errands he was required to run tomorrow.
負責任的家管列出他明天要跑腿的事項。

point　run an errand 意為「跑腿」。

---

08 **method**
★
★ [`mɛθəd]
★
ｎ 方法，條理，秩序
同 technique 方法
　　system 方式
　　means 方法
　　approach 方法
　　way 方式

I'm writing to inquire how many shipping methods you provide.
我寫信來詢問你們提供哪些運送方法。

point　I'm writing to 常在多益測驗的書信題目第一句話出現，後面加目的。

Taking shuttle buses is the fastest method to go to the hotel you are going to stay at.
搭接駁車是去你即將要下榻的飯店最快的方式。

point　Taking shuttle buses 為 Ving 當主詞，動詞為單數。

CH 10
物流運輸與貿易

Chapter 092

10 物流運輸與貿易

09 inventory

['ɪnvənˌtorɪ]

 n 存貨清單，詳細目錄

同 list 清單
listing 清單
catalogue 目錄

The system can track inventory immediately.
這個系統可以立即追蹤存貨。

The inventory showed that the product was out of stock.
存貨顯示這個產品已經沒貨了。

point out of stock 意為「無庫存」。

10 payment

['pemənt]

n 付款，報償，懲罰

同 salary 薪水
wage 薪資
pay 薪資
earnings 收入

You should pay partial payment in advance before you move to the rental house.
在你搬到租屋處之前，你要事先支付部分的款項。

point in advance 意為「事先」。

One of the most popular payment methods nowadays is cash on delivery.
貨到付款是現在最受歡迎的付款方式之一。

11 warehouse

['wɛrˌhaʊs]

n 倉庫，貨棧

同 storeroom 儲藏室
storehouse 倉庫

There are many products stored in the warehouse.
倉庫裡儲藏了很多商品。

point stored 前面省略了 which are。

We are running low on the inventory, so I will order more office supplies from the warehouse tomorrow.
我們快要沒有庫存了，所以我明天會從倉庫訂更多辦公室用品。

point be running low on + N 意為「某東西快要沒有了」。

12 shipping

['ʃɪpɪŋ]

n 運輸，船舶

同 delivery 傳送

The shipping company apologized for sending the goods to the wrong address.
運送公司因為把貨送到錯誤的地址而道歉。

point apologize for + N / Ving 意指「為……而道歉」。

When you order gifts from online stores, you should also consider both the shipping fee and delivery time.
當你從網路商店訂購禮物時，要記得也把運費及運送時間考量進去。

point shipping fee 意為「運費」。

13 **express**
★
★
★
[ɪkˈsprɛs]
- **V** 表達,陳述,快遞
- **n** 快車,快遞
- **a** 明確的,快遞的
- **ad** 用快遞
- 衍 expression (n.) 表達

The workshop will provide participants hands-on exercise of expressing themselves.
工作坊將會提供參加者實際表達自己的實作活動。

(point) hands-on (a.) 親身實踐的;實際動手做的。

DEK Electronics also offers customers express delivery service.
DEK 電子公司也提供顧客快遞服務。

(point) 延伸詞彙:express train 意為「快車」。

14 **deliver**
★
★
★
[dɪˈlɪvɚ]
- **V** 投遞,傳送,發表,接生
- 同 convey 傳送
  carry 搬運
  transport 運輸

We'll deliver your order as soon as we receive your partial payment.
一旦收到你們的部分款項,我們就會寄出你們的訂單。

(point) as soon as = once,意味「一……就……」。

The customer service representative contacted the shipping company to confirm whether the product the client ordered had been delivered.
客服代表聯絡運送公司以確定顧客訂的產品是否已經被寄出。

(point) shipping company = delivery company,意為「運送公司」。

15 **delivery**
★
★
★
[dɪˈlɪvərɪ]
- **n** 投遞,傳送,交貨,分娩
- 同 conveyance 運送
  carriage 馬車
  transportation 運輸

The sales negotiated the delivery time with his clients.
這名業務和他的客戶協商運送時間。

The delivery person said only a recipient with ID could sign for the parcel.
快遞說只有有身分證的收件者才能簽收包裹。

(point) parcel (n.) 包裹(英式),package (n.) 包裹(美式)。

16 **ship**
★
★
★
[ʃɪp]
- **n** 船艦
- **V** 用船運,郵寄,運送
- 同 boat 船
  ferry 渡輪
  yacht 遊艇

People are boarding the passenger ship.
人們正在登船。

(point) passenger ship 是主要用來載人,非載貨物,像是渡輪。

The frozen food is being shipped to Asia.
冷凍食品正被運往亞洲。

(point) is being shipped 為現在進行被動式,表示「正在被運送」。

CH 10

物流運輸與貿易

10 物流運輸與貿易

---

17 shipment
★
★ [`ʃɪpmənt]
★
n 裝運，運輸的貨物
同 cargo 貨物

We called the delivery company to confirm the shipment status of our latest order.
我們打給遞送公司確認我們最新的訂單運送狀況。

point 確認運送狀況為多益測驗常考的情境。

Our clients will receive the shipment details **once** the goods are sent.
一旦貨物被寄出去，我們的客戶將會收到出貨明細表。

point 此句中 once 為連結詞，表示「一……就……」。

---

18 overseas
★
★ [`ovɚ`siz]
★
a 海外的，國外的
ad 在海外，在國外
同 abroad (a.) 國外的
　 foreign (a.) 外國的
反 domestic (a.) 國內的

The telephone meeting with overseas coworkers was interrupted due to the sudden power **outage**.
與海外同事的電話會議因為突然的停電而被中斷。

point outage 表示「斷電；中斷供應」。

He was hired simply **due to** his profound experience in overseas trade.
他會被僱用單純是因為他對海外貿易的豐富經驗。

point due to + N = because of + N，表示「因為」。

---

19 carrier
★
[`kærɪɚ]
n 運送人，送信人，置物架
同 transporter 輸送者
　 letter carrier 送信者
衍 carry (v.) 運送

We **have cooperated with** this carrier for more than 10 years.
我們已經和這家運輸公司合作超過十年了。

point cooperate with 意為「與……合作」。

What is the best telecom carrier in this area?
哪一家電信公司是這區最棒的？

---

20 path
★
★ [pæθ]
★
★
n 小徑，途徑，路線
同 road 道路
　 route 路線

Due to the construction, drivers were suggested to take a different path to avoid the **traffic jam**.
因為施工，駕駛們被建議要開另一條路才能避免塞車。

point traffic jam = traffic congestion，意為「塞車」。

The receptionist led me to **the path to** the back door.
接待人員引導我到通往後門的小路。

point the path to... 意為「通往……的道路」；the path to success... 意為「通往成功的道路」。

21 **cargo**
★
★ [`kɑrgo]
★ **n** (船、飛機、車輛裝載的)
貨物
同 freight 貨物

The ship which could carry a cargo of 5,000 tons was damaged due to the storm.
這艘能載五千噸貨物的船因為暴風雨損壞了。

 point due to = because of，意為「因為」，後加名詞或 Ving。

A cargo plane landed at an airport in America yesterday.
昨天一台貨運飛機在美國的機場降落。

---

22 **railroad**
★ [`reɪˌrod]
n 鐵路，鐵路公司
同 rail transportation system
鐵路運輸系統
railroad line 鐵路路線
railway 鐵路

The company sends the majority of the goods by railroad.
公司用鐵路運送大部分的貨物。

 point goods 指「貨物」，一定要有 -s。

When you are planning a trip by train, remember to check the railroad timetable and fares.
當你計劃要搭火車旅行時，記得確認火車時刻表及票價。

point fare 指交通工具的票價。toll 則是指過路費、長途電話費。

---

23 **van**
★ [væn]
n 小貨車，有蓋貨車
同 truck 卡車
lorry 卡車

Goods are being loaded into the van.
貨物正被裝進貨車。

point 要記得 be being p.p. 的時態為「現在進行被動式」，若出現在圖片題，則要有「人」在圖片中才能選，因為貨物是需要被裝進貨車，而不會自己主動裝進貨車。

There were three vans parked along the street.
有三輛貨車沿著街道停著。

point along 意為「沿著」。

---

24 **logistics**
★ [lo`dʒɪstɪks]
n 後勤，物流，運籌

The specific criterion is used to select logistics service providers.
這個特定的標準是用來挑選物流服務供應商的。

The director of Logistics proposed a new plan to streamline the work process and improve workflow.
物流部主任提出一個新的計畫以簡化工作過程及增強工作流程。

 point streamline (v.) 簡化；使流線型。

211

25 **afraid**

★
★
★

[ə`frɛd]

a 害怕的，恐懼的

同 frightened 受驚的
scared 害怕的
terrified 恐懼的

反 bold 勇敢的
courageous 英勇的
daring 大膽的

Due to the inclement weather, I am afraid that the shipment won't arrive as planned.
因為天候不佳，貨物恐怕沒辦法如期抵達。

point 天候不佳是多益測驗中造成交通及運送延誤的常見原因。

I used to be afraid of public speaking, but not now anymore.
我以前很怕公眾演講，但現在不會了。

point used to + V 意為「過去習慣做……」。

26 **assure**

★
★

[ə`ʃʊr]

v 保證，擔保，使確信

同 convince 使確信
ensure 保證

衍 assurance (n.) 保證

Kenda Manufacturing Inc. assured us the products would be shipped as planned.
肯達公司向我們擔保產品會如期運出。

point as planned 意為「如期地」。

The babysitter assured the boy's parents that their son would be safe.
褓姆向小男孩的父母保證他們的小孩會很安全。

27 **bid**

★

[bɪd]

v 命令，吩咐，出價

n 出價，喊價

同 offer (v.) 提議
attempt (v.) 試圖

Bangkok is bidding to host the next Universiade.
曼谷正在爭取主辦下一屆的世界大學運動會。

point bid to 意為「爭取；競爭」。

The client gave the project to the company that made the lowest bid.
客戶將這項計畫給了投標出價最低的公司。

28 **enterprise**

★

[`ɛntɚˌpraɪz]

n 事業，進取心，企業

同 firm 公司
undertaking 企業
operation 運行
industry 企業
corporation 公司
establishment 企業

The International firm's latest enterprise this quarter is to expand market share.
這間跨國公司這季最新的雄心壯志就是擴大市場占有率。

point market share 意為「市場占有率」。

The subcontractor was chosen because they have shown a great deal of enterprise in arranging the project.
選擇這間承包商的原因是他們在安排專案上展現了大量的進取心。

point a great deal of = a lot of + N，意為「許多的……」。

29 **bidder**

★ [`bɪdɚ]

n 出價人，投標人，命令者

同 buyer 買家
collector 收藏家
purchaser 買家

Competition between bidders is usually severe.
投標者之間的競爭通常都很激烈。

Once the transaction is completed, you are required to send your winning bidder an invoice for the purchase.
一旦交易完成，你必須要寄購買的發票給你的得標者。

30 **negotiate**

★
★ [nɪ`goʃ͜ɪet]

v 談判，協商，洽談

同 discuss 討論
settle 解決
conclude 決定

衍 negotiator (n.) 磋商者

The sales negotiated the price with the major manufacturer of plastic.
業務和主要的塑膠製造商協商價錢。

The senior manager's attempt to negotiate a three percent pay increase with his supervisor still failed.
資深經理與上司協商薪水提高百分之三的試圖仍然失敗了。

 從句首到 supervisor 皆為主詞。

31 **between**

★
★ [bɪ`twin]
★

prep 在⋯⋯之間

Usually, regular delivery takes between four and seven days.
通常，一般運送服務會花四到七天。

 between A and B 意為「在兩者之間」。

There is a huge gap between the photographs taken by professional and amateur photographers.
專業和業餘攝影師所拍的照片有很大的差距。

 taken 前省略了 that / which are。

32 **surplus**

★ [`sɝpləs]

a 過剩的，剩餘的

n 過剩，剩餘物，盈餘

同 excess (n.) 超額量
remainder (n.) 剩餘物
residue (n.) 殘餘

反 shortage (n.) 缺少
lack (n.) 缺乏

Food surpluses are the main issue that the country is facing.
食物過剩是這個國家主要面臨的議題。

 相關詞彙：oversupply 供應過多，oversufficiency 過剩，remains 剩餘物。

Chapter 095

10 物流運輸與貿易

---

33 negotiable
★
★
[nɪˋgoʃɪəbl]

a 可協商的，可轉讓的

同 unsettled 未定的
undecided 未決定的
debatable 可爭論的

The rate is fixed and not negotiable.
這價格是固定的，且不可協商。

point 相關詞彙：flexible 有彈性的，open to modification 開放修改的，
discussable 可討論的。

The graduate just received a non-negotiable salary job offer.
這名畢業生剛剛得到一個沒辦法討論薪水空間的工作機會。

---

34 courier
★
[ˋkʊrɪɚ]

n 信差，導遊，情報員

同 messenger 送信人
conveyor 搬運者

The confidential document must be sent by a reliable courier.
這份機密文件必須由一個值得依賴的信使送件。

AKL is the biggest global business courier service provider in the world.
AKL 是世界上最大的全球商業快遞服務商。

---

35 obvious
★
[ˋɑbvɪəs]

a 明顯的，顯著的，
平淡無奇的

同 clear 清晰的
plain 清楚的
evident 明顯的
apparent 顯然的

反 obscure 模糊的

The participant's obvious mistake in his singing made him lose the competition.
參賽者歌聲中的明顯錯誤讓他輸了比賽。

point participant (n.) 參賽者，participate (v.) 參與，participation (n.) 參與。

The disadvantages in the contract are obvious to the company.
這些合約中的不利條件對那家公司而言是顯而易見的。

---

36 carefully
★
★
★
[ˋkɛrfəlɪ]

ad 小心謹慎地，仔細地

同 cautiously 小心地
meticulously 極注意地

反 carelessly 粗心大意地

Mr. Porzingiz carefully moved the furniture on display.
波辛吉斯先生仔細地搬運正在展示中的家具。

point on display 意為「展示中」。

It is suggested that drivers drive carefully in bad weather conditions.
駕駛們被建議在天氣狀況不好時要特別小心地開車。

37 **screen**

★
★
★

[skrin]

n 螢幕，遮蔽物，掩護
v 遮蔽，電影拍攝，選拔
同 monitor (n.) 螢幕

The monitor screen was broken during the move.
監視器螢幕在運送過程中壞了。

Some applicants were screened out by the oral interview.
有些面試者在口試時被篩選掉了。

point be screened out 意為「篩選」。

38 **liberal**

★

['lɪbərəl]

a 心胸開闊的，開明的，自由的
n 自由主義者
同 open-minded (a.) 心胸寬的
enlightened (a.) 開明的
反 conservative (a.) 保守的

Unlike my classmates' parents, mine are rather liberal-minded.
不像我同學的父母，我的父母相當開明。

point mine 在此句代表 my parents 的意思。

It's of great importance to hold a liberal attitude toward that issue.
對那個議題保持開放態度是很重要的。

39 **drive**

★
★
★

[draɪv]

v 開車，驅動，幹勁
n 驅車旅行，車程
同 propel (v.) 驅策
push (v.) 推進
urge (v.) 激勵

Whenever it rains, I drive particularly cautiously.
每當下雨，我開車總是特別謹慎。

point whenever 表示「不論何時」，使用時都表常態，故使用現在式。

The new kind of scooter is eco-friendly because it is driven by electricity.
新型的摩托車是對生態友善的，因為是用電來驅動。

point be driven by 意為「被……給驅動」。

40 **driver**

★
★

['draɪvɚ]

n 司機，駕駛員，驅動程式

His driver's license was suspended for six months due to violation of traffic rules.
他因為違反交通規則，駕駛執照被吊銷六個月。

point suspend 意為「暫停；懸浮；中止；勒令停職」。

The taxi driver took a detour since the road was closed temporarily.
因為道路暫時封閉，計程車司機繞道而行。

point 相關詞彙：road closure 為「道路封閉」，是名詞，常會是道路施工的結果。

CH 10
物流運輸與貿易

41 **freight**
★ [fret]

n 貨物，運費
v 裝貨於，運送貨物
同 shipment (n.) 貨物
　 load (n.) 貨物

Usually, buyers pay the freight.
通常是買家付運費。

After the customer placed an order, the company freighted the goods to Japan.
在顧客下訂單後，公司把貨物運往日本。

 place an order 意為「下訂單」。

---

42 **essence**
★ [ˈɛsn̩s]

n 本質，要素，精華
同 nature 本質
　 substance 本質

Delivering goods on time is of the essence.
準時送達貨物非常重要。

point of the essence = essential = important，意為「重要的」。

The painter totally captures the essence of tranquil country life.
畫家完全捕捉到寧靜鄉村生活的精華。

point 相關詞彙：spirit 精神，core 核心。

---

43 **domestic**
★ [dəˈmɛstɪk]

a 家庭的，國內的，馴養的
同 private 私人的
　 household 家庭的
反 foreign 外國的
　 international 國際的

After the domestic news, we will listen to the international news.
在國內新聞之後，我們會聽到國際新聞。

point 在多益測驗中常出現這類的廣播題型。

The sales explained the difference between domestic cars and foreign cars to his clients.
這名業務向他的客戶解釋國產車與進口車的差別。

---

44 **restriction**
★
★ [rɪˈstrɪkʃən]

n 限制，約束，規定
同 limitation 限制
　 limit 極限
　 constraint 限制
　 regulation 羢則
反 freedom 自由
　 flexibility 彈性

Parking restrictions are clearly written in the brochure.
停車規定被清楚地寫在小冊子裡。

Drivers who do not follow speed restrictions will be fined.
不遵守時速限制的駕駛會被罰錢。

Logistics & Trade

45 economy
★
★
[ɪˋkɑnəmɪ]
n 節約，節省，經濟
衍 economical (a.) 經濟的
economize (v.) 節約

He will be flying economy class this time.
他這次飛經濟艙。

point 延伸詞彙：business class 商務艙、first class 頭等艙。

The natural disaster had a serious effect on the local economy.
這個天災對當地經濟有很嚴重的影響。

46 distributor
★
[dɪˋstrɪbjətɚ]
n 分配者，批發商
同 provider 供應者
supplier 提供者

Our distributor renewed the contract with us this morning.
今早我們的經銷商與我們更新了合約。

As the sole distributor of this product, we are allowed to give you some discounts.
身為這個產品的獨家經銷商，我們能夠給你一些折扣。

point sole distributor 意為「獨家經銷商」，只有該商家能夠賣某特定產品。

47 security
★
★
★
[sɪˋkjurətɪ]
n 安全，防護，保證
同 soundness 健全
protection 保護
反 danger 危險

The night shift security guard reported that someone broke the windows of the building.
晚班警衛報告有人打破建築的窗戶。

point morning / afternoon / night shift 意為「早／午／晚班」。

The Administration Committee considered installing security cameras for security purposes.
管委會考量為了安全用途安裝監視攝影機。

point 相關詞彙：safety 安全。

48 register
★
★
★
[ˋrɛdʒɪstɚ]
v 登記，註冊
同 enroll 登記
enter 進入
sign up 註冊
apply 申請

To register, please visit our official website.
要註冊，請參訪我們的官方網站。

point 這句話很常出現在多益閱讀測驗文章最後一行。

The consultant will introduce how to register for on-site training classes.
顧問會介紹如何註冊在公司內的訓練課程。

point on-site 意指「在現場的」，off-site 意指「不在現場的」。

CH 10

物流運輸與貿易

217

49 currency
★
[`kɝənsɪ]

n 通貨，貨幣，通用
同 money 錢
　　cash 現金

The country will use new currency next year.
這個國家明年將會使用新貨幣。

Excuse me, can I change currency here?
不好意思，請問我能在這裡換錢嗎？

point 延伸詞彙：exchange rate 意為「匯率」。

---

50 acceptable
★
★
[ək`sɛptəbl̩]

a 可接受的，令人滿意的
同 pleasant 令人愉快的
　　agreeable 宜人的
反 unacceptable 無法接受的
衍 acceptance (n.) 接受

Taking many days off during the high season is not acceptable.
在旺季休很多天假是不行的。

point high season = peak season 意為「旺季」；low season = slack season 意為「淡季」。

Both parents and teachers should teach children socially acceptable behavior.
家長和老師都需要教兒童學社會上認可的行為舉止。

point both... and... 意為「兩者都」。

---

51 entrance
★
★
[`ɛntrəns]

n 入口，進入
同 entry 進入
　　doorway 出入口
　　gate 大門
　　gateway 入口處
　　lobby 門廳
反 exit 出口

To the left of the entrance is the storage room.
入口的左邊是儲藏室。

point 相關詞彙：supply room (ph.) 補給室，warehouse (n.) 倉庫。

With his student ID card, he got 10% discount on the entrance fee.
因為有學生證，他享有九折入場費優惠。

point entrance fee = admission fee，意為「入場費」。

---

52 collection
★
★
[kə`lɛkʃən]

n 收集，收藏品，大量
同 compilation 匯集
　　pile 大量
衍 collectible (a.) 可收集的

The bidder has a wide collection of antiques.
這名出價者有很廣泛的古董收藏。

There's quite a collection of pens in the supply room.
儲藏室裡有一大堆筆。

point 此處 collection 意為「一堆（東西）」。

53 behavior
★ [bɪˋhevjɚ]
🄽 行為，舉止，反應
🄸 conduct 行為
　　manner 舉止
　　action 行動
🄳 behavioral (a.) 行為的

The child was punished for his bad behavior.
這個孩子因為他的壞行為而被處罰。

People were astonished at the businessman's immoral behavior.
人們對於那個商人不道德的行為感到訝異。

point be astonished at 意為「對……感到訝異」。

54 procurement
★ [proˋkjurmənt]
🄽 獲得，採購
🄸 procurance 取得
　　procural 獲得
　　acquisition 獲得

Attached is the procurement contract template.
附檔為採購合約範本。

We have a limited budget for the procurement of camping gear.
我們在露營裝備上預算有限。

point gear 作為「工具；設備；衣服」的意思解釋時只能當不可數名詞，作為「齒輪；傳動裝置；排檔」的意思解釋時為可數名詞或不可數名詞。

55 doubt
★ [daut]
🅅 懷疑，不相信，恐怕
🄽 懷疑，不相信，疑問
🄸 uncertainty (n.) 不確定
　　unsureness (n.) 不確定
　　suspicion (n.) 懷疑
　　query (n.) 疑問
🄡 certainty (n.) 確實
　　trust (n.) 相信

I never have any doubts that you would win the bid.
我從來都沒有懷疑過你會得標。

point win the bid 意為「得標」。

I am having doubts about the quality of the shoes you bought from the flea market.
我對你從跳蚤市場買回來的鞋子品質感到懷疑。

point 相關字彙：second-hand store = thrift store，意為「二手物店」。

56 thus
★ [ðʌs]
★
★
🄰🄳 如此，因此
🄸 consequently 結果
　　therefore 因此
　　accordingly 因此

Thus, we require a 2-month security deposit.
因此，我們要求兩個月的安全押金。

point deposit = partial payment，意為「訂金；部分款項」。

The author has not explained when the initiation of his interest in reading was thus far.
到目前為止，作家還沒有解釋何時他對閱讀開始有興趣。

point thus far 意為「迄今」。

CH 10

物流運輸與貿易

10 物流運輸與貿易

---

57 defeat
★ [dɪ`fit]

V 戰勝，擊敗，使失敗
n 失敗，戰敗，擊敗
同 beat (v.) 勝過
　　conquer (v.) 戰勝
反 lose (v.) 輸掉

The new company defeated his opponent by the user-friendly and approachable design.
這間新創公司以容易操作且平易近人的設計戰勝了其對手。

point user-friendly（容易使用的）和 approachable（平易近人的）為常用來形容商品的正向形容詞。

After the commercial break, Mr. Jason will introduce his new publication, *Learn From Your Defeats*.
廣告後，傑森先生會介紹他的新書《從挫折中學習》。

point 多益聽力測驗 Part 4 廣播情境中常有這樣的句子，要注意。

---

58 debt
★ [dɛt]

n 債，借款
衍 bill (n.) 帳單
　　account (n.) 帳單
　　financial obligation
　　(ph.) 債務
　　charge 索價
　　financial statement
　　(ph.) 財務報表

In addition to his full-time job, he also took a part-time job to pay his debts.
除了他的正職工作以外，他還有個兼差來付他的債務。

point in addition to + N / Ving 意為「除了……之外」。

The middle-aged man got into debt after the failure of his business.
這名中年男子在經商失敗後開始舉債。

point get into debt 意為「向人借錢；負債」。

---

59 commerce
★ [`kɑmɝs]

n 商業，貿易
同 trade 交易
　　business 商業
　　bargain 協議
　　dealing 買賣

Usually, capital cities are the nerves of commerce.
首都通常會是商業的中樞。

The new brand has been trying to expand their commerce to the European market.
這個新品牌一直嘗試擴大它們的商業範圍到歐洲市場。

---

60 beware
★ [bɪ`wɛr]

V 當心，小心，注意
同 be careful 小心
　　watch out 注意
反 be careless 疏忽

There are more pickpockets during the high season, so beware.
旺季時有比較多扒手，所以要小心。

Beware not to be late when you meet with your clients.
在和客戶見面時，當心別遲到。

61 accessible
★
★ [æk`sɛsəbl̩]
★
a 可接近的，可進入的，
可使用的
同 approachable 可接近的
available 可用的

The newly established subway line makes the capital city more accessible to the tourists from airports.
新建的地鐵線讓從機場來的旅客更容易到達首都。

---

62 accessibility
★
★ [æk͵sɛsə`bɪlətɪ]
n 易接近，易受影響

The restaurant has great accessibility to the subway station.
這家餐廳離地鐵站很近。

 point great accessibility to... 意指「很接近……；取得……很方便」。

The editor chooses the topic every month by its accessibility to general readers.
編輯依據對於普遍讀者來說，容易理解的程度來挑選每個月的主題。

point 此句為每個月都會做的事情，屬於常態，故使用現在式。

---

63 crew
★
★ [kru]
n 全體機員，一組工作人員
同 team 團隊
unit（全體）一員
party 一夥人
staff 工作人員

Please follow the cabin crew's instructions.
請遵守機艙組員的指示。

The film crew attended the premiere of the movie.
電影製作團隊出席電影的首映會。

point film crew = movie crew，意為「電影製作團隊」。

---

64 cordially
★
[`kɔrdʒəlɪ]
ad 熱誠地，友善地
同 warmly 溫暖地
amiably 友好地
genially 親切地
heartily 熱誠地
反 indifferently 冷漠地

The host of the B&B received me so cordially that I really enjoyed my stay there.
民宿老闆熱情地款待我，所以我真的很享受住在那裡。

point B&B = breakfast and bed，意為「民宿」（提供早餐的住宿）。

The representatives of the two companies shook hands cordially as they met.
兩家公司的代表一見面就熱情地握手。

point as = when，意為「當……」。

10 物流運輸與貿易

---

65 wait
★
★ [wet]
★ **V** 等待，耽擱，伺候

I am waiting for the parcel I ordered from the online store yesterday.
我正在等我昨天上網訂購的包裹。

> (point) 注意此句中時態不一致的用法，多益測驗若挖空格在 am waiting 那邊，不要看到 yesterday 就選過去式。

For your safety, all the passengers should wait in the queue.
為了您的安全，所有的乘客都必須排隊。

> (point) wait in the queue 為英式英文，美式為 line up。

---

66 density
★ [`dɛnsətɪ]

n 密集，密度
同 denseness 濃厚
　　thickness 密度
衍 dense (a.) 稠密的

Traffic is heavy in this town because of the high population density.
因為高度的人口密度，這個城鎮的交通很擁擠。

The report shows the density of the population in two capital cities.
這份報告指出這兩個首都的人口密度。

---

67 disrupt
★ [dɪs`rʌpt]

V 使分裂，使混亂
同 disturb 擾亂
反 organize 組織
　　arrange 安排

Traffic was severely disrupted owing to the strike.
交通因為罷工被嚴重地擾亂。

> (point) owing to = because of = due to + N，意為「因為」。

A secretary rushed into the conference room, disrupting the meeting.
這名祕書衝進會議室，打斷了會議。

> (point) 此句為分詞構句，省略兩句中的連接詞，祕書的動作為主動，故把第二句動詞改成 Ving (disrupting)。

---

68 station
★ [`steʃən]
★
★ **n** 車站，電視臺，崗位，
　　身分
同 position 位置

Due to the delay, a lot of passengers were waiting at the station platform.
因為延誤，很多乘客在火車月台等車。

> (point) due to + N = because of + N，意指「因為」。

Local residents gathered outside city hall to oppose the construction of the nuclear power station.
當地居民聚集在市政府的外面，抗議核電廠的建造。

> (point) nuclear power station = nuclear power plant，意為「核電廠」。

69 evidence
★
[`ɛvədəns]
n 證據，證人，跡象
同 proof 證據
confirmation 確證
verification 證明
affirmation 證實

He didn't have enough evidence to sue his neighbor for breaking into his home.
他沒有足夠證據告他的鄰居闖空門。

point break into a home 意為「闖空門」。

The police found a lot of evidence of the company's illegal dealings with other firms.
警察發現這間公司和其他公司有很多非法交易。

point dealings 意指「（商業上的）活動，往來；交易」。

---

70 avenue
★
★
★
[`ævə͵nju]
n 大街，通道，途徑
同 road 道路
street 街道

This is the only avenue to success.
這是唯一一條通往成功的途徑。

Go straight for two blocks and turn left on Maple Avenue. The bank will be on your left.
直走兩個街區然後在楓葉大道左轉。銀行就會在你的左邊。

---

71 plane
★
★
★
[plen]
n 平面，程度，飛機
a 平的，平坦的
同 airplane (n.) 飛機
aircraft (n.) 航空器
aeroplane (n.) 飛機（英式）

CH 10
物流運輸與貿易

When passengers board a plane, they have to turn off their electronic devices.
當乘客登機時，他們必須關掉電子裝置。

point 相關詞彙：takeoff (n.) 起飛, take off (ph.) 起飛；脫去衣物。

Employees who keep their work on a high plane can receive performance bonuses.
維持工作表現在高水平的員工可以收到績效獎金。

point on a high plane 意為「在高水平」。

---

72 boat
★
★
★
[bot]
n 小船，輪船
v 划船
同 ship (n.) 船
vessel (n.) 船

The products will be shipped by boat by the end of this month.
這些產品會在這個月底前以船運的方式寄出。

point by... 表示「在……（時間點）以前」。

The famous tourist attraction is famous for its boating activity.
這個有名的旅遊景點是以划船活動為著名。

point be famous for 意為「以……為著名」。

73 vessel

★ [ˈvɛsḷ]

n 船艦，容器，血管

同 boat 船
ship 船

A **cargo** vessel is approaching the harbor.
這艘貨船正接近港灣。

(point) cargo 表示「貨物」，會出現在多益聽力測驗的 Part 1 圖片題，要注意。

I bought several metal and wooden vessels from the **clearance sale**.
我從清倉大拍賣中買了許多金屬容器及木製容器。

(point) 延伸詞彙：annual sale 週年慶，semi-annual = biannual **sale** 年終特賣，end-of-season sale 換季特賣，year-end sale 年終特賣，back-to school sale 開學季特賣。

---

74 route

★
★
★ [rut]

n 路線，路程，途徑

同 way 路
course 路線
direction 方向
passage 通行

This is the quickest route to go to the lecture hall.
這是去演講廳最快的路線。

The road is being repaved, so please **take an alternate route**.
這條路正在重鋪，所以請行駛另一條路。

(point) take an alternate route = take another route，意為「行駛另一條路」。

---

75 subway

★
★
★ [ˈsʌbˌwe]

n 地鐵，地下通道

同 railway 鐵路
metro 地鐵
rapid transit system
捷運系統
underground 地下鐵（英）
tube 地下鐵（英）

The **newly** built subway line brings convenience to the local residents.
新建的鐵路線帶給當地居民便利。

(point) newly 為副詞，修飾形容詞 built（build 動詞「建造」的過去分詞）。

We chose this **hostel** for our accommodation simply because it was near the subway station.
我們選擇這家青年旅舍單純是因為它離地鐵站很近。

(point) hostel 意為「青年旅舍」，hotel 意為「旅館」。

---

76 bend

★ [bɛnd]

v 彎曲，致力於，屈服於

n 彎曲，轉彎處

反 straighten (v.) 使挺直

The **janitor** bent over and scrubbed the sink.
工友彎腰並刷水槽。

(point) janitor (n.) 管理員；看門人；照管房屋的工友。

The road takes a sudden bend to the left.
這條路突然轉向左邊。

Test 1

一、請寫出下列單字的中文意思。

① negotiable _____   ⑥ assure _____

② acceptable _____   ⑦ delivery _____

③ inventory _____   ⑧ density _____

④ domestic _____   ⑨ logistics _____

⑤ surplus _____   ⑩ method _____

二、請寫出符合下列句意的單字。

① Traffic was severely _____ owing to the strike.
交通因為罷工被嚴重地擾亂。

② We called the delivery company to confirm the _____ status of our latest order.
我們打給運送公司確認我們最新的訂單運送狀況。

③ We are running low on the inventory, so I will order more office supplies from the _____ tomorrow.
我們快要沒有庫存了,所以我明天會從倉庫訂更多辦公室用品。

解答

1. ① 可討論的,可轉讓的 ② 可接受的,令人滿意的 ③ 清單,存貨,詳細目錄 ④ 國內的,家庭的 ⑤ 過剩的;餘額 ⑥ 保證,確信 ⑦ 遞送,交貨 ⑧ 濃度,密度 ⑨ 後勤,物流 ⑩ 方法,條理
2. ① disrupted ② shipment ③ warehouse

Test 2

一、請選擇符合下列文意的單字。

Ⓐ express   Ⓑ compensate   Ⓒ bidder
Ⓓ essence   Ⓔ carrier   Ⓕ enterprise

① Once the transaction is completed, you are required to send your winning _____ an invoice for the purchase.

② The International firm's latest _____ this quarter is to expand market share.

③ DEK Electronics also offers customers _____ delivery service.

④ Delivering goods on time is of the _____.

⑤ We have cooperated with this _____ for more than 10 years.

二、請寫出下列片語的中文意思。

① be famous for   _____   ⑤ get into debt   _____

② on display   _____   ⑥ be astonished at   _____

③ win the bid   _____   ⑦ owing to   _____

④ place an order   _____   ⑧ thus far   _____

解答

1. ①C ②F ③A ④D ⑤E
2. ① 以……聞名 ② 展示中 ③ 得標 ④ 下訂單 ⑤ 向人借錢；負債 ⑥ 對……感到訝異 ⑦ 因為
   ⑧ 迄今

Chapter 11
零售購物與訂單

以下多益必考單字，你認識哪些？

- [ ] percent (p.229)
- [ ] retail (p.228)
- [ ] participant (p.229)
- [ ] confirmation (p.230)
- [ ] warranty (p.235)
- [ ] quality (p.235)
- [ ] selection (p.232)
- [ ] inspect (p.237)
- [ ] merchandise (p.234)
- [ ] attention (p.243)
- [ ] nevertheless (p.245)
- [ ] purchase (p.232)
- [ ] order (p.243)
- [ ] address (p.231)
- [ ] compensate (p.233)
- [ ] expiration (p.234)
- [ ] guarantee (p.234)
- [ ] decide (p.236)

Chapter 101

11 零售購物與訂單

01 discount
★★★
['dɪskaunt]
n 折扣，折現
v 打折，漠視，低估
同 reduction (n.) 減少
deduction (n.) 扣除
markdown (n.) 減價
price cut (ph.) 降價

During the anniversary sales, all the organic food will be discounted.
在週年慶期間，所有的有機物都會打折。

The housewife buys products from the discount store from time to time.
這名家庭主婦偶爾會從這家折扣商店買東西。

point from time to time = sometimes，意為「偶爾」。

---

02 grand
★★★
[grænd]
a 雄偉的，崇高的，傲慢的
同 awe-inspiring 令人驚嘆的
superb 宏偉的
striking 突出的
majestic 雄偉的
反 inferior 低等的
unimpressive 普通的

The department store's grand opening attracted many people.
這間百貨公司的盛大開幕吸引了許多人。

point grand opening 意為「盛大開幕」，若在多益閱讀測驗的文章標題中看到這個片語就可以知道是新店家的開幕。

The view of Grand Canyon National Park is breathtaking.
大峽谷國家公園的景觀讓人目不轉睛。

---

03 retail
★★★
['ritel]
v 零售
n 零售
反 wholesale (n.) 批發

The retail store was newly renovated.
這家零售店最近被翻修了。

The position requires applicants with experience in retail.
這份工作需要有零售經驗的求職者。

point in retail 意為「在零售方面」。

---

04 retailer
★★★
['ritelɚ]
n 零售商，零售店
[rɪ'telɚ]
n 詳述者，傳播者
同 seller 銷售者
retail merchant 零售商人
反 wholesaler 批發商

The big electronics retailer provides special discounts for VIPs only.
這家大型電子產品零售店只提供貴賓特別的折扣。

The retailer had already sold off the existing surplus before the holiday season.
零售商在假日季節前就已經把剩餘商品都賣光了。

point holiday season（假日季節）為十一月底（感恩節前後）到一月初（新年）。

05 **percent**

★

[pɚˋsɛnt]

n 百分比，部分

衍 a hundred percent
(ph.) 百分之百

You can get a 10 percent discount if you use this coupon.
如果你使用這張折價券，你可以得到九折的優惠。

According to the research, the company's market share is 20 percent.
根據研究，這家公司的市場占有率是百分之二十。

point market share 意為「市場占有率」。

06 **percentage**

★

[pɚˋsɛntɪdʒ]

n 百分率，比例，部分

同 ratio 比率
part 部分
proportion 比例

The annual sales successfully attracted a large percentage of the customers.
週年慶成功吸引了很多顧客。

point a large percentage of 意為「很高的比率」。

People in this country consumed a high percentage of the energy last year.
這個國家的人們去年消耗掉很多能源。

07 **participant**

★
★
★

[parˋtɪsəpənt]

n 參與者，關係者

同 competitor 競爭者
player 參賽者

All participants will receive the vacuum coupons.
所有參加者都可以得到這台吸塵器的折價券。

point coupon = voucher，意為「禮券；折價券」。

Please reply to this email as soon as you receive it so that we can calculate the number of participants.
一收到信時就請馬上回覆，這樣我們才能計算參賽人數。

point as soon as 意為「一⋯⋯就⋯⋯」。

08 **participate**

★
★
★

[parˋtɪsəˏpet]

v 參與，分享，分擔

同 take part 參與
engage 使忙於
join 參加
get involved with 涉入
share 分享

Thank you for participating in the beach cleanup.
感謝您參加淨灘活動。

Loads of people participated in the strike to fight for labor rights.
許多人參加罷工以爭取勞工權利。

point loads of = a lot of，意為「許多」。

09 coupon
★
★
★
['kupɑn]

n 優待券，配給券，聯票

同 voucher 打折優惠券

The customer received a coupon **as** compensation for the wrong shipment.
這名顧客因為運送錯誤而收到一張折價券當作補償。

point as 解釋為「當作」。

Every participant in the conference will receive one **meal coupon**.
每位研討會參加者都會收到一張餐券。

point meal coupon 為餐券，用這張券可以領取餐點。

10 unauthorized
★
★
[ˌʌnˋɔθəˏraɪzd]

a 未經授權的，未經許可的

同 uncertified 未經證明的
unlicensed 沒有執照的
unwarranted 無保證的
unapproved 未經同意的

衍 authorize (v.) 授權

All the retailers are not allowed to sell unauthorized products in this region.
所有的零售商都不能在這區域賣未經授權的商品。

The Rubio Software's advanced techniques **used to prevent the unauthorized copying of data** have been proved to be rather successful.
魯比歐軟體公司用來防止未經授權的資料複製技術已經被證實相當成功。

point used to prevent the unauthorized copying of data 用來修飾前面的 techniques。

11 confirmation
★
★
★
[ˌkɑnfɚˋmeʃən]

n 確定，批准

同 verification 確認
proof 證明
testimony 證據

衍 confirm (v.) 證實

Once you place an order, we will send you a confirmation letter.
一旦你下了訂單，我們就會寄給你一封確認信。

point once = as soon as，意為「一⋯⋯就⋯⋯」。

The journalists are still awaiting official confirmation of the exact number of the unemployed.
記者們還在等待官方發布的確切失業人口。

12 reflect
★
[rɪˋflɛkt]

v 反映，表現，思考

同 mirror 反射
反 absorb 吸收
衍 reflection (n.) 反射

The palm trees reflected in the swimming pool.
棕櫚樹倒影在泳池。

These figures reflected several huge changes in consumer behavior.
這些數據顯示出消費者行為的一些巨大改變。

13 submit

★
★ [səbˋmɪt]
★ Ⅴ 使服從，屈從，提交
同 yield 使屈服
comply 順從
accept 接受
surrender 投降
反 defy 公然反抗
resist 抵抗

Please submit the questionnaire before you leave the conference room.
離開研討會室前請提交問卷。

Customers who shop in the online stores are not allowed to make changes when an order is submitted.
在網路商城購買東西的顧客，在訂單提交後不能做更改。

 who shop in the online store 修飾前面的 customers。

14 identify

★ [aɪˋdɛntəˏfaɪ]
Ⅴ 確認，識別，鑑定
同 recognize 認出
distinguish 區別
衍 identification (n.) 識別
identical (a.) 完全相同的

It's important for clerks to identify their customers' needs in a short time.
對於店員來說，一下子就認出顧客的需求是相當重要的。

He identified the singer by his voice.
他藉由聲音來認出這位歌手。

15 renew

★
★ [rɪˋnju]
★ Ⅴ 更新，復原，重新開始
同 resume 繼續
restart 重啟
recommence 重新開始
衍 renewal (n.) 更新

Subscribers can get a 10 percent discount if they renew the contract this week.
訂閱者如果在這週更新合約，他們可以得到九折的優惠。

point 延伸詞彙：subscribe (v.) 訂閱。

You can renew your membership by completing the online form or calling the customer service department instead.
你可以藉由完成線上表格，或是直接打給客服部來延續會籍。

point 易混淆詞彙：form (v.) 形成 (n.) 表格；形式／ from (prep.) 從⋯⋯；來自／ forum (n.) 論壇。

16 address

★
★ [əˋdrɛs]
★ n 地址，演說
Ⅴ 致詞，處理
同 lecture (n.) 演講
talk (n.) 演講

When you purchase things online, make sure the address is correct.
當你在線上購物時，請確保地址是正確的。

Whenever some problems come out, the senior manager always addresses them right away.
每當有問題，這位資深經理總是馬上處理。

point solve / address / attend to the problems 意為「處理問題」。

231

11 零售購物與訂單

17 selection
★ [sə`lɛkʃən]
n 選擇，選手，選集
同 assortment 分類
　　choice 選擇
　　collection 收集
衍 selective (a.) 有選擇性的

There are some problems in the selection process.
挑選過程中有些問題。

The store offered a wide selection of diamond rings and silver accessories.
這間店家提供多種鑽戒及銀飾品。

point a wide selection of 意為「多種」。

---

18 catalog
★
★ [`kætəlɔg]
★
n 目錄，登記
v 將……編入目錄，記載
同 directory (n.) 目錄
　　list (n.) 清單

The enclosed catalog contains our latest products.
附檔的目錄中包含了我們的最新產品。

point 「附件」很常在書信中出現，attachment 也是「附件；附檔」的意思。

The catalog should be reprinted since there are some mistakes on both the prices and the product descriptions.
這個目錄需要被重印，因為有些價錢和產品敘述上的錯誤。

point both... and... 意為「兩者皆是」。

---

19 pattern
★ [`pætən]
n 花樣，典型，模式
同 design 設計
　　figure 插圖

The designer chose the dress because of its floral pattern.
設計師選擇那件裙子，因為它的花朵圖案。

point choose-chose-chosen 為「選擇」的動詞三態。

The analyst analyzed the customers' shopping records and found some patterns.
分析師分析消費者的購買紀錄並找出一些模式。

---

20 purchase
★
★ [`pɝtʃəs]
★
v 購買，努力取得
n 購買，所購之物
同 buy (v.) 購買
　　acquire (v.) 獲得
　　obtain (v.) 獲得
反 sell (v.) 販賣

Thanks for purchasing items at Julie's grocery store.
感謝在茱莉的雜貨店購買商品。

The pop singer's concert tickets can only be purchased online.
這名流行歌手演唱會的門票只能在網路上買得到。

21 **compensate**
★
★ [ˋkɑmpənˌset]

Ⅴ 補償，賠償，抵銷

同 repay 償還
pay back 還錢
reimburse 補償

Nothing can compensate for the loss of family members.
什麼也不能彌補失去家人的損失。

The online store compensated the customer with free delivery and coupons.
這個網路商城用免費的運送及折價券來彌補這位客人。

 compensate... with... 意為「用⋯⋯補償」。

---

22 **compensation**
★
★ [ˌkɑmpənˋseʃən]

ⁿ 補償，賠償金，報酬

同 repayment 付還
payment 支付
reimbursement 償還

She received some coupons in compensation for the damaged goods.
她得到一些折價券，作為貨品損壞的補償。

 coupon = voucher，意為「折價券」。

The job is demanding but the compensation is better than my previous one.
這份工作要求很高，但工資比我上一份工作還要好。

 compensation 在此句等於 salary，意為「薪水」。

---

23 **depend**
★
★
★ [dɪˋpɛnd]

Ⅴ 信賴，依靠，取決於

同 be dependent on 依賴
衍 dependency (n.) 依靠

The charges will depend on how many pieces you purchase.
價錢會依你買了多少件而定。

Whether we'll hold the company picnic depends on weather conditions.
我們是否會舉行公司野餐要看天氣狀態而定。

 多益測驗中的交通工具延誤原因常為 severe / inclement weather，意為「天候不佳」。

---

24 **entitle**
★ [ɪnˋtaɪt!]

Ⅴ 給⋯⋯權力（資格，稱號）

同 qualify 使合格
authorize 授權給
allow 允許
permit 許可
grant 准予
enable 賦予

Students who show their student ID card are entitled to a discount.
出示學生證的學生可享有折扣。

The best-selling author's latest novel, entitled *Home*, is available online.
那位暢銷作者名為《家》的最新小說可在網路上買到。

 相關詞彙：best seller (ph.) 暢銷書。

25 refund
★
★ [rɪˋfʌnd]
★ v 退還，歸還
[ˋriˌfʌnd]
n 退還，償還金
同 repay (v.) 償還
restore (v.) 歸還
反 send (v.) 寄送
give (v.) 給予

You can get the refund if you keep the receipt and invoice.
如果你有留著收據跟發票，你就能退款。

Please read the return and refund policy carefully before you buy something from online shops.
你在網路商店買東西前，請仔細閱讀退換貨政策。

point return and refund policy 意為「退換貨政策」。

---

26 expiration
★ [ˌɛkspəˋreʃən]
n 終結，期滿，截止
同 termination 結束
反 start 開始
beginning 開始
衍 expire (v.) 終止

Consumers are suggested to read the expiration date labels before they make purchases.
消費者被建議購買前要看有效日期標籤。

point make purchase = purchase = buy，意為「購買」。

This coupon is invalid now because it has passed its expiration date.
這張折價券已經無效了，因為已經過了有效期限。

point 延伸詞彙：valid (a.) 有效的。

---

27 guarantee
★ [ˌgærənˋti]
v 擔保，保障
n 保證，保證書，抵押品
同 promise (n.) 承諾
assurance (n.) 保證

We provide a two-year guarantee on all the products.
我們所有的產品都有提供兩年保固。

The shop can replace the product as long as it is still under guarantee.
商店說會給我們退換那個產品，只要它還在保固期內。

point under guarantee 意為「在保固期內」。

---

28 merchandise
★ [ˋmɝtʃənˌdaɪz]
★
★ n 商品，貨物
v 買賣，促銷
同 goods (n.) 貨物
stock (n.) 存貨
commodity (n.) 商品
product (n.) 產品

Should you have any problems with your merchandise, please contact us.
如果你對商品有任何問題，請聯絡我們。

point should = if，意為「如果」。

The sales tried hard to merchandise the new product line.
該業務努力想要推銷這條新產品線。

point 此句的 merchandise = promote，意為「推銷」。

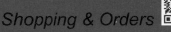

29 warranty

★
★
★

['wɔrəntɪ]

n 保證書，擔保，授權

同 guarantee 保證
assurance 保證
promise 承諾
commitment 承諾

You will not be charged for repairs as long as your cellphone is under warranty.

只要你的手機還在保固期內，維修就不會被收費。

point be under warranty 意為「保固期間內」。

If you would like to repair the blender you purchased from us, please bring the warranty card, invoice and receipt.

如果您想要修理您從我們這裡買的果汁機，請帶著保固卡、發票及收據。

point 有時退換貨也會提到要提供 serial number（序號）。

---

30 necessity

★
★
★

[nə`sɛsətɪ]

n 必需品，必然性

同 prerequisite 不可缺的
indispensable thing / item
必需品

衍 necessary (a.) 需要的

Due to budget constraints, the housewife only bought necessities when she went grocery shopping.

因為預算限制，這名家庭主婦去買菜時只買必需品。

Is there any necessity to update the existing system?

有必要更新現存的系統嗎？

---

31 quality

★
★
★

['kwɑlətɪ]

n 品質，特性，才能

同 standard 標準
grade 等級
class 等級
classification 分類

Coco Clothing, Inc., takes pride in providing high-quality, timeless and classic clothes.

可可衣服店以提供高品質、不退流行且經典的服務為傲。

point take pride in 意為「引以為傲」。

The company is known for the high quality of its dairy production.

這公司以高品質的乳製品聞名。

point be known for 意為「以……聞名」。

---

32 attract

★
★
★

[ə`trækt]

v 吸引，引起

同 draw 吸引
appeal 吸引

These candies are brightly colored in order to attract children.

這些糖果都有著鮮艷的色彩以吸引小孩。

The store provides a discount for the first time buyer to attract more potential customers.

店家提供給第一次消費的顧客優惠以吸引更多潛在的顧客。

point 常見優惠：buy one get one free 買一送一。

235

Chapter 105

11 零售購物與訂單

---

33 decide
★
★
★
[dɪ`saɪd]

v 決定，下決心

同 determine 決定
make up one's mind
下定決心
come to a decision
做出決定
reach a decision 做決定

反 hesitate 猶豫

He decided to purchase the **RV** entirely **on credit**.
他決定完全用分期付款的方式買那台休旅車。

point recreational vehicle = RV，意為「休旅車」。on credit 意為「分期付款」。

After consideration, the financial director decided the budget for that project.
在考量之後，財務部主任決定了那個專案的預算。

---

34 decision
★
★
★
[dɪ`sɪʒən]

n 決定，決心，判斷

同 resolution 決心
conclusion 結論
settlement 解決
determination 決心

反 hesitation 猶豫

She always reaches her purchase decisions by checking the online reviews of the products.
她總是看網路上的商品評價來決定是否購買。

The assistant was told to make the decision **on his own**.
助理被告知要自行做決定。

point on one's own 意為「獨自地」。

---

35 complete
★
★
★
[kəm`plit]

a 完整的，全部的，附帶的
v 完成，結束

同 accomplish (v.) 完成
achieve (v.) 達到
fulfill (v.) 完成

反 start (v.) 開始

衍 completion (n.) 完成

The famous **line** of the movie is "You make my life complete."
這部電影的著名台詞是：「你讓我的生命完整了。」

point 延伸詞彙：slogan (n.) 口號。

Once you get the form completed, we will deliver your order **straight away**.
一旦你完成表格，我們就會立即送出你的訂單。

point straight away = immediately，意為「立即地；馬上」。

---

36 upon
★
★
[ə`pɑn]

prep 在……上面，一旦，根據

Upon seeing his desired watch, he became an impulse buyer.
一看到他想要的手錶，他馬上變成衝動性購物者。

After negotiation, my clients **agreed upon** the extension of the delivery period.
在協調之後，我的客戶同意運送期間的延長。

point agree on / upon 意為「對……意見一致」。

37 **fold**

★

[fold]

Ⅴ 折疊，交叉，籠罩

Ⅵ 褶痕，褶皺

同 enfold (v.) 包住
wrap (v.) 包
envelop (v.) 包住

反 open (v.) 打開

The shopping bag can be folded and put into your pocket.
這個購物袋能夠被折起來放到你的口袋中。

The housekeeper folded the sheet neatly.
這名管家整整齊齊地疊起床單。

38 **inspect**

★
★
★

[ɪn`spɛkt]

Ⅴ 檢查，審查，檢閱

同 test 試驗
survey 調查
study 研究
scan 審視

The customer carefully inspected the mugs for damage when he received the package.
顧客收到包裹時仔細地檢查馬克杯有無損壞。

(point) 相關詞彙：examine 檢驗，check 檢查，investigate 調查，observe 觀察。

An officer inspected the central heating system in the building.
一位官員檢查這棟大樓的中央溫控系統。

39 **premium**

★
★
★

[`primɪəm]

Ⅵ 獎金，保險費

ⓐ 優質的，高價的

同 excellent (a.) 出色的

If you are satisfied with the trial version, you can pay $100 for premium service package.
如果你對試用版很滿意，你可以付一百元來享用進階版的套裝組合服務。

(point) 新制多益閱讀測驗中，店家提供給顧客的套裝組合可能有 basic package（入門款），或是 advanced / premium package（進階款）。

He is currently between jobs so that he can't afford to pay life insurance premiums.
他目前待業中，所以他不能負擔人壽保險費。

(point) be between jobs 意為「待業中」。

40 **accessory**

★
★

[æk`sɛsərɪ]

Ⅵ 附件，配件，從謀

反 essential (a.) 必要的
principal (a.) 主要的

I bought some accessories that go well with my dress for tonight's event.
我買了一些能搭配我今晚活動要穿的洋裝的配件。

(point) go well with 意為「能與……搭配得好」。

Refresh your bathroom with our latest accessories.
用我們最新的浴室配件來使你的浴室煥然一新吧。

Chapter 106

11 零售購物與訂單

---

41 cabinet
★
★ [`kæbənɪt]
★
n 櫥櫃，內閣
同 council 議會
　　ministry 內閣
　　official adviser 幕僚

The president decided to reshuffle his Cabinet.
總統決定要重組他的內閣。

I purchased this **cabinet** online to keep my collection of old **china** in.
我在網路上買了這個櫥櫃用來收藏我的古瓷器收藏品。

(point) china 意為「瓷器」。

---

42 cart
★
★ [kɑrt]
★
n 手推車，馬車
v 運送，搬運
同 trolley (n.) 手推車

After Sean completed his shopping, he wheeled the cart to the **checkout counter**.
在西恩完成購物後，他將推車推到結帳櫃台。

(point) 延伸詞彙：check in 旅館入住；登機，check out 結帳退房。

When Emma **is under stress**, she put whatever she likes into her shopping cart and pays the bill with her credit card.
當艾瑪有壓力的時候，她會把她喜歡的商品都放到購物車，然後用信用卡付款。

(point) be under stress 意為「承受壓力」。

---

43 crowd
★
★ [kraud]
n 人群，一堆
同 flock (n.) 人群
　　pack (n.) 一夥
衍 crowded (a.) 擁擠的

During the **anniversary** sale, a huge crowd of people shop in the department stores.
在週年慶期間，一大群人在百貨公司裡消費。

(point) anniversary (a.) 週年的；週年紀念的 (n.) 週年紀念；週年紀念日。

The hotel lobby was crowded with foreign tourists who were waiting to check in.
飯店大廳擠滿了等著辦理入住手續的外國旅客。

---

44 exclusive
★
★ [ɪk`sklusɪv]
★
a 除外的，獨有的，高級的
n 獨家新聞
衍 exclusive interview (ph.) 專訪

According to the exclusive news, DK Company is going to acquire FR Company next month.
根據獨家新聞，DK 公司將會在下個月收購 FR 公司。

(point) acquire (v.) 收購，acquisition (n.) 收購／ merge (v.) 併購，merger (n.) 併購。

He paid the **annual fee** to become a member of that exclusive club.
他付了年費以成為高級俱樂部的成員。

(point) 延伸詞彙：tuition fee 學費。

45 **exclusively**

★
★ [ɪkˋsklusɪvlɪ]

ad 專門地,獨佔地

同 completely 徹底地
absolutely 絕對地
totally 完全地
only 唯一地
utterly 完全地

The discount is exclusively for those first time customers.
只有首購的消費者才享有此優惠。

(point) be exclusively for 意為「專門給⋯⋯」。

We shop exclusively at Harrods'.
我們專門在哈洛德百貨公司購物。

(point) 英文的人名後加 -s 常用來表達店家名稱,例如:Jenny's,意為「珍妮的店」。

---

46 **toll**

★ [tol]

n 通行費,使用費,傷亡人數

v 徵稅

同 tariff (v.) 徵收關稅

Please call the toll-free number if you have any problems with our products.
如果你對我們的產品有任何疑問,請打這支免付費電話。

(point) toll-free 電話為對方付錢的電話,打電話的那方不需付錢。

Drivers need to stop at the toll booths and pay the toll.
駕駛們必須要停在收票站,並付過路費。

(point) booth 意為「亭;棚」,相關詞彙:telephone booth 電話亭。

---

47 **suite**

★ [swit]

n 套房,一套家具,系列

Jessie finally can afford to rent a suite downtown so that she can cut down on the time she spends on her commute.
潔西終於能負擔租市中心的套房,因此她能夠減少通勤時間。

(point) commute (n. / v.) 通勤。

The couple just bought a bathroom suite since it was on sale.
這對夫妻因為打折買了一套浴室家具。

(point) a bathroom suite 意為「一套浴室家具」,例如洗手台和馬桶。

---

48 **cupboard**

★
★ [ˋkʌbɚd]

n 碗櫃,壁櫥,櫥櫃

同 closet 衣櫥
cabinet 櫥櫃

We ordered a customized cupboard that can fit the size of our kitchen.
我們訂了一個可以符合我們廚房尺寸的客製化櫥櫃。

(point) customized = tailor-made,表示「客製化的」

The furniture company came to my house to measure the size of my kitchen to make the cupboard.
家具行來我家測量廚房的尺寸,以便製作櫥櫃。

11 零售購物與訂單

49 load
★
★
★
[lod]

n 負擔，重任，裝載量
v 裝載，使充滿，大量給予
同 loading (n.) 裝貨

The truck is being loaded with the gear for camping.
這台卡車正在被裝載著露營用的器具。

(point) is being loaded 為正在進行被動式，若在多益測驗 Part 1 圖片題中出現，必須要有「人」在圖片裡才能選。

Whenever it is the end of season sale, there are a load of people in the department stores shopping for clothes.
每當換季拍賣的時候，百貨公司總是有很多人在買衣服。

---

50 blender
★
[`blɛndɚ]

n 攪拌機
同 mixer 攪拌器
　food processor 食物處理機

I read the manual to know how to make juice with the new blender.
我讀說明手冊來了解如何用這台新的果汁機打果汁。

I complained about the defective food blender to the Customer Service Department and I received a new one right away.
我向客服部抱怨食物攪拌機的缺陷，然後我隨即就收到一台全新的食物攪拌機。

---

51 plug
★
[plʌg]

n 塞子，插頭
v 塞住，堵塞
同 clog (v.) 塞滿

When I am taking a nap, I use ear plugs to prevent the noises from the construction sites.
我在午睡時戴耳塞來隔絕工程噪音。

(point) prevent... from... 意為「避免……」。

After purchasing the lamp from the mall, I put the electric plug into the socket to check whether it worked.
從商場買了燈後，我將插頭插到插座裡來確認是否可用。

---

52 auction
★
[`ɔkʃən]

n 拍賣
v 拍賣
同 vendue (n.) 公開拍賣
　sale (n.) 拍賣

Since we are going to redecorate our home, let's go to a furniture auction for some good bargains.
既然我們要重新裝潢家裡，我們去家具拍賣會買些特價品吧。

(point) bargain (n.) 特價品 (v.) 殺價。

Some of the paintings and antiques were auctioned last year.
去年拍賣了一些畫和古董。

53 **bottom**

★
★
★

['bɑtəm]

n 底部，臀部
v 基於，降至最低點
a 最低的，最後的
同 base (n.) 基部
　　end (n.) 最後
反 top (n.) 上面

There is no room for bargaining, $200 is my bottom line.
沒有殺價的空間，兩百元是我的底價。

(point) bottom line 意為「底線；底價」。

Don't put the commonly used books on the bottom shelf.
別把常用的書放在最下層的架子上。

(point) commonly used 意為「經常使用的」。

54 **pure**

★

[pjur]

a 純粹的，道地的，完全的
同 absolute 完全的
　　simple 單純的
　　unmixed 純粹的
反 mixed 混合的
衍 purify (v.) 淨化

The sweater is more expensive because it is made of pure wool.
這件毛衣比較貴，因為是由純羊毛製成。

(point) be made of 意為「由……製成」。

The couple shared their romance in the wedding. They said they met each other by pure accident.
這對情侶在婚禮上分享他們的羅曼史。他們說他們的相遇純屬偶然。

55 **various**

★
★
★

['vɛrɪəs]

a 不同的，各式各樣的，
　　許多的
同 different 不同的
　　many 很多
　　varied 多變的
反 single 單一的

Department stores sell various goods that fit different people's needs.
百貨公司賣很多種商品，能符合不同人的需求。

(point) goods (n.) 意指「貨物」，要加 -s。

The safety inspector examined the existing problems in various ways.
該名安全檢查員以不同的方式來檢視現有的問題。

(point) 延伸詞彙：safety inspection 意為「安全檢查」。

56 **accidental**

★

[ˌæksə'dɛntl̩]

a 意外的，偶然的，附屬的
同 casual 偶然的
　　unexpected 意外的
　　unintended 非故意的
反 deliberate 故意的
衍 accident-prone
　　(a.) 特別容易出事的

We can refund you money if the damage is accidental.
如果這個損壞是意外造成的，我們可以退你錢。

I didn't mean to forget to bring your passport—it was accidental.
我不是故意要忘記帶你的護照的 —— 只是個意外。

241

11 零售購物與訂單

57 argue
★
★
★
[`argju]

V 爭論，主張，說服

同 debate 辯論
　 dispute 爭論

反 agree 同意

衍 argument (n.) 爭論

The couple were tired of arguing about the percentage of the travel budget.
這對夫妻已經疲於爭吵旅遊預算的比例。

point be tired of + N / Ving 意為「疲於……」。

The consumers who received defective products argued with the clerk in the hope of returning them.
收到瑕疵產品的消費者和店員爭執著，希望能夠換貨。

point in the hope of + N / Ving 或是 in the hopes that + S + V 意為「希望……」。

58 boot
★
[but]

n 靴子

V 猛踢，趕走

同 kick (v.) 踢

All the boots are on sale.
所有的靴子都在特價。

point be on sale 意為「特價中」。

The mechanic put a toolkit in the boot of his car.
技師在他汽車後車廂裡放了一個工具箱。

point boot 當名詞時也可當「汽車後車廂」。

59 blanket
★
★
[`blæŋkɪt]

n 毛毯

V 覆蓋，掩蓋

同 covering (n.) 毯子
　 quilt (n.) 被子

The fabric of the new blanket is as durable as the old one.
新毯子的布料和舊的一樣耐用。

point as... as 意為「和……一樣」。

The playground was blanketed with snow.
操場被雪覆蓋。

point be blanketed with 意為「被……覆蓋」。

60 carpet
★
[`kɑrpɪt]

n 地毯

V 鋪地毯

同 rug (n.) 毛皮地毯
　 mat (n.) 草蓆
　 covering (n.) 毯子

衍 mattress (n.) 床墊

Ed's Floor Covering, Inc. sells a wide variety of carpets and rugs.
艾德地毯公司販售各式各樣的地毯與地墊。

Come to our newly renovated showroom and select a carpet that suits your living room.
來我們最新翻修的展示間，挑選適合您家客廳的地毯。

point 多益測驗題目的敘述常常會問店家有什麼是新的，會用到 recently（最近的），此時閱讀測驗的文章或聽力測驗裡若出現 newly，後面的句子就是答案。

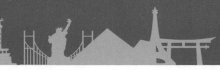

61 briefcase
★
[`brif͵kes]
n 公事包
衍 backpack (n.) 後背包
handbag (n.) 手提包
carry-on baggage
(ph.) 手提行李

The leather briefcase caught the designer's attention immediately.
這個皮製的手提包馬上就吸引該名設計師的目光。
(point) catch one's attention 意為「吸引注意」。

The man is carrying a black briefcase.
男生正提著一個黑色公事包。
(point) 要特別注意多益聽力測驗圖片題中,人與衣物、配件的關係。

62 attention
★
★
★
[ə`tɛnʃəl]
n 注意,專心,照顧
同 care 照料
consideration 關心
反 absent-mindedness
心不在焉
inattention 粗心

Attention shoppers, the store will be closed in 30 minutes. Enjoy your shopping!
消費者請注意,我們會在三十分鐘後打烊。享受您的購物吧!
(point) 「Attention shoppers」為多益聽力測驗 Part 4 常見的開頭,從此句就可以知道地點為商場。

The cut and the texture of the trousers really caught my attention!
這褲子的剪裁還有質地真的很吸引我!
(point) 其他常見談論衣物的詞彙:fabric 布料、durable 耐用的、waterproof 防水的、windproof 防風的。

63 order
★
★
★
[`ɔrdɚ]
n 順序,命令,訂購
v 命令,訂購,整理
同 sequence (n.) 順序
arrangement (n.) 安排
organization (n.) 條理

You can either place an order online or call the sales directly.
你可以在網路上下訂單或直接打給業務。
(point) place an order 意為「下訂單」。

Don't worry since all is in order.
別擔心,因為一切都準備就緒了。
(point) all is in order 意為「一切準備就緒」。

64 grocery
★
★
★
[`grosərɪ]
n 食品雜貨店,食品雜貨
同 grocery store 雜貨店

Anne's grocery was popular among the local residents.
安的雜貨店很受當地居民的歡迎。
(point) inhabitant, dweller, habitant 皆可指「居民」。延伸詞彙:tenant 房客,landlord 房東,citizen 市民。

The retired lady is considering using her pension to run a grocery store.
這名退休的女士在考慮使用她的退休金開一家雜貨店。
(point) consider + Ving 意為「考慮做……」。

Chapter 109

11 零售購物與訂單

---

65 browse
★
★
[braʊz]
★
Ⅴ 瀏覽，吃草
ⁿ 瀏覽，吃草
同 scan (v.) 粗略地看
　 skim (v.) 瀏覽
　 glance (v.) 瞥見
　 look (v.) 瞥
衍 browser (n.) 瀏覽器

If you would like to know more about our latest catalog, browse our official website.
如果你想要知道更多我們最新的目錄，瀏覽我們的官網。

point browse our official website 這句更常在多益測驗中表現為：visit our official website，意為「拜訪我們的官網」。

The commuter spent fifteen minutes browsing in the bookstore near the train station.
通勤者花了十五分鐘在車站旁的書店裡瀏覽圖書。

point spend 時間 + Ving 意為「花時間做……」。

---

66 sort
★
[sɔrt]
ⁿ 種類，性質，方式
Ⅴ 分類，挑選，區分
同 type (n.) 類型
　 kind (n.) 種類
　 variety (n.) 多樣化
　 category (n.) 種類
　 classification (n.) 分類

The clerk sort out the products according to the expiration date.
店員依照有效日期來分類產品。

point sort out 意為「分類」。

The newlyweds have a lot in common; for example, they enjoy the same sort of movie.
這對新婚夫妻有很多共通點，例如，他們喜歡同一類電影。

point have a lot in common 意為「有很多共同點」，have little in common 意為「有很少共同點」。

---

67 period
★
[`pɪrɪəd]
★
ⁿ 時期，週期，句點
同 term 任期
　 span 一段時間
　 phase 時期
　 session 期間
　 duration 持續期間

During the anniversary sales period, the store's business hours will be extended.
在週年慶期間，店家的營業時間會延長。

After a three-month probationary period, the assistant was offered a full-time contract.
在三個月的試用期後，這名助理得到全職的契約。

point 延伸詞彙：a 7-day trial 意為「一週試用期」。

---

68 reply
★
[rɪ`plaɪ]
★
★
ⁿ 回答，答覆
Ⅴ 回答，答覆
同 respond (v.) 作答
　 answer (v.) 回答
反 ask (v.) 詢問

As long as we receive your order, we'll reply to your email right away.
只要我們收到你的訂單，我們就會馬上回信。

Replying to customers' letters is the assistant's first priority.
回覆顧客信件是這個助理每天的第一優先事項。

point Replying to customers' letters 為 Ving 當主詞，動詞用單數。

69 **nevertheless**

★
★ [ˌnɛvəðəˈlɛs]

ad 不過，然而

同 nonetheless 仍然
　 yet 然而
　 though 然而
　 notwithstanding 儘管
　 regardless 無論如何
　 anyway 無論如何

Living expenses in this city are higher, but the assistant still prefers to live here nevertheless.
縱使這個城市的生活開銷比較高，助理還是選擇住在這裡。

E-commerce is increasing in popularity; nevertheless, some people still make purchases in real stores.
電子商務逐漸流行，但有些人仍然在實體店面消費。

(point) 相關詞彙：however 然而，still 然而。

70 **measurement**

★
★ [ˈmɛʒɚmənt]

n 測量，尺寸，長度

同 quantification 量化
　 computation 計算
　 calculation 計算
　 appraisal 估量
　 weighing 秤重
　 size 尺寸

The experienced tailor took the groom's measurements.
經驗豐富的裁縫師量了新郎的尺寸。

(point) take one's measurement 意為「量某人的尺寸」。

Buyers need to check their measurements before purchasing clothes online.
買家應該要在線上購買衣服前確認他們自己的尺寸。

71 **halfway**

★ [ˈhæfˈwe]

a 中途的，不徹底的
ad 在中途，不徹底地

同 midway (a.) 中途的
　 middle (a.) 中間的
　 mid (a.) 中央的
　 central (a.) 中心的

Don't give up! You are halfway to your goal.
不要放棄！你已經在往目標的路上了。

Some of our customers were not satisfied with the halfway measures provided by our customer service department.
有些顧客不滿意我們客服部提供的不徹底的措施。

(point) provided 由 that / which were provided 簡化而來。

72 **vendor**

★
★ [ˈvɛndɚ]

n 小販，賣主，自動販賣機

同 seller 賣家
　 salesperson 售貨員
　 retailer 零售商
　 wholesaler 批發商
　 merchant 商人
衍 vending machine
　 (ph.) 販賣機

The street vendor greeted his customers with a warm smile.
街頭小販用一個溫暖的微笑和他的客人打招呼。

(point) with 意為「用；伴隨著」。

After negotiating a price, the purchaser finally signed a contract with the vendor.
在議價後，買方終於和賣方簽合約。

(point) purchaser, buyer, customer, consumer, client 皆可指「購買的人；顧客」。

11 零售購物與訂單

---

110

73 bulk
★
★
★
[bʌlk]
n 體積，大塊，大多數
v 變得重要，擴大，膨脹
同 mass (n.) 大量
hugeness (n.) 龐大
largeness (n.) 巨大
majority (n.) 多數
反 minority (n.) 少數

You can get a 10% discount if you buy the product in bulk.
如果你大量購買這個產品，就可以得到百分之十的折扣。
(point) 多益測驗情境中若提到 in bulk（大量），常常也會提到 discount（折扣）或 save money（省錢）。

Actually, the bulk of the book is written by the famous writer's assistant but not by himself.
實際上，這本書的大部分都是由那位知名作家的助理寫的，而不是他本人。

---

74 unaware
★
★
★
[ˌʌnə`wɛr]
a 不知道的，未察覺到的
同 ignorant 不知道的
unknowing 不知道的
unmindful 不留心的
inattentive 不注意的
反 aware 知道的
conscious 意識到的

The director was unaware of the potential threats that the decision might bring to the company.
主任並沒有注意到那個決定可能會帶給公司的潛在威脅。
(point) be unaware of + N / Ving 意為「沒有注意到……」。

The customer who requested to return the vacuum was unaware that he forgot to bring the receipt and invoice.
要求吸塵器換貨的顧客沒有注意到他忘了帶發票及收據。

---

75 turnover
★
★
★
[`tɝnˌovɚ]
n 翻轉，營業額，流動率
同 revenue 收入
income 收入
yield 收益
sales 銷售

During the annual sale, the retail store had a high turnover.
在週年慶期間，零售店有很高的銷售量。

The company's turnover rate is low because it provides employees great learning opportunities and decent salaries.
公司的人員流動率很低，因為它提供員工好的學習機會及很棒的薪水。

---

76 invoice
★
★
★
[`ɪnvɔɪs]
n 發票，發貨單
v 開發票，列入清單
同 bill (n.) 帳單
account (n.) 帳單
statement (n.) 結算單

We have attached the invoice to the receipt.
我們已經將發票黏在收據上了。
(point) attach... to 意為「黏上」。

Please bring the invoice if you would like to return the product you purchased from our store.
如果你想要退掉從我們店裡買的產品，請帶著發票。
(point) 多益閱讀測驗中若有提到退貨，常會要求顧客提供 invoice（發票）、serial number（序號）和 receipt（收據）。

Question

以下題目完全擬真新制多益 Part 5，請選出最符合句意的選項。

1. Every ------- in the conference will receive one meal coupon.
   (A) participation
   (B) participate
   (C) participants
   (D) participant

2. ------- you place an order, we will send you a confirmation letter.
   (A) Although
   (B) What
   (C) Whether
   (D) Once

3. Customers who shop in the online stores are not allowed to make changes when an order -------.
   (A) submitted
   (B) submits
   (C) is submitted
   (D) was submitted

4. The online store ------- the customer with free delivery and coupons.
   (A) decided
   (B) compensated
   (C) purchased
   (D) reflected

5. ------- you have any problems with your merchandise, please contact us.
   (A) Should
   (B) In case of
   (C) Regarding
   (D) As

6. If you would like to repair the blender you ------- from us, please bring the warranty card, invoice and receipt.
   (A) was purchased
   (B) purchasing
   (C) purchased
   (D) to purchase

>> 正確答案與解析請翻至下一頁查看

Answer

● 正確答案與解析

1. 每位參加會議的人都會收到一張餐券。

(A) 參加 (n.)　　　　　　　　　(B) 參加 (v.)

(C) 參加者（名詞複數）　　　　(D) 參加者（every + 單數名詞）

正確答案 (D)

2. 一旦你下了訂單，我們就會寄給你一封確認信。

(A) 雖然　　　　　　　　　　　(B) 什麼

(C) 是否　　　　　　　　　　　(D) 一旦……就 (conj.)；曾經 (adv.)

正確答案 (D)

3. 在網路商城購買東西的顧客，在訂單提交後不能做更改。

(C) 現在式（這句話是事實）+ 被動式（訂單被提交）

正確答案 (C)

4. 這個網路商城用免費的運送及折價券來彌補這位客人。

(A) 決定　　　　(B) 彌補　　　　(C) 購買　　　　(D) 反映

正確答案 (B)

5. 如果你對商品有任何疑問，請聯絡我們。

(A) 如果 (conj.) = If；應該（助動詞）(B) 以防萬一 (prep.)

(C) 有關 (prep.)　　　　　　　(D) 因為 (conj.)

正確答案 (A)

6. 如果您想要修理您從我們這裡買的攪拌機，請帶著保固卡、發票及收據。

(C) 購買（過去式），意為「已經買了」

(D) 購買（不定詞，前面要有動詞）

正確答案 (C)

Chapter 12
行銷銷售

以下多益必考單字，你認識哪些？

- [ ] promote (p.252)
- [ ] advertise (p.251)
- [ ] recognize (p.254)
- [ ] performance (p.255)
- [ ] client (p.250)
- [ ] estimate (p.256)

- [ ] customize (p.253)
- [ ] awareness (p.261)
- [ ] include (p.268)
- [ ] precisely (p.265)
- [ ] representative (p.251)
- [ ] ultimate (p.263)

- [ ] addition (p.268)
- [ ] complain (p.256)
- [ ] increase (p.262)
- [ ] mention (p.258)
- [ ] demand (p.250)
- [ ] incentive (p.267)

111

12 行銷銷售

01 client
★
★
★
[`klaɪənt]

n 委託人，顧客，客戶
同 customer 顧客
shopper 顧客
consumer 消費者
patron 老顧客

All the materials must be sent to our **clients** by the end of this week.
所有的原料都必須要在這週結束前寄給客戶。

point 相關詞彙：purchaser / buyer 買家。

My assistant sent the **latest** product catalog to all clients.
我的助理寄最新的產品目錄給所有的客戶。

point latest 意為「最新的」。

---

02 customer
★
★
★
[`kʌstəmɚ]

n 顧客，傢伙（口語）
同 regular 老顧客
patronage 顧客
反 buyer 買家
businessman 商人
businessperson 商人
shop owner 店主

The clerk tried to settle the dispute between the two **customers**.
店員試著解決兩名顧客間的爭吵。

point 相關詞彙：shopper 購物者，consumer 消費者，patron 老主顧。

The demanding client phoned the customer service department to report the clerk's misbehavior.
這位要求很多的客戶打電話到客戶服務部門來回報店員的不良行為。

---

03 demand
★
★
★
[dɪ`mænd]

v 要求，請求，需要
n 要求，請求，需求
同 request (v.) 要求
call (v.) 要求

The demanding clients requested a refund.
這名苛求的客戶要求退費。

point demand（要求）加上 ing 變成形容詞，意為「苛求的」。

According to the statistical result, the global demand for food is rising.
根據統計結果，全球食物需求正在上升。

---

04 display
★
★
★
[dɪ`sple]

v 陳列，展出，表現
n 展覽，陳列，表露
同 exhibit (v.) 展覽
show (v.) 展現
present (v.) 呈現
反 hide (v.) 隱藏
conceal (v.) 隱藏

A golden **medal** was displayed on his desk.
他的桌子上展示了一塊金牌。

point 易混淆字：metal (n.) 金屬／mental (a.) 心理的。

Sometimes creative product displays can influence sales performance.
有時候具有創意的商品陳列會影響銷售表現。

05 **advertise**
★
★ [`ædvɚ͵taɪz]
★ **Ⅴ** 做宣傳，做廣告，公布
同 publicize 宣傳
promote 宣傳
make public 公布

The company advertises their products by holding campaigns.
這家公司藉由辦活動來為他們的產品打廣告。

(point) hold 意為「舉辦」。

Nowadays, not many companies advertise their products in the newspaper.
現在沒有很多公司會在報紙上打他們產品的廣告。

06 **advertisement**
★
★ [͵ædvɚ`taɪzmənt]
★ **ⁿ** 廣告，宣傳，公告
同 commercial 廣告

In the annual budget meeting, members of the Financial Department had disagreements on the amount of money they should spend on advertisements next year.
在年度預算會議中，財務部的成員們對於明年廣告要花多少錢有歧異。

(point) have disagreement on sth. 意為「在某事上有歧異」。

We know target consumers from the contents of the advertisements.
我們可以從廣告的內容中得知目標消費者群。

07 **represent**
★
★ [͵rɛprɪ`zɛnt]
★ **Ⅴ** 表現，代表，聲稱，
提出異議
同 indicate 象徵
present 表現

Mr. Turner will represent IT department to attend the 30th Technology conference.
透納先生將會代表資訊科技部門去參加第三十屆科技研討會。

This new policy represents that the company will use the new sales reporting system.
新政策代表公司將會使用新的回報銷售系統。

08 **representative**
★
★ [͵rɛprɪ`zɛntətɪv]
★ **ａ** 典型的，代表性的
ⁿ 典型，代表
同 typical (a.) 典型的
characteristic (a.) 典型的
反 atypical (a.) 非典型的
unrepresentative
(a.) 非代表性的

Red telephone booths are one of the representatives of the U.K.
紅色電話亭是英國代表物之一。

The board elected Ms. Mcgee as our sales representative.
委員會選了麥基女士擔任業務代表。

(point) elect A as + O 意為「選 A 做為……」。

12  行銷銷售

112

09 **campaign**
★
★ [kæm`pen]
★
n 戰役，運動，活動
v 從事運動，參加競選
同 action (n.) 活動
activity (n.) 活動

Over the past few weeks, the marketing team worked overtime to prepare for the campaign.
在過去這幾週以來，行銷團隊持續加班以準備行銷活動。

The campaign successfully attracted many potential customers by offering appealing discounts.
這個行銷活動成功地藉由提供誘人的折扣來吸引許多潛在顧客。

---

10 **project**
★
★ [`prɑdʒɛkt]
★
n 方案，計畫，工程
[prə`dʒɛkt]
v 計劃，投射，闡述
同 scheme (n.) 方案
plan (n.) 計畫
衍 projection (n.) 規劃

The marketing team is in charge of the new project.
行銷團隊負責這個新專案。

(point) be in charge of 意為「負責」。

The purpose of the banquet is to thank all members' contributions to the scientific research project.
宴席的主要目的就是要感謝所有成員對這個科學研究專案的貢獻。

---

11 **promote**
★
★ [prə`mot]
★
v 晉升，促進，發起
同 encourage 助長
foster 促進
boost 提升
stimulate 激發
反 obstruct 阻塞
impede 妨礙

The company promotes their products in TV commercials.
這間公司藉由電視廣告來推廣它們的產品。

(point) commercial (n.) 商業廣告 (a.) 商業的。

Recently, ways to promote products have changed dramatically.
近期以來，推銷商品的方式已經改變了很多。

---

12 **promotional**
★
★ [prə`moʃənl]
★
a 增進的，獎勵的，宣傳的
衍 promotional video
(n.) 廣告宣傳片

You can enter the promotional code and get a 10 percent discount.
你可以輸入這個折扣碼，以得到九折優惠。

(point) 英文的 10 percent discount 也就是中文的九折。

The leading actor and actress of the new movie went on a promotional tour to four different countries.
新電影的男女主角去了四個國家巡迴宣傳電影。

13 launch

★
★

[lɔntʃ]

V 發射，發動，發起

n 發射，發行

同 start (v.) 起始
　 begin (v.) 開始

The company launches new products every year.
這間公司每年都有新產品上市。

(point) 此句為常態，動詞使用現在式。

I wonder when the production will finish since it will influence our product launch schedule.
我想知道何時會生產完畢，因為這會影響我們產品上市的行程。

(point) since 在此句意為「因為」。

---

14 satisfy

★
★
★

[`sætɪsˌfaɪ]

V 使滿意，符合，使確信

同 please 使高興
　 content 使滿意

反 dissatisfy 使不滿
　 frustrate 使灰心

The customer was not satisfied with the service the store provided.
顧客不滿意店家提供的服務。

(point) be not satisfied with 意為「不滿意」。

Officials were satisfied with the consistency in the production of protective clothing and masks.
主管單位很滿意防護衣及面具生產的穩定性。

---

15 custom

★

[`kʌstəm]

n 習俗，慣例，習慣

a 訂做的

同 tradition (n.) 傳統

Respect every country's customs when you travel to different nations.
當你到不同國家旅遊時，要尊重每個國家不同的習俗。

(point) 相關詞彙：convention 習俗。

---

16 customize

★
★
★

[`kʌstəmˌaɪz]

V 訂做，客製化

同 modify 修改
　 adapt 使適合

The vacation package can be customized according to your needs.
這個假期套裝組合可以依你的需求客製化。

(point) needs (n.) 需求。

One of the biggest features of this electronic device is that you can customize the user interface.
這個電子裝置的最大特點之一就是你可以客製化使用者介面。

(point) user interface 意為「使用者介面」。

Chapter 113

12 行銷銷售

17 recognize
★
★
★
[ˋrɛkəgˏnaɪz]

Ⅴ 識別，認可，賞識

同 identify 認出
acknowledge 認識

反 overlook 忽略
ignore 忽視

He is an internationally recognized photographer.
他是個國際間認可的攝影師。

I can barely recognize my client who I have not seen for more than 10 years.
我幾乎認不得那位超過十年不見的客戶。

point barely = hardly = scarcely = rarely，意為「幾乎不」。

18 suggest
★
★
★
[səˋdʒɛst]

Ⅴ 提議，暗示，使聯想

同 propose 提議
recommend 建議
advocate 提倡
advise 建議
urge 力勸

衍 suggestion (n.) 建議

I suggested partnering with the marketing department.
我建議和行銷部門合夥。

point suggest + Ving 意為「建議做……」。

The firm suggested his employees minimize the amount of luggage they carry when they go on a business trip.
公司建議員工出差時將攜帶的行李最小化。

19 advice
★
★
[ədˋvaɪs]

n 勸告，忠告，消息

同 recommendation 勸告
suggestion 建議
proposal 提議

Customers can write down their advice on the feedback sheet.
顧客可以把他們的建議寫在回饋單。

When you are making a decision about your major, will you take your parents' advice or follow your heart?
當你在選科系時，你會採取你父母的意見還是順從你的心呢？

point make a decision = decide = determine，意為「決定」。

20 formal
★
★
[ˋfɔrml]

a 正式的，拘謹的，形式上的

同 official 正式的
legal 正當的
authorized 經授權的

反 informal 非正式的
unofficial 非正式的

The sales is required to wear formal clothes while visiting his clients.
當業務拜訪他的客戶時，他被要求穿著正式的衣服。

Our company usually holds formal events, like the product launch, in 5 star hotels.
我們公司通常在五星級飯店舉辦正式活動，像是產品發表會。

point product launch 意為「產品上市」。

CH 12

行銷銷售

21 initiation
★
[ɪnɪʃɪˋeʃən]
n 開始，入會，啟蒙
同 beginning 開始
　 starting 開始
　 commencement 開端
反 completion 完成
　 finish 結束

The consultant charged these new clients high initiation fees.
顧問向這些新客戶收取高額的入會費。

The service initiation date will be the day when the two parties sign the contract.
服務開始的日期，將會從雙方簽訂合約的那天開始。

point 易混淆字：contract (n.) 合約／contact (n. / v.) 聯絡。

---

22 performance
★
★
★
[pɚˋfɔrməns]
n 表演，履行，成果，機器性能
同 presentation 上演
　 achievement 成績

Unfortunately, the sales performance was considerably lower than we expected.
很不幸地，銷售表現比我們預期的低很多。

point considerably 意為「相當地」，修飾形容詞 lower。

The graph shows the estimate of the sales performance this season.
這個圖表展示了這季的預估銷售表現。

---

23 assistance
★
★
★
[əˋsɪstəns]
n 幫助，援助
同 help 幫助
反 opposition 反抗
衍 assistant (n.) 助手，助理
　 assist (v.) 幫助

But for your assistance, I would not have finished the task.
要不是有你的幫助，我可能無法完成這任務。

point but for 表示「要不是」。此句為「與過去事實相反」的假設句。

With the assistance of the Marketing and Sales Department, the campaign ran smoothly.
有行銷和業務部門的幫助，這個活動執行得很順利。

---

24 consumption
★
★
[kənˋsʌmpʃən]
n 消耗，消耗量，消費
同 depletion 消耗
　 expenditure 支出

Meat consumption has continued to rise since last year.
從去年開始，肉的消耗量就一直在上升。

Conspicuous consumption has gradually become a trend in this country.
炫耀式消費在這個國家逐漸變成一個趨勢。

point conspicuous (a.) 明顯的，出色的，炫耀的。

25 consume
★
★
★
[kən`sjum]

Ⅴ 消耗，花費，毀滅

同 eat up 用完
use up 消耗
spend 花費
waste 揮霍

The latest research indicated that the amount of gasoline that the average American consumes annually is considerable.
最新研究指出美國人一年平均所使用的石油數量相當驚人。

point 相關詞彙：annually 每年地，monthly 每月（的）地，weekly 每週（的）地，daily 每天（的）地。

Children who consume too much sugar might have a higher possibility of diabetes.
攝取太多糖分的小孩有更高的機率會得到糖尿病。

point 關係代名詞 who 後的動詞 consume 是跟著主詞來做變化，主詞為複數 children，因此也選擇複數動詞 consume。

26 estimate
★
★
★
[`ɛstə,met]

Ⅴ 估計，估價
[`ɛstəmət]

Ⅱ 估計，估價，看法

同 rough calculation (ph.) 粗略計算
rough guess (ph.) 粗略猜想
approximate price / cost / value (ph.) 大約價格

Please give us an estimate of the likely cost.
請給我們一個可能花費的估價。

point 多益測驗中，店家之間的書信往來常常會問到報價。相關詞彙：approximation 接近額，evaluation 估價，appraisal 估價，estimation 估計。

It was difficult to estimate the sales performance next quarter.
很難估計下一季的銷售表現。

27 assign
★
★
[ə`saɪn]

Ⅴ 分配，指定，歸於

同 allot 分配

衍 assignment (n.) 任務

The team leader assigned everyone's tasks.
組長指派了每個人的任務。

The sales was assigned to visit his clients in Germany.
這名業務被指派去拜訪他在德國的客戶。

28 complain
★
[kəm`plen]

Ⅴ 抱怨，發牢騷，投訴

同 grumble 抱怨
moan 悲嘆
whine 哀訴

The sales is always complaining about his clients' urgent cancellation of appointments.
這名業務總是在抱怨他客戶的緊急取消預約。

Many customers complained that the annual fee was too pricy.
很多顧客抱怨年費很貴。

point 相關費用詞彙：processing fee = handling fee 手續費，service fee 服務費，late payment fee 滯納金。

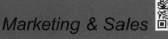
29 **complaint**

★★★ [kəmˋplent]

n 抱怨，抗議，控訴

同 objection 異議
murmur 低聲抱怨

反 approval 贊成

The waiter received a complaint letter owing to his poor service.

因為這名服務生差勁的服務，他收到一封抱怨信。

point owing to = due to = because of = thanks to + N 意為「因為⋯⋯」。

The customer service department should attend to every customer's complaint.

客戶服務部要處理每一個顧客的抱怨。

point attend to 意為「處理」。

30 **consumer**

★★★ [kənˋsjumɚ]

n 消費者

同 customer 顧客
client 顧客

He is a price-conscious consumer but not an impulse shopper.

他是一個對價格敏感的消費者，而不是一個衝動型購物者。

point 延伸詞彙：impulse shopping 表示「衝動型購物」。

Many companies use embedded marketing technique to increase customer awareness of their products subtly.

許多公司用置入性行銷的方式來隱隱約約地提高消費者對他們產品的注意。

point build / create / increase / raise customer awareness 意為「建立／提高消費者意識」。

31 **commitment**

★★★ [kəˋmɪtmənt]

n 承諾，信奉，罪刑

同 dedication 奉獻
devotion 奉獻
loyalty 忠誠
faithfulness 忠誠

衍 committed (a.) 忠誠的

The sales made a commitment to expand the customer base.

這名業務承諾要擴大客戶群。

point customer base = consumer base，意為「客戶群」。

The senior specialist shows a commitment to work.

這名資深專員展現了對工作的奉獻精神。

32 **breathe**

★ [brið]

v 呼吸，輕聲說，散發

同 inhale and exhale 吸入呼出

I almost can't breathe because the room is too stuffy.

我幾乎不能呼吸了，因為這房間太悶。

We need some creative product packaging to breathe life into this old product.

我們需要一些有創意的包裝來給這個老產品注入活力。

point breathe (new) life into sth. 意為「為某物注入活力」。

12 行銷銷售

33 expand
★
★
★
[ɪkˈspænd]

V 展開，擴張，發展

回 enlarge 擴大

反 contract 縮小
shrink 收縮

衍 expansion (n.) 擴展

Expanding customer base is always the first priority to this top sales.
對於這個頂尖業務而言，擴大顧客群一直都是第一優先的事情。

point customer base 意為「客戶群」。

The company expands its business by opening more branches in different cities.
這間公司藉由在不同城市開更多的分店來擴大營運。

---

34 strategy
★
★
★
[ˈstrætədʒɪ]

n 戰略，策略，計謀

回 scheme 計畫

The consultant is skillful at planning customized marketing strategies for different cases.
這名顧問很擅長為不同案件計劃出客製化的行銷策略。

point be skillful at 意為「擅長」。

One of the strategies to motivate employees is to provide opportunities for professional training.
其中一個鼓舞員工的策略就是提供專業訓練的機會。

---

35 mention
★
★
[ˈmɛnʃən]

V 提到，提名表揚

n 提及，提名表揚

回 state (v.) 陳述
declare (v.) 宣告
indicate (v.) 指出
present (v.) 提出

Just as I mentioned before, we will launch our new product at the end of this month.
就如同我先前所提及的，我們會在這個月底將新產品上市。

The senior executive had mentioned the merger in the board meeting.
高級行政主管曾經在董事會會議上提到合併案。

point board meeting 意為「董事會會議」。

---

36 abroad
★
★
[əˈbrɔd]

ad 在國外，在外面

One of my colleagues has been saving money for five years in order to study abroad.
我其中一個同事已經為了出國讀書存錢五年了。

point has been saving 為現在完成進行式，強調時間「五年」。易混淆字：board 委員會；木板／ aboard 在飛機上。

The senior sales was sent abroad to sign a crucial contract with his client in America.
這位資深業務被派去美國跟客戶簽一份重要的合約。

point was sent 為被動式，意為「被派出去」。contract 和 contact「聯繫」易混淆，要注意。

37 characteristic

★ [ˌkærəktəˈrɪstɪk]

a 典型的，獨特的
n 特徵，特性
同 typical (a.) 典型的
usual (a.) 通常的
normal (a.) 通常的
habitual (a.) 慣常的

He has a sociable characteristic, which makes him good at sales.
他有著善於社交的個性，這讓他善於銷售。
point which 代替前面的 He has a sociable characteristic。

It's characteristic of her that she is always punctual.
總是準時是她的特性。

38 workshop

★
★
★ [ˈwɜkˌʃɑp]

n 工作坊，研討會
同 seminar 研討會
conference 研討會
session 講習會

There will be one addition to today's workshop.
今天的工作坊會新加入一項活動。
point 多益聽力測驗中，演講或講座類的情境常會有行程增加或變動的內容。

Participants in the workshop will learn some practical skills in dealing with consumer complaints properly.
工作坊的參加者將會學到一些適當處理顧客抱怨的實際技巧。

39 helmet

★ [ˈhɛlmɪt]

n 頭盔，安全帽

The foreman warned all the workers to wear helmets while working in the construction site.
工頭提醒所有的工人在工地工作時一定要戴安全帽。

The company is planning for a series of campaigns to increase the sales volume of helmets.
為了要增加安全帽的銷售量，公司正計劃一連串的銷售活動。
point sales volume 意為「業績」。

40 below

★
★ [bəˈlo]

prep 在……下面，低於
ad 在下面，低於
同 beneath (prep.) 在……之下
under (prep.) 在……下面
反 above (prep.) 在……上面

The company phased out the products whose sales performance is below the average.
這家公司淘汰銷售表現低於平均的產品。
point phase out 意為「逐漸停止；逐步淘汰」。

The information below is for those who are going to attend the seminar.
以下資料是要給那些即將參加研習的人們。
point 相關詞彙：seminar 研習會，conference 會議，workshop 工作坊。

行銷銷售

41 billion
★ [`bɪljən]

n 十億，無數

衍 billions upon billions of
(ph.) 無數億

The annual sales volume of the new air conditioner is 4 billion.
這台新的冷氣年度銷售業績為四十億。

The government invested one billion in the public transportation.
政府投資了十億在公共交通工具上。

---

42 amaze
★ [ə`mez]

v 使驚奇，使驚愕

同 astonish 使吃驚
surprise 使驚訝

反 bore 使厭煩
tire 使疲勞

I was amazed at the efficiency of the newcomer.
這位新人的效率使我讚嘆。

The start-up's creative and innovative commercials always amaze me.
這間新創企業有創意又創新的廣告總是讓我很驚豔。

point 此句話表示一種常態，表示一直以來都會發生的事情，所以用現在式。

---

43 ambiguous
★ [æm`bɪgjʊəs]

a 含糊不清的；引起歧義的

同 uncertain 含糊的
vague 模糊的

反 clear 清楚的
obvious 明顯的
specific 明確的

The sales was asked to modify the contents of the contract because the manager thought they were too ambiguous to understand.
該名業務被要求修改合約內容，因為經理覺得太模稜兩可，讓人很難懂。

point too...to... 意為「太……以致於不能……」。

People can feel the ambiguous feeling between Jack from the Sales Department and Tina from the Marketing Department.
人們可以感覺到業務部的傑克與行銷部的堤娜有曖昧。

---

44 bold
★ [bold]

a 英勇的，大膽的，放肆的

同 courageous 英勇的
brave 勇敢的
fearless 無懼的

反 timid 膽小的
unadventurous
無冒險精神的

The marketing strategy is quite bold and innovative.
這個行銷策略相當大膽且創新。

They repainted the showroom in bold colors to attract customers' attention.
他們用色彩鮮豔的油漆重新粉刷展示區以吸引顧客的目光。

point attract one's attention 意為「吸引某人注意」。

45 **awareness**

★
★
★

n 察覺，覺悟，體認
同 consciousness 意識
　　attentiveness 專注

The firm attempted to raise consumers' environmental awareness by reducing the packages of the products, but in vain.

這間公司試圖藉由減少產品包裝來喚醒消費者的環保意識，但徒勞無功。

point in vain (ph.) 徒勞無功。

The awareness of work-life balance has increased dramatically.

對於工作與生活平衡的意識已經大幅地提升。

46 **slogan**

★
['slogən]

n 口號，標語
同 jingle 廣告短句
　　saying 格言

The company's creative advertising slogan impressed many people.

這間公司的創意廣告口號讓很多人印象深刻。

The campaign slogan failed to convey the politician's belief.

這個競選口號沒能傳達這名政治人物的信仰。

point fail to 意為「做……失敗」。

47 **valuable**

★
['væljuəbl]

a 貴重的，有價值的
n 貴重物品，財產
同 costly (a.) 貴重的
　　expensive (a.) 昂貴的
反 valueless (a.) 無價值的
　　cheap (a.) 便宜的
　　worthless (a.) 無價值的

The experience of working abroad is valuable to the candidate.

國外工作的經驗對這名面試者而言很寶貴。

point candidate, applicant, talent, individual 皆可指「求職者」。

The marketing team made a valuable contribution to the promotion of new products.

行銷團隊對推廣新產品做出了寶貴的貢獻。

point 相關詞彙：precious 貴重的，priceless 無價的，valued 寶貴的，prized 被珍視的，treasured 珍視的。

48 **resolute**

★
['rɛzə.lut]

a 堅決的，堅定的，果敢的
同 decided 果斷的
反 irresolute 優柔寡斷的

The movie director was resolute in the decision to change the leading actor.

電影導演對於換掉主角的決定十分堅決。

The manager took resolute steps to promote the sales performance.

經理採取果決的措施以提升銷售表現。

point 相關詞彙：determined 下決心的，resolved 斷然的。

12 行銷銷售

49 neglect
★
[nɪgˋlɛkt]
v 忽視，疏忽，漏做
n 忽略，疏忽，疏漏
同 disregard (v.) 忽視
　　ignore (v.) 忽略
　　skip (v.) 省略
衍 neglectful (a.) 疏忽的

We will never neglect our customers' needs.
我們絕不會忽略我們顧客的需求。

point need 當名詞「需求」時為複數。

In order to leave a good impression on the interviewer, you should not neglect your appearance.
為了給面試官留下好的印象，你不該不修邊幅。

point neglect one's appearance 意為「不修邊幅」。

50 increase
★
★
[ɪnˋkris]
★
v 增加，增大
[ˋɪnkris]
n 增大，增強
同 enlarge (v.) 擴大
　　climb (v.) 爬升
反 decrease(v.) 下降
　　reduce(v.) 減少

The director anticipated an increase in sales this quarter.
主任期待這季銷售增加。

point 相關詞彙：grow (v.) 成長，rise (v.) 上升，expand (v.) 擴張。

Our impressive promotional materials have successfully increased potential customers' interest in our products.
我們令人印象深刻的文宣品已經成功地增加潛在顧客們對商品的興趣。

point promotional material 意為「文宣品」。

51 further
★
[ˋfɝðɚ]
★
a 更遠的，進一步的
ad 而且，另外
v 促進，助長，推動
同 distant (a.) 遠的
　　extra (a.) 額外的
　　far (a.) 遠的

The sales believes that increasing professional knowledge can further his career.
這名業務相信增加專業知識可以推動他的事業發展。

point 此句的 further 為動詞，意為「促進」。

Feel free to let me know if you have any further questions.
如果你還有什麼問題，請隨時跟我說。

52 backyard
★
[ˋbækjɑrd]
n 後院

The real estate agent's client preferred this house, particularly the spacious backyard.
房屋仲介的客戶喜歡這棟房子，尤其是那寬廣的後院。

point 延伸用語：real estate agency 意為「房屋仲介業」。

Liam planted the seeds he bought from the nursery in the backyard.
利亞姆在後院種他從苗圃買回來的種子。

53 **image**
★

[ˈɪmɪdʒ]

n 形象，影像，象徵

v 想像，反映

同 impression (n.) 印象
idea (n.) 構想
concept (n.) 概念

衍 imagine (v.) 想像

Brand images matter!
品牌形象很重要！

point matter (n.) 事情；問題 (v.) 要緊；重要；有關係。

The politician has donated a great deal of money in order to improve his public image.
這名政治人物為了提升自己的公眾形象，已經捐出了大量的錢。

point a great deal of 意為「大量的」。

54 **disagree**
★
★

[ˌdɪsəˈgri]

v 不一致，意見不合，爭論

同 contradict each other 反駁
conflict 衝突
contrast 使對比

反 agree 同意

The manager partially disagreed with the project proposed by the marketing department.
經理有些部分不贊同行銷部門提出的專案。

point 相關詞彙：disapprove of 不同意，oppose 反對，differ 不同。

Whoever disagrees with the plan can propose other alternatives.
不論是誰不同意這個計畫，都可以提出其他的替代方案。

55 **certainly**
★

[ˈsɝtənlɪ]

ad 無疑地，必定，當然

同 unquestionably 無疑地
surely 當然
definitely 肯定地
undisputedly 無疑地
undoubtedly 肯定地

反 possibly 可能

We certainly dedicated ourselves to providing the top service.
我們當然會致力於提供最頂尖的服務。

point dedicate oneself to + Ving 意為「致力於」。

She will certainly be promoted given her outstanding sales performance.
有鑑於她傑出的銷售表現，她當然一定會被升遷。

point given + N 或 given that + S + V 意為「考慮到……；有鑑於……」。

56 **ultimate**
★

[ˈʌltəmɪt]

a 最後的，根本的，極限的

同 eventual 最終的
last 最後的
final 最終的
concluding 最後的
conclusive 最終的

反 peripheral 外圍的

The ultimate purpose of this campaign is to expand the consumer base and increase sales.
行銷活動的最終目標就是要擴大顧客群和增加銷售。

point consumer base 意為「顧客群」。

The travel magazine described the fancy restaurant as "the ultimate in luxury".
旅遊雜誌描述這間奢華的餐廳為「豪華的極致」。

point the ultimate in sth. 意為「……中最好的例子；……的極致」。

263

12 行銷銷售

57 backup
★
[`bæk͵ʌp]
n 備用，備用物
a 備用的
同 substitute (n.) 代替物
   fill in (ph.) 臨時代替

The marketing manager has two backup plans for the event next week.
行銷經理有兩個下週活動的替代計畫。

Currently, the backup system can only be activated by the managerial position.
目前只有管理階級能啟動後備系統。

---

58 among
★
★
★
[ə`mʌŋ]
prep 在……之中
同 surrounded by 被環繞
   in the company of 被陪伴
   amid 在……之中

Her sales performance is the most outstanding one among her colleagues.
她的銷售表現是同事間最棒的。

point among + N意為「在……之中」表達一個範圍，常與最高級連用。

The sensitive transfer student looked uncomfortable among the new classmates.
這個敏感的轉學生在新同學之中看起來很不自在。

point sensitive 在多益測驗中也常指機器或儀器是「靈敏的；敏感度高的」。

---

59 thrive
★
[θraɪv]
v 繁榮，成功，茁壯成長
同 blossom 生長茂盛
   advance 提前
   succeed 成功
反 decline 衰退
   fail 失敗
   die 平息

With the new marketing strategies, Ms. Fultz's restaurant has started to thrive.
隨著新的行銷策略，富爾茲女士的餐廳開始蓬勃發展。

point 相關詞彙：flourish 茂盛，prosper 繁榮，bloom 興盛。

Contrary to what people believed, the fancy boutique surprisingly throve in this area.
和人們相信的相反，奢華的精品店在這一區驚人地蓬勃發展。

point contrary to 意為「與……相反」。

---

60 target
★
[`tɑrgɪt]
n 目標，靶子
v 把……作為目標，對準
同 goal (n.) 目標
   object (n.) 目標
   aim (n.) 目的
   purpose (n.) 目的

Unfortunately, the sales volume failed to meet our sales target.
很不幸地，業績並沒有達到我們的銷售目標。

When you design any products, identifying your target users is particularly essential.
當你設計任何產品時，知道你的目標使用者是特別重要的。

point target user 意為「目標使用者」，target customer 意為「目標顧客」。

61 relation

★
★

[rɪ`leʃən]

n 關係，親戚，敘述

同 relationship 關係
association 聯想
alliance 結盟
bond 聯繫

The police didn't see any relation between the two incidents.
這個警察並不覺得這兩個意外有任何關連。

 相關詞彙：connection 關係，correlation 關聯，link 關係。

The marketing department has a good relation with the sales department because the two divisions have cooperated many times.
行銷部門和業務部門有著良好的關係，因為這兩個部門曾經合作過很多次。

 division (n.) 部門。

62 prolong

★
★
★

[prə`lɔŋ]

v 延長，拉長，拖延

同 lengthen 延長
extend 延伸

反 shorten 縮短

The hotel guest decided to prolong his stay by another two weeks.
飯店客人決定要多停留兩個禮拜。

Since you are our VIP, you are allowed to prolong the time of payment.
因為你是我們的貴賓，所以可以延長付款日期。

 since = because = as，意為「因為」，後面接 S + V。

63 precisely

★
★

[prɪ`saɪslɪ]

ad 精確地，清晰地，
嚴格地

同 exactly 確切地
promptly 正好

反 imprecisely 不嚴密地

衍 precise (a.) 精確的

The new system can precisely predict the market demand based on the past sales volume.
新系統能夠根據過去的銷售量來精確預測市場需求。

It was precisely because of the quality of the food and the efficient staff that I hired the restaurant to cater for my daughter's wedding.
正是因為那家餐廳食物的品質及有效率的員工，讓我僱用他們來幫我女兒的婚禮辦宴席。

 cater for 意為「承辦（宴席）」。

64 persuasion

★

[pə`sweʒən]

n 說服

衍 persuade (v.) 說服
convince (v.) 說服

Somehow, I felt his persuasion was convincing.
不知怎地，我覺得他那些說服的話令人信服。

The retailer was finally compromised by the sales' persuasion.
零售商最終因為業務的說服而妥協了。

12 行銷銷售

---

65 object
★
★ [`ɑbdʒɪkt]

n 物體，目標，受詞

[əb`dʒɛkt]

v 反對

同 target (n.) 目標
goal (n.) 目標
oppose (v.) 反對

反 accept (v.) 接受

I objected to the project that was proposed by the Marketing Department.
我反對行銷部門提出的案子。

(point) object 後面搭配 to 意為「反對」。

The object to the activity is to increase your hands-on experience.
活動的目的是增加你們親自動手做的經驗。

---

66 modification
★
★ [ˌmɑdəfə`keʃən]
★

n 修改，變更，緩和

同 alteration 更改
adjustment 調整
change 改變
adaptation 調整

Some further modifications are being carried out by the staff.
員工們正在進行更進一步的修改。

(point) carry out = implement，意為「執行」。

Our clients asked for modification to the contract.
我們的客戶要求對合約做修改。

---

67 moderately
★
★ [`mɑdərɪtlɪ]

ad 適度地，普通地，溫和地

同 fairly 相當地
reasonably 適度地

The campaign was moderately successful.
這個行銷活動只是普通成功。

The hotel is moderately priced, yet the service is rather great.
這間旅館收價合理，但服務很棒。

(point) yet = but，意為「但是」。

---

68 fundamental
★
★ [ˌfʌndə`mɛntl]

a 基礎的，根本的，主要的

n 基本原則，根本法則

同 basic (a.) 基本的
foundational (a.) 基礎的
elemental (a.) 基本的
elementary (a.) 基礎的
original (a.) 本來的
prime (a.) 最初的

The biology textbook introduced some fundamental differences between the two similar plants.
生物課本介紹了這兩種相似植物間的一些基本差異。

(point) fundamental difference 意為「基本差異」。

The fundamental purpose of the policy is to reduce operating costs.
這個政策的根本宗旨是降低營運成本。

(point) fundamental purpose 意為「根本宗旨」。

69 incentive
★

[ɪnˈsɛntɪv]

n 刺激，動機，激勵

a 刺激的，鼓勵的

同 encouragement (n.) 鼓勵
incitement (n.) 激勵

反 disincentive (n.) 抑制因素

The new policy provides incentives to those who successfully reach their sales goals.
新政策提供獎勵給那些成功達成銷售目標的人。

Many companies set their factories in this region because of tax incentives.
很多公司因為減稅而在這個區域設立工廠。

 factory = plant，意為「工廠」。

---

70 implication
★

[ˌɪmplɪˈkeʃən]

n 牽連，涉及，暗示

同 inference 推論
hint 暗示
indication 指示

The Marketing Department wondered about the implications of the new policy.
行銷部門想知道新政策會帶來的影響。

I am afraid that the manager does not totally realize the implications of the announcement.
恐怕經理沒有完全了解這個宣布的含義。

 I am afraid that + S + V 意為「我恐怕……」。

---

71 fluent
★

[ˈfluənt]

a 流利的，流暢的

同 articulate 善於表達的
eloquent 有說服力的
expressive 生動的
communicative 暢談的

反 inarticulate 口齒不清的

His goal is to become a fluent Japanese speaker.
他的目標就是成為一個流暢的日語口說使用者。

The sales is fluent in Spanish, and that's why he will be relocated to South America.
那名業務的西語很流利，這就是為什麼他將會被調到南美洲的原因。

---

72 hesitation
★

[ˌhɛzəˈteʃən]

n 躊躇，猶豫

同 delay 延遲
hanging back 畏縮不前
waiting 等待
uncertainty 不確定

反 determination 堅定

His hesitation indicated that he actually was not willing to help us.
他的猶豫點出了他其實不願意幫我們。

point be willing to 意為「願意」。

Without any hesitation, he signed the contract right after he saw the proposal.
他在看到提案後，沒有任何猶豫就簽了合約。

point without any hesitation 意為「沒有任何猶豫」。

12 行銷銷售

73 intend
★
★ [ɪnˋtɛnd]
★ Ⅴ 想要，打算，意指
同 plan 計畫
　 mean 意圖

The client didn't intend to renew the contract.
客戶並不打算續約。

The course is intended for students who plan to study abroad.
這門課是為了那些計劃出國的學生開設的。

74 include
★
★ [ɪnˋklud]
★ Ⅴ 包括，包含
同 incorporate 包含
　 encompass 包含
反 exclude 不包括
　 delete 刪去

The package includes both company brochures and two free samples.
這一袋包含了公司手冊及兩個免費的樣品。

point brochure (n.) 小冊子，請熟悉發音，常會在多益聽力測驗中出現。

The tenant asked his landlord whether the rent included utility fees.
房客問房東這個房租是否有包含水電雜費。

point 相關詞彙：comprise 包括，involve 包含，contain 包含。

75 exclude
★
★ [ɪkˋsklud]
Ⅴ 排除在外，開除，排斥
同 keep out 勿進
　 eliminate 排除
　 rule out 排除
反 accept 接受
　 include 包含

He was excluded from school for bad behavior, such as constantly cheating on exams.
他因為不良行為，像是不斷考試作弊，被學校開除了。

It's crucial to have an alternative plan because we can't exclude the possibility that it will rain.
有個替代方案是很重要的，因為我們不能排除會下雨的可能性。

point alternative (a.)（計畫或方法）可替代的 (n.) 可替代的計畫或方法。

76 addition
★
★ [əˋdɪʃən]
★ ℕ 附加，增加的人或物
同 supplement 增補
反 subtraction 減少
衍 additional (a.) 附加的

Before we start, I would like to announce that there is an addition to our schedule.
在開始之前，我想要宣布我們有增加一項行程。

point 多益聽力測驗 Part 4 的獨白中，介紹會議或研討會的常見情境之一為「增加行程」。

With her 10 years of experience in marketing, I believe that Annie will be an excellent addition to our team.
安妮有十年的行銷經驗，我相信她的到來將會為我們團隊增加一位出色的成員。

point with + N 意為「伴隨著」。

Test 1

● 一、請寫出下列單字的中文意思。

① consumption ＿＿＿＿＿　⑥ ultimate ＿＿＿＿＿

② performance ＿＿＿＿＿　⑦ advertisement ＿＿＿＿＿

③ backup ＿＿＿＿＿　⑧ commitment ＿＿＿＿＿

④ custom ＿＿＿＿＿　⑨ increase ＿＿＿＿＿

⑤ slogan ＿＿＿＿＿　⑩ campaign ＿＿＿＿＿

● 二、請寫出符合下列句意的單字。

① With the new marketing strategies, Ms. Fultz's restaurant has started to ＿＿＿＿＿.
隨著新的行銷策略，富爾茲女士的餐廳開始蓬勃發展。

② The new system can ＿＿＿＿＿ predict the market demand based on the past sales volume.
新系統能夠根據過去的銷售量來精確預測市場需求。

③ The new policy provides ＿＿＿＿＿ to those who successfully reach their sales goals.
新政策提供獎勵給那些成功達成銷售目標的人。

解答

1. ① 消耗，消耗量　② 表演，績效　③ 備份，替補物；備用的　④ 習俗，慣例；訂做的　⑤ 口號，標語
　　⑥ 最後的，根本的，最重要的　⑦ 廣告，公告　⑧ 承諾，保證，致力於　⑨ 增加，增長
　　⑩ 運動，活動；參加活動
2. ① thrive　② precisely　③ incentives

Test 2

一、請選擇符合下列文意的單字。

Ⓐ awareness	Ⓑ target	Ⓒ disagree
Ⓓ further	Ⓔ neglect	Ⓕ hesitation

① The firm attempted to raise consumers' environmental _____ by reducing the packages of the products, but in vain.

② We will never _____ our customers' needs.

③ The sales believes that increasing professional knowledge can _____ his career.

④ Without any _____, he signed the contract right after he saw the proposal.

⑤ Unfortunately, the sales volume failed to meet our sales _____.

二、請寫出下列片語的中文意思。

① be skillful at	_____	⑤ fail to	_____
② be willing to	_____	⑥ a great deal of	_____
③ carry out	_____	⑦ in vain	_____
④ have access to	_____	⑧ board meeting	_____

解答

1. ① A ② E ③ D ④ F ⑤ B
2. ① 擅長 ② 願意 ③ 執行 ④ 進入；有管道 ⑤ 失敗 ⑥ 大量的 ⑦ 徒勞無功 ⑧ 董事會會議

Chapter 13
社會經濟

以下多益必考單字，你認識哪些？

☐ donate (p.272) ☐ industrial (p.278) ☐ worldwide (p.284)

☐ sponsor (p.275) ☐ architect (p.280) ☐ dedication (p.278)

☐ generous (p.274) ☐ resident (p.281) ☐ description (p.281)

☐ benefit (p.275) ☐ acknowledge (p.287) ☐ volunteer (p.276)

☐ initiate (p.277) ☐ boundary (p.288) ☐ adequate (p.283)

☐ approve (p.279) ☐ citizen (p.284) ☐ funding (p.273)

13 社會經濟

---

01 rate
★
★
[ret]

n 比率，速度，價格，等級

同 speed 速度
　　pace 步速
　　tempo 節奏

Fortunately, the unemployment rate is decreasing.
很幸運地，失業率正在下降。

 point　unemployment rate 意為「失業率」。

We negotiated the rate with the freelance photographer.
我們和那位自由攝影師協商拍攝價錢。

point　freelance (a. / adv.) 從事自由職業的 (n.) 自由職業者 (v.) 當自由職業者。

---

02 range
★
★
[rendʒ]

n 系列，範圍，級別

同 extent 程度
　　scope 範圍

I would appreciate it if you could tell me the price range.
如果你可以告訴我價格範圍，我會很感激。

Applicants for this scholarship are in the 19-22 age range.
這些申請獎學金的申請者年齡介於十九至二十二歲之間。

point　application (n.) 申請，apply for + 事項／職位 (ph.) 申請。

---

03 region
★
★
★
[`ridʒən]

n 地區，領域

同 area 區域
　　territory 領土
　　division 區域
　　section 區域
　　sector 分區

There has been a steady decrease in the unemployment rate in this region.
這個區域的失業率有著很穩定的下降。

point　相關詞彙：district 地區，area 區域，zone 地區。

The authority in this region had difficulty implementing the plan.
此區域的當局在執行計畫上有困難。

point　have difficulty / trouble + Ving 意為「做……有困難」。

---

04 donate
★
★
[`donet]

v 捐獻，贈送

同 give 給予
　　make a donation of 捐贈
　　contribute 捐獻

反 keep 保有
　　receive 收到

The mayor donated $1,000,000 dollars to the orphanage secretly.
市長祕密地捐給孤兒院一百萬元。

They donated all of the proceeds they generated from this event.
他們捐出在這個活動得到的所有營收。

point　proceeds, profits, earnings, returns, income, revenue 皆可表達「營收」。

05 donation
★
★
[do`neʃən]

n 捐獻，捐款，捐贈物

同 contribution 捐獻
handout 捐贈物
grant 授予物
offering 捐獻物

反 receipt 收到

The donation will be used to build a local library.
捐款會被用來蓋當地的圖書館。

The businessman's generous donation rescued many homeless people.
那位商人慷慨的捐款拯救了許多無家可歸的人。

---

06 program
★
★
★
[`progræm]

n 節目，計畫，課程，程式

同 show 表演
scheme 計畫
plan 計畫

衍 programmer (n.) 程式設計師

The TV program is family-oriented.
這個電視節目適合闔家觀賞。

point -oriented 意為「以……為導向的」。

The welfare program is designed to help those unemployed people.
這個福利制度是設計用來幫助那些失業的人們。

---

07 funding
★
★
★
[`fʌndɪŋ]

n 資金，基金

同 money 金錢
capital 資本
fund 資金

Some people suggested that universities should provide more funding to academic resources like libraries.
有些人建議大學應該要提供更多資金給學術資源，例如圖書館。

The project was terminated in that the organization failed to apply for funding from the government.
這個專案被終止了，因為這個組織沒能從政府那裡申請到資金。

point in that (conj.) 因為。

---

08 fundraiser
★
[`fʌnd‚rezɚ]

n 資金籌集人，
資金籌集活動

Mr. Aldridge was appointed as a fundraiser and required to organize a charity event.
艾德里奇先生被指派為資金籌集者，且被要求統籌一個慈善活動。

point be appointed as... 意為「被指派為……」。

The event planner was totally exhausted because he was organizing a fundraiser for the local public library.
這名活動籌劃者累壞了，因為他正在為當地的公立圖書館舉辦資金籌募的活動。

point exhausted = tired (a.) 疲累的。exhausted 疲累的程度比 tired 還高。

273

09 foundation
★
★
[faʊnˈdeʃən]
★

n 創辦，基礎，基金，機構

同 institution 機構

The foundation is established to help the poor.
這個基金會設立的目的是為了幫助窮人。

These rumors are without foundation.
這些謠言沒有根據。

point without foundation 意為「沒有根據」。

---

10 government
★
★
[ˈgʌvɚnmənt]
★

n 政府，政體，管理

同 administration 管理
　　regime 政體
　　authority 當局
　　council 議會
衍 govern (v.) 管理

The final decision will be made by several senior government officials.
幾個政府高級官員會做出最後的決定。

point make a decision 意為「做決定」。

The central government's new policy to raise tariffs on imported cars has greatly influenced several businesses.
中央政府提高進口車關稅的新政策已經大大地影響許多企業。

point 主詞為 The central government's new policy to raise tariffs on imported cars，動詞用單數的 has influenced。

---

11 generous
★
[ˈdʒɛnərəs]

a 慷慨的，寬厚的，豐富的

同 plentiful 豐富的
　　ample 豐富的
反 ungenerous 不大方的
　　stingy 吝嗇的
　　strict 嚴厲的
　　harsh 嚴酷的

The senior manager received a generous pay increase.
那名資深經理得到大幅度加薪。

point pay increase 意為「加薪」。

It was generous of you to help those victims.
你幫助那些災民，心腸真好。

point 相關詞彙：charitable 仁慈的，unselfish 無私的。

---

12 generosity
★
[ˌdʒɛnəˈrɑsətɪ]

n 慷慨，寬大的行為

同 kindness 仁慈
　　charity 仁愛
　　liberality 慷慨
反 selfishness 自私
　　thoughtlessness 不體貼

His generosity to the poor is admired by people.
人們讚嘆他對窮人的慷慨。

point 相關詞彙：liberality 慷慨，generousness 寬大。

The assistant was impressed by his supervisor's generosity.
助理對他上司的慷慨印象深刻。

CH 13

社會經濟

13 sponsor

★
★

['spɑnsɚ]

n 主辦者，贊助者，保證人

v 發起，倡議，贊助

同 supporter (n.) 支持者

The sponsor provided every participant one new cellphone as a reward.
贊助商提供每位參加者一支手機當作獎勵。

The charity concert was sponsored by many businesses in this commercial area.
慈善演唱會是由這個商業區中的許多企業所贊助。

 延伸詞彙：residential area 意為「住宅區」，industrial area 意為「工業區」。

---

14 sponsorship

★

['spɑnsɚˌʃɪp]

n 贊助，資助

同 support 支持
help 幫助
aid 幫助
assistance 協助

The marketing department was looking for sponsorship for the carnival.
行銷部門正在找尋嘉年華會的贊助。

There are many benefits that corporate sponsorship can bring to a company.
企業贊助可以為一間公司帶來很多利益。

---

15 benefactor

★

['bɛnəˌfæktɚ]

n 捐助者，施主，恩人

同 supporter 支持者
donator 捐贈者
patron 贊助者
sponsor 贊助者
contributor 貢獻者

A wealthy benefactor bought several school buses for the small school.
一位很富有的捐助者買了很多台校車給這所小學校。

 wealthy = rich = affluent，意為「富有的」。

The homeless person received financial support from an anonymous benefactor.
這位無家可歸的人收到匿名捐助者的金錢幫助。

---

16 benefit

★
★

['bɛnəfɪt]

n 利益，好處，津貼

v 得益，有益於，受惠

同 advantage (n.) 好處
profit (n.) 益處

反 disadvantage (n.) 缺點

衍 beneficial (a.) 有益的

Employee benefits include a holiday bonus, annual bonus, and compensatory leave.
員工福利包含節慶獎金、年終獎金還有補休。

point 延伸詞彙：sick leave 病假、personal leave 事假、annual leave 特休、marriage leave 婚假。

For those who are laid off can receive unemployment benefit.
那些被解僱的人可以領取失業救濟金。

point be laid off 意為「被解僱」。

17 **volunteer**
★
★
[ˌvɑlənˈtɪr]

n 志願者，義工
v 自願，自願給予
衍 voluntary (a.) 志願的

After retiring from his company, he worked as a volunteer in the hospital.
從公司退休之後，他在醫院當義工。

point work as + 職位頭銜，意為「擔任……」。

Surprisingly, my neighbor volunteered to water my plants while I was out of town.
令人意外地，我的鄰居主動提出要在我出城時幫我的植物澆水。

point out of town 意為「出城」。

18 **renewal**
★
★
[rɪˈnjuəl]

n 更新，復原，繼續
衍 urban renewal
(ph.) 都市環境改造

This letter is to confirm your renewal of the mobile contract.
這封信是來確認你的手機續約。

Urban renewal project will be the focus of today's meeting.
今天的會議焦點將會是都市更新計畫。

19 **recognizable**
★
[ˈrɛkəgˌnaɪzəbl]

a 可辨認的，可承認的
同 visible 看得見的
反 imperceptible 察覺不出的
衍 recognize (v.) 認出
recognition (n.) 識別

The local government decided to build an instantly recognizable landmark in this area.
當地政府決定要在這區域蓋一個一眼就能認出的標誌性建築物。

point 相關詞彙：identifiable 可識別的，noticeable 顯著的，distinguishable 可辨別的，notable 顯著的，observable 顯著的。

The marketing consultant helped his client establish a recognizable brand identity.
行銷顧問幫助他的客戶建立有鑑別度的品牌身分。

point help + O + V 意為「幫助某人做某事」。

20 **apply**
★
★
★
[əˈplaɪ]

v 申請，應用，實施，使起作用
衍 applicant (n.) 申請人
application (n.) 申請
application form
(ph.) 申請表格

He is currently between jobs now and he plans to apply for jobs next month.
他目前失業中，他計劃下個月去求職。

point be between jobs 意為「失業中」。

Due to her excellent academic performance, Liz is qualified to apply for the scholarship.
因為優異的學術表現，莉茲有資格能申請獎學金。

point be qualified to 意為「夠資格」。

CH 13

社會經濟

21 handling
★
[ˋhændlɪŋ]
n 觸摸，操作，管理
同 management 管理
　　conduct 處理

The mayor made his reputation with his handling of the flood.
這名市長因處理水災而聲名大噪。

The reporter interviewed the manager about his handling of the financial crisis.
記者採訪該經理對財務危機的處理方式。

---

22 initiate
★
★
[ɪˋnɪʃˌet]
v 開始，創始，開始實施
同 start off (ph.) 開始
　　launch (v.) 開始
　　establish (v.) 設立
反 complete (v.) 完成
　　finish (v.) 結束

The executive committee promised to initiate a charity concert.
執行委員會承諾發起慈善演唱會。

A series of reforms will be initiated to improve quality of life.
將會發起一連串的改革以改進生活品質。

point a series of 意為「一連串」。

---

23 initiative
★
★
[ɪˋnɪʃətɪv]
n 主動，進取心，新作法
a 開始的，初步的
衍 take the initiative (ph.) 採取主動

The volunteer took an initiative part in the beach cleanup activities.
義工主動參加淨灘活動。

point take part in 意為「參加；出席」。

The sales might not be qualified for the position due to his lack of initiative.
這名業務可能不適合這個職位，因為他缺乏進取心。

---

24 insure
★
[ɪnˋʃur]
v 保證，確保，投保
同 assure 擔保
　　guarantee 保證
衍 insurance (n.) 保險

The bracelet is insured for 1 million dollars.
該手鐲投保了一百萬元。

point 常見首飾：earrings 意為「耳環」，necklace 意為「項鍊」。

Some insurance companies are reluctant to insure old people.
有些保險公司不願意為老人提供保險。

point be reluctant to 意為「不願意」，be willing to 意為「願意」。

Chapter 124

13 社會經濟

25 responsible
★
★
★
[rɪ`spɑnsəbḷ]

a 需負責的，負責任的

同 trustworthy 值得信賴的
reliable 可依賴的
dependable 可依靠的

反 irresponsible 無責任感的
untrustworthy 不可信賴的

The responsible wedding planner organized everything well.
負責任的婚禮顧問把每件事情都統籌得很完善。

Creating socially responsible image **is** considerably **beneficial to** a business.
創造對社會負責的形象是對一個企業相當有益的。

point be beneficial to 意為「有益的」。

---

26 dedication
★
★
[ˌdɛdə`keʃən]

n 奉獻，專心致力，
奉獻精神

同 loyalty 忠誠
faithfulness 忠實

反 laziness 懶惰
indifference 冷漠

衍 dedicate (v.) 奉獻

The city council's **dedication** to the town's economy was admirable.
市議會對這個城鎮經濟的付出令人敬佩。

point 相關詞彙：commitment 獻身，devotion 奉獻，devotedness 奉獻，wholeheartedness 全心全意。

The candidate showed dedication and **loyalty** to his job.
求職者在工作上展現了奉獻及忠誠。

point dedication（奉獻）和 loyalty（忠誠）為求職廣告中常見描述求職者的正向辭彙。

---

27 damage
★
★
★
[`dæmɪdʒ]

n 損失，賠償金

v 損害，毀壞

同 harm (v.) 傷害
destruction (n.) 破壞

反 repair (v.) 修復
improve (v.) 改善

The foundation is restoring the building damaged by the earthquake.
這個組織正在恢復被地震毀損的建築。

Drinking too much has caused serious damage to his liver.
喝太多酒使他的肝嚴重受損。

---

28 industrial
★
★
★
[ɪn`dʌstrɪəl]

a 工業的，產業的

n 工業公司

同 manufacturing (n.) 工業

衍 industrious (a.) 勤奮的

An industrial design coffee shop just opened in my neighborhood.
我家附近有間工業風咖啡廳才剛開幕。

The industrial designer **aimed to** design approachable products.
這名工業設計師旨在設計平易近人的產品。

point aim to + V 意為「瞄準；目的在於……」。

CH 13

社會經濟

29 **industry**
★
★
★ **n** 工業，企業，勤勉
同 business 企業
trade 商業
field 專業

The experienced foreman has worked in the construction industry over the past two decades.
這名經驗豐富的工頭已經在建築業做了二十年。

The economy of Las Vegas heavily relies on the tourism industry.
拉斯維加斯的經濟大大地仰賴旅遊業。

 rely on = depend on，意為「依賴」。

30 **industrialize**
★ [ɪn`dʌstrɪəˌlaɪz]
★
v 使工業化
衍 industrialized countries (ph.) 工業化國家

The government decided to industrialize more rapidly.
政府決定要更快速地工業化。

Many rural areas in this nation have begun to industrialize since 1875.
這個國家的很多鄉村地區自從一八七五年已開始工業化。

31 **approve**
★ [ə`pruv]
★
★
★ **v** 贊成，認可，讚許
同 accept 接受
agree 同意
support 支持
admire 讚賞
反 reject 拒絕
deny 否認
衍 approval (n.) 贊成

Lia's parents finally approve that she could go to the summer camp overseas.
麗亞的父母終於贊同她可以去海外的夏令營。

 overseas 可當形容詞和副詞，此處當副詞。當形容詞常見的搭配為 overseas market 海外市場、overseas student 外國留學生、overseas company 海外公司。

The city council didn't approve the plan, so many people will go on strike next week to show their positions.
市議會沒有批准這項計畫，因此很多人下週會罷工來表明他們的立場。

 stand, standpoint 皆可表達「立場」。

32 **commit**
★ [kə`mɪt]
v 做，犯罪，承諾，託付
同 carry out 實行
perform 履行
effect 實現
accomplish 實現
衍 committed (a.) 忠誠的

The single mother committed her entire life to taking care of her disabled child.
這名單親媽媽投注她的一生照顧她那個有殘缺的孩子。

 commit time / money to + Ving 意為「投入時間或金錢做……」。

The government was requested to commit to holding international sport events.
政府被要求致力於辦理國際運動活動。

279

Chapter 125

13 社會經濟

---

33 habitat ★
[`hæbə,tæt]
n 棲息地，產地
同 home 家園
　 habitation 住所

Deforestation will seriously influence the habitat of many creatures.
砍伐森林將會嚴重影響很多生物的棲息地。

The foundation aims to preserve natural habitats for wild animals.
這機構旨在保護野生動物的自然居住地。

---

34 architect ★ ★
[`ɑrkə,tɛkt]
n 建築師，設計師
同 designer 設計師

In addition to designing, the architect is excellent in photography as well.
除了設計，這名建築師也很擅長攝影。

(point) as well = too，意為「也是」。

Due to environmental concerns, the architect is inclined to design green buildings.
因為環境議題，這位建築師傾向於設計綠建築。

(point) be inclined to 意為「傾向於」。

---

35 architecture ★ ★
[`ɑrkə,tɛktʃɚ]
n 建築學，建築風格，建築物
同 construction 建築
　 structure 建築物
　 building 建築物

The style of the architecture is highly regarded by many designers worldwide.
這個建築風格被世界各國的設計師高度推崇。

(point) be highly regarded 意為「被高度推崇」，這樣的詞彙若在選項中用 popular（受歡迎的）也是同義。

We can see several examples of Japanese architecture in Taiwan because Taiwan used to be colonized by Japan.
我們可以在台灣看到許多日式建築範例，因為台灣過去被日本殖民。

(point) 兩句話時態不同，第一句為事實，用現在式。第二句為過去的事實，用過去式。

---

36 according ★ ★ ★
[ə`kɔrdɪŋ]
a 相符的，和諧的
衍 accord (v.) 符合

According to the research, the unemployment rate is gradually rising.
根據研究，失業率逐漸上漲。

Jane will be late for the board meeting due to the delay of her flight according to her secretary.
根據珍的祕書所說，因為班機的延誤，珍將會晚到委員會會議。

(point) 會議常見字：take meeting minutes 做會議紀錄，meeting agenda 會議議程。

37 construction

[kənˋstrʌkʃən]

n 建築物，建造，構造，
意義

衍 construct (v.) 建造
reconstruction (n.) 重建

Workers are repaving the road in the construction site.
工人們正在鋪工地的路。

point repave the road = resurface the road 表示「鋪路」，為多益測驗圖片題中常見的情境。

My niece has been working in the construction industry for 10 years.
我的姪女已經在建築業工作十年了。

point nephew 表示「姪子」，industry 表示「工業；產業」。

---

38 resident

[ˋrɛzədənt]

n 居民，定居者
a 居住的，內在的
同 inhabitant (n.) 居民
dweller (n.) 居住者
衍 residence (n.) 居住

The residents of the small town are expecting the new fitness center which will be completed in 2 months.
小鎮的居民正期待著兩個月內即將完工的健身中心。

point will be completed 為未來被動式，表示「將會被完成」。

Residents should attend the annual neighborhood assembly to vote for the new policy.
居民應該要參加一年一度的里民大會來為新政策投票。

point vote for + sth. 意為「為某事投票」。

---

39 residential

[͵rɛzəˋdɛnʃəl]

a 居住的，住宅的，
學生住宿的
同 domiciliary 住宅的
反 nonresidential 非居住的

Many people hold the opinion that nuclear power plants should not be built in residential areas.
很多人抱持著核電廠不該建造在住宅區的想法。

point hold the opinion, think, suggest, indicate 都可作為「認為；指出；表示」。

It is rather normal that rents in business districts are higher than the ones in residential areas.
商業區房子的租金比住宅區還高是相當正常的。

---

40 description

[dɪˋskrɪpʃən]

n 描寫，敘述，種類
同 explanation 說明
illustration 說明
衍 describe (v.) 形容
subscription (n.) 訂閱
prescription (n.) 處方箋

When the victim was interviewed, he gave the reporter a detailed description.
當受災戶被採訪時，他對記者做出詳細的描述。

A job description of this position is also included in the advertisement.
這個職位的工作描述也包含在廣告中。

13 社會經濟

---

41 reputation
★
[ˌrɛpjəˈteʃən]

n 名譽，名聲，聲望
同 fame 名聲

The company has a good reputation since it donates money to the charities on a regular basis.
這間公司有很好的名聲，因為它會定時捐款給慈善機構。

(point) on a regular basis = regularly，意為「經常地」。

The business has a worldwide reputation for having complete and well-organized employee benefits.
這家公司完整且有架構的員工福利譽滿全球。

(point) benefits 在此句為「福利」的意思，一般常用來表示「利益；好處」。

---

42 affect
★
★
[əˈfɛkt]

v 影響，使感動，罹患
同 impact 產生影響
infect 傳染
move 使感動
touch 使感動

Those who inhabit coastal villages are easily affected by typhoons.
住在海邊村莊的人們很容易被颱風影響。

Business executives revealed thousands of employees would be deeply affected once the new policy was implemented.
主管透露一旦實施新政策，成千上萬名員工將會深深被影響。

(point) thousand 當單位詞時不加 s，例如 six thousand 意為「六千」。

---

43 nationality
★
[ˌnæʃəˈnælətɪ]

n 國籍，民族
同 citizenship 公民身分
衍 nation (n.) 國家
national (a.) 國際的

Citizens who have dual nationality are forbidden to apply for this scholarship.
有雙重國籍的市民不能申請這項獎學金。

(point) forbid, ban, prohibit 意為「禁止」。

The Sociology course consists of students of five different nationalities.
社會學這堂課由五種不同國籍的學生所組成。

(point) consist of, compose, contain, comprise, constitute 皆可指「組成」。

---

44 strike
★
[straɪk]

n 打擊，罷工，攻擊

A large-scale strike is being held in front of the city hall.
大型的罷工正在市政廳前方舉行。

(point) large-scale 意為「大型規模的」。

The strike has seriously influenced thousands of passengers to Paris.
罷工已經嚴重地影響上千名前往巴黎的乘客。

45 adequate

★ [`ædəkwɪt]

🅐 足夠的，適當的，
差強人意的

🔄 enough 足夠的
sufficient 足夠的
suitable 適合的

🔄 inadequate 不適當的
insufficient 不足夠的

The chairman of the company took adequate measures to solve the urgent problem.
董事長採取適當的措施去解決這個緊急的問題。

point measure 在此句為名詞「方法」的意思，也可當動詞「測量」，例如 measure the height of the wall 意為「測量牆的高度」

The welfare program for the elderly in this small town is barely adequate.
這小鎮針對年長者的福利計畫不多。

point barely 意為「幾乎不」，具有否定意味，其同義字為 scarcely, hardly, rarely。

46 urban

★ [`ɝbən]

🅐 城市的，居住在城市

🔄 modern 現代的

🔄 rural 鄉村的

衍 urbanize (v.) 都市化

The urban facilities in this city are maintained regularly.
這個城市的設施都會被定期維修。

point frequently, usually, often, repeatedly 都表示「經常地」。

To pursue better job opportunities, many people move to urban areas.
為了追求更好的工作機會，很多人搬進市區。

point job opportunity 單純指工作機會；但 job offer 為已被錄取的工作邀約或機會。

47 enlarge

★ [ɪn`lɑrdʒ]

🅥 擴大，放大照片，詳述

🔄 magnify 放大

🔄 reduce 減少
diminish 減少

衍 enlargement (n.) 擴大

Meg enlarges her English vocabulary by listening to English songs and watching TV series.
梅格藉由聽英文歌及看影集來擴大英文詞彙量。

point 相關詞彙：expand 擴展，broaden 擴大，amplify 增強。

The police officer enlarged the photo to speculate who might be the possible suspect.
警察放大照片來推敲誰是可能的嫌疑犯。

point suspect (n.) 嫌疑犯；(v.) 懷疑。

48 agricultural

★ [ˌægrɪ`kʌltʃərəl]

🅐 農業的，務農的

衍 agricultural show
(ph.) 農業博覽會
agriculture (n.) 農業

The agricultural development in this town has progressed dramatically.
這個城鎮的農業發展進步很大。

He is proficient in agricultural knowledge.
他專精於農業知識。

point be proficient in 意為「專精於」。

283

13 社會經濟

49 immigrant
★
[`ɪməgrənt]
n 移民，僑民
a 移民的，移入的
同 foreigner (n.) 外國人
　　settler (n.) 移居者
反 emigrant (n.) 移出者
衍 immigrate (v.) 移民

There are **a variety of** restaurants in this district since many immigrants from different nations settle down here.
這區有很多不同種類的餐廳，因為很多來自不同國家的移民在這裡定居。

point a variety of = various，意為「多樣化的」。

We **are qualified to** apply for immigrant visas.
我們符合申請移民簽證的資格。

point be qualified to + N / V 意為「具有……的資格」。

---

50 worldwide
★
★
[`wɜld.waɪd]
a 全球的，世界的
ad 在全世界
同 global (a.) 全球的
　　international (a.) 國際的
　　universal (a.) 全球的
反 local (a.) 當地的

The influence of a worldwide recession is considerable.
全世界經濟衰退的影響很大。

The **merger** of the two companies made headlines worldwide.
兩家公司的合併成為全球性的頭條新聞。

point 易混淆字：merge (v.) merger (n.) 合併／ acquire (v.) acquisition (n.) 收購。

---

51 civil
★
[`sɪv!]
a 平民的，國民的

The mayor of the city indicated that voting is a **civil right**.
市長指出投票是公民的權利。

point civil right 意為「公民權利」。

My best friend is a **civil servant**.
我最好的朋友是一位公務人員。

point civil servant = public servant，意為「公務人員」。

---

52 citizen
★
★
[`sɪtəzṇ]
n 市民，公民，居民
同 civilian 市民
　　inhabitant 居民
　　resident 居民
　　native 原住民

The amusement park provides discounts for **senior citizens**.
這間遊樂園提供老年人折扣優惠。

point senior citizen 為對年長者較有禮貌的說法。

How to **apply to** become a U.S. citizen?
要如何申請成為美國公民？

point apply to + 單位／ apply for + 職位；想要的東西。例：I apply to the bank for a loan.（我向銀行申請貸款。）

53 **citizenship**
★
[ˈsɪtəznˌʃɪp]
n 公民權，公民身分

The government took his citizenship away.
政府取消了他的國籍。
(point) take away 意為「取消；奪走」。

After living in that country for 10 years, he finally gained citizenship.
居住在那個國家十年後，他終於取得公民身分。

54 **downtown**
★
★
[ˌdaunˈtaun]
n 城市商業區，鬧區
ad 在城市商業區，
在市中心
同 city center (ph.) 市中心
反 uptown (n.) 住宅區

The public transportation downtown usually is significantly advanced than the one in rural areas.
市中心的大眾運輸通常都會比鄉村區域更加進步。
(point) significantly 表示「重要地；較大地」，常在多益測驗中修飾形容詞。

Property rental downtown is gradually increasing due to the establishment of the new shopping mall and subway line.
因為新建立的購物商城及地鐵線，商業區的租金逐漸上漲。
(point) 延伸詞彙：rent 租金、landlord 房東、tenant 房客、tenancy 租期。

55 **remote**
★
★
[rɪˈmot]
a 遙遠的，冷淡的，遙控的
同 distant 遠的
far 遠的
反 near 近的
close 接近的

The remote control was broken so I could not use it to switch channels.
遙控器壞掉了，所以我沒辦法使用它來切換頻道。
(point) 表示東西壞掉，還可以用這些形容詞：defective 有缺陷的、out of order 發生故障。

Aboriginals who live in remote areas are more likely to preserve their cultures and customs.
住在遙遠地區的原住民比較有可能保存他們的文化及習俗。
(point) 延伸詞彙：customs 複數形式為「海關」。

56 **pollute**
★
[pəˈlut]
v 污染，弄髒，敗壞
同 contaminate 汙染
infect 感染
反 purify 淨化
衍 pollution (n.) 汙染

Riding bicycles will not pollute the air, but driving cars will.
騎腳踏車不會汙染空氣，但開車會。

Chemical waste from upstream polluted the river badly.
來自上游的化學廢料嚴重污染了河川。
(point) 延伸詞彙：downstream 意為「下游」。

285

57 alley
★ [ˋælɪ]

n 小巷，胡同，小徑
同 lane 小巷
  corridor 通道
  path 小徑
  aisle 通道

The alley was not well-lit, so the government installed some street lights.
這條小巷光線不佳，所以政府安裝了一些路燈。

point well-lit 意為「光線充足」。

Your suggestions will only lead us down a blind alley.
你的建議根本行不通。

point blind alley 意為「死胡同；行不通的方法」。

---

58 geography
★ [ˋdʒɪˋɑɡrəfɪ]

n 地理學，地形，地勢
衍 geographic (a.) 地理的
  geographical (a.) 地理的

I read the National Geographic Magazine yesterday and it brought me some new insights about the geography of the province.
我昨天讀了國家地理頻道雜誌，這讓我對於這個省的地理有些新的想法。

The tour guide majored in Geography, which makes his introduction more professional than other tour guides.
這名導遊是地理系，這讓他的介紹比其他導遊更加專業。

point major in 意指「主修⋯⋯科系」。

---

59 variation
★ [ˌvɛrɪˋeʃən]
★

n 變化，差別，變異
同 kind 種類
  sort 分類
  type 類型
衍 variety (n.) 多樣化

With the increasing number of nonnative English speakers, there are more and more variations of pronouncing the same word.
隨著使用英語的非母語人士數量的增加，同一個字發音的變異也越來越多。

point with 表示「隨著」。

We can observe the price variation of food before and after a typhoon.
我們可以觀察到颱風前後食物價格的變動。

---

60 involvement
★ [ɪnˋvɑlvmənt]

n 參與，牽連，財政困難
同 participation 參加
衍 involve (v.) 牽涉

To successfully carry out the plan, we need people's involvement.
為了成功執行計畫，我們需要人民的投入。

After investigation, the police found that the deal didn't include any political parties involvement.
經過調查後，警察發現沒有任何政黨參與這筆交易。

CH 13

社會經濟

61 acknowledge

★ [əkˋnɑlɪdʒ]

Ⅴ 承認，表示感謝，打招呼

同 recognize 認可

　　admit 承認

反 deny 否認

The victim of the typhoon wrote a letter to the charity to acknowledge their help.

某位颱風受災戶的災民寫了一封信感謝這間慈善機構的幫助。

point acknowledge one's help 意為「感謝某人的幫助」。

She is widely acknowledged to be one of our best actresses.

她被廣泛地認為是最棒的女演員之一。

point be acknowledged = be recognized，意為「被認可」。

---

62 acknowledgement

★ [əkˋnɑlɪdʒmənt]

ⓝ 承認，致謝，確認

同 recognition 承認

反 denial 否認

The celebrity made no formal acknowledgement of his scandal.

該位名人沒有正式承認他的醜聞。

point formal 意為「正式的」。相反詞為 less formal（不那麼正式），或是 casual（非正式的）。

We sent the company a certificate in acknowledgment of their effort for the society.

我們寄給這間公司一張感謝狀，以感謝他們對這社會所做的努力。

point in acknowledgment of 意為「以感謝」。

---

63 adopt

★

★ [əˋdɑpt]

Ⅴ 採取，收養，接受

同 accept 接受

　　embrace 欣然接受

反 refuse 拒絕

　　reject 拒絕

衍 adoption (n.) 採用

The couple decided to adopt a child from Africa.

這對夫妻決定要從非洲領養小孩。

Since there are a lot of stray dogs on the streets, it would be better if you could adopt dogs but not purchase them.

因為現在街上有很多流浪狗，如果你能夠用領養代替購買會很棒。

point it would be better if you 意為「如果你⋯⋯這樣將會很好」。

---

64 acquisitive

★ [əˋkwɪzətɪv]

ⓐ 渴望得到的，貪婪的，自私的

同 greedy 貪心的

　　materialistic 功利主義的

衍 acquire (v.) 獲得

　　acquisition (n.) 獲得

He is acquisitive of fortune and fame.

他十分貪財及渴望名聲。

point fortune (n.) 一大筆錢；命運。make a fortune 意為「賺大錢」。

Most people judge a person by his or her salary since we live in an acquisitive society.

很多人用一個人的薪水來判斷這個人，因為我們生活在一個求取功利的社會中。

Chapter 129

13 社會經濟

---

65 **assurance**
★
★ [əˋʃurəns]

n 保證，把握，信心

同 guarantee 保證

衍 assure (v.) 保證

Despite the government's repeated assurances that the unemployment rate would not rise, many people have doubts about it.
儘管政府不斷保證失業率不會上升，很多人抱持著懷疑的態度。

point despite = in spite of + N，意指「儘管；雖然」。

The candidate was hired because he was experienced and also he spoke with calm assurance.
這名求職者被僱用的原因是他很有經驗，而且說話時冷靜而自信。

---

66 **behave**
★ [bɪˋhev]

v 表現，表現良好，起作用

同 conduct oneself well
表現良好
act properly 表現得體
show good manners
展現禮貌

She was chosen to be the role model because she always behaves like an elegant lady.
她被票選為模範，因為她的行為舉止總是像個優雅的女性。

The police were admired by the people in this small town because they behaved courageously in the face of danger.
警察被小鎮的人們擁戴，因為他們面對危險時表現得十分勇敢。

---

67 **boundary**
★ [ˋbaundrɪ]

n 邊界，界線，範圍

同 border 邊界
frontier 邊境
borderline 邊界

The bridge marks the boundary between the two cities.
這座橋是兩個城市的分界線。

point mark the boundary 意為「劃下分界線」。

Building a power plant within the city boundary might not be a good suggestion.
把發電廠建在市區內可能不是一個好建議。

---

68 **subside**
★ [səbˋsaɪd]

v 消退，平息，下沉

同 lessen 減少
soften 變弱

反 intensify 加強
worsen 惡化

These effects will not subside until the government makes an official announcement.
這些影響不會停止，直到政府做出官方宣布。

point 相關詞彙：alleviate 減輕，fade 褪去，weaken 變弱，decline 衰退，terminate 結束。

As time goes by, public criticisms gradually subside.
隨著時間的流逝，大眾的批評逐漸消失。

CH 13

社會經濟

---

69 **anxiety**
★
[æŋˋzaɪətɪ]

🄝 焦慮，掛念，渴望

🄟 fear 害怕
　nervousness 緊張
　tension 緊繃
　stress 壓力

🄬 anxious (a.) 焦慮的

The high unemployment **rate** has caused us much anxiety.
高度的失業率使我們極為擔心。

(point) rate (n.) 速率；費用。要記得也有「費用」的意思，多益常考。

The contract workers felt a lot of anxiety about the **performance evaluation**.
契約工對績效評估感到非常不安。

(point) performance evaluation 意為「績效評估」。

---

70 **amplify**
★
★
[ˋæmpləˌfaɪ]

🅅 放大，擴大，詳述

🄟 magnify 放大
　escalate 上升

🄰 reduce 減少
　quieten 使安靜

Some local residents **objected to** the noises from amplified music concerts.
有些當地居民反對使用擴音演唱會的噪音。

(point) object to 意為「反對」。

The graduate's anxiety seemed to be **amplified** since the graduation season was approaching.
因為畢業季的接近，畢業生的焦慮似乎被放大了。

(point) 相關詞彙：increase 增加，raise 提高，heighten 升高。

---

71 **national**
★
★
[ˋnæʃənl̩]

🄰 國家的，國民的

🄝 國民，國人

🄟 state (a.) 國家的
　civic (a.) 公民的
　domestic (a.) 國內的

🄰 local (a.) 本地的
　international (a.) 國際的

During National Holiday periods, flight tickets are **considerably** more expensive than usual.
在國慶假日期間，機票都比平常貴得多。

(point) considerably (adv.) 相當，非常。用來強調比較級的程度。

The aborigines wear traditional national costume on special **occasions**.
原住民在特別場合穿傳統的民族服裝。

(point) occasion 意為「場合；時機」，搭配 on 這個介係詞。

---

72 **union**
★
★
[ˋjunjən]

🄝 一致，聯盟，工會

🄟 association 公會
　trade union 貿易聯盟
　alliance 同盟
　league 聯盟

The union always defends their member's jobs and rights.
公會總是捍衛會員的工作及權利。

The union **launched a** huge **strike** and it seriously caused traffic problems.
公會發動了一場大型罷工，造成嚴重的交通問題。

(point) launch a strike 意為「發動罷工」。

73 **majority**
★
★ [mə`dʒɔrətɪ]
- n 大多數，成人
- 同 bulk 大量
  mass 大量
- 反 minority 少數
- 衍 major (a.) 主要的

The majority of participants showed a positive attitude toward e-learning.
大部分的參與者對於線上學習有很正向的態度。

point show a positive attitude 意為「展現正向態度」。

Surprisingly, contrary to what the committee expected, the vast majority of citizens approved of the proposal.
出乎意料地，和委員會預期的相反，很大一部分的市民同意這個提議。

point approve of 意為「贊成；同意」，approve 意為「核准」。

74 **legalize**
★ [`ligḷͺaɪz]
- V 使合法化
- 同 admit 承認
  authorize 授權
- 反 prohibit 禁止
- 衍 legitimate (a.) 合法的
  legitimize (v.) 使合法

So far, gambling has not been legalized by the government.
到目前為止，政府還沒讓賭博合法化。

The authority is considering legalizing recreational marijuana.
當局正在考慮將娛樂用大麻合法化。

point consider + Ving 意為「考慮做……」。

75 **fund**
★
★ [fʌnd]
★
- n 資金，存款
- V 提供資金，積累
- 同 finance (v.) 籌措資金
  capitalize (v.) 供給資本
  sponsor (v.) 贊助
  subsidize (v.) 資助

The event planner is responsible for organizing the fund-raising dinner herself.
活動策畫者自己要負責統籌募款晚宴。

point be responsible for = be in charge of，意為「負責」。

The construction was prolonged due to the shortage of funds and severe weather.
因為缺少資金及惡劣的天氣，這個工程被延誤了。

76 **population**
★
★ [ͺpɑpjə`leʃən]
★
- n 人口，全部居民，總數

Ever since last year, the population of the city has been decreasing.
自從去年以來，城市的人口就一直在下降。

point Ever since 意為「自從」，常與完成式連用。

Due to convenient public transportation and well-organized welfare programs, the population of the city has risen gradually.
因為便利的大眾交通及完善的福利制度，城市的人口逐漸上升。

Question

以下題目完全擬真新制多益 Part 5，請選出最符合句意的選項。

1. We negotiated the ------- with the freelance photographer.

   (A) worldwide　　(B) approve　　(C) rate　　(D) dedication

2. The authority in this region had difficulty ------- the plan.

   (A) to implement　　　　(B) implementing

   (C) implement　　　　　(D) implementation

3. Property rental downtown is gradually increasing ------- the establishment of the new shopping mall and subway line.

   (A) due to　　(B) since　　(C) as　　(D) because

4. Mr. Gasol has received unemployment ------- for three months ever since he was laid off.

   (A) variation　　　　　(B) infrastructure

   (C) alley　　　　　　　(D) subsidy

5. The project was terminated in that the organization failed to apply for ------- from the government.

   (A) funding　　　　　(B) involvement

   (C) sponsor　　　　　(D) fundraiser

6. The charity concert was sponsored by many ------- in this commercial area.

   (A) enlarges　　(B) adopts　　(C) generous　　(D) businesses

>> 正確答案與解析請翻至下一頁查看

Answer

🔘 **正確答案與解析**

1. 我們和那位自由攝影師協商拍攝價錢。
   (A) 全世界的　　　(B) 贊成　　　　(C) 速度，價格　(D) 奉獻
   正確答案 (C)

2. 此區域的當局在執行計畫上有困難。
   (B) 執行（動詞進行式），have difficulty + Ving 意為「有……困難」
   正確答案 (B)

3. 因為新建立的購物商城及地鐵線，商業區的租金逐漸上漲。
   (A) 因為 (prep.) + N / Ving　　　　(B) 因為 (conj.) + S + V
   (C) 因為 (conj.) + S + V　　　　　(D) 因為 (conj.) + S + V
   正確答案 (A)

4. 自從蓋索先生失業以來，他已經拿失業補貼金三個月了。
   (A) 變化　　　(B) 基礎設施　　　(C) 小巷　　　(D) 津貼
   正確答案 (D)

5. 這個專案被終止了，因為這個組織沒能從政府那裡申請到資金。
   (A) 資金　　　(B) 參與　　　(C) 贊助商　　　(D) 資金籌集人
   正確答案 (A)

6. 慈善演唱會是由這個商業區中的許多企業所贊助。
   (A) 擴大　　　(B) 採用　　　(C) 大方的　　　(D) 企業
   正確答案 (D)

Chapter 14
餐飲住宿

以下多益必考單字，你認識哪些？

- [ ] accommodate (p.294)
- [ ] specialize (p.300)
- [ ] combine (p.302)
- [ ] advanced (p.299)
- [ ] consequently (p.309)
- [ ] several (p.311)

- [ ] especially (p.308)
- [ ] typical (p.310)
- [ ] expertise (p.297)
- [ ] average (p.302)
- [ ] indoors (p.308)
- [ ] distinctive (p.303)

- [ ] sensible (p.311)
- [ ] particular (p.312)
- [ ] assist (p.299)
- [ ] firm (p.298)
- [ ] reservation (p.294)
- [ ] steady (p.302)

Chapter 131

14 餐飲住宿

01 accommodate
★
★ [əˋkɑməˏdet]
★ ☑ 能容納，適應，提供
同 provide 提供
    supply 供給
    adapt 適應
    adjust 調整

The newly renovated hostel can accommodate up to 100 people.
新裝修的青年旅館可以容納高達一百人。
point up to 意為「高達」。

The bank accommodated the applicants with loans.
銀行提供給申請人貸款。
point accommodate sb. (with sth.) 意為「提供某人（某事物）；幫某人的忙」。

02 accommodation
★
★ [əˏkɑməˋdeʃən]
★ ⋂ 適應，調節，住處
同 housing 住房
    lodging 寄宿
    residence 居住
    arrangement 安排
    adaptation 適應

The hotel manager said they could not provide accommodation for 200 people at such short notice.
旅館經理說沒有辦法在臨時通知的狀況下提供兩百人的住處。

Please inform us of your travel plan so that we can arrange accommodation for you.
請通知我們您的旅遊計畫，如此一來，我們才能幫您安排住宿。
point inform sb. of sth. 意為「通知某人某事」。

03 reserve
★
★ [rɪˋzɝv]
☑ 儲備，保留，預約
⋂ 儲備物，儲備金
同 keep 保留
    preserve 保存
    store 儲存
    retain 保留

The largest conference room has been reserved for the annual meeting.
最大的會議室已經被預訂給年度會議使用。
point annual (a.) 每年的，annually (adv.) 每年地。

The school plans to bring students to the nature reserve for their field trip.
這所學校計劃帶學生到自然保育區戶外教學。
point 此句的 reserve 為名詞「保護區」的意思。

04 reservation
★
★ [ˏrɛzɚˋveʃən]
★ ⋂ 保留，預訂（房間、座位），保護區
同 booking 預訂

After I booked a hotel room online and paid for it by credit card, I called the hotel to confirm my reservation.
在上線上訂房並用信用卡付款後，我打給飯店確認我的訂房。
point 易混淆字：confirm (v.) 確認／conform (v.) 遵從。

Should you have any problems about your reservation, feel free to contact us.
如果你有任何關於預約的問題，敬請聯絡我們。
point should = if，意為「如果」。contact 後面不能加 with。

CH 14

餐飲住宿

05 tenant
★
[`tɛnənt]

n 房客，承租人，住戶

衍 landlord (n.) 房東

The tenant finally decided to extend the rental lease.
房客最後決定要延長租約。

The tenant transferred the monthly rent to the landlord's account.
房客匯每月房租到房東的帳戶。

point transfer money to 意為「轉帳給……」。

06 cafeteria
★
★
★
[ˌkæfəˈtɪrɪə]

n 自助餐館

同 restaurant 餐廳
dining hall 餐廳

衍 café (n.) 小餐館
buffet (n.) 自助餐

The staff in the new cafeteria is very efficient. I got my food soon after I finished my order.
新餐館的員工相當有效率，我一點完餐就拿到我的食物了。

point soon after 意為「不久之後」，在此句當連接詞。

I am craving for today's special in that cafeteria near our company. Do you want to come with me?
我很想吃在公司附近的那家自助餐館的今日特餐。你要跟我一起去嗎？

point be craving for + N / Ving 意為「渴望；想要……」。

07 landmark
★
★
[ˈlændˌmɑrk]

n 地標，里程碑

同 turning point 轉捩點
milestone 里程碑
monument 紀念碑

The travel guide introduced the top 10 landmarks in the world.
導遊介紹了世界前十大地標。

The restaurant is usually fully booked because it is located near the main landmarks.
這間餐廳常常會全部被訂滿，因為它坐落於幾個主要地標旁。

08 charge
★
★
★
[tʃɑrdʒ]

n 費用，掌管，責任
v 收費，控告，充電

同 accuse (v.) 指控

Do you charge an extra fee for this service?
這服務有額外收費嗎？

point additional fee 也等於「額外的費用」。

These guidebooks are free of charge.
這些旅遊書免費。

point be free of charge 意為「免費」。

09 cater
★
★ [`ketɚ]
★
Ⅴ 承辦宴席，迎合
同 provide 提供
　supply 供給
　serve 服務

The new company provides customized service to cater for customers' particular needs.
那家新公司提供的客製化服務符合消費者的特殊需求。

point customized、custom-made、tailor-made 都可表達「客製化的」。

It's rather difficult for a novel to cater for many different tastes.
一本小說要能滿足觀眾的不同愛好是相當難的事情。

point taste 在此句當作品味。taste of the food 意為「食物的味道」。

---

10 catering
★
★ [`ketərɪŋ]
★
ｎ 提供飲食及服務

Mayson restaurant is responsible for the catering of my daughter's wedding.
梅森餐廳負責辦理我女兒的婚禮外燴。

point be responsible for = be in charge of + N / Ving，意為「負責」。

Since we don't have enough budget for our trip, we should find a self-catering accommodation.
因為我們沒有足夠的旅遊預算，所以我們必須找到有提供煮菜設備的住處。

point self-catering 意為「自理飲食的」。

---

11 recommendation
★
★ [ˌrɛkəmɛnˋdeʃən]
★
ｎ 推薦（信），建議，優點
同 advice 建議
　suggestion 建議
　proposal 提議

Thanks to the tour guide's recommendation, we had a wonderful dinner.
幸虧有導遊的推薦，我們享用了一頓美好的晚餐。

point thanks to + N / Ving 意為「幸虧；因為……」。

The manager made recommendations to the engineer's report.
經理對這名工程師的報告提出建議。

---

12 recommend
★
★ [ˌrɛkəˋmɛnd]
★
Ⅴ 推薦，建議，使受歡迎
同 advocate 主張
　endorse 贊同
　commend 推薦
　nominate 提名
反 reject 拒絕

The local people recommended us some delicious but not famous restaurants.
當地人推薦給我們好吃但不有名的餐廳。

I recommend having a physical checkup once a year.
我建議一年去一次健康檢查。

point recommend + Ving 意為「建議做……」。

13 **chef**

★
[ʃɛf]

n 主廚，廚師

同 cook 廚師

In this workshop, the chef will demonstrate a variety of authentic Mexican dishes.

在這個工作坊中，廚師將會展示不同的道地墨西哥料理。

point a variety of = various，意為「不同的」。

The chef apprentice has good culinary skills.

那位廚師學徒有很棒的烹調技術。

point culinary (a.) 烹飪的。

---

14 **serve**

★
★
★
[sɜv]

v 為……服務，供應，任職，招待

同 work for 為……工作
be employed by 被僱用
have a job with 與……工作

The food served in the restaurant is average.

那家餐廳供應的食物很普通。

point served 前面省略了 which is。

I think the bill is due tomorrow, if my memory serves me right.

如果我沒記錯的話，我想帳單是明天到期。

point if my memory serves me right 意為「如果我沒記錯的話」。

---

15 **preference**

★
★
[ˋprɛfərəns]

n 喜好，偏愛，優先權

同 choice 選擇

衍 prefer (v.) 偏好

The employees of the restaurant are required to remember the meal preferences of their customers.

這家餐廳的員工被要求記得顧客們的用餐偏好。

point be required to + V 為被動式，表示「被要求做……」。

Our company provides gifts or certificates on employees' birthdays and you can choose according to your preference.

我們公司在員工生日時提供禮物或是禮券，你可以依照你的偏好來選擇。

point according to + N 表示「根據……」。

---

16 **expertise**

★
★
★
[ˌɛkspɚˋtiz]

n 專門知識，專門技術

同 expertness 特別技能
proficiency 精通
competence 能力
knowledge 知識
mastery 熟練

Cooking is not really my area of expertise.

烹飪真的不是我的專長。

The specialist is known for his expertise in marketing strategy.

這名專家以其在行銷策略方面的專業知識而聞名。

point be known for 意為「以……為人所知」。

14 餐飲住宿

17 service

★
★
★

['sɝvɪs]

n 服務，幫助，招待

同 assistance 協助
help 幫忙
aid 幫助

衍 serve (v.) 服務

The customer complained about the poor service he received.
這名顧客抱怨他受到的不良服務。

point he received 前面省略了 that，整個用來修飾前面的 service。

Please note that we request a 10 percent service fee.
請注意我們要求百分之十的手續費。

point please note that 意為「請注意」，在多益測驗中以此句開頭的段落，後面常有考題重點。

---

18 entirely

★
★
★

[ɪn'taɪrlɪ]

ad 完全地，徹底地

同 absolutely 絕對地
completely 完全地
totally 完全地
wholly 完全地

反 partially 部分地
slightly 稍微地

The newlyweds purchase the RV entirely on credit.
那對新婚夫妻完全用分期付款來購買那台休旅車。

point on credit 意為「分期付款」。RV = recreational（娛樂）vehicle（車輛），意為「休旅車」。

---

19 firm

★
★
★

[fɝm]

a 穩定的，堅定的

v 使穩固，使牢固

n 公司，商行

同 solid (a.) 結實的
stable (a.) 穩定的
steady (a.) 穩固的

反 unstable (a.) 不穩的

He has established his own firm right after he graduated from college.
他從大學畢業後馬上就建立了自己的公司。

point firm, company, business, concern, venture, start-up 皆可表達「公司」。

So far, our opponent hasn't made any firm decisions.
到目前為止，我們的對手還沒做出任何確切的決定。

---

20 diet

★
★

['daɪət]

n 飲食，食物

v 節食，忌食

同 food and drink (ph.) 飲食

She is trying this popular diet to lose weight for her wedding day.
她正在為了婚禮嘗試這個流行的飲食方式來減重。

point for 表示「為了」。

Diets differ in different countries around the world.
飲食在世界上各個國家都不同。

21 **advanced**

★
★
★

[əd`vænst]

a 先進的，高級的，年邁的

同 leading 領導的
high-level 高級的

反 beginner (n.) 初學者

衍 advance (v.) 前進

We expect our sales people to have advanced English level because they are required to visit foreign clients frequently.

我們期待我們的業務能有高階的英文能力，因為他們經常需要拜訪外國客戶。

point be required to 表示「被要求」，為多益測驗中常見的敘述。

I will work as an intern in that hotel reception desk this year because I have taken advanced Japanese.

我今年將會在那家旅館接待台當實習生，因為我曾經修過高階日文。

point take + 科目，意為「修……課」。

22 **assist**

★
★
★

[ə`sɪst]

v 幫助，支持，出席，參加

同 support 支持
facilitate 促進

反 oppose 反對

衍 assistance (n.) 協助
assistant (n.) 助手

The hotel porter assisted me in carrying my luggage.

飯店搬運工幫我搬行李。

My colleague assisted me with my presentation slides, including the contents and the design.

我同事協助我的簡報頁面，包含了內容和設計。

point presentation（簡報）的相關討論，像是字體大小、簡報內容，是多益聽力測驗常見的主題之一。

23 **consideration**

★
★
★

[kənsɪdə`reʃən]

n 考慮，動機，體貼

同 thought 想法
contemplation 沉思
review 複審
discussion 討論

衍 considering (prep.) 考慮到

When it comes to deciding at which hotels to stay, budget is an important consideration.

若提到決定要住哪間飯店，預算是個重要的考量。

point When it comes to + Ving 意為「若提到……」。

The board couldn't make any final decisions since the proposal needed further consideration.

委員會沒辦法做出最終決定，因為計畫還需要更多考量。

24 **tender**

★

[`tɛndɚ]

a 柔軟的，敏感的，微妙的

同 gentle 溫和的
soft 柔軟的
warm 溫暖的

The steak house got great reviews because its steak is tender and juicy.

這家牛排館的評價相當好，因為它的牛排相當嫩且多汁。

point review (v.) 複習 (n.) 評價。

The teacher is always very tender and patient toward her students.

老師總是對她的學生很溫柔且有耐心。

14 餐飲住宿

25 cuisine
★
[kwɪˋzin]
ⁿ 烹飪，菜餚
同 food 食物

All you can eat buffets provide different kinds of cuisines.
吃到飽餐廳提供各式各樣的菜餚。

point 相關詞彙：culinary art 意為「廚藝」。

The small costal town's local cuisine is strong on seafood.
這個沿海小鎮的當地特色菜是海鮮。

point costal 為「海岸的；沿海的」。

---

26 specialize
★
★
[ˋspɛʃəlˌaɪz]
ᵛ 專門從事，詳細說明
同 specify 詳細指明
反 diversify 使多樣化
　 generalize 概括
衍 special (a.) 特別的

He particularly specializes in interior design.
他特別專精於室內設計。

point interior designer 意為「室內設計師」。

My company hired a restaurant that specializes in Thai food to cater for the year-end banquet.
我公司僱用專營泰國菜的餐館來為尾牙辦外燴。

point cater for 意為「為⋯⋯辦外燴」。

---

27 specialty
★
★
[ˋspɛʃəltɪ]
ⁿ 專業，特性，特產
同 strength 實力
　 talent 天資
　 skill 技能
　 gift 天賦

The candidate was employed due to her personality rather than specialty.
求職者因為她的個性被僱用，而非專長。

point rather than = instead of，意為「而不是；而非」。

The regular always orders today's specialty.
那名常客總是點每日特餐。

point 延伸詞彙：be out of order 意為「壞了」，in order to + V = in order that + S + V 意為「為了⋯⋯」。

---

28 return
★
★
★
[rɪˋtɝn]
ᵛ 返回，回答，反駁
同 go back 返回
　 come back 回來
　 get back 回來
反 depart 離開
　 set out 開始

Please return the tray after you finish your meal.
用完餐後，請歸還托盤。

Please return the damaged items to this address within seven days.
請在七天內退回損壞產品到這個地址。

point damaged 為過去分詞，修飾 items。

CH 14

餐飲住宿

29 condition
[kənˋdɪʃən]
★
★
★
n 情況，條件，身分
V 決定，使適應
同 circumstance (n.) 情況
situation (n.) 狀況
position (n.) 形勢
context (n.) 環境
setting (n.) 環境

The sanitary conditions of this restaurant still can be improved.
這家餐廳的衛生條件仍有待改進。

point 相關詞彙：surroundings 環境，environment 環境。

Customers can receive a full refund only on certain conditions.
消費者只有在一些特定的情況才能收到全額退款。

point on certain conditions 意為「在一些特定的情況」。

30 notice
[ˋnotɪs]
★
★
★
n 公告，通知，注意
V 注意，通知，提到
同 attention (n.) 注意
observation (n.) 察覺
awareness (n.) 察覺
announcement (n.) 宣布

The driver ignored a notice on the wall, and still parked there.
駕駛忽略牆上的公告牌，仍然在那裡停車。

The diner noticed that the meal prices had been raised.
用餐者注意到餐點的價格漲了。

point diner (n.) 用餐者；路邊小餐館，dine (v.) 用餐。

31 regular
[ˋrɛgjələ]
★
★
★
a 規則的，定期的，普通的
n 常客
同 continual (a.) 不間斷的
recurrent (a.) 週期性的
periodic (a.) 週期的
constant (a.) 不斷的
反 irregular (a.) 不規則的

Ms. Yamagata, a well-known architect, is a regular at this cafeteria.
知名建築師山形女士，是這家食堂的常客。

point 延伸詞彙：patron (n.) 贊助者；老顧客。

We sincerely apologize that the escalator is currently out of service for regular maintenance.
手扶梯目前因為例行的維修暫停服務，我們誠摯地向您道歉。

point out of service 意為「暫停服務」。out of stock 意為「缺貨」。

32 lease
[lis]
★
★
n 租約，租賃物，租期
V 出租，長期租用
同 contract (n.) 契約
rental (n.) 租賃
rent (v.) 租
tenancy (n.) 租賃期
tenure (n.) 任期

The tenant renewed the rental lease with his landlord.
這名房客向房東更新了租約。

You need to pay a two-month deposit to lease this flat.
你必須付兩個月的租金來租這間房子。

point deposit (n.) 租金，在多益測驗題目中也常寫成 partial payment，意為「部分的付款」。

14 餐飲住宿

---

33 steady
★
★
['stɛdɪ]
ⓐ 穩固的，不變的，沉著的
ⓢ stable 穩定的
　　firm 穩固的
　　fixed 固定的
　　secured 牢固的
　　unshakeable 不可動搖的
ⓐ unstable 不穩定的
　　loose 鬆的

There was a steady increase in the sales of the newly opened pizzeria.
這家新開的披薩店的銷售有著穩定的增長。

It's impossible for the price of vegetables to remain steady before the coming of a typhoon.
在颱風來之前，蔬菜的價格要維持不變是不可能的。
point　remain + a. 意為「維持……」。

---

34 residence
★
★
★
['rɛzədəns]
ⓝ 居住，住所，官邸
ⓢ habitation 居住
　　home 家
　　house 房子
ⓓ resident (n.) 居民
　　residential (a.) 居住的

Besides the apartment downtown, the Wangs own a summer residence in the suburbs.
除了市區的公寓，王家在郊區也有夏季住宅。
point　the + 某姓氏，意為「某姓氏的一家人」。

In order to decrease the money spent on rent, I live in the hall of residence.
為了省房租錢，我住在學生宿舍。
point　spent 前面省略了 which is，意為「花在房租上的錢」。

---

35 average
★
★
★
['ævərɪdʒ]
ⓐ 平均的，一般的，中等的
ⓝ 平均數，平均水準，中等
ⓥ 平均，平均達到
ⓢ medium (a.) 中等的

I won't say the food is tasty but it's just average.
我不會說這食物很好吃，但就只是很普通。
point　相反詞彙：excellent 傑出的，exceptional 例外的，extraordinary 非凡的，extreme 極度的。

---

36 combine
★
★
[kəm'baɪn]
ⓥ 結合，聯合
ⓢ unite 聯合
　　integrate 整合
　　merge 合併
ⓐ separate 分開
　　split up 分開
ⓓ combination (n.) 結合

The bartender tried to invent a new drink by combining different juices and alcohol.
這位酒保藉由混合不同的果汁和酒來試著發明出新的飲料。
point　by 為介係詞，後面加 Ving。

I've heard that the CEO plans to combine the two departments.
我聽說執行長計劃要合併兩個部門。
point　I've heard that 意為「我聽說」。

37 distinctive
★
★ [dɪˈstɪŋktɪv]

a 有特色的，特殊的

同 discriminative 有區別的
unusual 獨特的
different 不同的

反 common 普通的
usual 通常的

衍 distinguish (v.) 區別

I am impressed by the distinctive taste of the new drink.
我對這個新飲料的獨特味道感到印象深刻。

(point) be impressed by 意為「對……感到印象深刻」。

The mascot wore a distinctive costume, warming up the baseball game.
吉祥物穿戴著特別的服裝，為棒球比賽暖場。

(point) 此句為分詞構句，省略連接詞（and）及第二句的主詞（the mascot）。

CH 14
餐飲住宿

---

38 hospitality
★ [ˌhɑspɪˈtælətɪ]

n 好客，殷勤招待

同 kindness 好意
generosity 慷慨
cordiality 熱誠

反 inhospitality 不好客

I am writing to thank you for your hospitality during my stay at your place.
我是寫信來感謝您在我入住期間的熱情款待。

(point) I am writing to + V 意為「我是寫信來……」，後面會加主旨。

I was impressed by the hospitality of the owner of the B&B so that I left a positive review on the internet.
我被民宿主人的好客深深感動，所以我在網站上留了好評。

---

39 taste
★
★
★ [test]

n 味覺，味道，感受

v 嚐，體驗，感到

同 experience (v.) 經驗
sample (v.) 體驗
try (v.) 嘗試

As a top clothes designer, he has an incredibly good taste in fashion.
身為一個頂尖的服裝設計師，他有極好的時尚品味。

The Spanish cuisine in that restaurant tastes fantastic. No wonder it is recommended by a lot of celebrities.
這家餐廳的西班牙料理嚐起來棒極了。難怪很多名人推薦它。

---

40 heater
★ [ˈhitɚ]

n 加熱器，暖氣機

同 stove 暖爐
furnace 火爐
electric fire 電爐

The water heater is broken. Can you call someone to fix it?
熱水器壞掉了，你可以打電話找人來修嗎？

The sales performance of heaters is rising as the weather is getting cold.
因為天氣越來越冷，暖氣的銷售表現正在上漲。

(point) is rising, is getting cold 用進行式表達「越來越……」。

303

Chapter 136

14 餐飲住宿

---

41 ★ **bake**
[bek]
ⓥ 烘烤，烘乾
回 roast 烤
　 toast 烤

Laura baked some chocolate cookies for the potluck this weekend.
蘿拉為這週末的百樂聚烤一些巧克力餅乾。

point potluck 是一種派對形式，每一位客人要帶一道菜到主人的家。

During my summer vacation, I learned how to bake by attending cooking classes.
在暑假時，我上廚藝課學如何烤麵包。

---

42 ★ **baker**
[ˋbekɚ]
ⓝ 麵包師，麵包店店主

After she graduated from the School of Cookery, she became a baker.
她從廚藝學校畢業之後，成為了麵包師傅。

point cookery 為「烹調法；烹調術」。

The baker has won several prizes and that's why his bread is so popular.
這位麵包師傅曾經贏得過許多獎項，這就是為什麼他的麵包如此受歡迎。

point has won 表示經驗，用完成式。

---

43 ★ **bakery**
[ˋbekərɪ]
ⓝ 麵包店，烘烤食品

The new bakery provided buy one get one free discounts, and it successfully attracted many customers.
這家新的麵包店提供買一送一的優惠，成功吸引到很多客人。

point buy one get one free 表示「買一送一」。

The bakery gives out fresh bread to the poor every day.
這家麵包店每天都會給窮苦人家新鮮麵包。

---

44 ★★★ **appetite**
[ˋæpəˌtaɪt]
ⓝ 食慾，胃口，愛好
回 craving 渴望
　 hunger 食慾

Bon appétit!
祝你有好的食慾。

point 此句為法語，但英語系國家的人也很常使用。

Working out in a gym for 2 hours has given me a good appetite.
在健身房運動了兩小時使我食慾大振。

point Working out in a gym for 2 hours 為此句的主詞，動詞用單數。

CH 14

餐飲住宿

45 vegetarian
★ [ˌvɛdʒəˈtɛrɪən]
🅰 吃素的，素食主義的
🅝 素食者，食草動物
🔲 vegan (n.)
嚴守素食主義的人

In order to attract more potential customers, the restaurant provides vegetarian food.
為了吸引更多潛在的客人，該餐廳提供素食餐點。
point potential 意為「潛在的；有潛力的」，也可以形容有潛力的求職者：potential candidate。

In Taiwan, more and more people become vegetarians for health reasons but not religious reasons nowadays.
現今台灣有越來越多人因為健康因素變成吃素者，而非宗教原因。
point more and more 也可以替換成 increasingly，意為「逐漸增加地」。

46 vegetable
★ [ˈvɛdʒətəbl]
🅝 蔬菜，植物，植物人
🔲 produce 農產品

Irene is not picky and she eats all kinds of vegetables.
愛玲不挑食，所有的蔬菜她都吃。
point picky 意為「挑剔的」。

My neighbor goes grocery shopping every week. She usually buys dairy products, vegetables, and some necessities.
我的鄰居每週都會去買菜，她通常都會買乳製品、蔬菜和一些生活必需品。
point dairy product 意為「乳製品」，像是牛奶和起士。

47 crowded
★ [ˈkraʊdɪd]
🅰 擁擠的，閱歷豐富的
🔲 packed 擁擠的
congested 擁塞的
full 滿的
🔣 crowd (n.) 人群

It was too crowded to stand in the countdown party in the hotel.
在飯店裡的跨年倒數派對，人多到都站不穩了。

Walking on the crowded city streets, people watch out for their bags to avoid being robbed.
走在擁擠的城市街上，人們看好他們的包包以免被搶。
point 此句為分詞構句，簡化前的句子為 When people walk on the crowded city streets, they watch out for their bags to avoid being robbed.

48 bay
★ [be]
🅝 灣，間隔區
🅥 吠叫，咆哮

The luxurious 5 star villa is situated in a bay.
這豪華的五星級別墅坐落於海灣內。

The company rents a storage bay to store their heavy machines.
公司租了一個有隔間的儲藏室來放置他們的重型機器。

Chapter 137

14 餐飲住宿

---

49 **barbecue**
★
[ˋbɑrbɪkju]

n（戶外）燒烤
v 燒烤
同 BBQ (n.) 燒烤

For environmental protection, participants of the barbecue party should bring their own bottles.
為了保護環境，烤肉派對的參加者要帶他們自己的水瓶。

I purchased a barbecue grill online with the promotional code.
我使用折扣碼在網路上買了一個烤肉架。

point buy、purchase、procure 都有「購買」的意思。

---

50 **delicious**
★
★
[dɪˋlɪʃəs]

a 美味的，可口的
同 appetizing 開胃的
mouthwatering
令人垂涎欲滴的
tasty 美味的
反 distasteful 味道差的

She is a professional gourmet, and she can introduce every delicious restaurant in this town.
她是一個專業的饕客，她可以介紹這城鎮裡每一家好吃的餐廳。

The ravioli is delicious but the price is too steep.
這義大利餃很好吃，但價錢太貴了。

point steep (a.) 陡峭的；（價格）過高的。

---

51 **allergy**
★
[ˋælədʒɪ]

n 過敏症，反感
同 allergic reaction 過敏反應
衍 allergic (a.) 過敏的

Before I booked a restaurant for my clients, I asked them whether they had any food allergies.
在我為我的客戶訂餐廳時，我問他們是否有會過敏的食物。

He was sent to the hospital owing to the life-threatening allergies.
他因為有生命危險的過敏反應，而被送到醫院。

point owing to + N 意為「因為……」。

---

52 **weight**
★
★
[wet]

n 重量，負擔，重要性

Eating too much junk food makes people gain weight.
吃太多垃圾食物會讓人增重。

point Ving 為主詞，動詞單數。make, let, have（使役動詞）+ V，意為「使……」。

The traveler was fined for the luggage that exceeded the weight limit.
旅客因為超過重量限制的行李而被罰錢。

point that exceeded the weight limit 修飾前面的 luggage。

CH 14

餐飲住宿

53 **variety**
★
★ [vəˈraɪətɪ]
★
🄝 多樣化，種類
🔄 difference 差別
　　dissimilarity 不同

All you can eat buffet restaurants provide customers with a wide variety of foods.
吃到飽餐廳提供顧客多樣化的食物。

point 用餐相關字：dine (v.) 用餐，diner (n.) 用餐的人；小餐館。

Add variety to your clothing options so that you can look more refreshed.
讓你的衣服選擇增加多樣性，這樣你就能看起來更煥然一新。

---

54 **bubble**
★ [ˈbʌbḷ]

🄝 水泡，氣泡，沸騰
🄥 沸騰，冒泡，情緒高漲
🔄 globule (n.) 水珠

Bubble tea is popular among people in Taiwan.
珍珠奶茶很受台灣人歡迎。

point bubble tea = pearl milk tea = bubble milk tea = boba，意為「珍珠奶茶」。

Once the water in the pot is beginning to bubble, you can put all the materials into it.
一旦鍋裡的水開始冒泡，你就可以放入所有的食材。

---

55 **carryout**
★ [ˈkærˌaʊt]

🄝 外賣食品
🄐 外帶的，外賣的
🔄 takeout (n.) 外賣
　　takeaway (n.) 外賣食物

If he is in a hurry, he usually buys lunch from the carryout near the train station.
如果他在趕時間，他通常都會從火車站旁的外賣餐館買午餐。

point be in a hurry 意為「匆忙；趕時間」。

The popular restaurant also offers carryout service.
這間有名的餐廳也提供外帶服務。

point 易混淆字：carry out (v.) 施行。

---

56 **suitable**
★
★ [ˈsutəbḷ]
★
🄐 適當的，合適的
🔄 acceptable 可以接受的
　　satisfactory 令人滿意的
　　fit 適合的
🔄 unsuitable 不適合的
　　inappropriate 不適當的
　　unfit 不合適的

I don't think the accommodation is suitable for me due to budget constraints.
因為預算限制，我不覺得這住宿適合我。

point be suitable for 意為「適合」。

It's difficult for the executive to determine which applicant is more suitable for this position since most of them are over-qualified.
主管很難決定哪位申請者比較合適，因為他們大部分都比這職位所需要的條件還要好很多。

307

Chapter 138

14 餐飲住宿

---

57 namely
★
[`nemlɪ]

ad 即，那就是
同 that is 那就是
　　that is to say 那就是說

The recipe is the secret of the store, namely that only the main chief knows it.
這個食譜是店家的祕密，也就是說，只有主廚知道。
point 延伸詞彙：cook (n.) 廚師，cooker (n.) 廚具。

---

58 indoors
★
[`ɪn`dorz]

ad 在室內，在屋裡
反 outdoors 在戶外

The host of the B&B invited his guests to come indoors.
民宿主人邀請他的客人進到屋內。
point B&B = bed and breakfast，意為「民宿」。

The experienced event planner decided to hold the event indoors just in case of bad weather conditions.
為避免天候不佳，經驗豐富的活動籌劃者決定把活動辦在室內。
point in case + S + V = in case of + N / Ving，意為「以免；以防」。

---

59 unsatisfactory
★
★
★
[ˌʌnsætɪs`fæktərɪ]

a 令人不滿的，
　　不符合要求的
同 disappointing 失望的
　　dissatisfying 不滿的
　　undesirable 令人不快的
　　disagreeable 不愉快的
反 satisfactory 滿意的

Both the new restaurant's service and the food were unsatisfactory.
新餐廳的服務和食物都令人不滿意。
point both A and B 意為「兩者皆是」。

The sales performance of this model was unsatisfactory; therefore, the company had a meeting to discuss the possible solutions.
這個型號的銷售表現不盡理想，因此公司開會討論可能的解決方法。

---

60 especially
★
★
★
[ə`spɛʃəlɪ]

ad 特別，尤其，格外
同 exceptionally 例外地
　　particularly 尤其
　　specially 特別地
　　extremely 極度地

The fashion blogger is especially particular about what she wears.
時尚部落客對衣著尤其講究。
point what she wears 意為「她所穿的衣服」，整句當 about 的受詞。

The wallpaper and carpet were chosen especially for the hotel lobby.
壁紙和地毯是特別選來用在飯店大廳的。

61 decade
★
★　['dɛked]
★
　n 十年
　衍 annual (a.) 一年一次的
　　　yearly (a.) 一年一次的

The manager has worked for IDF Investment for two decades.
這名經理已經為 IDF 投資公司工作了二十年。

Ann's diner has served excellent cuisine for the local residents over the past three decades.
安的餐館已經為當地居民提供美味菜餚超過三十年了。

point diner (n.) 餐館;用餐的人。

62 globe
★
★　[glob]
　n 地球儀,地球,球狀
　同 world 世界
　　　earth 地球
　　　universe 宇宙
　衍 global (a.) 全球的

Rice is the staple food in many parts of the globe.
米飯在地球上許多地方是主食。

point staple (n.) 主要商品 (a.) 主要的。

The marathon has attracted 3,000 people around the globe.
這場馬拉松已經吸引了全球各地三千人來參加。

63 consequently
★
★　['kɑnsə͵kwɛntlɪ]
★
　ad 結果,因此
　同 as a result 因此
　　　in consequence 結果
　　　thus 如此
　　　therefore 因此
　　　accordingly 於是
　　　hence 因此

The building inspection will be carried out in two hours; consequently, employees should leave the building within one hour.
建物檢查會在兩小時內實施,因此員工要在一小時內離開大樓。

point 此兩句分別呈現出 consequently 兩種連接句子的方式:用 and 連接放句中、用分號「;」連接放句中。

64 vacant
★
★　['vekənt]
　a 空著的,空虛的,茫然的
　同 empty 空的
　　　unengaged 沒事的
　　　uninhabited 無人居住的
　反 full 滿的
　　　occupied 已佔用的

The seat is vacant for now.
這個座位暫時沒人坐。

point for now 意為「暫時地」。

The hotel did not have any vacant rooms.
這家旅館沒有任何空房。

Chapter 139

14 餐飲住宿

65 underestimate
★
★ [ˈʌndəˈɛstəˌmet]
v 低估，輕視
[ˈʌndəˈɛstəmɪt]
n 低估
同 underrate (v.) 低估
反 overestimate (v.) 高估
　　overrate (v.) 高估

The pizzeria is totally underestimated. It's delicious but not famous.
這家披薩店完全被低估了，很好吃，但卻不有名。

The tennis player lost the final in that he underestimated his opponent.
那名網球選手輸了決賽，因為他低估了他的對手。

point in that = because = since = as，意為「因為」。

---

66 typical
★
★ [ˈtɪpɪkl]
★ **a** 典型的，特有的，象徵的
同 distinguishing 有區別的
　　particular 特殊的
反 atypical 非典型的
　　abnormal 不正常的
　　exceptional 例外的

It's typical European weather and you will get used to it.
這只是典型的歐洲天氣，你會習慣的。

point get used to 意為「習慣……」。

The backpacker had the local food which is typical in the south of the country.
背包客吃了這個國家南方特有的當地食物。

point 相關詞彙：representative 代表性的，classic 典型的，distinctive 有特色的。

---

67 takeout
★ [ˈtekˌaut]
n 外賣，外賣餐館
a 外賣的
同 takeaway (n.) 外賣食物
　　carryout (n.) 外賣餐食
　　ready meal (ph.) 外賣

If you are in a hurry, you can order food from the takeout counter.
如果你正在趕時間，你可以去外帶櫃台點餐。

point takeout counter 意為「外帶櫃台」，「內用」可以說 for here。

This is our takeout menu, which is different from the one for customers who eat in the restaurant.
這是我們的外帶菜單，和給在餐廳內用的客人看到的菜單不同。

point be different from 意為「不同於」。

---

68 renovation
★
★ [ˌrɛnəˈveʃən]
★ **n** 更新，修理，恢復活力
同 makeover 改觀
　　updating 更新
　　improvement 改善
　　upgrading 升級

After renovation, the store has successfully attracted many customers.
在裝修後，店家成功吸引了許多顧客。

The hotel is under renovation and will reopen next year.
飯店在整修，明年會再重新開張。

point 相關詞彙：restoration 整修，reconstruction 重建，repair 修復，remodeling 改建。

CH 14

餐飲住宿

69 sensible

★
★
★

[`sɛnsəbl]

a 明智的，合情理的，
察覺到的

同 rational 理性的
logical 具邏輯的
sound 明智的
realistic 注重實際的

反 foolish 愚笨的

It would be sensible to make a reservation before you visit that famous restaurant.
去那家有名的餐廳前先訂位是明智的。

(point) 相關詞彙：practical 實際的，thoughtful 考慮周到的，reasonable 合理的，wise 明智的，intelligent 有智慧的，clever 聰明的。

The company was not sensible of the threats that the decision might bring to their reputation.
公司沒有察覺到這個決定可能會帶給它們名聲的威脅。

70 superb

★
★

[su`pɝb]

a 宏偉的，極好的，一流的

同 superior 優秀的
supreme 至上的
remarkable 非凡的
marvelous 了不起的

反 poor 粗劣的
inferior 低等的

Both food quality and the decor of this Japanese restaurant are superb.
這家日本料理的食物品質及裝潢都是一流。

(point) both A and B 兩者皆是／either... or 兩者其一／neither... nor 兩者皆非。

The city fitness center provides citizens superb sports facilities.
城市體適能中心提供市民頂尖的運動設施。

(point) citizen, resident, habitant 皆可指「居民」。

71 substitute

★
★

[`sʌbstəˌtjut]

v 替代

n 替代物

a 代替的

同 deputy (n.) 代理
proxy (n.) 代理人
alternative (a.) 替代的

If you would like to have a low-calorie meal, you can substitute tofu for beef in this recipe.
如果你想吃低卡路里的餐點，這道菜中你可以用豆腐取代牛肉。

(point) 相關詞彙：replace 取代。

The school will hire a substitute teacher because the regular teacher is on sick leave.
因為原本的老師請病假，學校將會僱用一名代課老師。

(point) on sick leave 意為「請病假」。

72 several

★
★
★

[`sɛvərəl]

a 幾個的，數個的

同 some 一些
a number of 一些
a few 少數
a handful of 少數

There are several reasons why diets differ around the world.
有很多原因導致飲食在世界各地有所不同。

The workplace was forced to close after several workplace accidents happened.
在發生很多工作意外後，這個工作場所被迫關閉。

(point) workplace accident 意為「工作意外」。

73 prohibit
★
★ [prə`hɪbɪt]
★ **V** 禁止，妨礙，阻止
同 forbid 禁止
ban 禁止
bar 禁止
反 permit 許可
allow 允許
authorize 授權

The government **prohibited** people **from** drinking alcohol in all the train stations.
政府禁止人民在所有火車站飲酒。
point prohibit sb. from Ving 意為「禁止某人做……」。

The kid's parents prohibited him from eating junk food.
小孩的父母禁止他吃垃圾食物。

---

74 preserve
★
★ [prɪ`zɝv]
★ **V** 保存，維護，保護
同 conserve 保存
protect 保護
maintain 維護
反 consume 消耗

The container is used to preserve food, **such as** jam.
這個容器是用來保存食物的，像是果醬。
point such as + N / Ving，意為「例如……」。

The policy is to preserve endangered species.
這個政策是為了保護瀕臨絕種的物種。

---

75 particular
★
★ [pə`tɪkjələ]
★ **a** 特殊的，挑剔的，詳細的
同 specific 特殊的
distinct 有區別的
separate 個別的
peculiar 特有的
反 careless 隨便的
easy-going 隨和的

If you have nothing particular to do this evening, maybe you can grab a bite with us.
如果你今晚沒有什麼特別的事要做，也許你可以跟我們一起去吃點東西。
point grab a bite 意為「簡單吃點東西」。

The gourmet enjoys food from different countries, Japanese food **in particular**.
這名美食家喜歡不同國家的食物，尤其是日本料理。
point in particular 意為「尤其是」。

---

76 gather
★
★ [`gæðə]
★ **V** 收集，積蓄，猜想
同 collect (v.) 收集
put together (ph.) 組合
accumulate (v.) 累積
反 scatter (v.) 分散

People gathered in the hotel lobby, waiting to check in.
人們聚集在飯店大廳，等著辦理入住手續。
point 多益聽力測驗 Part 1 圖片題中常有「人們聚集」這樣的敘述，要注意。

The assistant finally gathered the courage to say no.
這名助理終於鼓足勇氣說不。

Test 1

一、請寫出下列單字的中文意思。

① average ＿＿＿＿＿＿ ⑥ decade ＿＿＿＿＿＿

② suitable ＿＿＿＿＿＿ ⑦ steady ＿＿＿＿＿＿

③ expertise ＿＿＿＿＿＿ ⑧ specialize ＿＿＿＿＿＿

④ variety ＿＿＿＿＿＿ ⑨ recommend ＿＿＿＿＿＿

⑤ accommodation ＿＿＿＿＿＿ ⑩ distinctive ＿＿＿＿＿＿

二、請寫出符合下列句意的單字。

① After I booked a hotel room online and paid for it by credit card, I called the hotel to confirm my ＿＿＿＿＿＿.
我在線上訂房並用信用卡付款後，打給飯店確認我的訂房。

② We expect our sales people to have ＿＿＿＿＿＿ English level because they are required to visit foreign clients frequently.
我們期待我們的業務能有高階的英文能力，因為他們經常需要拜訪外國客戶。

③ The container is used to ＿＿＿＿＿＿ food, such as jam.
這個容器是用來保存食物的，像是果醬。

解答

1. ① 平均的；平均 ② 適當的，相配的 ③ 專門的知識，專長 ④ 多樣的，老於世故的
⑤ 房間，適應 ⑥ 十年 ⑦ 穩定的，沉著的；穩固 ⑧ 專門從事，詳細說明 ⑨ 推薦，建議
⑩ 特別的，有特色的
2. ① reservation ② advanced ③ preserve

Test 2

一、請選擇符合下列文意的單字。

Ⓐ return	Ⓑ entirely	Ⓒ consideration
Ⓓ residence	Ⓔ preference	Ⓕ charge

① The employees of the restaurant are required to remember the meal _____ of their customers.

② When it comes to deciding at which hotels to stay, budget is an important _____.

③ Besides the apartment downtown, the Wangs own a summer _____ in the suburbs.

④ Please _____ the damaged items to this address within seven days.

⑤ The travelers stayed _____ at hostels instead of hotels, which saved them a great sum of money.

二、請寫出下列片語的中文意思。

① grab a bite _____　　⑤ instead of _____

② on sick leave _____　　⑥ get used to _____

③ be in a hurry _____　　⑦ owing to _____

④ in case of _____　　⑧ in particular _____

解答

1. ① E　② C　③ D　④ A　⑤ B
2. ① 吃東西　② 請病假　③ 匆忙，趕時間　④ 以防萬一　⑤ 而不是　⑥ 習慣　⑦ 因為　⑧ 尤其是

Chapter 15
交通觀光

以下多益必考單字，你認識哪些？

☐ commute (p.316)   ☐ absolutely (p.330)   ☐ capture (p.331)

☐ depart (p.318)   ☐ destination (p.319)   ☐ passenger (p.326)

☐ luggage (p.316)   ☐ flight (p.318)   ☐ leave (p.329)

☐ agency (p.323)   ☐ itinerary (p.316)   ☐ breathtaking (p.327)

☐ promise (p.324)   ☐ expire (p.325)   ☐ fare (p.317)

☐ scenery (p.328)   ☐ arrive (p.321)   ☐ brochure (p.323)

15 交通觀光

01 commute
★
★
★
[kə`mjut]
V 通勤，交換，改變
n 通勤
同 travel (v.) 遊歷
　　exchange (v.) 交換

It takes Hans two hours to commute from home to school so he rents a suite which he can afford near the campus.
從家裡通勤到學校要花漢斯兩小時的時間，所以他在校園附近租了一個他可以負擔得起的套房。

point　suite [swit] 意為「套房」，請注意讀音，別與 suit [sut] 搞混。

When you have passion for your job, you can commute the pressure for the pleasure.
當你對你的工作有熱情時，你就能夠化壓力為快樂。

point　have passion for... 意為「對某事有熱情」。

02 commuter
★
★
[kə`mjutɚ]
n 通勤者
同 passenger 乘客

The subway company is going to carry out a commuter benefits program to attract more passengers.
地鐵公司即將推出通勤者福利計畫以吸引更多的乘客。

point　carry out 表示「執行」。

The commuter train was delayed due to the inclement weather.
市郊往返的火車因為不好的天氣而誤點。

point　inclement 表示「惡劣的」，是多益測驗中飛機誤點的常見原因（天候不佳）。

03 luggage
★
★
★
[`lʌgɪdʒ]
n 行李
同 baggage 行李
　　valise 手提旅行袋

The woman put her luggage next to the bed.
這名女士把行李放在床邊。

You should pay the fee for your overweight luggage.
你必須要為你的超重行李付罰金。

04 itinerary
★
★
★
[aɪ`tɪnəˌrɛrɪ]
n 旅程，路線，旅行計畫
同 schedule (n.) 行程

When can you finalize the itinerary? I need to check it today.
你何時可以將行程表定案？我今天必須確認。

The travel agency said that there will be an addition to the itinerary.
旅行社說行程表將會有一項新增的行程。

point　「新增行程」為多益聽力測驗中研討會常見的情景。

CH 15

交通觀光

05 **fare**
★
★
★
[fɛr]

n 票價，乘客，食物
同 fee 費用
　 charge 收費
　 toll 道路通行費

Fares are usually lower in the low season.
淡季的機票價格通常都會比旺季還低。

(point) 延伸詞彙：high season 意為「旺季」。

The assistant of the Human Resources Department called the travel agency to confirm the fare for the excursion for the annual employee trip.
人資部的助理打給旅行社以確定年度員工旅遊的票價。

06 **direct**
★
★
★
[dəˋrɛkt]

a 直接的，恰好的
ad 直接地
v 指示，針對，導演
同 straight (a.) 直的
反 indirect (a.) 不直接的

The receptionist directed the guest's call directly to the personnel department.
接待員直接把訪客的電話轉給人事部門。

(point) direct ones call to 意為「轉接」。

The documentary directed by the young director won several awards.
那名年輕導演所導的紀錄片贏得許多獎項。

07 **directly**
★
★
★
[dəˋrɛktlɪ]

ad 直接地，筆直地，即刻
conj 一……就……
同 instantly (adv.) 立即

You can contact the landlord Mrs. Rudd directly if you are willing to rent the apartment.
如果你願意租這間公寓，你可以直接聯絡房東路德太太。

In regard to machinery breakdowns, we will send an experienced technician to your office directly to help you.
有關機器的故障，我們將會派一位有經驗的技師直接到你的辦公室幫你。

(point) in regard to = about，意為「有關」。

08 **customs**
★
★
[ˋkʌstəmz]

n 關稅，海關

The customs officer confiscated the dairy products in the passenger's baggage.
海關人員沒收了該名旅客行李內的乳製品。

The government plan to increase the customs tariffs of the product to protect the local market.
政府計劃要增加這項產品的關稅，以保護當地的市場。

(point) tariffs 意為「關稅」。

317

09 **depart**
★
★ [dɪˋpɑrt]
★ **V** 離開
同 go away 走開
　 fly out 搭飛機離開
　 set off 出發
　 take off 起飛
反 reach 到達
　 arrive 抵達
　 stay 留下

The inbound flight will depart at 7:30. Passengers are suggested to wait at the gate in advance.
回程的班機會在七點半起飛，乘客們被建議要提早到登機門等。
point depart 意為「離開」，也就是起飛。

Before the boss departed, the secretary had arranged everything, including the accommodation, flight ticket, and tour schedule.
在老闆出發前，祕書已經安排好所有的事情，包括住宿、機票及旅遊行程。
point including 為介系詞，後加 Ving 及名詞。

10 **departure**
★
★ [dɪˋpɑrtʃɚ]
★ **n** 離開
反 arrival 抵達

Passengers should check the latest status of their flights on the departure board.
乘客們應該要在出境顯示板上確認他們班機的最新狀況。
point 延伸詞彙：arrival board 入境顯示板。

VIPs can enjoy the refreshments in the departure lounge.
貴賓們可以享用候機室的點心。
point refreshments 為「點心、茶點」的意思，是多益測驗中會議行程表裡休息時段常見的詞彙。

11 **board**
★
★ [bord]
★ **n** 木板，牌子，董事會
V 上（飛機、車、船等），
　 寄宿
同 committee (n.) 委員會
　 council (n.) 議會

All the passengers are boarding the airplane.
所有的旅客正在登機。

Tina is in charge of preparing refreshments for the monthly board meeting.
提娜負責準備每月的董事會會議茶點。

12 **flight**
★
★ [flaɪt]
★ **n** 班機，飛行

If you had booked the flight ticket one year before your trip, you would have gotten a better fare.
如果你在旅行的一年前就訂機票，你就可以得到較佳的票價。
point had booked 表示過去完成式，用來表示與過去事實相反。

While the passenger was waiting for the flight to Russia, he heard an airport announcement.
當該乘客在等待前往俄羅斯的班機時，他聽到一則機場廣播。

13 **claim**

★
★
★

[klem]

v 要求，聲稱，需要

n 要求，主張，所有權

同 assert (v.) 斷言
declare (v.) 宣布
maintain (v.) 主張
affirm (v.) 斷言

Go to the baggage claim area and get your luggage.
去行李領取處拿你的行李。

(point) baggage claim area 為機場拿回行李的行李輸送帶區。

DMU Corporation claimed they didn't imitate their opponent's idea.
DMU 公司聲稱他們並沒有模仿其競爭者的點子。

14 **cruise**

★
★

[kruz]

v 巡航，航行

n 航遊，坐船旅行

同 sail (v.) 航行
travel (v.) 旅行
trip (n.) 旅行
voyage (n.) 旅程
journey (n.) 旅程

Eason used the website to know whether he got the best deal on the river cruise.
易森用這個網站來知道他買的河上航遊是不是最划算的價錢。

(point) deal 表示「交易」。單獨講 deal 表示為「成交；一言為定」。

The cruise ship can accommodate 100 guests in total.
這艘大型郵輪總共可以容納一百位來賓。

(point) in total 意為「總數」。

15 **delay**

★
★
★

[dɪ`le]

v 延期，耽擱，延誤

n 延遲，耽擱

同 hold up (ph.) 延誤
put off (ph.) 延遲
prolong (v.) 延長

反 advance (v.) 前進
forward (v.) 向前

Due to the flight delay, Mr. Johnson cancelled his dental appointment.
因為班機延誤，強森先生取消他的牙醫預約。

(point) 取消牙醫預約這個情境很容易在多益聽力測驗 Part 3 和 Part 4 中出現，可以多留意。

After considering the market trend, the company delayed the product launch until next quarter.
在考量市場趨勢後，公司延遲產品上市到下一季。

(point) 相關詞彙：defer 推遲，detain 使耽擱，postpone 延緩。

16 **destination**

★
★
★

[ˌdɛstə`neʃən]

n 目的地，目標，終點

同 end of the line 終點線
goal 終點
target 目標
objective 目標
purpose 目的

Attention passengers, the next stop is our destination.
乘客請注意，下一站為我們的終點站。

(point) 這樣的句子會出現在多益聽力測驗中交通工具的廣播，要注意。

After considering his time and budget, he finally decided his travel destination.
在考慮時間跟預算後，他終於決定了他的旅遊目的地。

15 交通觀光

---

17 yacht ★

[jɑt]

n 遊艇,快艇

v 駕快艇,乘遊艇

同 boat (n.) 船

The celebrity owns a private luxury yacht.
這位名人擁有私人遊艇。

point luxury 在此處當形容詞「奢侈的」,也可當名詞「奢侈品」。

It's a beautiful day. Do you want to go yachting with me this afternoon?
今天天氣很好,你下午要不要跟我一起去搭快艇?

point go + Ving 意旨「從事……活動」。

---

18 aircraft ★

[ˈɛrˌkræft]

n 航空器,飛機

同 airplane 飛機
jet 噴氣式飛機
aeroplane 飛機

The flight attendant sincerely apologized for the late arrival of the aircraft.
空服員真摯地對飛機的誤點表示抱歉。

point apologized for + N / Ving 意為「為……而道歉」。

Be careful of the size limit of the carry-on luggage that you are going to take to the aircraft.
請注意你要帶上飛機的隨身行李的尺寸限制。

point carry-on luggage 為不須託運、可帶上飛機的隨身行李,會有尺寸及重量的限制。

---

19 airline ★★★

[ˈɛrˌlaɪn]

n 航空公司,航線

衍 low cost airline (ph.) 廉價航空公司

The airline canceled the flight owing to the unpleasant weather conditions.
因為天候不佳,該航空公司取消了這班班機。

point owing to = because of = due to + N / Ving 表示「因為」。

I use this website to compare the cost of the flight tickets of different airline companies to get the best deal.
我用這個網站來比較不同航空公司的票價,以取得最佳優惠。

point deal意為「交易」;deal with = cope with = handle意為「處理」。

---

20 airport ★★★

[ˈɛrˌport]

n 機場,航空站

同 airfield 小航空站
aerodrome 機場

We take the shuttle bus to the airport.
我們搭接駁車到機場。

point shuttle bus 為往返兩地的交通車,例如從車站到旅館。

CH 15

交通觀光

21 **arrive**

★
★
★

[ə`raɪv]

Ⅴ 到達，抵達，成功

同 come 來
reach 到達
get to 到達

反 leave 離開
depart 離開

By the time we arrived at the station, they had gone.
我們抵達車站時，他們已經走了。

point 本句有兩個動詞，had gone 為「過去完成式」，較早發生，arrived 為「過去式」，較慢發生。

My boss asked Joanna to pick up the client from the airport, so she needed to arrive there earlier.
我的老闆叫喬安娜到機場接客戶，所以她必須要提早到那裡。

point pick up 有很多意思：「接機；撿起來；搭訕」。

22 **arrival**

★
★
★

[ə`raɪv l]

ｎ 到達，到來，
到達的人或物

同 coming 到來

反 departure 離開
going 離去
leaving 離開

The spring new arrival sale will end this Friday.
春季新貨特賣會在這週五結束。

point arrival 在此句的意思為「新貨」。

The train has been delayed for a long time. Now the new approximate time of arrival is 7:45.
這班火車已經延誤好一陣子了。現在最新的大約抵達時間為七點四十五分。

point approximate 的副詞為 approximately，意為「大約地」，等於about。

23 **fuel**

★
★

[`fjuəl]

ｎ 燃料，刺激因素

Ⅴ 供給燃料，刺激

衍 fueled (a.) 加燃料的

The newly updated hybrid car can reduce the consumption of fossil fuels.
新升級的油電混合車能夠減少化石燃料的消耗。

point newly 為副詞，修飾形容詞 updated。

Before the long road trip, he fueled his car with petrol.
在長程旅行前，他把車子加了油。

point 此處 fuel 為動詞，「增添燃料」的意思。

24 **gate**

★
★
★

[get]

ｎ 大門，出入口，觀眾數

同 gateway 入口處
doorway 出入口
entrance 入口
exit 入口

Passengers on flight EAR569 please go to Gate 7.
搭乘 EAR569 的乘客請至七號登機門。

It is believed that working hard is the gate to success.
人們相信努力工作是通往成功的大門。

point it is believed that 意為「人們相信……」。

Chapter 144

15 交通觀光

25 **valid**
★
★ [`vælɪd]
★ **a** 有根據的，有效的
圓 authentic 有效的
　　legally acceptable 合法的
反 invalid 無效的
衍 validate (v.) 使生效

Make sure your passport is valid before you go abroad.
在你出國前，請確認你的護照是有效的

Holland Corporation gave the customer a voucher that was valid for three months.
荷蘭公司給這位客人三個月效期的折價券。

---

26 **guide**
★
★ [gaɪd]
★ **n** 導遊，指南，入門書
v 帶領，指導，管理
圓 direct (v.) 指導
　　lead (v.) 領導
衍 guidance (n.) 指導
　　guideline (n.) 指導方針

The travel guide is pretty professional in that he is familiar with the history and the culture of the local town.
這名導遊相當專業，因為他很熟悉這個小鎮的歷史及文化。
point in that 是連接詞，意為「因為」。

As soon as I asked the receptionist the location of the lecture hall, she guided me to the right place.
我一問接待人員演講廳的地點，她馬上就帶我到那裡。
point as soon as 意為「一……就……」。

---

27 **guidebook**
★ [`gaɪd͵buk]
n 旅行指南，手冊
圓 handbook 旅行指南

The guidebook provides informative information about Paris and even includes the suggested travel schedules.
這本旅遊書提供許多有關巴黎的有用資訊，甚至包括了建議的旅遊行程。

Under his guidance, we finished the task sooner than we expected.
在他的協助下，我們比預計的還要早完成任務。
point under one's guidance 意為「在某人的協助之下」。

---

28 **agenda**
★
★ [ə`dʒɛndə]
★ **n** 議程，日常工作事項
圓 schedule 行程
　　itinerary 旅程

Please send me a copy of the travel agenda.
請寄給我一份旅行行程表。

We can finalize the conference agenda by the end of the month.
我們可以在月底前完成會議行程表。
point finalize (v.) 完成；確定，最終確定。

29 brochure
★
★ [bro`ʃur]
★ n 小冊子
同 booklet 小冊子
pamphlet 小冊子
catalogue 目錄
leaflet 傳單
printed matter 文宣

In the orientation, every new recruit will receive a brochure related to the company history and employee benefits.
在員工訓練中，每位新成員將會收到介紹公司歷史及員工福利的小冊子。

point 請注意 brochure 的發音，常在新制多益聽力測驗中出現。

The assistant had ordered 500 brochures for the new campaign a month ago.
這位助理一個月前就為了新的行銷活動訂了五百本小冊子。

CH 15

交通觀光

---

30 agency
★
★ [`edʒənsɪ]
★ n 代辦處，經銷處，
★ 行政機構
同 bureau 局
office 政府機關
organization 機構

The travel agency provides a wide variety of packages to travelers.
旅行社提供旅客多樣化的套裝行程。

point a variety of = various 意為「多樣的」。

I will visit the agency of that overseas company to apply for some necessary documents tomorrow.
明天我會去那家海外公司的代辦處申請一些必要的文件。

point apply for + N 意為「申請……」。

---

31 agent
★
★ [`edʒənt]
★ n 代理人，仲介，起因
同 deputy 代理人

The real estate agent informed his clients of the date to visit the new building.
那位房仲通知他的客戶參訪那棟新建築的日期。

point inform sb. of sth. 意為「通知某人某事」。

After I paid the deposit, the travel agent sent me the itinerary of the travel.
在我付訂金後，旅行社人員寄給我行程表。

point deposit 意為「訂金」。

---

32 package
★
★ [`pækɪdʒ]
★ n 包裹，包裝，一包
v 打包，包裝
同 box (n.) 一盒
carton (n.) 紙盒

DKL Telecommunication Company provides two packages for different customers.
DKL 電信公司提供兩種組合給不同的顧客。

Discounted package tours are available to VIPs only.
特價的套裝行程只有貴賓能買。

point be available to 意為「可用的」。

15 交通觀光

---

33 promise
★
[ˈprɑmɪs]
Ⅴ 承諾，保證，有指望
ⁿ 諾言，前途
圓 guarantee (v.) 保證
　 assure (v.) 擔保

I promise I will send the itinerary to you before you come back.
我發誓我會在你回來之前把行程表寄給你。

point itinerary, schedule 皆可表達「行程表」。

The government has promised that they will try to reduce the unemployment rate.
政府已承諾會試著減低失業率。

point promise that + S + V 意為「允諾做……」。

---

34 pack
★
★
[pæk]
ⁿ 包裝，背包，一夥
Ⅴ 擠滿，包裝，駁運
圓 container (n.) 容器
　 package (n.) 包裹
　 parcel (n.) 包裹

The hotel guests had packed their luggage before they checked out.
飯店房客在辦理退房前就已經把所有行李都打包好了。

point 時間比較早發生：使用過去完成式 had packed。時間較晚發生：使用過去式 checked out。

The trains in the morning are usually packed with commuters.
早上的火車通常都擠滿了通勤者。

point be packed with 意為「充滿」。

---

35 announce
★
★
★
[əˈnɑʊns]
Ⅴ 宣布，通知，聲稱，播報
圓 declare 宣布
　 publish 發表
　 report 報告

The policy has been announced by the authorities, which means that everyone should adhere to it.
這個政策已經被當局宣布了，就意味著每個人都必須遵守它。

point which 代替逗點前的整句話，為關係代名詞。

The pilot announced that the flight would take off as long as the weather conditions were acceptable.
機長宣布只要天氣狀況許可，班機就會起飛。

point as long as 意為「只要」。

---

36 announcement
★
★
★
[əˈnɑʊnsmənt]
ⁿ 通告，宣布，預告
圓 declaration 宣布
　 statement 聲明
　 report 報告

The announcement is made to ask passengers to mind their personal belongings.
這個宣布是要請乘客們注意他們的個人物品。

point 延伸詞彙：belong to 意為「屬於」。

Please pay attention to the announcement to know the flight's updated departure time.
請注意聽通知以得知班機出發的更新時間。

CH 15

交通觀光

37 **entire**

★
★
★

[ɪnˈtaɪr]

a 全部的，全然的
n 全部，整體
同 whole (a.) 全部的
　　complete (a.) 完整的
　　total (a.) 完全的
　　full (a.) 充分
反 partial (a.) 部分的

The industry expert will take a few days off and take his entire family to Australia for vacation.
這名產業專家將會休幾天假，帶他的全家人去澳洲度假。

It took him an entire two weeks to finish the financial summary.
完成財務摘要花了他整整兩週。

point financial summary 常在多益測驗中改寫成 financial report。

38 **expire**

★
★

[ɪkˈspaɪr]

v 期滿，終止，死亡
同 end 結束
　　finish 結束
　　terminate 終止
反 begin 開始
衍 expiration (n.) 終結

My passport will expire soon.
我的護照快過期了。

Holy renewed her annual membership before it expired.
荷利在她的年度會員過期前就續會了。

39 **carry**

★
★
★

[ˈkærɪ]

v 運送，傳達，攜帶，資助
同 bring 攜帶
　　fetch 取物
　　convey 傳達
　　transport 運輸
衍 carrier (n.) 運送人

All passengers should follow the size limit of carry-on baggage.
所有乘客都必須遵守隨身攜帶行李的尺寸限制。

point carry-on 意為「（乘飛機時）隨身攜帶的」，不須託運。

40 **rise**

★
★
★
★

[raɪz]

v 上升，高出，起立
n 增加，提升，加薪
同 arise (v.) 升起
　　increase (v.) 增加
　　mount (v.) 登上
反 fall (v.) 跌落
　　decline (v.) 下降

Some employees decided to ask their employer for a pay rise.
有些員工決定和他們的雇主要求加薪。

point pay rise 意為「加薪」。

Since the travel agency offered special discounted packages, the sales volume has risen.
自從旅行社推出特惠套裝行程後，業績就上升了。

41 allowance
★
★
[əˈlaʊəns]
n 津貼，零用錢
同 money 錢
衍 allow (v.) 允許

Have you received the travel allowance for your business trip to New York?
你已經收到去紐約出差的旅遊津貼了嗎？

When you pack your luggage, be careful of the weight since the luggage allowance for you flight is 20 kilograms.
當你打包行李時，請注意重量，因為你的班機允許乘客攜帶的行李重量限額是二十公斤。

---

42 regulation
★
★
★
[ˌrɛɡjəˈleʃən]
n 規則，管理，調整
同 rule 規則
order 秩序
act 法案
law 法律
衍 regulate (v.) 管理

The traffic regulations are strictly carried out by the local government.
當地政府嚴厲地執行交通法規。
point carry out = implement = put... into practice，意為「執行」。

All safety regulations should be followed in order to work more efficiently and safely.
所有的安全規則都該被遵守，工作才能更有效率且安全。
point in order to + V / that + S + V，意為「為了……」。

---

43 passenger
★
★
★
[ˈpæsn̩dʒɚ]
n 乘客，旅客
同 commuter 通勤者
traveler 旅客
rider 搭乘者
voyager 旅客

Attention passengers, the next train is to Springfield. Please wait on platform 2.
乘客們請注意，下一班車是往史普林菲爾德，請在第二月台等候。
point 從第一句 Attention passengers 就可以推敲出多益聽力測驗的背景和交通工具有關。

The flight attendants reminded all the passengers to get their boarding passes ready when they boarded the plane.
空服員提醒所有乘客在登機時準備好登機證。
point boarding pass 登機證、passport 護照、(electronic) ticket（電子）機票，皆為多益測驗中機場情景常見的必需文件。

---

44 ferry
★
★
[ˈfɛrɪ]
n 渡輪，渡口
同 ship 船

The only way to go to that small town is by ferry.
去那個小鎮的唯一方法就是搭渡輪。

The ferry service is temporary not available because of the strike.
渡輪服務因為罷工的關係，暫時不提供服務。
point temporary（暫時的）的相反為 permanent（永久的）。

45 rapid
★

['ræpɪd]

a 迅速的，險峻的

同 fast 快的
　quick 快的
　swift 快速的
　prompt 敏捷的

反 slow 慢的

衍 rapidly (adv.) 迅速地

The delivery company is known for its rapid and accurate service.

這間貨運公司以快速且精確的服務而聞名。

point be known for... 意為「以……而聞名」。

The new intern showed rapid progress in writing English emails.

新的實習生在寫英文書信上進步很快。

CH 15

交通觀光

---

46 traffic
★
★
★

['træfɪk]

n 交通，貿易，運輸

同 transport 運輸
　transportation 運輸

Do not violate the traffic rules or you will be fined.

不要違反交通規則，不然你就會被罰款。

point fine 在此句當動詞，意為「罰款」。比較此句語意：You will be fine.（你會沒事的。）這裡的 fine 為形容詞「很好的」。

You can go straight when the traffic light is green.

綠燈時你就可以直行。

point traffic light 意為「紅綠燈」。

---

47 breathtaking
★

['brεθ,tekɪŋ]

a 驚人的，極其美麗的

同 spectacular 壯觀的
　awesome 令人驚嘆的
　wonderful 極好的
　marvelous 非凡的

The travel magazine ranked the Great Canyon as one of the most breathtaking tourist attractions.

該旅遊雜誌評比美國大峽谷為最令人歎為觀止的名勝之一。

The photographer recorded the breathtaking view of the waterfall using a drone.

該名攝影師用空拍機來記錄這瀑布的驚人美景。

point 請注意 photographer 的重音在第二音節 [fə'tɑgrəfɚ]。

---

48 heritage
★

['hεrətɪdʒ]

n 遺產，繼承物，傳統

同 inheritance 繼承
　estate 遺產

I was amazed by the natural heritage sites, and I thus took tons of pictures.

這個自然遺跡使我感到驚豔，所以我拍了許多照片。

point thus 為副詞，表示「因此」，不能連接兩個句子，故用 and 連接。

147

15 交通觀光

49 scenery
★
★
[ˋsinərɪ]
n 風景，景色
同 landscape 風景
　　view 景色
衍 scene 景象

I'm totally attracted to the natural scenery here.
我完全被這裡的自然美景給吸引住了。
point be attracted to... 意為「被……吸引」。

I have always wanted to see the spectacular scenery of Europe in person.
我一直都想親眼看看歐洲的壯觀景色。
point in person = personally，表示「親自地」。

---

50 coach
★
★
[kotʃ]
n 教練，巴士，公車
v 訓練，輔導
同 tutor (n.) 家教
　　teacher (n.) 教師
　　instructor (n.) 指導者
　　trainer (n.) 教練員

I'm flying coach.
我搭經濟艙。
point 延伸詞彙：first class 頭等艙、business class 商務艙、economy class = coach 經濟艙。

After work, she coaches students in Physics as her part-time job.
她在下班後輔導學生物理作為她的兼職工作。
point 延伸詞彙：full-time 全職的。

---

51 spray
★
[spre]
v 噴灑，濺散
n 水花，噴霧
同 splash (v.) 濺潑

The cleaning company comes to this building to spray insecticide once a quarter.
清潔公司每一季會來這棟樓噴一次殺蟲劑。
point 延伸詞彙：twice a quarter 一季兩次，three times a quarter 一季三次。

The tour guide asked us to wear raincoats so that we would not get wet from the spray.
導遊要我們穿雨衣，這樣我們就不會被水花濺濕。

---

52 zone
★
[zon]
n 地帶，區域，範圍
同 area 地區
　　region 區域
　　section 地段
　　territory 領域

When you fly to different time zones, you might have the problem of jet lag.
當你飛到不同時區，你可能會有時差的問題。
point have problem / difficulty of N / Ving 意為「做……有問題」。

People who live in temperate zones enjoy mild weather.
住在溫帶的人們享受溫和的氣候。
point temperate zone 意為「溫帶」。

53 **suitcase**

★
★

['sut,kes]

n 手提箱，小型旅行箱

同 baggage 行李
　　luggage 行李
　　traveling bag 旅行袋

The suitcase is too heavy to carry.
這個手提箱太重以至於搬不動。

point too... to... 意為「太……以至於不能……」。

I packed all the souvenirs in my suitcase.
我把所有的紀念品打包到我的手提箱裡。

point 延伸詞彙：souvenir shop 為「紀念品店」。

54 **aisle**

★
★

[aɪl]

n 走道，通道

同 corridor 走廊
　　passageway 通道
　　alley 小巷

The security guard is in charge of guiding the visitors to the conference room which is at the end of the aisle.
警衛負責帶訪客到走廊盡頭的會議室。

55 **cabin**

★
★

['kæbɪn]

n 客艙，駕駛艙，小屋

同 hut 小屋

反 mansion 大廈
　　palace 皇宮

Children are fond of playing in the log cabin.
孩子們喜歡在小木屋裡玩。

point be fond of 意為「喜歡」，後加 Ving。

No cabin passengers are allowed to use their cellphones while planes are taking off.
當飛機起飛時，所有的機上乘客都不能使用手機。

56 **leave**

★
★
★

[liv]

v 離開，遺棄，辭去，丟下

同 depart 離開
　　go 離去

反 arrive 到達

They will take the early plane to leave for London.
他們會搭早班飛機動身前往倫敦。

point leave for 意為「前往」。比較此句的語意：I will leave London tomorrow.（我明天會離開英國。）

I left a message for Johnson, "I left your report on your desk".
我留言給強森：「我把你的報告留在你的桌上」。

point leave a message 表示「留言」，take a message 意為「抄寫留言」。

15 交通觀光

---

148

57 ★ ★

handbook
[`hænd,buk]

n 手冊,旅行指南
同 manual 手冊

According to the gardening handbook, excess water is not beneficial to the plants.
根據這本園藝手冊,過多的水對盆栽不好。

(point) plant 除了是「盆栽」,也可指「工廠」。

---

58 ★

blossom
[`blɑsəm]

n 花
v 開花,發展,生長茂盛
同 bloom (v.) 開花
flower (n.) 花

Many people travel to Japan to see the cherry blossoms during March.
很多人為了看櫻花在三月時去日本旅行。

(point) during + N 意為「在……期間」。

After graduating from college, she gradually blossomed into a gorgeous lady.
在大學畢業之後,她逐漸變成一位美麗動人的女士。

---

59 ★ ★

absolutely
[`æbsə,lutlɪ]

ad 絕對地,完全地
同 totally 完全地
utterly 十足地
definitely 絕對地
completely 完全地
反 relatively 相對地

Excellent language ability is absolutely a plus when you are looking for jobs.
找工作時,優異的語言能力絕對能為你加分。

(point) sth. is a plus 意為「某事是加分的」。

---

60 ★

accumulate
[ə`kjumjə,let]

v 累積,積聚
同 collect 收集
increase 增加
反 decrease 減少
scatter 分散
衍 accumulation (n.) 累積

Don't violate the traffic rules again. The accumulated fines will cost you a fortune.
不要再違反交通規則了,這些累積起來的罰金會花你很多錢。

(point) 相關詞彙:pile up 積累,save up 儲備,store up 收藏,gather 積聚。

I have accumulated many travel guidebooks since 2010.
自從二〇一〇年開始,我已經收集了許多旅遊書。

(point) 完成式常與 since 連用。

61 boom
★ [bum]
Ⅴ 暴漲，興旺
ⁿ 繁榮
同 thrive (v.) 興盛

The boom in language learning makes more people desire to study abroad.
語言學習的興旺使更多人想出國讀書。

---

62 bound
★ [baʊnd]
Ⅴ 跳躍，劃界線，限制
ⁿ 跳躍，邊界，範圍
ⓐ 受束縛的，有義務的
同 leap (v.) 跳躍
　　jump (v.) 跳
　　spring (v.) 彈起
衍 bounce (v.) 彈起

The train is bound for Manchester.
火車開往曼徹斯特。

> point　be bound for 意為「開往」。

Once the cellphone application was launched, the senior engineer knew it would be bound to fail.
手機應用程式一推出，資深的工程師就知道這注定會失敗。

> point　be bound to 意為「注定要」。

---

63 capital
★
★ [ˋkæpət!]
ⁿ 首都，資本，大寫字母
ⓐ 致命的，資本的，
　　大寫字母的
同 fund (n.) 資金
衍 capitalize (v.) 供給資本
　　capitalization (n.) 資本化

London is the capital city of the United Kingdom, and attracts many tourists from around the world every year.
倫敦是英國的首都，每年都吸引很多來自不同國家的遊客。

You can write capital letters when you would like to highlight some points.
你可以用大寫字母來強調一些重點。

> point　stress, spotlight, emphasize, give an emphasis to 皆可表達「強調」。

---

64 capture
★
★ [ˋkæptʃɚ]
Ⅴ 補捉，佔領，迷住
ⁿ 獲得，戰利品
同 apprehend (v.) 捕捉
　　arrest (v.) 逮捕

You are welcome to take pictures to capture the breathtaking views.
歡迎你照相來記錄這令人讚嘆的景色。

> point　相關詞彙：catch 抓住，seize 抓住。

The predator captured the prey in no time.
掠食者馬上就抓到了獵物。

> point　shortly, immediately, instantly, instantaneously 皆可表達「不久」。

15 交通觀光

65 **season**
★
★
★
[ˈsizṇ]

n 季節，旺季，時令
v 調味

We always avoid going abroad during the holiday season to get cheaper tickets.
我們總是避免在度假旺季時出國，才能買到便宜的票。

point holiday season 意為「度假旺季」。

During the peak season, our company usually hires more temporary workers.
在生意旺季時，我們公司通常都會僱用更多臨時工。

---

66 **safety**
★
★
[ˈseftɪ]

n 安全，安全設施
同 protection 保護
　　security 安全
反 danger 危險

Safety is the first concern when the backpacker chooses travel destinations.
當該名背包客選擇旅行目的地時，安全是第一個考量。

To ensure your safety, please follow the safeguard instructions.
為了確保你的安全，請遵守救生員指示。

point please + V 意為「請做……」，為祈使句。

---

67 **journey**
★
★
[ˈdʒɝnɪ]

n 旅行，行程
v 旅行
同 trip (n.) 旅行
　　tour (n.) 旅遊
　　expedition (n.) 遠征

The photographer took many pictures to record his journey.
攝影師拍了很多照片以記錄他的旅程。

point 相關詞彙：travel (n.) 旅行，voyage (n.) 旅程。

---

68 **inconvenience**
★
★
[ˌɪnkənˈvinjəns]

n 不便，麻煩
v 造成不便，打擾
同 trouble (n.) 麻煩
　　bother (v.) 打擾
　　problem (n.) 問題
　　difficulty (n.) 難處
反 convenience (n.) 方便

We sincerely apologize for the inconvenience caused by the delay of the flight.
我們真誠地為延誤的班機帶來的不便道歉。

point caused 由 which / that was caused 簡化而來。

The road was closed due to the serious traffic collision, which inconvenienced many commuters.
道路因為嚴重的車禍而封閉，造成許多通勤者的不便。

point traffic collision, car accident, crash 皆可指「車禍」。

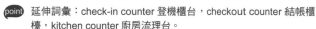

CH 15

交通觀光

---

69 **entry**
★
★
　['εntrɪ]
　n 進入，入口，項目，登記
　同 admission 進入許可
　　 admittance 入場許可
　　 access 進入
　反 departure 離開

The tour guide was waiting for his team members at the entry to the museum.
導遊在博物館的入口處等他的團員。

(point) 相關詞彙：entrance 入口。

---

70 **voucher**
★
★
★
　['vautʃɚ]
　n 票券，優惠券
　同 coupon 優惠券
　　 ticket 票券

Unfortunately, the voucher is not valid anymore.
很不幸地，該現金券不再有效。

Passengers who take the delayed flight EK309 please come to the counter to get a meal voucher.
搭乘延誤的 EK309 號班機的乘客請到櫃台來領取餐券。

(point) 延伸詞彙：check-in counter 登機櫃台，checkout counter 結帳櫃檯，kitchen counter 廚房流理台。

---

71 **transfer**
★
★
　[træns`fɝ]
　v 轉換，改變，轉乘
　['trænsfɝ]
　n 移交，轉讓，調任
　同 move (v.) 移動
　　 convey (v.) 轉運
　　 shift (v.) 轉移

The operator transferred Sam's call to the Personnel Department.
接線生轉接山姆的電話給人事部門。

(point) transfer one's call to 意為「轉接某人的電話給……」。

With this comprehensive guidebook, it's not difficult to transfer from one subway line to another.
有了這本詳盡的旅遊書，從一個地鐵線轉到另一個地鐵線一點都不難。

(point) transfer from A to B 意為「從 A 轉到 B」。

---

72 **hence**
★
★
　[hεns]
　ad 因此，從現在起
　同 accordingly 因此
　　 therefore 因此
　　 thus 因此

The road is being repaired, and hence it is closed temporarily.
道路正在修復中，因此暫時被封閉。

(point) hence 為副詞，因此需要 and 來連接兩個句子。

The weather conditions were not good; hence most of the flights were cancelled.
天候不佳，因此大部分的航班都被取消了。

(point) 分號「;」有連接詞的作用，用來連接兩個句子。

Chapter 150

15 交通觀光

73 terminal
★
★
★
[ˋtɝmənḷ]

a 末端的，終點的，晚期的
n 航廈，終點站
同 end (n.) 盡頭
extreme (n.) 末端
反 first (n.) 第一個

The next stop is the terminal station.
下一站是終點站。

The coach will take you to terminal 2 rather than terminal 3.
客運會載你到第二航廈而不是第三航廈。

point rather than = instead of，意為「取而代之」。

74 severe
★
★
★
[səˋvɪr]

a 嚴重的，劇烈的，苛刻的
同 terrible 嚴重的
alarming 告急的
worrying 令人擔心的
反 minor 次要的
gentle 溫和的
slight 輕微的

Due to the severe weather conditions, the flight was delayed.
因為惡劣的天氣，班機延誤了。

point 多益測驗中飛機延誤常是因為天氣的原因。

The government is facing severe criticism owing to the failure to address problems immediately.
政府目前正因為沒有立即處理問題而遭到嚴厲的批評。

point 相關詞彙：serious 嚴重的，critical 批判的，awful 十分的，extreme 極度的。

75 recently
★
★
★
[ˋrisn̩tlɪ]

ad 最近，近來
同 lately 最近
latterly 近來
just now 現階段
反 a long time ago 很久以前
past 過去

Recently, he has started to learn Spanish.
他最近開始學西班牙語。

Recently, the tire factory has been transformed into a famous tourist attraction.
最近，輪胎工廠被改造成有名的旅遊景點。

76 exposure
★
[ɪkˋspoʒɚ]

n 暴露，揭露，曝光
同 revelation 暴露
disclosure 揭發
unveiling 揭開
uncovering 揭露

Increasing language exposure is the best and the most efficient way to learn a new foreign language.
增加對語言的接觸就是一個最棒且最有效率的學習新外語的方法

point Increasing language exposure 為 Ving 當主詞，動詞單數。

When you go to tropical countries, remember to apply sunscreen and limit your exposure to sun.
當你去熱帶國家時，記得塗防曬乳及不要長時間曬太陽。

point sunscreen (n.) 防曬乳，不是 sun cream。

Question

⬤ 以下題目完全擬真新制多益 Part 5，請選出最符合句意的選項。

1. Due to the ------- weather, the flight was delayed.
   (A) frequent
   (B) breathtaking
   (C) inclement
   (D) rapid

2. Make sure your passport is ------- before you go abroad.
   (A) capital   (B) valid   (C) expire   (D) terminal

3. The assistant had ordered 50 ------- for the new campaign a month ago.
   (A) commuters
   (B) belongings
   (C) announcement
   (D) brochures

4. The travel agency said that there will be an addition to the -------.
   (A) itinerary   (B) backpack   (C) guidebook   (D) suitcase

5. They will take the early plane to leave ------- London.
   (A) in   (B) for   (C) on   (D) to

6. -------, the tire factory has been transformed into a famous tourist attraction.
   (A) Absolutely   (B) Directly   (C) Severely   (D) Recently

>> 正確答案與解析請翻至下一頁查看

Answer

● 正確答案與解析

1. 因天候不佳,航班延誤。

(A) 經常的　　　　(B) 驚人的　　　　(C) 惡劣的　　　　(D) 迅速的

正確答案 (C)

2. 在你出國前,請確認你的護照是有效的。

(A) 重要的　　　　(B) 有效的　　　　(C) 期滿　　　　(D) 末端的;航廈

正確答案 (B)

3. 這位助理一個月前就為了新的行銷活動訂了五百本小冊子。

(A) 通勤者　　　　(B) 所有物　　　　(C) 宣布　　　　(D) 小冊子

正確答案 (D)

4. 旅行社說行程表將會有一項新增的行程。

(A) 行程　　　　(B) 後背包　　　　(C) 旅遊書　　　　(D) 行李箱

正確答案 (A)

5. 他們會搭早班飛機動身前往倫敦。

(B) leave for 意為「動身前往」

正確答案 (B)

6. 最近,輪胎工廠被改造成有名的旅遊景點。

(A) 完全地　　　　(B) 直接地　　　　(C) 嚴重地　　　　(D) 最近地

正確答案 (D)

Chapter 16
醫療健康

DAILY REPORT SCHEDULE

08:15

以下多益必考單字,你認識哪些?

☐ effective (p.339)   ☐ contain (p.343)   ☐ conclusion (p.341)

☐ success (p.339)   ☐ treatment (p.348)   ☐ professional (p.346)

☐ excess (p.341)   ☐ except (p.353)   ☐ lately (p.346)

☐ confirm (p.338)   ☐ importance (p.351)   ☐ decline (p.354)

☐ breakthrough (p.344)   ☐ conclusion (p.341)   ☐ prescription (p.349)

☐ license (p.351)   ☐ create (p.352)   ☐ pharmacy (p.342)

16 醫療健康

---

01 **proceed**
★
★
[prə`sid]

Ⅴ 繼續進行，著手，出發

同 go 出發
　continue 繼續

反 stop 停止

衍 proceeds (n.) 收益

The award ceremony is now proceeding smoothly.
頒獎典禮現在正順利進行中。

The patient had decided to proceed with the medical treatment.
病人已經決定要進行那個醫療療程。

---

02 **expectation**
★
★
★
[ˌɛkspɛk`teʃən]

ⓝ 期待，預期，前程

同 anticipation 期待
　expectancy 期望
　outlook 展望

衍 expect (v.) 期待

It's unlikely for me to get a promotion this year since I failed to fulfill the manager's expectations.
今年我是不可能升遷了，因為我沒能達到經理的期望。

point　fail to + V 意為「做……失敗」。

With the improvements in both nutrition and medical techniques, life expectation is generally longer than before.
隨著營養及醫療技術的進步，平均壽命普遍比以前還長。

point　life expectation 意為「平均壽命」。

---

03 **confirm**
★
★
★
[kən`fɝm]

Ⅴ 證實，確定，批准

同 affirm 證實
　assert 斷言

反 deny 否認

衍 confirmation (n.) 證實

I am calling to confirm your dental appointment with Dr. Barea.
我打來確認您與巴雷亞醫生的牙醫預約。

point　schedule / reschedule an appointment 意為「排程預約／重新安排預約」。

The hotel reservation has been confirmed by both telephone and e-mail.
飯店訂房預約已經用電話和電子郵件確認了。

---

04 **effect**
★
★
★
[ɪ`fɛkt]

ⓝ 效果，結果，影響

Ⅴ 造成，產生，達到

同 result (n.) 結果
　consequence (n.) 結果
　outcome (n.) 後果

反 cause (n.) 原因

The medicine will take effect in 5 minutes.
藥效會在五分鐘內見效。

point　take effect 意為「產生預期的或要求的結果；生效」。

Using electronic devices for a long time might have a harmful effect on our eyes.
長期使用電子產品可能會對人們的眼睛造成不良的影響。

point　have a harmful effect on 意為「對……有不良的影響」。

05 **effective**

★
★ [ɪ`fɛktɪv]
★
🅰 有效的，起作用的
🔄 successful 成功的
constructive 有助益的
helpful 有幫助的
🔄 ineffective 無效的
incompetent 無能的

The Spring treadmill makes your fitness training more effective.
春天跑步機讓你體能訓練更有效。

(point) 相關詞彙：productive 有成效的，powerful 效力大的。

The new policy will be effective next Monday.
新政策下週一會生效。

(point) 多益閱讀測驗中有時會考新政策何時生效，認出 effective 這個字很重要。

06 **beneficial**

★
★ [ˌbɛnə`fɪʃəl]
🅰 有益的，有幫助的，有利的
🔄 helpful 有幫助的
useful 有用的
🔄 unwholesome 有害身心的
useless 無用的
🔄 benefactor (n.) 贊助人

Sponsoring international competition is beneficial to a company's reputation.
贊助國際比賽有助一家公司的商譽。

(point) Sponsoring international competition 為主詞，動詞用單數 is。

Taking some supplements like vitamin C and B complex is beneficial to your health.
吃一些營養食品，像是維他命 C 和維他命 B 群有益健康。

07 **schedule**

★
★ [`skɛdʒul]
★
🄽 時間表，計畫表，清單
🅅 列入時間表，安排，預定
🔄 timetable (n.) 時間表
agenda (n.) 議程

The schedule is enclosed in the envelope.
行程表在隨信附上的信封裡。

Due to schedule conflicts, he called the clinic to cancel the scheduled medical appointment.
因為行程衝突，他打給診所取消已排好的醫療預約。

(point) 延伸詞彙：reschedule (v.) 重新排程。

08 **success**

★
★ [sək`sɛs]
★
🄽 成功，成功的人（或物）
🔄 successfulness 成功
victory 勝利
triumph 勝利
🔄 successful (a.) 成功的
succeed (v.) 成功

The success of the event has brought the team a lot of confidence.
這個活動的成功已經帶給團隊許多信心。

With the advance in medical technology, the success rate for this treatment is very high.
隨著醫療科技的進步，這種治療方式的成功率非常高。

(point) with 在此句意為「隨著」。

Chapter 152

16 醫療健康

09 intense
★
[ɪnˋtɛns]
ⓐ 強烈的，極度的，熱情的
同 acute 劇烈的
　severe 嚴重的
　extreme 極度的
反 mild 溫和的
衍 intensive 密集的

The player felt intense pain in his back and then was sent to the hospital immediately.
球員突然覺得背部一陣劇痛，接著就立即被送到醫院。

She hardly could stand the intense heat and just passed out.
她不能忍受高溫，暈了過去。

point hardly = barely = rarely = scarcely，意為「幾乎不」。

10 enhance
★
★
★
[ɪnˋhæns]
ⓥ 提高，增加，改善
同 increase 增加
　build up 增進
　upgrade 提高
　escalate 增加
反 decrease 減少
　diminish 減少

Regular physical training enhances your health.
規律的體能訓練可以強化你的健康。

point 相關詞彙：boost 提升，intensify 強化，elevate 使上升，amplify 增強，strengthen 加強。

Many office workers take language courses after their full-time jobs to enhance their career prospects.
很多上班族在正職工作下班後上語言課程，以增強他們的工作前景。

point 延伸詞彙：part-time (a.) 兼職的。

11 fit
★
★
★
[fɪt]
ⓐ 適合的，健康的，能勝任的
ⓥ 相稱，使適合，安裝
同 healthy (a.) 健康的
　in shape (ph.) 健康的
反 unfit (a.) 不合適的

Slogans should be short and catchy, such as, "Go to the gym and stay fit."
廣告口號應該要簡短好記，像是「去健身房，保持健康。」

The clerk kept saying that the dress fitted her customer well.
店員不斷地說這裙子很適合她的客人。

point keep + Ving 意為「保持做……」。

12 fitness
★
[ˋfɪtnɪs]
ⓝ 健康，適合
同 health 健康
　strength 力量
反 unfitness 不適當

You can buy the one-month fitness center pass.
你可以買那個健身中心的一個月通行證。

Physical fitness and training shouldn't be ignored in formal education.
體能健康及訓練不該在正規教育中被忽略。

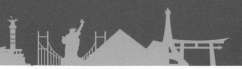

CH 16

醫療健康

13 excess

★

[ɪkˋsɛs]

n 超過，過量，無節制

[ɛkˋsɛs]

a 過量的，額快的，附加的

同 surplus (n.) 過剩

反 inadequate (a.) 不夠的
　 scarce (a.) 不足的

The speaker mentioned that an excess of kindness is not always a good thing.
講者提到過分善良不見得總是件好事。

People who are diagnosed with diabetes should have a healthy and balanced diet to get rid of excess weight.
被診斷出有糖尿病的人們要有健康且均衡的飲食以減輕過量的體重。

point get rid of 意為「去除」。

14 effort

★
★
★

[ˋɛfɚt]

n 努力，成就

同 attempt 企圖
　 try 嘗試
　 endeavor 努力

He goes to the gym to work out regularly in an effort to keep fit.
爲了讓體態良好，他定期去健身房健身。

point 此句為描述「習慣」，使用現在式。

Your efforts won't be wasted because the dots will be connected eventually.
你的努力不會被浪費，因為這些點終究都會被串聯起來。

point eventually (adv.) 最後，終於。

15 regularly

★
★
★

[ˋrɛgjələˌlɪ]

ad 有規律地，定期地，整齊地

反 irregularly 不規律地

衍 regulate (v.) 管理
　 regulation (n.) 規則

Sunbathing regularly might be harmful to your skin.
定期的日光浴可能會對你的皮膚不好。

point be harmful to 意為「對……有壞處」。

One of the employee benefits is that the company holds training sessions regularly.
員工福利之一就是公司會定期舉辦訓練課程。

16 conclusion

★
★
★

[kənˋkluʒən]

n 結論，終結，議定

同 ending 結局
　 finish 結束
　 close 結束

反 beginning 開始

衍 conclude (v.) 結束

Don't jump to conclusions too soon.
不要太快下結論。

In conclusion, take the prescription medicine twice a day and keep a balanced diet.
總而言之，一天吃兩次處方藥並保持均衡的飲食。

point in conclusion = in summary，意為「總而言之」。

Chapter 153

16 醫療健康

17 permanent
★
★

[ˈpɝmənənt]

a 永久的，固定性的

同 enduring 持久的
continuing 不間斷的

反 temporary 暫時的

This doctor introduced three main reasons for permanent hearing loss.
這位醫生介紹了三種主要永久性失聰的原因。

Usually, permanent workers will receive a pay raise every year.
一般來說，全職員工每年都會有加薪。

18 instruct
★
★
★

[ɪnˈstrʌkt]

V 指示，命令，教導，訓練

同 order 命令
command 命令
direct 指揮
require 要求

衍 instruction (n.) 指示

He instructs people how to use the gym equipment in the local community center.
他在當地的社區中心教人們如何使用健身器材。

point 此句以現在式來表達現況。

The employees are instructed to submit their daily work reports.
員工們被指示每天要交工作報告。

19 pharmacy
★
★

[ˈfɑrməsɪ]

n 藥房，製藥業

同 drugstore 藥房

She has worked in the pharmacy ever since she graduated from college.
自從大學畢業以來，她一直都在這間藥局工作。

point since 常與完成式連用。

A bachelor's degree in Pharmacy is one of the most crucial requirements for this position.
對這個職位來說，藥學學士學位是其中一個最關鍵的必要條件。

point one of the Ns 意為「其中一個」，名詞使用複數，代表一堆群體。

20 stationary
★

[ˈsteʃənˌɛrɪ]

a 不動的，定居的，停滯的

同 immobile 不動的
motionless 靜止的

反 dynamic 動態的

Jo goes to the gym to work out twice a week and she likes to use treadmills and stationary bikes.
喬一週去健身房鍛鍊兩次，她喜歡使用跑步機和健身車。

point stationary bike 意為靜止的腳踏車，也就是健身車。

Many people live a stationary lifestyle, which means they spend plenty of time lying, sitting, reading and watching TV, instead of doing physical exercise.
很多人過著靜態的生活，他們花很多時間躺著、坐著、看電視，而不是做運動。

point 易混淆字：stationery (n.) 文具。

CH 16

醫療健康

---

21 blockage

★

['blɑkɪdʒ]

n 封鎖，妨礙

同 obstruction 障礙

衍 block (v.) 封鎖

The experienced plumber cleared the blockage immediately.

這位經驗豐富的水電工馬上清除了阻塞。

point 在國外 plumber 為「水管工人」，而 electrician 為「電工」。但台灣是合在一起叫做「水電工」。

A blockage in arteries might cause a heart attack and stroke.

動脈阻塞可能會造成心臟病和中風。

point 延伸詞彙：sunstroke 意為「中暑」。

---

22 duration

★
★
★

[dju`reʃən]

n 持續，持續時間

同 period 期間
term 任期

The duration of the health check-up is one hour.

健康檢查所需要的時間是一小時。

point 「健康檢查」的其他講法：physical examination / check-up / health examination。

The typhoon was of short duration.

颱風持續的時間很短。

point of + N 有形容詞的作用。

---

23 contain

★
★

[kən`ten]

v 包含，容納，控制

同 include 包含

反 exclude 不包含

The package contains some free samples.

這個裹裡包含了一些免費的樣品。

Milk contains calcium, which is beneficial to adolescents.

牛奶富含鈣，這對青少年有益。

point be beneficial to 意為「對……有益」。

---

24 instance

★

['ɪnstəns]

n 實例，情況，場合

同 example 例子

衍 instant (a.) 立即的
instantaneous (a.) 瞬間的
instantly (adv.) 立即地

Andy is quite responsible; for instance, he always tells his deputy what to do in detail when he takes a leave.

安迪相當負責，舉例來說，他要請假時總是會很詳細地告訴他的職務代理人要做什麼。

point in detail 此處為副詞，意為「詳細地」。

In most instances young people can recover from surgery sooner than the elderly.

在大部分的情況下，年輕人比起年長者能更快在手術後復原。

point recover from 意為「從……復原」。

343

25 **proximity**
★ [prɑk`sɪmətɪ]
　🆝 接近，鄰近，親近
　🔄 vicinity 附近地區
　　 closeness 接近
　　 nearness 接近

My house is in close proximity to the gym, which makes exercise a lot more convenient.
我家十分接近健身房，非常方便我去運動。

🔵point a lot, considerably, significantly 都可用來修飾比較級。

When choosing a place to live, proximity to a supermarket is extremely essential to me.
當選擇要住的地點時，接近超市對我來說很重要。

🔵point important, crucial, critical, significant, major, key 都可表達「重要的」。

26 **purify**
★ [`pjʊrəˏfaɪ]
　🆅 淨化，精煉
　🔄 cleanse 淨化
　　 refine 精煉
　🔁 stain 染污
　📋 pure (a.) 純粹的

Doing yoga purifies my thoughts because I only focus on my body movements without being bothered by other things.
做瑜伽能夠淨化我的想法，因為我只需要專注在我的身體動作而不用被其他事情打擾。

🔵point 原本被動式為 be bothered，但因為是在 without 介係詞後，因此變 being bothered。

27 **fiber**
★ [`faɪbɚ]
　🆝 纖維，質地，素質

For your health, you should eat vegetables that are high in fiber.
為了你的健康著想，你該吃富含高纖維的蔬菜。

Synthetic fiber is welcomed by consumers due to its stain resistance functions.
因為防汙漬的功能，合成纖維在顧客間很受歡迎。

28 **breakthrough**
★ [`brekˏθru]
　🆝 突破，突破性進展
　🔄 development 發展
　　 discovery 發現
　　 advance 發展

The medical breakthrough sounds like the plot of a science fiction novel.
這個醫學發現聽起來就像科幻小說中的劇情。

I was impressed by the actor's breakthrough performance.
我對這名演員的突破性演出印象深刻

🔵point be impressed by 意為「對……印象深刻」。

29 basis
★
['besɪs]

n 基礎，根據，準則
同 base 基礎
foundation 基礎
principle 原則
衍 basic (a.) 基礎的
basically (adv.) 基礎地

My company gives out bonuses on the basis of employees' performance.
我們公司根據員工的工作表現來發獎金。
(point) give out 意為「發出」。

The government promotes new medical concepts based on a scientific basis.
政府倡導新的、有科學根據的醫療觀念。
(point) based on 意為「根據」。

30 activity
★
★
[æk'tɪvətɪ]

n 活動，活動力，活躍
同 movement 活動
energy 活力
反 inactivity 靜止
衍 action (n.) 動作
activate (v.) 使活潑
active (a.) 活躍的

My father loves outdoor activities, such as camping, hiking and biking.
我父親熱愛戶外運動，像是露營、健行及騎腳踏車。
(point) 延伸詞彙：indoor (a.) 室內的。

Tourists to that area please be careful since the volcanic activity is increasing.
要去那個地區的遊客請小心，因為那區的火山運動正在增加。
(point) 延伸詞彙：volcano 意為「火山」。

31 bind
★
[baɪnd]

v 捆，裝訂，黏合，約束
同 stick 黏貼
cohere 黏合
unite 聯合
join 連結
bond 連結
衍 binding (n.) 裝訂

The manager found himself in a double bind.
這位經理發現自己進退兩難。
(point) double bind 意為「進退兩難」。

Bandages are used to bind up patients' wounds.
繃帶用來綁住病人的傷口。
(point) be used to + V 意為「被用來做……」。

32 occupation
★
★
★
[ˌɑkjə'peʃən]

n 職業，消遣，佔據
同 profession 職業
career 職業
job 工作
衍 occupancy (n.) 佔有
occupied (a.) 已佔用的

If you have no idea how to choose an occupation, you can ask the consultant for help.
如果你不知道如何選擇職業，你可以請顧問幫忙。
(point) ask sb. for help 意為「尋求某人的幫忙」。

For busy people nowadays, exercising is a beneficial occupation.
對於忙碌的現代人而言，運動是一種有益的消遣。
(point) 延伸詞彙：recreation 也指「娛樂；消遣」。

345

醫療健康

33 **decent**

★

[`disnt]

a 正派的，體面的，還不錯的

同 proper 恰當的
correct 端正的
appropriate 合適的
apt 恰當的

反 indecent 下流的

The health professional earns a decent salary.
這名醫療專業人士收入相當好。

Mr. Saric who just transferred from the headquarters worked hard in order to have a decent standard of living.
為了要有體面的生活，剛從總部調來的薩利奇先生努力工作。

point transfer from A to B 意為「從 A 轉乘／調職到 B」。

34 **twice**

★

[twaɪs]

ad 兩次，兩回，兩倍

衍 think twice (ph.) 重新考慮
twice over
(ph.) 不只一次，而是兩次

Please take the tablets twice a day.
請一天吃兩次藥。

Normally, my associates attend training sessions twice a year.
通常我的同事一年參加兩次訓練課程。

35 **professional**

★
★
★

[prə`fɛʃənl]

a 職業的，專業的，內行的

n 職業選手，專家

同 non-manual (a.) 非勞力的

反 manual (a.) 體力的

衍 profession (n.) 職業

According to the professional, solar power is widely used in this country.
根據專業人士，太陽能在這個國家被廣泛使用。

point according to = based on，意為「根據」。

The journalist arranged a meeting with the health professional to ask his professional opinion on diabetes.
記者和那位醫療專業人士安排了會議，要問他有關糖尿病的專業看法。

point arrange / schedule a meeting 意為「安排會議」，reschedule a meeting 意為「重新排程會議」。

36 **lately**

★
★

[`letlɪ]

ad 近來，不久前

同 recently 最近
of late 最近以來

The sales representative has not visited the dealer lately.
這名業務最近都沒有去拜訪經銷商。

The patient told the doctor that he had stayed up late lately.
病人和醫生說他最近都熬夜。

point stay up late 意為「熬夜」。

37 examination
★
★
★
[ɪɡˌzæməˈneʃən]
Ⓝ 檢查，調查，考試
Ⓢ inspection 檢查
    check-up 檢查
    assessment 評估
    review 複審
衍 examiner (n.) 檢查人

He felt frustrated after he knew he failed the entrance examination.
他在知道自己沒能通過入學考試時非常沮喪。

Every employee receives a physical examination every year.
每個員工每年都要做身體檢查。

point every, each + 單數名詞。

---

38 degree
★
★
★
[dɪˈɡri]
Ⓝ 度數，程度，學位
Ⓢ level 等級
    stage 階段
    standard 標準
    grade 等級
    amount 數量
    extent 程度

Even though many medical professionals had warned the athlete that there was a degree of danger involved in the sport, he still insisted on doing it.
即使許多醫療專業人士已經警告那名運動員這運動有一定的危險，他仍然堅持去做。

point a degree of 意為「有一定程度的……」。

Having a bachelor's degree in marketing is a plus for this position.
擁有大學行銷學歷對這個職位很加分。

CH 16
醫療健康

---

39 breakdown
★
[ˈbrekˌdaʊn]
Ⓝ 故障，損壞，崩潰，細目
Ⓢ malfunction 故障
    failure 失敗
    crash 撞壞
衍 breakable (a.) 會破的

The patient received regular treatment because of his mental breakdown.
病人因為精神崩潰，定期接受治療。

The accountant sent the breakdown of the expenses through the internal mail system to the director of the financial department.
會計透過內部郵件系統將支出細目表傳給財務部主任。

---

40 warning
★
★
[ˈwɔrnɪŋ]
Ⓝ 警告，警報
Ⓐ 警告的，告誡的
Ⓢ caution (n.) 警告
    alarm (n.) 警報
衍 warn (v.) 警告

Loss of appetite might be a warning of some health-related problems.
失去胃口可能是一些健康相關問題的警告。

The security guard's timely warning saved many morning commuters' lives.
警衛及時的警告拯救了許多早晨通勤者的生命。

point timely 長得像副詞，但卻是形容詞，意為「及時的」。

Chapter 156

16 醫療健康

41 vital
★
★★
★
['vaɪtl]

a 生命的，充滿活力的
同 necessary 必要的
反 unimportant 不重要的
peripheral 周圍的
secondary 次要的

Regular exercise and a balanced diet are two vital tips for staying healthy.
規律的運動和均衡飲食是兩個保持健康的重要訣竅。

(point) 相關詞彙：essential 必要的，indispensable 不可或缺的，crucial 關鍵的，key 重要的。

It is vital that we should upgrade the software to make the system run faster.
重要的是我們必須要更新軟體讓系統運作加速。

(point) It is vital that + S + V 意為「……是重要的」。

---

42 treatment
★
★
['tritmənt]

n 對待，處理，治療（法）
同 therapy 治療
remedy 治療
衍 treat (v.) 處理

The patient received medical treatment.
病人接受醫療治療。

The group that received special treatment performed better than the other group.
有接受特別治療的小組比另一組的表現還要好。

---

43 supplement
★
★
★
['sʌpləˌmɛnt]

v 補充，補附錄
['sʌpləmənt]

n 增補，補充，附錄
同 addition (n.) 附加

The housewife particularly enjoys clipping coupons from Sunday newspaper supplements.
那位家庭主婦特別喜歡在週日報紙副刊中剪下折價券。

The patient was supposed to take vitamin supplements twice a week.
病人應該要一週服用兩次維生素補充劑。

---

44 spread
★
★
★
[sprɛd]

v 伸展，傳開，蔓延
n 抹醬
同 extend 延伸

The government is dealing with the spread of disease.
政府正在處理疾病的散播。

(point) deal with = cope with = handle，意為「處理」。

The store sells a variety of cheese spreads to satisfy different customers.
這家店賣各式各樣乳酪醬以滿足不同的顧客。

45 recover

★
★

[rɪˋkʌvɚ]

Ⅴ 恢復，重新獲得，挽回

同 recuperate 恢復
　 regain 收復

反 deteriorate 惡化
　 worsen 惡化

I am afraid that the patient will take one year to recover from the surgery.
恐怕病人要花一年才能從手術中復原。

(point) be afraid that + S + V 意為「恐怕……」。

Finally, it was British police that recovered the stolen masterpieces.
最終，是英國警察找回了被盜的傑作。

(point) It Is + 強調的事物 + that... 為強調句，意為「正是……」。

46 recovery

★
★

[rɪˋkʌvərɪ]

ⓝ 重獲，恢復，痊癒

反 deterioration 惡化

Both Mr. Hayward's coach and doctor were surprised at the speed of his recovery.
海渥德先生的教練和醫生都對他的復原速度感到驚訝。

(point) be surprised at 意為「感到驚訝」。

After the natural disaster, the small town began to show signs of economic recovery.
在天災後，小鎮開始有經濟復原的跡象。

47 prescription

★
★

[prɪˋskrɪpʃən]

ⓝ 處方，祕訣，指示

同 instruction 指示
　 order 命令
　 direction 指導

衍 prescribe (v.) 開處方

You can buy the medicine only when you have a doctor's prescription.
你只有在有醫生處方箋時才能買這個藥。

The audience asked the businessman in the pharmaceutical industry his prescription for success.
觀眾詢問在製藥業的企業家成功的訣竅是什麼。

48 persistent

★

[pɚˋsɪstənt]

ⓐ 堅持不懈的，持續的，持久的

同 constant 持續的
　 steady 不變的

反 occasional 偶爾的

衍 persistence (n.) 堅持
　 persist (v.) 堅持

The persistent ringing of the cellphone from the client annoyed the sales rep.
客戶不斷打來的電話鈴聲惹惱了這名業務。

(point) 相關詞彙：continuing 連續的，lasting 持續的。

The patient suffered from persistent headaches; therefore, he went to see a doctor.
病人受持續不斷的頭痛之苦，因此他去看醫生。

(point) therefore 為副詞，用分號連接兩個句子。

Chapter 157

16 醫療健康

49 nutrition
★
[njuˈtrɪʃən]
n 營養，營養物，營養學
同 nourishment 營養品
衍 nurture (v.) 養育
nutrient (a.) 營養的
nutritious (a.) 滋養的

This food provides nutrition that pregnant women need.
這個食物提供孕婦所需的營養。

The meal designed for patients contains a lot of nutrition.
為了病人設計的餐點含有許多營養。

---

50 obviously
★
★
[ˈɑbvɪəslɪ]
ad 明顯地，顯然地
同 clearly 明確地
evidently 明顯地
plainly 清楚地
visibly 明顯地
衍 obvious (a.) 明顯的

Obviously, the client was not willing to sign the contract.
很明顯地，這名客戶不願意簽約。
point be willing to 意為「願意……」。

When I looked at his pale complexion, I knew he was obviously sick.
當我看到他的蒼白面色時，我知道他顯然是生病了。

---

51 mild
★
[maɪld]
a 溫和的，溫暖的，溫柔的
同 gentle 溫和的
tender 溫柔的
soft 柔軟的
反 strong 強壯的
spicy 辛辣的

According to the forecast, tomorrow will be a mild day.
根據天氣預報，明天天氣會很暖和。

The patient only ate mild food that was easy to digest since he had a delicate stomach yesterday.
這位病患昨天只吃易消化的清淡食物，因為他腸胃不適。
point mild 此處指「食物清淡的」。

---

52 eliminate
★
[ɪˈlɪməˌnet]
v 排除，消滅，淘汰
同 get rid of 擺脫
反 keep 保持
stay 留下
remain 剩下

The magazine editor eliminated all the technical words from the article to make it more reader-friendly.
雜誌編輯將所有的專業術語從這篇文章中刪除，讓讀者較好閱讀。
point 延伸詞彙：eco-friendly 意為「對環境友善的」。

The virus can be gradually eliminated from your body by taking medicine and exercising.
透過吃藥和運動，病毒可以逐漸從你的體內排除。
point by 意為「藉由」，為介係詞，後面加 N / Ving。

53 mental

★
★
['mɛntḷ]

a 精神的，心理的，智力的

同 intellectual 智力的
rational 理性的
psychological 心理的
conceptual 概念上的

反 physical 身體的

衍 metal (a.) 金屬的

Mental health is as significant as physical health.
心理的健康跟生理的健康一樣重要。

point as... as 意為「和……一樣」。

The patient suffered from a mental disorder.
病人深受心理疾病之苦。

point suffer from 意為「深受……之苦」。

---

54 license

★
★
★
['laɪsn̩s]

n 特許，許可證

v 許可，發許可證給

同 permit (v.) 准許
authorize (v.) 授權

反 ban (v.) 禁止
forbid (v.) 禁止
prohibit (v.) 禁止

His driver's license was suspended owing to the traffic violations.
他的駕照因為交通違規被吊銷了。

point owing to = because of = due to + N / Ving，意為「因為」。

The pharmacy has been licensed to sell the medicine.
藥局獲得了這項藥品的銷售許可。

---

55 importance

★
★
★
[ɪm'pɔrtn̩s]

n 重要性，重要地位，傲慢

同 significance 重要

反 unimportance 不重要
insignificance 不重要

We should never ignore the importance of education.
我們絕對不能忽略教育的重要性。

The fitness trainer stressed the importance of healthy diets.
健身教練強調了健康飲食的重要性。

point stress the importance of 意為「強調……的重要性」。

---

56 hazardous

★
['hæzɚdəs]

a 有危險的，冒險的

同 dangerous 危險的

反 safe 安全的
secure 安全的
certain 有把握的

The article reported on some hazardous occupations in the world.
這篇文章報導了一些世界上危險的職業。

point 相關詞彙：risky 有風險的，unsafe 不安全的，insecure 不安全的。

It's believed that excessive drinking is hazardous to people's health.
人們相信過度飲酒有害健康。

57 harm
★
[hɑrm]

Ⅴ 損傷,傷害,危害
ⁿ 損傷,傷害,危害
ⓢ injury (n.) 受傷
　hurt (n.) 創傷
　damage (n.) 損害
反 benefit (n.) 益處

He meant no harm.
他並無惡意。

Excessive use of electronic devices will do you harm.
過量使用電子裝置對你有害。

point do sb. harm 意為「對(人)有害」。

---

58 harmful
★
★
[ˋhɑrmfəl]

ⓐ 有害的,不良的
ⓢ detrimental 有害的
　deleterious 有害的
　unfavorable 不利的
反 beneficial 有益的
　harmless 無害的

Drinking too much is harmful to your health.
喝太多對你的健康不好。

point 相關詞彙:injurious 有害的,damaging 有害的,unhealthy 不健康的,disadvantageous 不利的,negative 負面的。

Some people think seeing violence on television has a harmful effect on children.
有些人覺得在電視上看到暴力畫面會對小孩子有不良的影響。

---

59 create
★
★
[krɪˋet]

Ⅴ 創作,創造,設計
ⓢ generate 產生
　design 設計
　manufacture 製造
　construct 建造

The Café tries to create a cozy atmosphere by playing Jazz music.
這家咖啡廳藉由播放爵士樂來創造愜意的氣氛。

point 相關詞彙:produce 製造,make 製造,build 建造。

The medical consultant created a method to address the vicious cycle of sleeping late and waking up late.
那位醫療顧問發明了一個方法來處理熬夜又晚起的惡性循環。

point vicious cycle 意為「惡性循環」。

---

60 fiction
★
[ˋfɪkʃən]

ⁿ 小說,捏造,虛構的事
ⓢ novel 小說
　story 傳說
反 non-fiction 紀實文學
　fact 事實
　truth 事實

He enjoys the imaginary worlds in science fiction movies.
他享受科幻片中想像的世界。

The patient who suffered from mental disease had a hard time distinguishing fact from fiction.
這位有心理疾病的病人很難區分事實和虛構的事。

point distinguish A from B 意為「區分 A 和 B」。

61 except

★
★

[ɪkˋsɛpt]

prep 除……之外

V 除外，反對

同 other than (ph.) 除了
exclude (v.) 不包含

反 include (v.) 包含

The bookstore is open daily from 9:00 a.m. to 9:00 p.m., except Mondays.

書店每日都開放，從早上九點到晚上九點，除了星期一之外。

point 因為是「每個週一」，所以 Mondays 為複數。

The patient who just recovered from the surgery couldn't eat anything except some mild food.

剛從手術中復原的那位病人什麼都不能吃，除了一些清淡的食物以外。

CH 16

醫療健康

62 drastically

★

[ˋdræstɪklɪ]

ad 徹底地，激烈地

同 radically 激烈地
extremely 極度地
severely 嚴重地

Cutting calories drastically may not be a proper method to lose weight in the long run.

大幅度減少卡路里對於減肥來說，長期下來或許不是適當的方法。

The demand for nutritional supplement has increased drastically since last year.

營養食品的需求從去年開始已經大幅地上升。

point since 常與完成式連用。

63 disease

★

[dɪˋziz]

n 疾病，弊病

同 illness 疾病
sickness 患病
infection 感染

反 health 健康

Keep your room clean because disease is usually caused by germs.

保持你房間的乾淨，因為疾病通常是由病菌引起的。

point be caused by「由……所造成」。

The terrible disease has killed thousands of people in this district.

這個可怕的疾病已經帶走這個區域數千人的性命。

64 deficiency

★
★

[dɪˋfɪʃənsɪ]

n 不足，缺點，缺陷

同 insufficiency 不足
lack 缺少
shortage 短缺
inadequacy 不充分
shortfall 不足
scarcity 缺乏

反 surplus 過剩

People who suffer from calcium deficiency can take calcium tablets regularly.

有缺鈣的人們可以規律地攝取鈣片。

point suffer from 意為「身受……之苦」。

Today's meeting will address the deficiencies in the operating system.

今天的會議將會解決操作系統的缺陷。

point address = deal with = cope with = solve，意為「處理」。

353

Chapter 159

16 醫療健康

---

65 defense
★
★
[dɪˋfɛns]

n 防禦，保護，辯護

同 protection 保護

衍 defend (v.) 防禦
defensive (a.) 防禦的

Regular exercise and a balanced diet can improve people's natural defenses.
規律的運動和均衡的飲食可改善人們的自然防禦力。

Self-defense classes are getting popular these days.
自我防衛課程近日來變得越來越受歡迎。

---

66 decline
★
★
★
[dɪˋklaɪn]

v 下降，減少，婉拒

n 下降，減少，衰退

同 deteriorate (v.) 惡化
decay (v.) 衰敗
slide (v.) 下降

反 growth (n.) 成長
extension (n.) 伸展
inflation (n.) 膨脹

I declined his invitation because I had a dental appointment.
我婉拒了他的邀約，因為我有預約牙醫。

His interest in traveling declined after surgery.
在那場手術後，他對旅遊的興趣就遞減了。

---

67 fluctuate
★
★
[ˋflʌktʃuˏet]

v 波動，變動，動搖

同 shift 變動
alter 改變
alternate 交替

Oil prices fluctuate all the time.
油價總是在波動。

point 相關詞彙：vary 變化，differ 不同，change 改變，waver 搖擺，swing 擺動。

Whenever she is under pressure, her weight fluctuates considerably.
每當她處於壓力之下，她的體重起伏就很大。

---

68 consistently
★
[kənˋsɪstəntlɪ]

ad 一貫地，始終如一地

同 constantly 不斷地

反 inconsistently 不一致地

衍 consist (v.) 組成
consistency (n.) 一致

His design is consistently approachable and user-friendly.
他的設計一如往常的平易近人且好使用。

point 延伸詞彙：approach (v.) 接近，approachable (a.) 友善的；易接近的。

The foundation promotes the concept of vegetarian diets consistently.
這個組織堅持不懈地推廣素食飲食的概念。

69 concentrate
★ [`kɑnsɛnˌtret]

Ⓥ 集中，聚集，濃縮
Ⓢ focus 聚焦
　　direct 針對
　　centre 使集中
Ⓐ distract 使分心

I wore earplugs to keep me concentrating on my writing.
我戴耳機來讓自己保持專注於寫作。

point keep + O + concentrating 意為「使某人保持專注」。

Drink fresh juice instead of concentrated juice.
喝新鮮的果汁而不要喝濃縮果汁。

point instead of + N / Ving 意為「而不要……」。

---

70 blood
★ [blʌd]

Ⓝ 血，血統，家族關係
Ⓥ 從……抽血

John donates blood regularly.
約翰定期捐血。

point regularly = on a regular basis 意為「定期地」，frequently 意為「經常地」。

The player who has Russian blood performed well in the badminton world championships.
這位有俄羅斯血統的選手在世界羽球錦標賽中表現得非常好。

point blood 在此處意為「血統」。

---

71 adverse
★ [æd`vɝs]

Ⓐ 相反的，不利的，有害的
Ⓢ contrary 相反的
　　hurtful 有害的
　　opposite 對立的
Ⓐ beneficial 有益的
Ⓓ adversary (n.) 敵手

The drug is banned because of its adverse effects.
這個藥物因為副作用而被禁止。

point because of = owing to = due to = thanks to，意為「因為」。

Overuse of electronic devices is adverse to people's health.
過度使用電子裝置對人們的健康不好。

point overuse (n. / v.) 過度使用；濫用。

---

72 advisable
★ [əd`vaɪzəbl]

Ⓐ 可取的，適當的，明智的
Ⓢ suitable 適合的
　　wise 明智的
Ⓐ inadvisable 不聰明的
Ⓓ advisor (n.) 顧問

It's not advisable to drink tea with a lot of sugar when you have diabetes.
當你有糖尿病時，喝含糖量高的茶是不明智的。

73 yearly
★
★
[ˋjɪrlɪ]
🅰 每年的，一年一次的
🆎 每年，一年一度
🔄 annual (a.) 年度的
once a year (ph.) 一年一次
each / every year (ph.) 每年

It's vital for the manager to have a yearly physical.
對於經理來說，年度身體檢查很重要。

Subscribers can have a 10% discount by paying yearly.
訂閱者付一年份的金額，可以享有九折優惠。

point 延伸詞彙：subscribe (v.) 訂閱，subscription (n.) 訂閱。

---

74 bearable
★
[ˋbɛrəbl̩]
🅰 能耐的，忍得住的
🔄 tolerable 可忍受的
endurable 耐用的
🔺 unbearable 不能忍受的
intolerable 無法容忍的

The noise from the construction site was annoying but bearable.
工地的噪音很惱人但還可以忍受。

point 延伸片語：be under construction 意為「建造中」。

The painkillers prescribed by the doctor made the headache bearable.
這名醫生開的止痛藥讓頭痛變得可以忍受。

point prescribed 前面省略了 which were。prescription 意為「處方箋」。

---

75 patient
★
★
[ˋpeʃənt]
🅰 有耐心的，能容忍的
🔠 病人
🔺 impatient (a.) 不耐煩的

Somehow, the interviewer could tell the interviewee was not patient at all.
不知怎地，面試官可以得知這名求職者一點耐心都沒有。

Patients who would like to reschedule medical appointments should call the clinic three days before the scheduled time.
要更改醫療預約的病人應該要在預定的時間三天前打電話到診所。

point 請注意更改預約是多益測驗常見情境，常見原因為 be on a business trip「出差」。

---

76 cure
★
[kjʊr]
🆅 治癒，消族，糾正
🔠 治療，痊癒，藥
🔄 heal (v.) 治癒
remedy (n.) 治療

The prescription drug successfully cured me of my stomachache.
這個處方箋成功治好了我的胃痛。

point prescription (n.) 醫生開的處方箋，prescribed (a.) 處方的。

The best cure for obesity is exercise.
消除肥胖最有效的方法是運動。

point 延伸詞彙：obese (a.) 肥胖的。

Test 1

一、請寫出下列單字的中文意思。

① enhance _____ ⑥ beneficial _____

② spread _____ ⑦ concentrate _____

③ breakthrough _____ ⑧ examination _____

④ hazardous _____ ⑨ conclusion _____

⑤ instance _____ ⑩ drastically _____

二、請寫出符合下列句意的單字。

① Overuse of electronic devices is _____ to people's health.
過度使用電子裝置對人們的健康不好。

② I would like to _____ my scheduled medical appointment.
我想取消我預約好的醫療掛號。

③ The _____ drug successfully cured me of my stomachache.
這個處方箋成功治好了我的胃痛。

④ The pharmacy has been _____ to sell the medicine.
藥局獲得了這項藥品的銷售許可。

解答

1. ① 提高，增強 ② 伸展，蔓延，傳開 ③ 突破 ④ 有危險的，有危害的 ⑤ 情況，實例
⑥ 有益的，有用的 ⑦ 專心，集中，濃縮 ⑧ 檢查，調查，考試 ⑨ 結論，結束
⑩ 徹底地，大幅度地
2. ① adverse ② cancel ③ prescription ④ licensed

Test 2

○ 一、請選擇符合下列文意的單字。

> A recover   B obviously   C supplement
> D eliminated   E consistently   F tablets

① Please take the _____ twice a day.

② The virus can be gradually _____ from your body by taking medicine and exercising.

③ I am afraid that the patient will take one year to _____ from the surgery.

④ The patient was supposed to take vitamin _____ twice a week.

⑤ When I looked at his pale complexion, I knew he was _____ sick.

○ 二、請寫出下列片語的中文意思。

① deal with _____   ⑤ in case _____

② lead to _____   ⑥ be surprised at _____

③ a degree of _____   ⑦ transfer from A to B _____

④ all year round _____   ⑧ stay up late _____

解答

1. ① F ② D ③ A ④ C ⑤ B
2. ① 處理 ② 導致 ③ 有一定程度的 ④ 全年 ⑤ 以防萬一 ⑥ 感到驚訝 ⑦ 轉乘，調職 ⑧ 熬夜

Chapter 17
展覽表演

以下多益必考單字，你認識哪些？

☐ audience (p.360)   ☐ acquire (p.361)   ☐ significance (p.366)

☐ primarily (p.366)   ☐ respond (p.372)   ☐ entertain (p.362)

☐ flexibility (p.367)   ☐ extension (p.377)   ☐ prime (p.375)

☐ exhibition (p.362)   ☐ electric (p.361)   ☐ renowned (p.367)

☐ deserve (p.371)   ☐ exhibit (p.362)   ☐ arena (p.364)

☐ compete (p.373)   ☐ contemporary (p.373)   ☐ event (p.369)

17 展覽表演

01 landscape
★
['lænd,skep]

n 風景，景色

同 scenery (n.) 景色

The gallery features some watercolor landscapes.
這個展覽是以一些水彩風景畫為特色。

(point) 延伸詞彙：statue 雕像，sculpture 雕刻。

The photographer captured the breathtaking landscapes with his professional single-lens reflex camera.
攝影師用他的專業單眼相機捕捉了許多動人風景。

02 lead
★
★
★
[lid]

v 引導，領路，導致
n 領導，榜樣，主角

同 guide (v.) 指導
conduct (v.) 引導
show (v.) 引導
衍 leader (n.) 領導者

The manager encouraged one of his subordinates to lead the discussion.
經理鼓勵其中一位下屬引導討論。

(point) one of Ns 意為「其中一位」。

After 10 years, the experienced actor finally had an opportunity to play the lead in the new play.
十年後，這名經驗豐富的演員終於有機會在新戲中擔任主角。

03 eligible
★
★
['ɛlɪdʒəbḷ]

a 合格的，合適的
同 acceptable 可接受的
suitable 適合的
appropriate 合適的
反 ineligible 不適任的

Some people wonder whether she is eligible to enter the final.
有些人好奇她是否夠資格能進入決賽。

(point) 相關詞彙：entitled 賦予權力的，qualified 合格的，competent 有能力的。延伸詞彙：finalist (n.) 參加決賽者。

Only citizens who are eighteen and above are eligible to vote.
只有十八歲以上的公民有投票資格。

04 audience
★
★
★
['ɔdɪəns]

n 聽眾，觀眾，讀者
同 listener 聽眾
spectator 觀眾
attendee 出席者

The audience asked the speaker some questions after the dinner break.
聽眾在晚餐休息後問演講者一些問題。

(point) after the lunch break（在午餐休息後）／ after the Q&A session（在問答時間後）常出現在多益聽力測驗中。以此例句來說，常見的題目敘述是：「What are the audience suggested to do after the dinner break?」，答案就是「Talking to the speaker.」。

05 **perform**
★
★ [pɚˋfɔrm]
★
Ⓥ 履行,完成,演奏,運轉
同 execute 執行
accomplish 完成
fulfill 完成
反 neglect 忽視
omit 遺漏
衍 performance (n.) 表現

Most of the dancers performed well on the stage.
大部分的舞者在舞台上都表現得很棒。

The factory foreman found these tires that his company produced performed differently in cold and hot weather.
工廠監工發現公司生產的這些輪胎在天氣寒冷及炎熱時的性能表現不同。

---

06 **convince**
★
★ [kənˋvɪns]
★
Ⓥ 使確信,使信服,說服
同 persuade 說服
prove 證明

The actor was convinced that he performed well in the audition.
這名演員深信他在試鏡中表現得很好。

The businessman tried to convince the customers the effectiveness of the product by showing them research results.
這名商人試著藉由展現研究結果來說服客人商品的有效性。

 易混淆詞彙:effectiveness (n.) 有效性／ effective (a.) 有效的／ efficiency (n.) 效率／ efficient (a.) 有效率的。

---

07 **electric**
★
★ [ɪˋlɛktrɪk]
★
ⓐ 電的,電動的, 令人震驚的
衍 electrician (n.) 電工
electricity (n.) 電力
electronic (a.) 電子的

Frank's body suddenly shook when he touched the socket as if he had gotten an electric shock.
富蘭克在他碰觸插座時突然抖動身體,就好像他觸電一樣。

point as if 後面用過去完成式,表示與過去事實相反的假設語氣。

The concert stage was decorated with plenty of shining and artistic electric lights.
演唱會舞台用很多閃亮且有藝術感的電燈裝飾。

point 除了 electric light,多益測驗裡也常用 lighting fixture 來表示「照明設備,燈具」。

---

08 **acquire**
★
★ [əˋkwaɪr]
★
Ⓥ 取得,獲得,學到
同 achieve 達成
反 lose 失去
衍 acquisition (n.) 獲得
acquisitive (a.) 想獲得的

After saving money for three months, I finally acquired a ticket for the concert.
在存錢三個月之後,我終於弄到了一張音樂會的票。

point 相關詞彙:get 得到,attain 達到,obtain 得到,gain 獲得。

His responsibility acquired him a good reputation.
他的負責任使他得到好名聲。

Chapter 162

17 展覽表演

09 **entertainer**
★
★
[ˌɛntɚˋtenɚ]

🄝 表演者，專業演員
🄸 performer 表演者
　 artist 藝人
🄵 street entertainer
　 (ph.) 街頭藝人

The entertainer replayed the song **by** clicking that button.
表演者按那個按鈕來重新播放那首歌。
point by + N / Ving 意為「藉由……」。

The versatile street entertainer in the town square entertained his audiences with his excellent performance.
在城鎮廣場的多才多藝街頭藝人用他傑出的表演娛樂了他的觀眾。

---

10 **entertain**
★
★
[ˌɛntɚˋten]

🄥 使娛樂，招待，請客
🄸 delight 取樂
🄵 bore 使無聊
🄵 entertainment (n.) 娛樂

The comedy successfully entertained almost **every** viewer.
這齣喜劇成功地娛樂了幾乎每個觀賞者。
point every 後面的名詞都接單數。

All audiences were **entertained** by the amazing magic show.
所有觀眾都被這精彩的魔術秀給逗樂了。
point 相關詞彙：amuse 使歡樂，please 取悅，charm 使高興，cheer 振奮。

---

11 **exhibit**
★
★
★
[ɪgˋzɪbɪt]

🄥 展示，陳列，表現
🄝 展示品，展示會
🄸 exhibition (n.) 展覽
　 display (n.) 陳列
　 show (n.) 表演
　 showcase (n.) 陳列櫃

Please do not touch the exhibits.
請不要觸摸展示品。
point exhibit 當名詞「展示品」時為可數名詞。

The focus of the exhibit will be on Chinese paintings.
這個展覽的重點是中國畫作。

---

12 **exhibition**
★
★
★
[ˌɛksəˋbɪʃən]

🄝 展覽（會），表現，顯示
🄸 showing 陳列
　 presentation 演出
　 demonstration 示範

The exhibition successfully attracted people from around the world.
這個展覽成功地吸引世界各地的人。

The sculpture will **be on exhibition** until the end of this year.
這些雕塑作品將一直展出到年底。
point sth. be on exhibition 意為「某物被展出」。

CH 17

展覽表演

13 **enthusiastic**

★
★ [ɪnˌθjuzɪˋæstɪk]

a 熱情的，熱心的

同 eager 熱心的
earnest 熱心的
keen 熱衷的

反 unenthusiastic 冷淡的

衍 enthusiasm (n.) 熱心

In the board meeting, his proposal received an enthusiastic response.
在委員會會議上，他的提案獲得熱烈的回應。

(point) 相關會議用字：conference 研討會，seminar 研討會，meeting 會議，workshop 工作坊。

14 **accompany**

★
★
★ [əˋkʌmpənɪ]

v 陪同，伴隨，伴奏

同 go along with 伴隨著
escort 護送

Children must be accompanied by their parents to enter the swimming pool.
小孩們必須在父母的陪同下進入游泳池。

(point) be accompanied by 意為「由……陪同」。

She was chosen out of plenty of pianists because she accompanied magnificently.
她因為伴奏得精彩極了，因此從許多鋼琴家中脫穎而出。

(point) plenty of + N 意為「許多……」。

15 **feast**

★
★ [fist]

n 盛宴，享受，節日

v 盛宴款待，享受

同 banquet (n.) 宴會
festival (n.) 節日

A critic mentioned that the painting in the art exhibition is a feast for the eyes.
一個評論家提及在畫展的這幅畫令人賞心悅目。

(point) a feast for the eyes 意為「賞心悅目」。

After the final project, we treated ourselves to a fancy restaurant to feast on fine wine and delicious food.
在期末報告後，我們去一家高級餐廳犒賞自己，享用美酒與美食。

(point) feast on 意為「盡情享用」。

16 **breathless**

★ [ˋbrɛθlɪs]

a 氣喘吁吁的，屏息的

同 out of breath 上氣不接下氣

I was breathless after taking an aerobic dance class.
上完一堂有氧舞蹈課後我就氣喘吁吁了。

The audience were breathless when they watched the amazing magic show.
觀眾們在看魔術表演時都屏住呼吸。

Chapter 163

17 展覽表演

17 arena
★
[əˋrinə]
n 競技場，活動場所
同 field 比賽場
stadium 運動場
stage 舞台

The Olympic arena is under construction now.
奧運比賽場地正在施工中。

(point) be under construction 意為「正在施工」。

---

18 astonish
★
★
[əˋstɑnɪʃ]
v 使驚訝，吃驚
同 surprise 使驚訝
amaze 使驚奇
startle 使驚嚇
反 bore 使無聊
tire 使疲累

I was astonished that the driver's license was suspended.
我很訝異這名駕駛的駕照被吊銷了。

The stuntman's prestigious performance astonished all the audience.
特技演員傑出的表演震驚了所有觀眾。

(point) 延伸詞彙：stunt 為名詞，意為「特技」。

---

19 square
★
★
[skwɛr]
n 廣場，正方形
a 正方形的，公正的
同 plaza (n.) 廣場

Plenty of people gathered in the square to see the fantastic performance of the street artists.
很多人聚集在廣場看街頭藝人傑出的表演。

(point) gather 意為「聚在一起」，是多益測驗圖片題中常用來形容人們聚集在某地的動詞。

We used to put all the receipts in a square box.
我們以前常把所有的收據放在一個方形箱子裡。

(point) used to + 原形動詞，表示「過去習慣做……」。

---

20 act
★
[ækt]
n 行為，行動，節目
v 扮演，行動，起作用
同 execute (v.) 執行
function (v.) 運行
operate (v.) 操作
衍 action (n.) 行動
actor (n.) 演員
actress (n.) 女演員

The manager always reminds his subordinates to think well before they act.
經理一直以來都在提醒他的下屬要三思而後行。

(point) remind 的其他常用法：remind sb. of + N 意為「提醒某人……」。

He acted the main hero in the play, which brought overnight fame to him.
他在那齣戲中演主角，這讓他一夕之間爆紅。

(point) bring fame to sb. 意為「爆紅」，即一夕成名。

21 applaud
★
★
[ə`plɔd]

Ⅴ 鼓掌，稱讚，贊成

同 praise 讚揚
approve 贊成
support 支持

反 distain 污辱

The whole audiences applauded the amazing speech.
所有觀眾為這個精湛的演講鼓掌。

point 相關用語：win a round of applause 意為「贏得一陣掌聲」。

The manager applauded the assistant's responsibility and dedication to work.
經理讚美這位助理的負責任及對工作的盡心盡力。

---

22 accomplishment
★
★
★
[ə`kɑmplɪʃmənt]

ⁿ 成就，才藝，完成

同 achievement 達成
completion 完成
attainment 達到

反 failure 失敗

衍 accomplish (v.) 完成

His accomplishment in the interior design of that fancy restaurant has brought him confidence.
他在那間高級餐廳的室內設計成就已經帶給他信心。

The rookie singer just made her debut, and this gave her a sense of accomplishment.
這位新人歌手的初登場帶給她自己一種成就感。

point this 代替 The rookie singer just made her first debut。

---

23 actually
★
★
★
[`æktʃuəlɪ]

ad 實際上，真的，竟然

同 really 真的
truly 真的
in fact 事實上
indeed 確實

Actually, your performance is rather satisfactory and we would like to invite you to perform at my company's year-end party.
事實上，你的演出相當令人滿意，我想邀請你到我們公司的尾牙來表演。

point sb. be satisfied with 意為「人對……很滿意」，sth. be satisfactory 意為「某事令人滿意」。

I remembered he took a leave yesterday but I actually saw him in the company.
我記得他昨天請假，但我昨天真的竟然在公司看見他。

point take a leave 意為「請假」。

---

24 band
★
[bænd]

Ⅴ 聚集，聯合，團結
ⁿ 一夥，樂團

同 group (n.) 一群
league (n.) 同盟

反 divide (v.) 分開
split up (ph.) 分離

The band's vocalist doesn't sing well.
這樂團的主唱唱功不佳。

The facility is designed for females in the 18-21 age band.
該設施是為十八至二十一歲年齡階段的女性所設計的。

point 此句的 band 表示「數值的特定範圍」。

---

25 benchmark
★
[`bɛntʃˌmɑrk]
n 水準點，基準
同 standard 標準
　　target 目標

The magician's prestigious performances **set a** new **benchmark** for other magicians.
魔術師的傑出表現給了其他魔術師一個新的參照點。

point set a benchmark 意為「設下一個標準」。

The sales volume of this beverage became a benchmark for others.
這款飲料的銷售量變成其他飲料的標準。

---

26 primarily
★
★
[praɪˈmɛrəlɪ]
ad 首先，原來，首要地，根本上
同 first 第一
　　basically 基本上
　　fundamentally 基礎地
　　principally 主要地
　　essentially 本來

This space was primarily designed to be an **auditorium**.
這個空間原來是設計做為演藝廳的。

point 延伸詞彙：lecture hall 意為「演講廳」。

The sales representatives attended the workshop primarily because they would like to enhance their conversation skills.
業務代表參加工作坊的主要原因是他們想增進溝通技巧。

---

27 significance
★
★
★
[sɪgˈnɪfəkəns]
n 重要性，意義，意思
同 importance 重要性
　　meaning 意義
衍 significant (a.) 重要的
　　signify (v.) 表明

The style of the painting is **of** great **significance** to contemporary artists.
這幅畫的風格對當代藝術家來說具有重要意義。

point of significance = significant，意為「重要的」。

The singer was invited to promote the idea of gender equality due to the significance of his influence.
因為這位歌手帶來的影響的重要性，他被邀請推廣性別平等的觀念。

---

28 diversity
★
★
[daɪˈvɜsətɪ]
n 差異，多樣性
同 variety 多樣化
反 uniformity 一致
衍 diversification (n.) 多樣化
　　diverse (a.) 多變化的

The columnist introduced the **diversities** between two cultures.
專欄作家介紹了兩個文化的差異。

point 相關詞彙：dissimilarity 相異點，distinctiveness 區別性，contrast 對比。

The exhibition totally shows the diversity of species in this region.
展覽完全展現出這個區域的物種多樣性。

29 renowned

★
★
★

[rɪ`naʊnd]

a 有名的，有聲譽的

同 popular 受歡迎的
established 信譽卓著的
notable 著名的
prominent 著名的

反 notorious 惡名昭彰的

The renowned photographer's work is being exhibited in the local art center right now.
這位著名攝影師的作品正在當地的藝術中心展出中。

(point) 此句 work 為名詞，意為「作品」。相關詞彙：famous 有名的，distinguished 著名的，noted 有名的，celebrated 著名的，famed 有名的，well-known 出名的，prestigious 有名望的。

He is a renowned financial analyst because he can always interpret statistical data precisely and accurately.
他是個有名的財務分析家，因為他總是能很精確且正確地詮釋統計數據。

(point) analyst（分析家）為多益測驗長篇閱讀報導中會出現的人物。

30 alike

★

[ə`laɪk]

a 相同的，相像的
ad 一樣地，相似地

同 similar (a.) 相像的
identical (a.) 完全相同的
uniform (a.) 相同的
parallel (a.) 相同的

反 different (a.) 不同的

The members of the orchestra are required to dress alike.
管絃樂團的成員被要求穿得一樣。

(point) 延伸用語：chorus 意為「合唱團」。

In recent years, most portable electronic devices on the market all look alike.
近年來，大部分在市場上的可攜式電子裝置看起來都一樣。

(point) on the market 意為「在市場上」。

31 overall

★
★

[`ovɚ͵ɔl]

a 包括一切的，全部的

[͵ovɚ`ɔl]

ad 全面地，大體上

同 comprehensive (a.) 廣泛的

Overall, his performance was rather impressive.
整體來說，他的表演相當令人印象深刻。

The designer explained the overall design of the eco-friendly house to his client.
設計師向他的客戶解釋這棟綠建築的整體設計。

(point) eco-friendly 意為「對生態友善的」。

32 flexibility

★

[͵flɛksə`bɪlətɪ]

n 適應性，靈活性，彈性

同 pliancy 適應性
pliability 易適應性

反 rigidity 死板
inflexibility 缺乏彈性

Maintain flexibility while you are planning your daily schedule.
當你在計劃每日行程時，保持彈性。

The acrobat often stretches his body to improve flexibility.
雜技演員經常伸展以增強柔軟度。

Chapter 165

17 展覽表演

33 privilege
★
[`prɪvḷɪdʒ]

n 特權，榮幸，基本權利

同 right 權利
pleasure 榮幸
honor 榮譽

As a resident in this community, it's your privilege to use the gym and the swim pool.
身為這個社區的居民，使用健身房跟泳池是你的權利。
(point) as 意為「身為」。

The VIP had the privilege of entering the gallery without an invitation card.
貴賓擁有不用邀請函就可以進入藝廊的特權。

---

34 metropolitan
★
[ˌmɛtrə`pɑlətṇ]

a 大都會的，
（基督教）大主教轄區的
n 大城市人

同 city (n.) 都市
反 suburb (n.) 郊區
outskirt (n.) 郊外

The Metropolitan Museum of Art is a must-see when you travel to New York.
紐約大都會藝術博物館是去紐約必看的景點。
(point) must-see 意為「必看的景點」。

She has a hard time getting used to the pace of metropolitan life.
她很難適應都市生活的節奏。
(point) have a hard time + Ving 意為「做……有困難」。

---

35 inspiration
★
★
[ˌɪnspə`reʃən]

n 靈感，鼓舞人心的事物

同 innovation 革新
originality 創造力
衍 inspire (v.) 鼓舞
inspiring (a.) 激勵人心的

Reading a variety of books gave the designer plenty of inspiration.
閱讀多樣化的書帶給這名設計師許多靈感。
(point) a variety of = various，意為「多樣的」。

The painting provided the inspiration for his dance.
這幅畫提供了他在舞蹈上的靈感。

---

36 graceful
★
[`gresfəl]

a 優美的，典雅的，得體的

同 stylish 漂亮的
dignified 高貴的
反 stiff 僵硬的
衍 grace (n.) 優雅

The magician ended the show with a graceful pose.
魔術師以一個優雅的姿勢結束了這場秀。
(point) with 意為「伴隨著」。

Her graceful refusal didn't annoy us.
她得體的拒絕並沒有使我們生氣。
(point) 相關詞彙：elegant 簡練的，tasteful 高雅的，sophisticated 老於世故的，refined 優美的。

37 event
★
★
★
[ɪ`vɛnt]
n 事件，比賽項目，結果
同 episode 一個事件
incident 事件
affair 事情
circumstance 情況

Please reply to this letter if you would like to participate in the event.
如果您想參加這個活動，請回覆此信。

The event will be held at the end of this month.
這個活動將會在月底舉行。

point will be held 意為「將會被舉行」，為未來被動式。

---

38 emergency
★
★
[ɪ`mɝdʒənsɪ]
n 緊急情況，非常時刻
同 crisis 危機
urgent situation 緊急狀況

The emergency exit is at the end of the hall.
緊急出口在大廳的後端。

point emergency exit 意為「緊急出口」。

Remember to keep a toolkit in your car for emergencies.
以防緊急情況，記得要在你車上放一個工具箱。

CH 17
展覽表演

---

39 elegant
★
[`ɛləgənt]
a 雅緻的，漂亮的，精緻的
同 cultivated 文雅的
distinguished 高雅的
artistic 精美的
反 inelegant 粗魯的
clumsy 笨拙的

The dress is simple but elegant.
這件裙子很簡單卻優雅。

The elegant actress is definitely the best spokesperson for that product.
這個優雅的女演員絕對是那個產品的最佳代言人。

point spokesperson 意為「代言人」。

---

40 elaborate
★
[ɪ`læbərɪt]
a 精心製作的，詳盡的，複雜的
[ɪ`læbəˌret]
v 精心製作，詳盡闡述
同 intricate (a.) 錯綜複雜的
complex (a.) 複雜的
反 plain (a.) 簡樸的

The project manager elaborated on the abstract concept by using a concrete model.
專案經理用具體的模型來解釋這個抽象的概念。

point 易混淆詞彙：project manager 專案經理／ product manager 產品經理人。

The judges were amazed by her elaborate performance.
評審對她精心編造的表演感到驚訝。

point be amazed by 意為「感到驚訝」。

17 展覽表演

41 **dress code**
★
[drɛs][kod]

ph 穿衣規則，著裝標準

You should comply with the dress code when you attend the formal event.
當你參加那場正式活動時，你必須遵守服儀規定。

point comply with 意為「遵守」。

The dress code for this wedding ceremony was written in the invitation card.
邀請卡中寫著這場婚宴的服儀規定。

---

42 **drama**
★
★
[`drɑmə]

n 戲劇，戲劇性事件
同 play 戲劇
　　show 演出
　　stage play 舞台劇

I am fond of watching musical dramas.
我喜歡看音樂劇。

point be fond of 意為「喜歡」

People don't like to team up with her because she is such a drama queen.
人們不喜歡和她一組，因為她很愛大驚小怪。

point drama queen 意為「愛大驚小怪的人」。

---

43 **discourage**
★
★
[dɪs`kɝɪdʒ]

v 使洩氣，使沮喪，勸阻
同 prevent 防止
　　stop 停止
反 encourage 鼓勵
衍 discouragement (n.) 氣餒

Failing to participate in the final discouraged him.
無法參加決賽使他很沮喪。

point 此句的 final 為名詞，意為「決賽」。

---

44 **extra**
★
★
★
[`ɛkstrə]

a 額外的，附加的
ad 額外地，特別地
n 附加費用，額外的事物
同 additional (a.) 附加的
　　added (a.) 額外的
　　supplementary (a.) 追加的
　　further (a.) 另外的
反 included (a.) 包含的

We prepared extra copies, just in case.
為了以防萬一，我們準備了額外的份量。

point just in case 意為「以防萬一」。

Tom had no choice but to pay extra charges for his overweight luggage.
湯姆別無選擇，只能付超重的額外行李費用。

point have no choice but to + V 意為「除了做……別無選擇」。

45 disappear
★ [ˌdɪsə`pɪr]
Ⅴ 消失，不見，滅絕
同 vanish 消失
　 fade 褪去
反 appear 出現

My notepad disappeared during the move.
我的筆記本在搬家途中不見了。

As soon as the magician smiled to the audience, the dove suddenly disappeared.
魔術師一對觀眾笑，鴿子就突然不見了。

point as soon as 意為「一……就……」。

---

46 deserve
★ [dɪ`zɝv]
Ⅴ 應受（賞罰），應得
同 earn 掙得

As our VIP, you deserve this kind of premium service.
身為我們的貴賓，你值得這樣優質的服務。

point as + N 意為「身為……」。

He definitely deserved a long vacation after finishing the big project.
在完成這個大型專案後，他當然值得放一個長假。

CH 17
展覽表演

---

47 foresee
★ [for`si]
Ⅴ 預見，預知
同 anticipate 預期
　 predict 預料
　 forecast 預測
　 expect 預料

Upon watching the weather forecast, he foresaw that tomorrow's event would be canceled.
當他一看到天氣預報，他就預測明天的活動將會被取消。

point upon = as soon as，意為「一……就……」。

---

48 cross
★ [krɔs]
ⓝ 十字形，十字架
ⓐ 發怒的，交叉的
Ⅴ 橫穿，交叉，相交

The participant was very cross because he failed to enter the final.
參賽者非常生氣，因為他沒能進入決賽。

point 延伸詞彙：participate (v.) 參加／participation (n.) 參與。

Don't cross the road.
不要穿越馬路。

Chapter 167

17 展覽表演

---

49 creative

★
★

[krɪˋetɪv]

ⓐ 創造的，有創造力的

同 innovative 革新的
　original 獨創性的

反 conservative 守舊的

衍 create (v.) 創造

The creative warning sign catches people's attention immediately.
這個具有創意的警告標誌馬上吸引人們的注意。

The creative artist will attend the opening of the gallery tomorrow.
那位富有創意力的藝術家明天會去畫廊的開幕典禮。

point 延伸用字：Grand Opening 意為「盛大開幕」。

---

50 creation

★
★

[krɪˋeʃən]

ⓝ 創造，世界，作品

同 design 設計
　formation 構成
　invention 發明

衍 creativity (n.) 創造力

The newest creations of the wooden furniture have been included in the catalog.
最新的木製家具已經放在目錄上了。

The well-known industrial designer's new creation will be presented.
這位知名工業設計師將會發表新創作。

---

51 context

★
★
★

[ˋkɑntɛkst]

ⓝ 上下文，背景，環境

同 circumstance 情況
　condition 情況
　surrounding 環境

If you don't know the word's meaning, you can try to read it in context.
如果你不知道字的意思，你可以試著閱讀上下文。

The professor asked his students to analyze the drama based on its historical context.
教授請他的學生根據歷史背景來分析這齣戲劇。

point historical context = historical background，意為「歷史背景」。

---

52 respond

★
★
★

[rɪˋspɑnd]

ⓥ 回答，作出反應，
　承擔責任

同 answer 回答
　reply to 答覆

衍 response (n.) 回答

So far, the retailer hasn't responded to the sales representative's banquet invitation.
到目前為止，這名零售商還沒回應業務的宴席邀約。

Some citizens were satisfied with the way the mayor responded to the strike.
一些市民很滿意市長對於罷工的應對方式。

point be satisfied with 意為「（人）對……感到滿意」。

53 **contemporary**
★ [kən`tɛmpə‚rɛrɪ]
 a 當代的，同時代的
 n 同時代的人，現代人
 同 modern (a.) 現代的
 　 present (a.) 現在的
 反 old-fashioned (a.) 過時的
 　 out of date (ph.) 過時

He is one of the famous contemporary writers.
他是其中一位有名的當代作家。

The exhibition's topic is contemporary art.
展覽的主題是當代藝術。

point exhibition = expo = fair = exhibit，皆表示「展覽」。

---

54 **composition**
★ [‚kɑmpə`zɪʃən]
 n 作品，構成，合成物
 同 constitution 構造
 　 configuration 結構
 　 conformation 構造
 　 formation 構成

The composition is highly regarded by many contemporary artists.
這個作品被許多當代藝術家高度推崇。

It takes me 20 minutes to refine a writing composition.
修改作文花了我二十分鐘。

point it + takes / took + 人 + 時間 + to + V，意為「某人花時間做……」。

---

55 **compete**
★
★
★ [kəm`pit]
 v 競爭，對抗，比賽
 同 rival 競爭
 　 challenge 挑戰
 　 keep pace with 並駕齊驅

All the finalists are competing for the gold medal.
所有決賽參與者都在爭取金牌。

point compete... for 意為「爭取（某物）」。延伸字彙：final (n.) 決賽。

It's rather difficult for small grocery stores to compete with big supermarkets on price.
小型雜貨店很難在價錢上和大超市競爭。

---

56 **conventional**
★ [kən`vɛnʃənḷ]
 a 習慣的，普通的，
 　 過分拘泥的
 同 traditional 傳統的
 　 typical 典型的
 反 unconventional 非常規的
 衍 convention (n.) 會議

When you go to an interview, just wear formal and conventional clothes.
當你去面試時，穿正式且符合常規的衣服就好。

point 相關詞彙：regular 正常的，normal 一般的，standard 標準的，
　　ordinary 普通的，usual 平常的，common 普通的。

Conventional art will be displayed next Monday.
傳統藝術下週一將會被展出。

Chapter 168

17 展覽表演

---

57 briefly

★
★ [`brɪflɪ]
★

ad 簡短地，簡單地說

同 shortly 簡短地
temporarily 暫時地

反 permanently 永久地

The interviewee briefly introduced himself.
面試者簡短地介紹自己。

The judge commented on the participant's talk briefly.
評審簡短地評論參加者的演說。

---

58 delight

★
★ [dɪ`laɪt]

n 愉快，樂趣

v 使高興，取樂

同 enjoyment (n.) 樂趣
pleasure (n.) 愉快

反 disgust (v.) 使厭惡
displeasure (n.) 不滿

Much to her delight, she won the best employee of the year award.
使她高興的是她贏得了年度最佳員工獎。

At the year-end party, he delighted the audience with his hilarious performance.
在尾牙派對上，他用他的搞笑表演使觀眾開心。

point 相關派對名稱：retirement / farewell party 退休派對、graduation party 畢業派對。

---

59 imagine

★
★ [ɪ`mædʒɪn]
★

v 想像，猜想，料想

同 visualize 想像
envision 想像
picture 想像

It was hard to imagine that his coworker performed well on the stage given that he used to be quite timid.
有鑑於他的同事過去十分內向，很難想像他在舞台上表演得這麼好。

point given that 意為「考量到」。

The lecturer asked some participants to try to imagine delivering a speech in front of 100 people.
講師要一些參加者試著想像在一百人面前演講。

point deliver a speech = give a speech，意為「演講」。

---

60 outdoor

★
★ [`aʊt,dor]
★

a 戶外的，喜歡戶外活動的

同 open-air 露天的
out-of-door 戶外的
outside 外面的

反 indoor 室內的

The hotel provides several outdoor facilities, such as a swimming pool.
該飯店提供許多戶外設施，像是游泳池。

Would you like to go to the outdoor concert with me tonight?
你今晚要跟我一起去戶外演唱會嗎？

point Would you like to... 意為「你想要……嗎？」，表邀約。

61 **conserve**
★
★ [kənˋsɝv]
V 保存，保護，節省
N 蜜餞，糖漬食品
同 preserve (v.) 保存
protect (v.) 保護
save (v.) 節省
反 waste (v.) 浪費
衍 conservative (a.) 保守的
conservation
(n.) 保存，保育

The athlete conserved his energy for the international competition next month.
運動員為了下個月的國際賽事保存體力。
point conserve one's strength / energy 意為「保留體力」。

My coworker bought strawberry conserve from the souvenir shop.
我同事從伴手禮店買了草莓蜜餞。

62 **prime**
★
★ [praɪm]
a 最初的，基本的，主要的
同 principal 主要的
fundamental 基礎的
initial 最初的
反 secondary 第二的

The fancy restaurant only offers prime beef.
這間高級餐廳只賣上等牛肉。

The rent of the gallery is rather high, since it is situated in the prime location in the metropolitan area.
這間畫廊的房租相當高，因為它位於大都會區的黃金地段。
point city, downtown, urban area 皆可指「城市；市區」。

63 **blend**
★ [blɛnd]
V 混合，協調，相稱
同 compound 混合
mix 混合
反 divide 分開
separate 分離

The artists blended two colors together with a small brush.
藝術家用一把小刷子把兩個顏色混和在一起。

I particularly enjoy music that blends POP and EDM.
我特別喜歡混合流行樂及電音的音樂。
point EDM = Electronic Dance Music 意為「電子音樂」。

64 **token**
★ [ˋtokən]
N 象徵，代價券，紀念品
同 symbol 象徵
sign 標誌
representation 代表
mark 標誌

Participants who attend this activity will receive a £10 gift token.
參加這個活動的參加者可以收到一張價值十英鎊的禮券。
point 延伸詞彙：campaign 意為「行銷活動」。

By the same token, you should transfer partial payments before your stay.
同樣地，在你入住之前，你應該要先匯部分的款項。
point by the same token 意為「同樣地，由於同樣的原因」。

375

65 **procure**
★
[proˈkjur]

Ⅴ 努力取得，導致，達成
同 obtain 取得
　 acquire 獲得
衍 procurement (n.) 獲得

The painting procured for the exhibition is valuable.
為了展覽而設法取得的畫作相當貴重。

The specialist procured the confidential documents from the conference.
專員從研討會中取得這個機密文件。

point 延伸詞彙：confidential (a.) 機密的，confident (a.) 有信心的，considerable (a.) 大量的。

---

66 **invite**
★
★
★
[ɪnˈvaɪt]

Ⅴ 邀請，請求，招致
同 ask 邀請
　 summon 請求

You are invited to attend Joanna's retirement party.
你被邀請來參加喬安娜的退休派對。

point retirement party = farewell party，意為「退休派對」。

We are writing to invite you to perform for the Grand Opening Ceremony.
我們寫信來邀請你來為我們盛大開幕的儀式表演。

point Grand Opening 意為「盛大開幕」。

---

67 **debatable**
★
[dɪˈbetəbḷ]

ａ 有爭議的，有問題的
同 arguable 有疑義的
　 disputable 真假可疑的
　 questionable 有問題的
反 indisputable 明白的

The value of the painting is debatable.
這幅畫的價值是很有爭議性的。

It's debatable whether the product is eco-friendly.
這個產品是否對環境友善仍有爭議。

---

68 **enrich**
★
[ɪnˈrɪtʃ]

Ⅴ 使富裕，使豐富，使肥沃
同 boost 提高
　 refine 提煉
　 intensify 增強
反 devaluate 降低價值
　 impoverish 使貧窮

The editor once mentioned that an appreciation of art can enrich people's lives.
主編曾經提及藝術欣賞能豐富人們的生活。

point once (adv.) 曾經；一次 (n.) 一次 (conj.) 一旦。

The singer's life is greatly enriched by knowing his wife who has lot of in common with him.
認識了和他有很多共同點的老婆，讓這名歌手的生活變得非常充實。

point have a lot of in common 意為「有很多相似點」，have little in common 意為「有很少相似點」。

69 evolve
★
[ɪ`vɑlv]

Ⓥ 逐步形成，進化，發展

🟰 develop 發展
　 progress 進步
　 grow 發展

The exhibition will illustrate how humans evolve from apes.
這個展覽將會說明人類如何從猿猴進化而來。

Languages are always changing and evolving to fulfill users' needs.
語言一直不斷地改變及演化以滿足使用者的需求。

(point) 此句使用進行式來表達動作不斷反覆發生。

---

70 flawless
★
[`flɔlɪs]

ⓐ 無瑕疵的，完美的

🟰 undamaged 未損壞的
　 unmarked 無瑕疵的

反 flawed 有缺點的
　 defective 有缺陷的
　 faulty 有缺點的

Nothing is flawless.
沒什麼東西是完美的。

(point) 相關詞彙：perfect 完美的，unbroken 未受阻礙的，unblemished 無瑕疵的。

Both audience and the judges all agreed it was a flawless performance.
觀眾和評審都同意這是完美的表演。

(point) both A and B 意為「兩者皆是」。

---

71 extension
★
★
★
[ɪk`stɛnʃən]

ⓝ 伸展，延期，電話分機

🟰 addition 附加
　 increase 增加

反 decrease 減少
　 shortening 縮短

Here is the form for an extension of your visa.
這是延長簽證有效期的表格。

If you have any problems about the event, please call extension number 235.
如果你對於活動有任何疑問，請打分機號碼二三五。

---

72 priceless
★
[`praɪslɪs]

ⓐ 貴重的，無價的，極有趣的

🟰 precious 貴重的
　 valuable 值錢的

反 worthless 無價值的
　 cheap 廉價的

The collector has a large priceless collection of antiques.
這名收藏家有一大批無價的古董。

(point) 相關詞彙：expensive 昂貴的，invaluable 無價的，costly 貴重的，high-priced 高價的。

The exhibit is priceless and can't be sold.
這個展示品是無價的，且不能販售。

(point) exhibit (n.) 展示品 (v.) 展示。

17 展覽表演

73 judge
★
★
[dʒʌdʒ]
Ⅴ 審判，裁決，判斷
ⁿ 法官，鑑賞家
同 estimate (v.) 判斷

You can't judge a book by its cover.
不能以貌取人。

The judge complimented the participant's performance.
評審稱讚這名參賽者的表演。

---

74 betray
★
[bɪˋtre]
Ⅴ 背叛，出賣，洩露
同 cheat 不忠
衍 betray oneself
(ph.) 原形畢露

Those who made an illegal deal betrayed their conscience.
那些從事非法交易的人們出賣了自己的良知。

(point) Those who made an illegal deal 為主詞。

The experienced performer never betrays his nervousness when he is on stage.
這名經驗豐富的表演者從不在舞臺上表露緊張。

---

75 admittance
★
★
★
[ədˋmɪtəns]
ⁿ 進入，入場許可
同 permission 准許
access 進入
衍 admit (v.) 准許進入

The sign said, "No admittance"!
那個標示寫了：「禁止進入」！

Only those who have VIP invitation cards can have admittance to the charity event.
只有那些有貴賓邀請卡的人才可以進入慈善活動現場。

---

76 tangible
★
[ˋtændʒəbl̩]
ⓐ 有形的，有實體的，
實際的
同 touchable 可觸摸的
substantial 真實的
concrete 有形的
反 intangible 無形的

The gallery features tangible art forms, such as sculptures.
這個藝廊以可觸摸的藝術形式為特色，像是雕刻。

(point) form (n.) 形式；表格。fill out the form 意為「填寫表格」。

The list includes a wide range of tangible assets including vehicles, furniture, and machinery.
這個清單包含了一系列廣泛的有形資產，包含車輛、家具及機器。

(point) a range of 意為「一系列的」。

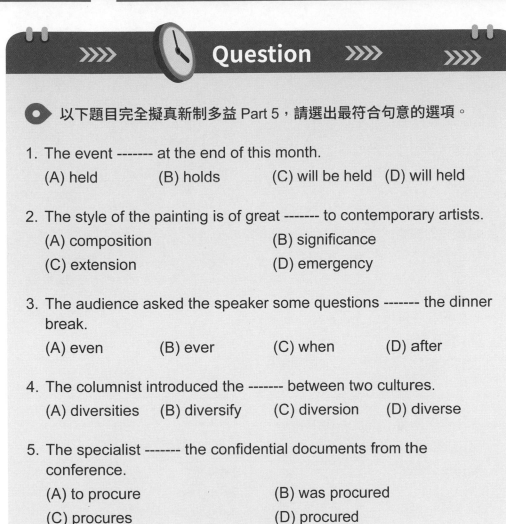

以下題目完全擬真新制多益 Part 5，請選出最符合句意的選項。

1. The event ------- at the end of this month.

   (A) held   (B) holds   (C) will be held   (D) will held

2. The style of the painting is of great ------- to contemporary artists.

   (A) composition   (B) significance

   (C) extension   (D) emergency

3. The audience asked the speaker some questions ------- the dinner break.

   (A) even   (B) ever   (C) when   (D) after

4. The columnist introduced the ------- between two cultures.

   (A) diversities   (B) diversify   (C) diversion   (D) diverse

5. The specialist ------- the confidential documents from the conference.

   (A) to procure   (B) was procured

   (C) procures   (D) procured

6. The exhibition ------- French sculptures.

   (A) performs   (B) features   (C) competes   (D) acquires

>> 正確答案與解析請翻至下一頁查看

 **Answer**

正確答案與解析

1. 這個活動將會在月底舉行。

   (C) 未來式（at the end of this month）+ 被動式（活動被舉行）

   正確答案 (C)

2. 這幅畫的風格對當代藝術家來說具有重要意義。

   (A) 作品　　　　(B) 重要性　　　(C) 延長　　　(D) 緊急事件

   正確答案 (B)

3. 這聽眾在晚餐休息後問演講者一些問題。

   (A) 甚至　　　　(B) 曾經　　　　(C) 當（連接詞 + S + V）

   (D) 之後（介係詞 + N；連接詞 + S + V）

   正確答案 (D)

4. 專欄作家介紹了兩個文化的差異。

   (A) 差異　　　　　　　　　(B)（使）多元化經營

   (C) 繞行路線　　　　　　　(D) 不同的

   正確答案 (A)

5. 專員從研討會中取得這個機密文件。

   (D) 意為「已取得」，事情已發生，所以用過去式

   正確答案 (D)

6. 這個展覽以法國雕刻而聞名。

   (A) 表演　　　　　　　　　(B) 以……為特色 (v.)；特色 (n.)

   (C) 媲美，比得上　　　　　(D) 取得

   正確答案 (B)

Chapter 18
表達與演講

以下多益必考單字，你認識哪些？

☐ guidance (p.382)   ☐ explain (p.399)   ☐ capability (p.385)

☐ summarize (p.389)   ☐ demonstration (p.383)   ☐ command (p.396)

☐ detail (p.385)   ☐ emphasis (p.399)   ☐ ceremony (p.397)

☐ introduction (p.386)   ☐ overcome (p.399)   ☐ avoid (p.387)

☐ motivate (p.391)   ☐ leading (p.385)   ☐ occasion (p.390)

☐ conduct (p.384)   ☐ prior (p.384)   ☐ background (p.389)

18 表達與演講

---

01 farewell
★
★ [ˈfɛrˈwɛl]
★
int 再會
n 告別，歡送會
同 good-bye (n.) 告別

Mr. Stephen has worked in New Insight Company for more than 25 years and next Monday will be his farewell party.
史蒂芬先生已經在新觀點公司工作超過二十五年了，下週一是他的退休餐會。

(point) farewell party = retirement party，意為「退休派對、餐會」。

---

02 guidance
★
★ [ˈgaɪdn̩s]
★
n 指導，引導，輔導
同 direction 指導
assistance 援助
衍 guide (v.) 引導
guideline (n.) 指導方針

The recipient of the best employee of the year award thanked her manager's guidance so that she could receive the honor.
年度最佳員工得獎人感謝她經理的指導，讓她得到這項殊榮。

(point) recipient 意為「受獎者；接收者」。

You can either join gyms or hire a fitness coach for personal guidance.
你可以加入健身房或請一個健身教練來幫你親自指導。

(point) either... or... 意為「兩者其一」。

---

03 college
★
★ [ˈkɑlɪdʒ]
★
n 大學，學院
同 university 大學
educational institution
教育機構

He will attend college this September.
他今年九月會上大學。

(point) attend 後面不加 to。

The founder of this college gave a speech in the graduation ceremony.
這所大學的創辦人在畢業典禮上演講。

---

04 infer
★
★ [ɪnˈfɝ]
v 推斷，推論，暗示
同 deduce 推論
reason 推理
work out 想出
conclude 推斷

It's rather easy for the secretary to infer what her supervisor actually means.
對於那名祕書而言，推敲出她上司真實的意思是相當容易的。

We could infer the hidden meaning from the key words that the speaker emphasized.
我們可以從講者強調的關鍵字來推論出隱含的意義。

05 base
★
★
[bes]
n 基底，基地
v 以……為基地
a 基礎的
同 bottom (n.) 底部
　　foundation (n.) 基礎
反 peak (n.) 頂端
　　top (n.) 頂部

His speech is based on several research results.
他的演講是根據許多研究結果而來。
point be based on = according to，意為「根據」。

I have business trips often but Taipei is still my base.
我經常需要出差，但台北仍然是我的基地。

---

06 demonstration
★
★
★
[ˌdɛmən`streʃən]
n 證明，示範，示威
同 proof 證明
　　confirmation 證實
　　affirmation 肯定
　　evidence 證據

With the speaker's detailed demonstration, everyone had a more comprehensive understanding of the topic.
伴隨著講者仔細的示範，每個人都對主題有更透徹的了解。
point with + N 意為「伴隨著……」。

Mr. Johansson gave us a demonstration of the machine on display.
喬韓森先生為我們示範如何使用展示中的機器。
point on display 意為「展示中」。

CH18
表達與演講

---

07 divide
★
★
[də`vaɪd]
v 劃分，分發，分裂
n 分開，分歧，分水嶺
同 split (v.) 分開
　　separate (v.) 分開
反 unify (v.) 聯合
　　join (v.) 連結

The instructor divided all the students into small discussion groups.
講師把所有學生分成幾個討論小組。
point divide... into 意為「將……分成」。

The white fence divides our house from our neighbor's.
這個白色籬笆將我們的房子和鄰居的隔開了。
point neighbor's = neighbor's house（鄰居的房子）。

---

08 division
★
★
[də`vɪʒən]
n 分開，分配，分裂，部門
同 section 部分
　　subdivision 細分
　　portion 部分
　　segment 部門
反 unity 聯合

Divisions among the executives have delayed the construction schedule.
主管間的意見紛歧已經延遲了工程進度。
point divisions among sb. 意為「（人）之間的分歧」。

She has worked in the company's export division for over 10 years.
她在該公司的出口部門工作已超過十年。

09 **founder**

★
★
★

[`faʊndɚ]

n 創立者，奠基者

v 船隻沉沒，失敗

同 creator (n.) 創造者
initiator (n.) 創始者

The founder of the company delivered a speech on that formal occasion.
這間公司的創立者在那個正式場合中演講。

point deliver a speech = make a speech，意為「演講」。

As the founder of the student affair association, she always has tons of creative and constructive ideas.
身為學生會的創立者，她總是有許多有創意及建設性的點子。

point tons of = a lot of，意為「大量地」。

10 **prior**

★
★

[`praɪɚ]

a 在先的，優先的，更重要的

ad 在前，居先

同 earlier (a.) 早先的
previous (a.) 先前的

反 later (a.) 較晚的

衍 prioritize (v.) 按順序處理

According to the agenda, the president's talk will be prior to Keith's presentation.
根據行程表，總裁的演講會在基斯的簡報前面。

point be prior to 意為「在……前面。」。

11 **expression**

★

[ɪk`sprɛʃən]

n 表達，表示，表情

同 look 表情
appearance 顯露

衍 express (v.) 表達

Based on the manager's facial expression, I don't think he will agree to the proposal.
根據經理的臉部表情，我不覺得他會同意這提案。

This kind of expression is not appropriate in formal speeches.
這樣的措辭在正式演講是不適當的。

12 **conduct**

★

[`kɑndʌkt]

n 行為，品行，舉動

[kən`dʌkt]

v 引導，處理，指揮

同 behavior (n.) 行為
performance (n.) 表現
demeanor (n.) 舉動
action (n.) 行為

He is not sociable and thus he might not know how to conduct himself at formal events.
他很不擅長社交，因此他有可能不知道該如何在正式場合表現。

point conduct oneself 意為「某人（在公共場所）的表現」。

The new policy will be conducted next week.
新政策下週會實行。

point conduct = implement = take sth. into practice / effect，皆可表示「執行」。

13 leading

★
★

['lidɪŋ]

a 領導的，主要的，
最重要的

同 main 主要的
major 主要的
prime 主要的

反 secondary 第二的
subordinate 次要的
minor 次要的

One of the leading businesses on Queen Street will hold an event in the square.
在皇后街的其中一家指標性公司將會在廣場舉辦活動。

(point) 延伸詞彙：campaign 意為「行銷活動」。

As a leading specialist on consumer behavior, Mr. Wiggins will deliver a speech after the banquet.
身為研究消費者行為的頂級專家，威金斯先生會在宴席後發表演講。

(point) 延伸詞彙：give a speech 意為「演講」。

14 detail

★
★
★

['ditel]

n 細節，詳情，詳述

v 詳細說明

同 fact (n.) 實情
item (n.) 項目

反 overview (n.) 概要
main idea (n.) 大意

The clerk explained the way to use the machine to the customer in detail.
店員仔細地向顧客解釋使用這台機器的方法。

(point) explain sth. to sb. 「向某人解釋某事」。

When you are presenting the proposal, mention the main idea first and then details.
當你正在報告提案時，先提及大意再講細節。

CH 18

表達與演講

15 detailed

★
★
★

['di'teld]

a 詳細的，精細的，複雜的

同 comprehensive 廣泛的
thorough 徹底的

反 general 一般的
brief 簡短的

Thanks to your detailed report, I am all clear now.
多虧你詳細的報告，我現在很清楚了。

The tour guide passed out a detailed map of this area.
導遊發下一張很詳細的此區地圖。

(point) pass out 意為「發下」。

16 capability

★
★
★

[ˌkepə'bɪlətɪ]

n 能力，才能，性能

同 potential 潛力
ability 能力

反 inability 無能
incompetence 無能

衍 capable (a.) 有能力的

He has the capability to deal with the demanding client alone.
他有能力獨自地應對那個要求很高的客戶。

(point) 相關詞彙：ability 能力，capacity 能力，competence 能力。

The speaker's topic is how to increase production capability.
演講者的主題是如何增進生產力。

(point) 多益測驗中常考「演講者的演講主題為何」。

17 **inventive**

★

[ɪnˈvɛntɪv]

ⓐ 發明的，有發明才能的

⑤ innovative 創新的
imaginative 有創造力的

衍 invention (n.) 發明
inventor (n.) 發明家
invent (v.) 發明

Participants were amazed by the lecturer's inventive powers.
出席者對講師的創造力感到驚奇。

point be amazed by 意為「對……感到驚奇」。

The industry expert is an inventive person who has given his colleagues many creative and effective suggestions.
這名產業專家曾經提供許多創新且有效的意見給他的同事，是個有創意的人。

---

18 **introduction**

★
★
★

[ˌɪntrəˈdʌkʃən]

ⓝ 介紹，引進，入門

衍 self-introduction
(ph.) 自我介紹
introductory (a.) 介紹的
introduce (v.) 介紹

Compared with the previous speaker, his introduction is rather informative.
和前一位講者相比，他的介紹相當有知識性。

point compared with 意為「與……相比」。

After the director's introduction to the firm, the sales started to introduce the newest model.
在主任介紹完公司後，業務開始介紹最新的機種。

point after 為介係詞和連接詞，後面分別加 N / Ving 和 S + V。

---

19 **instructor**

★
★
★

[ɪnˈstrʌktɚ]

ⓝ 指導者，教師，教練

⑤ trainer 訓練人
coach 教練
demonstrator 指示者
lecturer 講師

反 student 學生
pupil 學生

衍 instruct (v.) 指導

The instructor of the training session will be late due to the delay of his train.
因為火車的延誤，訓練課程的講師會遲到。

point 多益聽力測驗中常會一起提到 training 和 train，常造成聽力的混淆，要注意。

---

20 **hardly**

★
★
★

[ˈhɑrdlɪ]

ⓐⓓ 幾乎不，簡直不

⑤ scarcely 幾乎不
barely 僅僅
rarely 難得

He hardly delivers public speeches.
他很少公開演講。

He just recovered from surgery and hardly ate anything.
他才剛從手術中復原，幾乎什麼都沒吃。

21 complex
★
★
★
['kɑmplɛks]

ⓐ 複雜的，複合的
ⓝ 綜合設施，情結
ⓢ complicated (a.) 複雜的
　 involved (a.) 複雜的
　 intricate (a.) 錯綜複雜的

Smoking is not allowed in this complex.
在這棟建築內抽菸是不被允許的。

The topic of this speech is how to get rid of an inferiority complex.
這個演講的主題就是如何去除自卑情結。

(point) get rid of 意為「去除」。

---

22 housing
★
['haʊzɪŋ]

ⓝ 房屋，遮蔽物，外殼
ⓢ habitation 住處
　 residence 居住
　 home 家

After the lunch break, the highly acclaimed interior designer will give a talk on housing improvements.
在午休時間之後，這位有名的室內設計師將會主講有關改善住宅的議題。

(point) acclaimed 為被讚揚，相似字有 highly regarded, prestigious, prominent, famous, well-known, renowned，都能表達「有名的」。

The high cost of housing in big cities is the main reason why plenty of people would rather commute from suburbs to their companies.
大城市的高額房價是為何很多人寧願從郊區到公司通勤的原因。

(point) would rather 後面要用原形動詞。

> CH 18
>
> 表達與演講

---

23 excite
★
[ɪk'saɪt]

ⓥ 刺激，使興奮，使激動
ⓢ inspire 啟發
　 stimulate 刺激
　 stir up 使激動
ⓐ bore 使無聊

I don't drink coffee at night because it excites my nerves.
我晚上不喝咖啡，因為會刺激我的神經。

(point) in the evening / at night 皆可表達「晚上」。

His inspiring speech excited my interest in the psychology field.
他激勵人心的演講激發我對心理學領域的興趣。

---

24 avoid
★
★
★
[ə'vɔɪd]

ⓥ 避開，躲開，避免
ⓢ prevent 避免
　 keep away from 遠離
ⓐ face 面對
　 confront 面臨
ⓓ avoidance (n.) 逃避

You should avoid redundancy in your speech.
你的演講應避免贅詞。

(point) 延伸詞彙：redundant (a.) 多餘的。

I try to avoid going abroad in summer vacation because it's peak season.
我盡量不在暑假出國，因為是旺季。

(point) avoid + Ving 意為「避免做……」。

387

25 **banner**
★
[`bænɚ]
n 橫幅，旗幟
同 flag 旗幟

The school hung a welcome banner in front of the building to welcome the speaker.
學校掛上歡迎的橫幅在建築物前來歡迎演講者。

Some computer users download some applications to block banner advertisements.
有些電腦使用者下載一些應用程式來阻擋橫幅廣告。

point banner advertisement 為電腦網頁中的橫幅廣告。

---

26 **bearing**
★
[`bɛrɪŋ]
n 舉止，體態，關聯
同 posture 姿勢
demeanor 舉動
manner 舉止
attitude 態度
behavior 行為

People admire the politician's dignified bearing.
人們欣賞那名政治人物的莊重舉止。

The lecturer said all questions must have a bearing on the subject.
講者說所有的問題都必須與主題有關。

point 此句的 bearing 解釋為「關聯」。

---

27 **interrupt**
★
★
[ˌɪntəˋrʌpt]
v 打斷，中止，阻礙
同 interfere (with) 妨礙
intervene (in) 介入
衍 interruption (n.) 中止

Interrupting people while they are talking is considered impolite.
在人們講話時打斷他們被認為是不禮貌的。

point be considered (to be) 意為「被認為……」，要注意後面不是接 as。

If you can't understand anything, feel free to interrupt my speech.
如果你不了解任何事情，儘管打斷我的演講。

point 相關詞彙：break in (on) 插嘴，cut in (on) 插話，intrude (on) 打擾。

---

28 **suppose**
★
★
★
[səˋpoz]
v 猜想，認為，假定
同 guess 猜想
infer 猜想

The speaker supposed the audiences had a basic knowledge about herbs.
講者假定觀眾對藥草有基本的知識。

point 相關詞彙：assume 假定，presume 假設，expect 預期。

Do you suppose that the construction will be finished as planned?
你認為工程會如期完成嗎？

point as planned = as scheduled，意為「如期地」。

29 background
★
★
★
[`bæk͵graʊnd]
n 背景，經歷，幕後
同 surrounding 環境
　　framework 架構
反 foreground 前景
　　front 前面

Obviously, the audience hardly had any background knowledge on biotechnology.
很明顯地，聽眾沒有任何生物科技的知識。

 hardly = scarcely = rarely = barely，意為「幾乎不」。

Candidates with a marketing background are more likely to get the position.
有行銷經驗背景的求職者比較有可能取得那個職位。

---

30 summarize
★
★
[`sʌmə͵raɪz]
V 總結，概述
同 outline 概述
　　brief 做提要
反 elaborate 詳細說明

The financial director summarized the financial report in the meeting.
財務主任在會議中概述了財務報告。

 financial report 在多益閱讀測驗的選項中常用 financial summary 替換。

The host summarized the keynote speaker's talk and shared some of her opinions on the issue discussed.
主持人總結了主講人的演講內容，並分享她自己對那個討論議題的想法。

point discussed 前省略了 which (that) was，用來修飾 issue，意為「被討論的議題」。

---

31 retire
★
★
★
[rɪ`taɪr]
V 退休，撤退，就寢
同 retreat 撤退
　　withdraw 撤回
反 advance 前進
衍 retirement (n.) 退休

Since retiring from his job, he runs a grocery store in the small town.
退休之後，他在小鎮經營一家雜貨店。

point run 在此句為「經營」的意思。

The speakers introduced 5 essential money management strategies to retire early.
講師介紹五個可以達成早點退休的重要金錢管理策略。

---

32 mayor
★
★
★
[`meɚ]
n 市長，鎮長
衍 major (n.) 科系
　　　　(a.) 主要的

The mayor delivered a speech at the opening ceremony.
市長在開幕典禮上演講。

point deliver a speech 意為「演講」。

The mayor's secretary put his itinerary on his desk.
市長的祕書把他的行程放到他的桌上。

Chapter 175

18 表達與演講

33 remark
★
★

[rɪ`mɑrk]

n 言辭，評論，察覺
v 談論，覺察，評論
同 comment (n.) 評論
say (n.) 意見
observe (v.) 觀察
mention (v.) 提及

After some brief opening remarks, the guests helped themselves to some food and beverages.
在簡短的開幕致詞後，客人們盡情地去拿些食物跟飲料。

point opening remark 意為「開幕致詞」，多益測驗中常常出現，要特別注意。

The candidate's remarks on power plants have led to a discussion.
候選人對發電廠的評論已經引發了討論。

point plant = factory，意為「工廠」。

34 private
★
★
★

[`praɪvɪt]

a 私下的，祕密的，私立的
同 personal 個人的
individual 個人的
exclusive 獨有的
反 public 公開的

When making small talk, remember to avoid asking strangers private questions, like their age.
在閒聊時，記得要避免問陌生人私人問題，像是年紀。

It is absolutely improper that the manager asked his subordinates to deal with his own private things.
經理叫下屬幫他處理私事完全是不恰當的。

point deal with = cope with，意為「處理」。

35 previous
★
★
★

[`priviəs]

a 先前的，以前的
同 foregoing 前面的
preceding 在前的
earlier 早先的
former 在前的
反 following 接著的
next 下一個

Before we start today's class, let's review the previous lesson.
在我們開始今天的課程之前，讓我們先複習上一課。

point before 在此句為連接詞，連接兩個句子。before 還可以當介係詞，後面加 Ving / N。

The previous tenant repainted the wall by himself without telling his landlord.
先前的房客自己重漆了牆面，而沒有告訴房東。

36 occasion
★
★
★

[ə`keʒən]

n 場合，重大活動，時機
同 instance 情況
moment 時刻
event 事件
situation 狀況
circumstance 情況

The CEO wears a suit no matter what formal occasions he attends.
不論執行長參加什麼正式場合，他都穿西裝。

point no matter what = whatever，意為「不論什麼」。

The secretary, on occasion, forgets her supervisor's schedule.
祕書偶爾會忘記她上司的行程。

point on occasion 意為「偶爾」。

37 offensive
★
[əˋfɛnsɪv]

🅐 冒犯的，討厭的，進攻的

🔄 rude 粗魯的
disrespectful 無禮的

🔄 pleasant 舒適的
delightful 令人愉快的

衍 offense (n.) 冒犯

People found the politician's speech offensive.
人們覺得那個政治人物的演講很無禮。

point find sth. + a. 意為「覺得……」。

The assistant was laid off because of his offensive remarks.
那名助理因為冒犯的話而被解僱。

point lay off 意為「解僱」。

---

38 objective
★
★
[əbˋdʒɛktɪv]

🅝 目的，目標

🅐 客觀的，目標的

🔄 aim (n.) 目標
intention (n.) 意圖
purpose (n.) 目的
target (n.) 目標
goal (n.) 目標

Always keep your objectives in mind when you are making a speech.
當你演講時，要一直記得你的演講目的。

point keep... in mind 意為「記住……」。

The main objective of the new policy is to improve employee productivity.
新政策的主要目的是為了增強員工生產力。

point employee productivity 意為「員工生產力」，常常作為多益聽力測驗中演講者分享的主題。

CH 18
表達與演講

---

39 motivate
★
★
★
[ˋmotəˌvet]

🆅 給動機，刺激，激發

🔄 move 使感動
influence 影響
lead 引導

🔄 demotivate 使失去動力

A good teacher knows how to motivate students to learn.
一個好的老師知道如何鼓舞學生學習。

point 相關詞彙：inspire 啟發，stimulate 刺激，drive 驅動，prompt 激勵。

The speaker shared some highly effective ways to motivate employees.
講者分享了一些有效鼓勵員工的方式。

---

40 inadequate
★
★
[ɪnˋædəkwɪt]

🅐 不充足的，不適當的，不能勝任的

🔄 insufficient 不足的
limited 有限的

🔄 adequate 適當的
sufficient 足夠的

In fact, we didn't think the way he dealt with the problem was inadequate.
事實上，我們並不覺得他處理這問題的方式不適當。

point 在多益聽力和閱讀測驗中 In fact 後面常會加重要的訊息，要注意。

The presidential candidate's inadequate speech has raised a lot of criticism.
該名總統候選人不適當的演講已經引起很多批評。

41 lecture
★
★ [ˈlɛktʃɚ]
★ n 授課，演講，責備
Ⅴ 演講，講課，訓斥
同 speech (n.) 演講
address (n.) 演說
lesson (n.) 課程

The security guard guided the visitor to the lecture hall.
警衛引導訪客到演講廳。

Inspired by the speaker's lecture, I decided to take a minor.
我被這名講者的課程所啟發，因此我決定要修輔系。

point 此句為分詞構句，原句為 Because I was inspired by the speaker's lecture, ...。省略連接詞與主詞，was inspired 為被動語態，即保留動詞的過去分詞 inspired。

42 least
★ [list]
★ a 最小的，最少的，最不重要的
ad 最小，最少，最不
同 slightest (a.) 最小的
smallest (a.) 最小的
minimal (a.) 極微的
反 greatest (a.) 最大的
most (a.) 最多的

At least, we still can apply for the scholarship.
至少我們還可以申請獎學金。

point apply for 意為「申請」。

Last but not least, Professor Johnson will give us a talk on "sustainable energy".
最後，強森教授會為我們進行「可持續能源」的演講。

point Last but not least = finally，意為「最後」。

43 honor
★ [ˈɑnɚ]
★
★ n 榮譽，敬意，禮儀
Ⅴ 使榮譽，尊敬，實踐
同 privilege (n.) 殊榮
glory (n.) 光榮
fame (n.) 聲譽
反 dishonor (v.) 使丟臉
衍 honorary (a.) 名譽上的

The banquet was held to honor Mr. Turner, who had worked for the company for over thirty years.
這場餐宴是為了致敬已經為公司工作超過三十年的透納先生。

point 這樣的句子常出現在多益聽力測驗 Part 4 介紹退休人員的情境中，要注意。

The recipient said it was his honor to receive this award.
得獎人說得到這個獎項是他的榮幸。

44 gesture
★ [ˈdʒɛstʃɚ]
n 姿勢，手勢
Ⅴ 做手勢
同 sign (n.) 手勢

Some gestures are universal.
有些手勢是世界通用的。

point universal (a.) 共同的；通用的。

When you are making a speech, you can emphasize key points with gestures.
當你在演講時，你可以用手勢來強調關鍵字。

45 grateful

★
★
['gretfəl]

ⓐ 感激的，感謝的

同 thankful 感謝的
filled with gratitude
充滿感激的
appreciative 感謝的

反 ungrateful 忘恩負義的

In the ceremony, the software engineer said he felt grateful to work with many talented people.
在典禮上，軟體工程師表示他對於可以和很多有才華的人一起工作感到很感恩。

(point) talent (n.) 天賦；天才。

I'd be very grateful if you could send us your latest catalog as soon as possible.
如果你們可以盡快將最新目錄寄給我們，我們將感激不盡。

(point) as soon as possible 意為「盡可能地快」。

46 fluctuation

★
[͵flʌktʃuˋeʃən]

ⓝ 波動，變動，動搖

同 shift 轉變
alteration 改變
swing 擺動

反 stability 穩定

衍 fluctuate (v.) 波動

Some people who prefer stable lives can't stand the day-to-day fluctuations of the stock market.
有些比較喜歡穩定生活的人，沒辦法忍受股票市場每天的起伏。

(point) who prefer stable lives 為關係子句（等於形容詞子句），用來修飾前面的 Some people。

The speech focuses on the effects of climatic fluctuations.
這場演講聚焦在氣候變化的影響。

(point) 相關詞彙：change 改變，variation 變化。

CH 18

表達與演講

---

47 earn

★
★
★
[ɝn]

ⓥ 賺得，搏得，使得到

同 receive 收到
get 得到
obtain 獲得
gain 得到

It takes time to earn people's trust.
贏得人們的信任是相當花時間的。

(point) it takes time to... 意為「……是花時間的」。

He used to earn his living by being a columnist.
他過去靠當專欄作家賺錢。

(point) 延伸詞彙：freelance (n.) 自由職業者 (a.) 自由職業者的。

---

48 elevate

★
[ˋɛlə͵vet]

ⓥ 舉起，提高，振奮精神

同 raise 增加
lift (up) 舉起

反 lower 放下

衍 elevator (n.) 電梯
elevation (n.) 高度

The CEO's inspiring speech elevated the staff.
執行長那番鼓舞人心的演說使員工精神振奮。

All of the audiences' spirits were elevated by the song.
所有觀眾的精神都被這首歌振奮了。

(point) be elevated 為被動式，意為「被振奮」。

18 表達與演講

---

49 each
★
★
★
[itʃ]
pron 每個
ad 各個，各自，每一個
同 every one (ph.) 每一個

Ever since the two brothers' parents left them, they have taken care of each other.
自從倆兄弟的父母離開他們，他們就互相照顧彼此。

The sales managers from each branch took turns sharing their management experience.
每個分部的業務經理輪流分享他們的管理經驗。

point take turn + Ving 意為「輪流做……」。

---

50 drastic
★
[`dræstɪk]
a 激烈的，猛烈的，極端的
同 radical 極端的
sharp 銳利的
severe 嚴重的
反 mild 溫和的
moderate 適當的
衍 drastically (adv.) 激烈地

His proposal needed drastic revision before the presentation.
在簡報前，他的提案需要重大的修改。

point 相關詞彙：extreme 極度的，serious 重要的。

The officer's comments to the homeless person brought up some drastic arguments.
官員對遊民的評論引起了一些激烈的爭論。

---

51 discouraged
★
[dɪs`kɝɪdʒd]
a 灰心的，氣餒的
同 frustrated 挫敗的
depressed 消沉的
disappointed 失望的
反 cheerful 樂意的
encouraging 鼓舞的

If you can face your failures, there's nothing to feel discouraged about.
如果你可以面對你的失敗，沒有什麼可以為之感到氣餒的。

He was discouraged from pursuing his goal.
他在追尋自己的目標時受到阻礙。

point be discouraged from 意為「受阻於」。

---

52 discouragement
★
[dɪs`kɝɪdʒmənt]
n 沮喪，氣餒，洩氣
同 lack of enthusiasm
缺乏熱忱
lack of confidence
缺乏自信
pessimism 悲觀
反 optimism 樂觀
encouragement 鼓勵

Failing to attend the top university was a great discouragement to him.
沒能進入最棒的大學令他極其灰心喪氣。

point Failing to attend the top university 為 Ving 當主詞，動詞用單數。

If we think in a different way, discouragement can also help us grow.
如果我們換一個角度來想的話，沮喪也能幫助我們成長。

point 相關詞彙：depression 沮喪，disappointment 失望，hopelessness 無望，despair 絕望，gloom 憂鬱心情。

53 delegate

★
★

[ˋdɛləgɪt]

n 代表，會議代表

[ˋdɛləˏget]

v 委派代表，授權給

同 agent (n.) 代理人
representative (n.) 代表

The team leader knows how to delegate responsibilities to his members according to their abilities.
組長知道如何根據成員們的能力來授予責任。

point according to = based on，意為「根據」。

The senior engineer was delegated to present the prototype of the product.
資深工程師被派來報告產品的原型。

---

54 critic

★
★

[ˋkrɪtɪk]

n 批評家，評論家

同 commentator 時事評論者

衍 critical (a.) 緊要的
criticize (v.) 批評

People found the critic's comments informative.
人們覺得那位評論家的評論具有教育性。

point find + O + a. 意為「發現……處於……狀態」。

The movie critic attended the premiere of *Avengers* the day before yesterday.
那位電影評論家前天出席《復仇者聯盟》的首映會。

point the day before yesterday 意為「前天」。

CH 18

表達與演講

---

55 corporate

★
★
★

[ˋkɔrpərɪt]

a 團體的，公司的，共同的

同 collective 集體的
shared 共用的
joint 共同的
collaborative 合作的

反 individual 個人的

In the next session, Professor King will talk about corporate management.
在下一個階段，金教授會分享有關企業經營的主題。

point 此為多益聽力測驗中廣播常見的情境，常考演講主題，要注意。

The movie crew made a corporate effort to win the Academy Award for Best Picture.
這個電影團隊透過共同努力贏得了奧斯卡最佳影片大獎。

point corporate effort 意為「共同的努力」。

---

56 contrary

★
★

[ˋkɑntrɛrɪ]

a 相反的，對立的

n 相反，對立面

同 opposite (a.) 相反的
contradictory (a.) 對立的
incompatible (a.) 矛盾的

反 compatible (a.) 能共處的
same (a.) 一樣的

Contrary to the critic's predication, the candidate failed.
和那名評論家預期不同的是，那名候選人敗選了。

point candidate (n.) 候選人；求職者。

On the contrary, he has a good command of Spanish.
相反地，他西語能力極佳。

point have a good command of 意為「對……掌握度高」。

Chapter 178

18 表達與演講

57 receptionist
★
★
[rɪ`sɛpʃənɪst]
★
n 接待員，傳達員
衍 reception (n.) 接待會
recipient (n.) 受領者

The receptionist led the guests to the lecture hall.
接待員帶客人到演講廳。

The receptionist transferred my call to the person who is in charge of credit card business.
接線生轉接我的電話給負責信用卡業務的人員。

---

58 concept
★
★
[`kɑnsɛpt]
★
n 觀念，概念，思想
同 belief 看法
opinion 意見
view 觀點

The professor illustrated the abstract concept with two concrete examples.
教授用兩個具體的例子來說明這個抽象的概念。

(point) 相關詞彙：idea 概念，conception 觀念，notion 概念。

The speaker presented a new concept of work-life balance.
講者提出了一個工作與生活的平衡的新觀念。

---

59 command
★
[kə`mænd]
n 命令，指揮，掌握
v 命令，控制，指揮
同 order (v.) 命令
give orders to (ph.) 下命令
direct (v.) 指揮
instruct (v.) 命令
require (v.) 要求

From her presentation, we can confirm that she has a good command of public speaking.
從她的演講，我們可以證實她在公共演講上有很好的掌握。

(point) have a good command of 意為「對……有很好的掌握」。

All the police officers in this district are under his command.
這區所有的警察都是由他指揮。

(point) under one's command 意為「在某人的指揮之下」。

---

60 adapt
★
★
[ə`dæpt]
★
v 使適應，改編，改寫
同 adjust 改變以適應
modify 修改
accommodate 使適應
alter 改變
衍 adapter (n.) 改編者

The movie director is going to adapt the renowned writer's novel into a movie.
這名電影導演計劃要把暢銷作家的小說改編成電影。

When you are lecturing something difficult to people who don't have a certain background knowledge, try to adapt your lecture to them.
當你要對沒有特定背景知識的人們講一些很困難的事情時，試著把難度調整成適合聽眾的程度。

61 compliment
★ [`kɑmpləmənt]
- **n** 恭維，敬意，問候
- **v** 讚美，祝賀，表示敬意
- **同** acclaim (v.) 稱讚
  praise (v.) 讚揚
- **反** criticize (v.) 批評
- **衍** complimentary
  (a.) 讚美的，免費的

I will take this as a compliment.
我會把這個當作對我的讚美。

The manager complimented the newcomer on the meeting.
經理在會議上讚美那位新人。

 newcomer 意為「新來的人」。

62 ceremony
★
★
★ [`sɛrə‚monɪ]
- **n** 典禮，禮儀
- **同** celebration 慶典
  ritual 儀式
- **衍** wedding ceremony
  (ph.) 婚禮

The university invited a prestigious speaker to speak at the graduation ceremony.
這所大學邀請一位聲望很高的講師來畢業典禮演講。

 延伸詞彙：graduate (v.) 畢業 (a.) 畢業的 (n.) 畢業生。注意畢業生是 graduate，不是 graduater 或 graduator（刻度員）。

GTI Company was responsible for catering for her wedding ceremony.
GTI 公司負責她婚禮的外燴服務。

 catering (n.) 承辦酒席，cater (v.) 提供外燴服務。

63 career
★
★
★ [kə`rɪr]
- **n** 職業，經歷，生涯
- **同** job 工作
  profession 職業

Sometimes you need to get lost a little bit before you find your dream career.
有時你必須要迷失一下才能找到你夢想中的工作。

Some people decide their careers by their interests, while others choose jobs depending on their specialties.
有些人以他們的興趣來決定職業，但另一些人用專長來選擇工作。

 some... others 意為「有些人……另一些人」。

64 purely
★ [`pjurlɪ]
- **ad** 純粹地，完全
- **同** entirely 完全
  totally 完全
  completely 徹底地
- **衍** purify (v.) 淨化

It's purely voluntary to participate in the activity, not compulsory.
參加活動完全是志願性的，非強迫性。

They married purely for political reasons.
他們結婚單純是因為政治原因。

 for + N 意為「為了……原因」。

CH 18
表達與演講

65 irrelevant
★

[ɪ`rɛləvənt]

a 不恰當的，無關係的

同 unconnected 無關的
unrelated 無關的

反 relevant 有關的

The editor suggested the writer delete all the irrelevant and redundant words.
編輯建議作家刪除所有不相關及多餘的字。

(point) suggest + O + (should) + V 意為「建議某人做某事」。

What he said is totally irrelevant to the central argument.
他說的和中心論點完全不相關。

---

66 frequently
★
★
★

[`frikwəntlɪ]

ad 頻繁地，屢次地，經常地

同 habitually 慣常地
customarily 通常
routinely 慣常地

反 seldom 很少

The instructor collected many frequently asked questions, and answered them in the Q&A session.
講師收集許多經常被問到的問題，然後在提問時間回答。

(point) 相關詞彙：regularly 經常地，usually 通常，often 時常，normally 通常。

The personnel department holds workshops frequently.
人事部門經常辦工作坊。

(point) 延伸詞彙：conference, seminar 皆可指「研討會」。

---

67 composure
★

[kəm`poʒɚ]

n 平靜，鎮靜，沉著

同 self-possession 沉著
self-command 自制
calmness 冷靜

反 nervousness 緊張
discomposure 不安

Try to maintain composure even when you are in trouble.
即使當你陷入麻煩，也要試著保持鎮靜。

(point) be in trouble 意為「陷入困難」。

Don't lose your composure when you are on the stage.
別在舞台上失去你的鎮定。

(point) lose one's temper 意為「生氣」。

---

68 signify
★
★
★

[`sɪgnəˌfaɪ]

v 表示，表明，意味著

同 signal 示意
announce 宣布

反 withhold 保留
keep a secret 保守機密

He signified his consent by smiling.
他微笑以表示同意。

To the Asian actress Ms. Holland, the cooperation with the famous American actor signified another step to the international market.
對亞洲女演員何藍女士來說，和那位著名美國男演員的合作代表了通往國際市場的一步。

(point) 相關詞彙：mark 標誌，mean 代表，indicate 象徵。

69 **overcome**
★
★
[ˌovɚˋkʌm]

Ⓥ 戰勝，克服，壓倒

同 defeat 戰勝
  beat 獲勝
  conquer 征服

反 lose 失敗

He overcame all the difficulties and fulfilled his dream.
他克服了所有困難並實現了他的夢想。

 fulfill one's dream 意為「實現某人的夢想」。

Overcome your fear and step out of your comfort zone.
戰勝你的恐懼，踏出舒適圈。

---

70 **emphasis**
★
★
★
[ˋɛmfəsɪs]

Ⓝ 強調，重點，加強語氣

同 importance 重要性
  significance 重要
  stress 著重

衍 emphasize (v.) 強調

The government placed greater emphasis on the highway construction.
政府將更多的重心放在建造公路。

She tends to lay emphasis on the keywords by slowing down her speech.
她傾向藉由放慢講話速度來強調關鍵字。

 tend to 意為「傾向於」。

CH 18

表達與演講

---

71 **explain**
★
★
★
[ɪkˋsplen]

Ⓥ 解釋，說明，辯解

同 describe 敘述
  give an explanation of
  給出解釋

衍 explanation (n.) 說明

The lecturer explained the new system of reporting sales in detail.
講師仔細解釋新的回報銷售狀況的系統。

The friendly clerk kept explaining how to install the machine until the customer fully understood the procedures.
那名友善的店員不斷解釋如何安裝機器直到顧客完全了解步驟為止。

point keep + Ving 意為「不斷……」。

---

72 **distract**
★
[dɪˋstrækt]

Ⓥ 轉移，使分心，使苦惱

同 disturb 打擾

反 concentrate 專心

Nowadays, many pupils are easily distracted by social media.
現今非常多學生很容易被社群媒體分心。

 pupil = student，意為「學生」。

The shoplifter stole the luxury necklace by distracting the shop clerk.
這名順手牽羊者藉由使店員分心來偷走那條珍貴的項鍊。

---

73 definite
★
['dɛfənɪt]
a 明確的，肯定的，限定的
同 express 明確的
反 vague 模糊的
　　indefinite 不確定的
　　slight 不牢靠的

There is no definite definition of success.
成功沒有絕對的定義。

(point) 相關詞彙：explicit 明確的，precise 精確的，specific 明確的，exact 確切的。

The protesters in the square demanded a definite answer from the city council.
在廣場的抗議者要求市政府給出一個明確的答覆。

---

74 deep
★
[dip]
a 深的，極度的，玄妙的
同 extensive 廣泛的
　　profound 深奧的
反 shallow 淺的
衍 deepen (v.) 使變深

Take a deep breath before the presentation.
在簡報前，深呼吸。

The rapper is famous for his deep voice.
那名饒舌高手以他低沈的嗓音而聞名。

(point) be famous for 意為「以……而聞名」。

---

75 debate
★
[dɪ'bet]
v 辯論，討論，爭論
n 辯論，討論，辯論會
同 exchange of views
　　(ph.) 交換觀點
　　argument (n.) 爭執
衍 debatable (a.) 有爭議的

People are looking forward to the presidential debate tonight.
人們很期待今晚的總統選舉辯論。

(point) be looking forward to + N / Ving 意為「期待……」。

The Human Resources Department debated the details of the company trip earlier this morning.
人力資源部門今天稍早討論了員工旅遊的細節。

---

76 demonstrate
★
★
★
['dɛmən،stret]
v 證明，示範，示威
同 reveal 揭示
　　indicate 表明
　　signify 表示
　　signal 示意
　　show 展示
衍 demonstration (n.) 示範

Later, Mr. Matteo will demonstrate how to use the new kitchen utensils.
稍後，馬泰奧先生將會展示如何使用新的廚房器具。

The executive chef of Golden Resort will demonstrate this recipe after the talk.
高登度假村的執行主廚將會在演講之後示範這個食譜。

(point) 多益聽力測驗 Part 4 介紹演講者的題目，很容易在 after the talk, after the dinner / lunch, after the Q&A section 有個活動。

Test 1

🔘 **一、請寫出下列單字的中文意思。**

① interrupt _____ ⑥ inventive _____

② irrelevant _____ ⑦ explain _____

③ contrary _____ ⑧ demonstration _____

④ expression _____ ⑨ inadequate _____

⑤ motivate _____ ⑩ previous _____

🔘 **二、請寫出符合下列句意的單字。**

① The personnel department holds workshops _____.
人事部門經常辦工作坊。

② The _____ led the guests to the lecture hall.
接待員帶客人到演講廳。

③ In the next session, Professor King will talk about _____ management.
在下一個階段,金教授會分享有關企業經營的主題。

解答

1. ① 打斷,中止　② 不相關的,無關係的　③ 相反的,對立的;對立面　④ 表達,表情
　⑤ 刺激,激發,使有動機　⑥ 發明的,有創造才能的　⑦ 解釋,說明　⑧ 證明,示範,示威
　⑨ 不充足的,不適當的　⑩ 先前的,上一個的

2. ① frequently　② receptionist　③ corporate

Test 2

一、請選擇符合下列文意的單字。

Ⓐ occasions　　Ⓑ avoid　　Ⓒ prior
Ⓓ retire　　Ⓔ detailed　　Ⓕ inadequate

① The speakers introduced 5 essential money management strategies to _____ early.

② Thanks to your _____ report, I am all clear now.

③ The CEO wears a suit no matter what formal _____ he attends.

④ You should _____ redundancy in your speech.

⑤ The movie critic's _____ speech had risen a lot of criticisms.

二、請寫出下列片語的中文意思。

① be based on _____　　⑤ as scheduled _____

② get rid of _____　　⑥ have a good command of _____

③ cope with _____　　⑦ compare with _____

④ apply for _____　　⑧ on occasion _____

解答

1. ①D　②E　③A　④B　⑤F
2. ① 根據　② 去除　③ 處理　④ 申請　⑤ 如期地　⑥ 對……掌握度高　⑦ 與……相比　⑧ 偶爾

Chapter 19
傳播媒體

以下多益必考單字，你認識哪些？

☐ publish (p.407)　　☐ partial (p.418)　　☐ fulfillment (p.417)

☐ review (p.406)　　☐ avoidance (p.415)　　☐ author (p.411)

☐ subscription (p.409)　　☐ rapidly (p.410)　　☐ current (p.418)

☐ selective (p.404)　　☐ combination (p.411)　　☐ release (p.418)

☐ adventure (p.414)　　☐ pursue (p.420)　　☐ repetitive (p.417)

☐ acclaim (p.414)　　☐ sufficient (p.420)　　☐ accuracy (p.412)

傳播媒體

01 appearance
★
★
★
[əˈpɪrəns]

🅝 出現，演出，外表

🔁 figure 外形
　 form 外形
　 outline 輪廓
　 shape 形狀

衍 appear (v.) 出現

The idiom "Don't judge a book by its cover." means don't judge a person by his or her appearance.
「不要以貌取人」，這個諺語的意思是不要用人的外表來評斷一個人。

She made some television appearances lately because her video on the internet went viral.
她最近參加了一些電視演出，因為她在網路上的影片爆紅。

point　go viral 意為「廣為流傳」。

02 brand-new
★
[ˈbrændˈnu]

🅐 全新的，嶄新的

🔁 new 新的

反 old 舊的

The brand-new single became rather popular once it was released.
這首新單曲一推出就受到歡迎。

point　single 意為「單曲」，album 意為「專輯」。

He couldn't afford to buy a brand-new house, so he borrowed money from the bank.
他沒辦法負擔得起買那棟全新的房子，所以他向銀行借錢。

03 selective
★
★
[səˈlɛktɪv]

🅐 有選擇性的，淘汰的

🔁 discriminating 有差別的
　 discriminatory 有識別力的

反 indiscriminate 無差別的

Many parents nowadays are more selective about the TV programs for their children.
現在的父母對於給他們小孩看的電視節目更加嚴格篩選。

People who work in the fashion industry tend to be more selective in the outfits they wear.
在時尚界工作的人對於自己穿的衣服比較精挑細選。

point　延伸詞彙：show business 意為「演藝圈」。

04 nominate
★
★
★
[ˈnɑməˌnet]

🅥 提名，任命，指定

🔁 appoint 任命
　 designate 指定
　 assign 指定
　 name 提名

We all agreed to nominate John as the employee of the year.
我們都同意提名強為年度最佳員工。

point　the employee of the year 意為「年度最佳員工」。

Surprisingly, the film which was directed by a new director was nominated for an Academy Award.
令人意外地，這部由新導演所導的電影獲得奧斯卡提名。

point　film = movie，意為「電影」。

05 **nomination**

★
★
[ˌnɑməˋneʃən]

n 提名，任命

回 naming (n.) 命名

The judge explained the method of award nomination.
這個評審解釋了獎項提名的方式。

The results of Emmy nomination had been posted on the website before she got back to home.
在她回家之前，艾美獎提名結果早已經被發布在網頁上。

 had been posted 為過去完成式，時間發生較早，got 為過去式，時間發生較晚。

06 **nominee**

★
★
★
[ˌnɑməˋni]

n 被提名的人，被任命者

回 candidate 候選人

All the award nominees should reply to this email before this Friday.
所有的獎項提名人都須在本週五前回覆這封信。

The presidential nominee shared his opinion about financial issues.
該名總統候選人分享了他對財政議題的看法。

07 **comment**

★
★
★
[ˋkɑmɛnt]

n 批評，意見，評論

v 發表意見，評論，註解

回 remark (n.) 評論
observation (n.) 言論
statement (n.) 聲明

Feel free to leave comments below if you have questions.
如果你有問題，請儘管在下面留言。

He commented that the supporting actor in this drama outperformed the leading actor.
他評論這齣戲劇的男配角表現得比男主角還要好。

 supporting actor 意為「男配角」，leading actor = main actor 意為「男主角」。

08 **commentary**

★
★
[ˋkɑmənˌtɛrɪ]

n 評論，實況報導

回 narration 敘述
description 敘述
account 解釋
report 報導
review 評論

The factory tour has Chinese commentaries.
這個工廠導覽有中文解說。

My friends are watching the live running commentary on the basketball.
我的朋友正在看現場實況籃球報導。

 running commentary 意為「連續不斷的報導」。

09 **version**

★
[ˋvɝʒən]
★
★ **n** 版本,說法,改寫本
同 sort 類型
kind 種類
type 類型
class 級別
category 種類

The new version of the package is more appealing than the old one.
套裝組合的新版本比舊版的還要更吸引人。

point 因為前面提過 version,故後面的 one 代替 version。

The critic indicated that the original novel was superior to its film version.
評論家指出這部原作小說勝過它的電影版本。

point be superior to 意為「優於」。

10 **update**

★
[ʌpˋdet]
★
★ **v** 使現代化,更新
[ˋʌpdet]
n 最新情況,最新報導
同 modernize (v.) 現代化
renovate (v.) 更新
improve (v.) 改進
upgrade (v.) 提高
reform (v.) 改正

Stay tune for our hourly update.
請鎖定收聽我們每小時的更新。

point 多益聽力測驗的廣播中,如果問聽眾下一次什麼時候聽到廣播,題目出現 hourly 的話,就是指一小時後。

Please update the mailing list before this Friday because we need to send out the printed materials to our customers before the annual sale.
請在這週五前更新郵寄名單,因為我們要在週年慶之前寄文宣給我們的客戶。

point mailing list 意為「郵寄名單」。

11 **review**

★
[rɪˋvju]
★
★ **v** 再檢查,評論,回顧
n 複審,評論,複習
同 survey (n.) 調查
study (n.) 研究
research (n.) 研究

The professor asked his students to preview and review the reading materials.
教授要求學生預習和複習閱讀教材。

point ask sb. to 意為「請求某人去……」。

The movie got excellent reviews because the plot was unpredictable.
這部電影因為不老套的劇情而得到極高的評價。

12 **broadcast**

★
[ˋbrɔdˌkæst]
★
★ **v** 廣播,播放,散播
n 廣播,廣播節目
同 announce (v.) 宣布

Nowadays, many people do a live broadcast to earn money.
現在很多人靠線上直播賺錢。

The broadcast host interviewed his guests about the issue of off-shoring in the IT industry.
廣播主持人訪問他的來賓有關資訊產業外移的議題。

point off-shoring 意為「產業外移」,in-shoring 意為「產業內移」。

13 **journalist**
★
★ [ˋdʒɝnəlɪst]
★
n 新聞工作者，新聞記者

同 reporter 記者
　　correspondent 通訊記者
　　columnist 專欄作家
　　writer 撰稿人

The seminar is designed for journalists.
這個研習會是設計給新聞記者參加的。

Growing up in this culturally diverse city, the journalist knows how to speak three languages.
因為這位記者在這個多元文化的城市長大，所以他知道如何講三種語言。

14 **newsletter**
★
★ [ˋnjuzˏlɛtɚ]
★
n 時事通訊，商務通訊

衍 news 新聞

Have you read the monthly newsletter yet?
你讀每月的時事通訊了嗎？

point 如果多益測驗題目問「出版頻率」時，從這個句子敘述就可以知道是每月出版一次。

The assistant confirmed the format of newsletters because he would start to be responsible for editing them next quarter.
助理確認了時事通訊的格式，因為他下一季會開始負責編輯。

CH 19

傳
播
媒
體

15 **press**
★
★ [prɛs]

v 按壓，催促，強迫
n 報刊，新聞界

同 push (v.) 逼迫
　　depress (v.) 壓下
　　force (v.) 強迫
　　compress (v.) 壓緊

The entrepreneur tried to get press coverage for his business.
這名創業家試著讓媒體報導他的企業。

The journalist works for the national press, instead of the local press.
這位記者為那個全國性報刊工作，而不是地方性報刊。

16 **publish**
★
★ [ˋpʌblɪʃ]
★
v 出版，刊登，發表

同 issue 發行
　　produce 出版
　　print 出版

The science fiction novel will be published in this country once the contract is signed.
一旦契約簽訂，這本科幻小說就會在這個國家出版。

point once 在這句為連接詞，意為「一旦」。

The reader wrote to inquire how to get his article published in newspapers.
讀者寫信來詢問如何將他的文章刊登在報紙上。

point inquire (v.) 詢問，inquiry (n.) 詢問；問題。

17 **publisher**
★
★
★
['pʌblɪʃɚ]

🄝 出版者，出版社
🄢 publishing house 出版社
🄦 publication (n.) 出版品

Many publishers are eager to cooperate with the well-known writer.
很多出版社都渴望可以跟那位有名的作家合作。
(point) be eager to 意為「渴望」。

If you have submitted your article to the publisher, no further steps are required.
如果你已經把文章交給出版社，那就不用再做任何事了。

18 **publication**
★
★
★
[‚pʌblɪ'keʃən]

🄝 出版（物），發表，宣布
🄢 announcement 宣布
　 publishing 出版
　 printing 出版
🄦 publicize (v.) 宣傳

Professor Wright's publication is now available in electronic form.
萊特教授的出版品現在有電子版本。
(point) form (n.) 形式；表格。

The well-known industry expert will introduce his latest publication in the exclusive interview.
知名的產業專家會在獨家專訪中介紹他最新的出版物。

19 **editor**
★
★
★
['ɛdɪtɚ]

🄝 編輯，編者，校訂者
🄢 reviser 校訂者

The magazine editor of Life and Technology made a feature article about the new RT vacuum cleaner.
生活與科技雜誌的編輯做了一個 RT 吸塵器的專欄報導。
(point) feature article 意為「專欄報導」。

The chief editor of that fashion magazine was invited to attend the autumn fashion show.
那名時尚雜誌主編被邀請參加秋季時尚秀。

20 **edit**
★
['ɛdɪt]

🄥 編輯，校訂，剪輯
🄢 revise 修訂
　 modify 修改
　 adapt 改編
　 rewrite 改寫

She is responsible for editing the magazine.
她負責編輯那本雜誌。
(point) be responsible for = be in charge of，意為「負責」。

The senior specialist is editing his company's confidential documents.
這名資深專員正在編輯他公司的機密文件。
(point) confidential = secret，意為「機密的」。

21 subscribe
★
★ [səbˋskraɪb]
★
Ⅴ 訂閱，認捐
同 contribute 捐助
　 donate 捐獻

If you subscribe to the magazine today, we will offer you three free movie tickets.
如果你今天訂雜誌，我們會提供你三張免費的電影票。

Subscribe to the YouTube channel "NLL Speaking" to enhance your English ability.
訂閱 YouTube 頻道「NLL Speaking」以增進你的英文能力。

---

22 subscription
★
★ [səbˋskrɪpʃən]
★
ⁿ 訂閱，同意，署名，捐款

The subscription will end this month.
訂閱將於這個月到期。

Trend Magazine encourages their subscribers to renew their subscription by offering a 10% discount.
潮流雜誌藉由提供九折優惠來鼓勵訂閱者續訂。

CH 19
傳播媒體

---

23 collect
★
★ [kəˋlɛkt]
★
Ⅴ 收集，領取，募捐
同 gather 聚集
　 accumulate 累積
　 assemble 集合
衍 collectable (a.) 可收集的
　 collection (n.) 收集

The famous actress mentioned in an interview that collecting paintings is one of her hobbies.
那位知名的女演員在訪談中提到收集畫作是她的嗜好之一。

point　collecting painting 以 Ving 當主詞，動詞是單數（is）。

The new operating system will automatically collect all the mistakes to the online database.
這個新的作業系統會自動收集所有的錯誤到線上資料庫。

point　operating system（作業系統）縮寫為 OS。

---

24 entertainment
★
★ [ˌɛntɚˋtenmənt]
ⁿ 招待，娛樂，消遣
同 amusement 娛樂
　 pleasure 樂事
　 relaxation 消遣
　 enjoyment 樂趣
　 interest 興趣

Building department stores can provide local residents with more entertainment options.
建造百貨公司可以提供當地居民更多的娛樂選擇。

Entertainments like watching movies and going shopping are common among people of different ages.
娛樂活動像是看電影及購物，在不同年齡層中都很普遍。

point　among + 三者以上，意為「在……之中」。between + 兩者以上，意為「在……之間」。

25 **issue**
★
★
★
[ˈɪʃjʊ]

n 問題，爭議，發行物
v 發行，配給，出版
同 matter (n.) 問題
affair (n.) 事情
subject (n) 話題
topic (n.) 話題
question (n.) 問題

The authorities are **addressing** the issue right now.
當局目前正在處理這個問題。

point address, solve, deal with, cope with, tackle, handle, attend to + the problem 意為「解決問題；處理問題」。

The column covers a variety of diverse issues.
這個專欄涵蓋了各式各樣不同的議題。

26 **film**
★
★
★
[fɪlm]

n 電影，膠捲
v 拍成電影
同 movie (n.) 電影

Some people enjoy the humor and sarcasm in silent films.
有些人喜歡默劇中的幽默及諷刺。

The documentary film is surprisingly informative.
這部紀錄片意外地富有知識性。

27 **host**
★
★
★
[host]

n 主人，節目主持人
v 主辦，主持，招待
反 guest (n.) 賓客

The host's firm handshake totally showed his **hospitality**.
主人堅定的握手顯現了他的好客。

point 易混淆詞彙：hospital (n.) 醫院／hospitalize (v.) 住院。

The host of the broadcast introduced the following programs.
廣播主持人介紹了接下來的節目。

point 多益聽力測驗情境中，廣播或電視主持人若要介紹來賓，常提到的為來賓名字、頭銜、授課領域、出版品及演講主題。

28 **rapidly**
★
★
[ˈræpɪdlɪ]

ad 很快地，立即，迅速地
同 speedily 迅速地
swiftly 敏捷地
in a hurry 迅速地
promptly 敏捷地
反 slowly 慢地
衍 rapid (a.) 立即的

After the host of the TV program had a serious scandal, the **ratings** of the program dropped rapidly.
在這名節目主持人嚴重的醜聞後，節目的收視率快速下降。

point rating 意為「評比；收視率」。

Tickets for the singer's concert were all sold out rapidly **within** 10 minutes.
這個歌手的演唱會門票在十分鐘內就迅速賣光。

point within 意為「在……期間以內」。

29 combination
★
★
[ˌkɑmbə`neʃən]

Ⓝ 結合，聯合，組合
Ⓢ union 聯合
   cooperation 合作
   collaboration 合作
Ⓐ conflict 衝突
Ⓓ combine (v.) 結合

The song is the perfect combination of R&B and pop.
這首歌是 R&B 和流行樂的完美結合。

(point) 相關詞彙：blend 混合，mixture 混合。

I asked my mother how to reset a combination lock.
我問我媽媽如何重新設定密碼鎖。

(point) combination lock 意為「密碼鎖」。

30 energy
★
[`ɛnɚdʒɪ]

Ⓝ 活力，幹勁，能量
Ⓢ power 力量
   spirit 精神
   strength 力氣
Ⓓ energetic (a.) 精力旺盛的

Whenever I hear the broadcaster's voice, I am full of energy.
每當我聽到那位主播的聲音，我就充滿活力。

(point) be full of energy 意為「精力充沛」。

Green constructions are built to improve the sustainability of energy.
綠建築是建來增進能源的永續發展。

(point) 綠建築為能節省能源的建築。

31 scene
★
★
★
[sin]

Ⓝ 場面，景象，地點
Ⓢ sight 景色
   view 景色
Ⓓ scenery (n.) 風景

One of the critics mentioned that he was impressed by the scenes of the movie.
其中一位評論家指出他對電影的場景印象深刻。

(point) be impressed by... 表示「對……印象深刻」。

We need to go before you make a scene.
我們必須要在你當眾大鬧之前離開。

(point) make a scene 意為「製造事端，引人側目」。

32 author
★
★
★
[`ɔθɚ]

Ⓝ 作者，著作，創始人
Ⓥ 著作，開創
Ⓢ writer (n.) 作者
Ⓐ reader (n.) 讀者
Ⓓ authorize (v.) 授權
   authorization (n.) 授權
   authority (n.) 當局

The broadcast host interviewed one of the best-selling authors in the UK.
廣播主持人訪問英國的一位暢銷書作家。

The author has a special writing style, which is why he's popular.
這位作家有著很特別的寫作風格，這也就是他受歡迎的原因。

(point) which 代替的是前面提到的 The writer has a special writing style。

CH 19
傳播媒體

33 accuracy
★
★ [ˋækjərəsɪ]
★
n 正確，準確
同 exactness 確切
precision 精準
correctness 正確
反 inaccuracy 不正確
衍 accurate (a.) 正確的

Advanced language learners are more likely to reach both fluency and accuracy.
高階程度的學習者比較有可能同時達到語言的流暢度和準確性。

point both... and... 意為「兩者皆……」。

Magazine editors are required to make sure of the accuracy of the information in the articles.
雜誌編輯被要求確定文章中訊息的正確性。

point be required to + V 為被動式，意為「被要求做……」。

---

34 billboard
★
★ [ˋbɪl‚bord]
★
n 廣告牌，布告板
同 poster 海報

Due to the typhoon, the huge billboard fell to the ground.
因為颱風，大型廣告看板掉到地上。

point due to + N 意為「因為……」。

I bought a collection called Billboard Hot 100.
我買了一張告示牌排行榜百大熱門歌精選輯。

point Billboard 為美國音樂排行榜。

---

35 absurd
★
★ [əbˋsɝd]
a 不合理的，荒謬的，可笑的
同 irrational 荒謬的
silly 愚蠢的
反 logical 合邏輯的
reasonable 合理的

Some movie critics said the plot of the movie was too absurd and didn't make any sense.
有些電影評論家說這部電影的劇情太荒謬，而且不太合理。

point 相關詞彙：unreasonable 不合理的，senseless 愚蠢的，ridiculous 荒謬的，illogical 不合邏輯的。

Some employees went on strike this morning to oppose the absurd new policy.
一些員工今早罷工來表示反對那荒謬的新政策。

point reject, refuse , object to 也可表達「反對」。

---

36 binding
★ [ˋbaɪndɪŋ]
a 有約束力的
n 書的裝訂、封皮，鑲邊
同 compulsory (a.) 強制的
obligatory (a.) 義務的

After two countries sign the treaty, it is legally binding.
在兩個國家簽條約後，就具有法律約束力。

37 academy
★
★
[əˋkædəmɪ]
n 學院，大學，研究院
同 school 學校
　　college 大學
衍 academic (a.) 學術的

He dropped out from the Academy of Sciences.
他從科學院輟學了。

After working 20 years in the movie industry, the actress won Academy Awards for Best Actress.
在進入電影界二十年後，這名女演員贏得奧斯卡金像獎的最佳女主角。

 奧斯卡金像獎 Academy Awards 也稱為 The Oscars。

38 actor
★
[ˋæktɚ]
n 演員，男演員，行動者
同 performer 表演者

The actor disappointed his fans and followers due to his love affair with his assistant.
這名演員和助理的緋聞使他的粉絲和追蹤者失望。

 disappointed sb. 意為「使某人失望」。

The actor is known for his natural acting and warm smile.
這位演員以自然的演技和溫暖的微笑而聞名。

 be known for 意為「以……而聞名」。

39 actress
★
[ˋæktrɪs]
n 女演員
同 entertainer 表演者

The gorgeous actress was nominated for the best actress of the year.
這位美麗的女演員被提名為年度最佳女演員。

(point) be nominated 意為「被提名」，是在多益測驗中提到獎項時就很常見的字。

All of the actresses dressed up for the award ceremony.
所有女演員都盛裝出席頒獎典禮。

(point) dress up 意為「盛裝」。

40 action
★
★
★
[ˋækʃən]
n 行動，作用，情節，訴訟
同 movement 動作
　　deed 行為
衍 act (v.) 行動
　　activity (n.) 活動

The action movie got plenty of great reviews. Would you like to watch it with me?
那部動作片有很多好評。你要和我一起看嗎？

(point) 延伸詞彙：romance movie 愛情片，comedy 喜劇，tragedy 悲劇，adventure movie 冒險片，horror movie 恐怖片。

Most of the managers admire their employees who can take action and solve problems initially.
大部分的經理欣賞能主動採取行動解決問題的員工。

(point) initially 為「自動自發地」。

413

41 **acclaim**
★
★ [ə`klem]
★
　Ⅴ 歡呼，喝采，稱讚
　ⁿ 歡呼，喝彩，稱讚
　同 applaud (v.) 喝采
　　 praise (v.) 讚揚
　　 applause (n.) 嘉許

He is a highly acclaimed photographer and blogger.
他是一位被高度認可的攝影師兼部落客。
point　highly acclaimed 意為「被高度認可的」。

Both critics and netizens enthusiastically acclaimed the drama.
評論家和網民們熱情洋溢地稱讚這部戲劇。
point　netizen 網民 = internet 網路 + citizen 市民。

---

42 **adapter**
★ [ə`dæptɚ]
　ⁿ 改編者，轉接器
　衍 adapt (v.) 使適應

Mr. White, I would like to introduce you to Mr. Chen, the adapter of the play.
懷特先生，我想介紹你給陳先生認識，他是這部戲劇的改編者。
point　此為常見的介紹用語。

Did you buy the adapter for your computer online?
你在線上購買你電腦的轉接器嗎？

---

43 **adventure**
★ [əd`vɛntʃɚ]
　ⁿ 冒險，激動人心的經歷
　同 venture 冒險

My niece enjoys adventure movies and horror movies rather than action movies.
我的姪女喜歡冒險片和恐怖片勝過動作片。
point　rather than 為連接詞，前後要接一樣的詞性。

I regard a gap year as a kind of adventure.
我認為不上班或不上課一年是一種冒險。
point　gap year（空檔年）為暫時不上班或上課，去學習想學的事物或是去旅行。

---

44 **alert**
★ [ə`lɝt]
　ⁿ 警戒，警報
　Ⅴ 報警，使警覺，使注意
　ⓐ 警覺的，機敏的
　同 aware (a.) 察覺的
　　 careful (a.) 謹慎的
　反 careless (a.) 粗心的
　　 inactive (a.) 行動緩慢的
　　 unaware (a.) 不知道的

Spoiler alert.
小心有劇情透露。
point　spoiler 指「弄壞觀影心情的東西」，也就是在要講到有關電影或戲劇的重要情節時，會事先講 spoiler alert，來告訴讀者以下有劇情透露。

The sound of the alarm suddenly alerted the safety guard.
警鈴聲突然使警衛警覺了起來。

45 **animate**

★ [ˋænəmɪt]

a 有生命的，活的

[ˋænəˌmet]

v 賦予生命，使活潑，激勵

同 stir (v.) 激起
activate (v.) 使活潑

反 inanimate (a.) 無生命的

Jason's arrival at the party animated the party in that he was very sociable.
傑森的到來使派對氣氛活絡起來，因為他相當擅長交際。

point arrival 意為「到來；新貨到來」。

The news about winning the Best Movie of the year animated the whole film crew.
贏得年度最佳電影的新聞振奮了整個電影拍攝小組。

point 主詞為 The news of winning the Best Movie of the year，也就是這件事情振奮了電影小組。

46 **arise**

★
★ [əˋraɪz]

v 產生，上升，起來

同 awaken 叫醒
rouse 激起
wake 醒來

Josh is a heavy sleeper, and it's hard for him to arise early.
喬許是重度睡眠者，早起對他而言很難。

point heavy sleeper 指「睡得很熟，不容易叫醒的人」，相反的詞為 light sleeper。

Serious arguments arose between the producer and the film crew.
製作人和電影團隊之間起了嚴重的紛爭。

point 延伸詞彙：documentary 紀錄片，action movie 動作片，romance 愛情片。

47 **avoidance**

★
★ [əˋvɔɪdəns]

n 逃避，躲避，空缺

同 escaping 逃跑
prevention 妨礙

衍 avoid (v.) 避免

The avoidance of scandal and bad reputation is essential to a celebrity.
對於一個名人來說，避免醜聞及不好的名聲是相當重要的。

For the avoidance of doubt, the student discount can't be used with other offers.
為避免疑慮，學生優惠不得與其他優惠一起使用。

point for the avoidance of doubt 為書面語，意為「為避免疑慮」。

48 **coverage**

★
★ [ˋkʌvərɪdʒ]

n 覆蓋（範圍），新聞報導

同 reporting 報導
article 文章
news 新聞

The politician's huge donation to the charity got massive media coverage.
該名政治人物因為捐給慈善機構大筆捐款，而被媒體大量報導。

The vegetation coverage in this region is decreasing because of the weather change.
這個區域的植被覆蓋範圍因為氣候變遷而逐漸減少。

Chapter 187

19 傳播媒體

---

49 ★ behold

[bɪˋhold]

Ⅴ 看，注視

同 look at 看著
observe 觀察
view 觀看
watch 注視

All the pupils beheld the introduction video of the seven wonders quietly.
所有的學生安靜地看著世界七大奇景的介紹影片。

point seven wonders 意為「世界七大奇景」。

They beheld the night scene of the coastal city from the tall building.
他們從高樓看了那個沿海城市的夜景。

---

50 ★ blow

[blo]

Ⅴ 吹，錯失良機，傳播

同 gust 狂風勁吹
puff 一陣陣地吹

The birthday girl blew out the candles and made a wish.
壽星女孩吹蠟燭並許願。

point birthday girl 意為「（女生）壽星」，birthday boy 意為「（男生）壽星」。

I am convinced that the ending of the movie will blow you away.
我相信電影結局會讓你非常驚喜。

point blow sb. away 意為「使（某人）大為驚訝；令（某人）非常高興」。

---

51 ★ ★ repetitive

[rɪˋpɛtɪtɪv]

ａ 反覆的，嘮叨的

同 boring 無聊的
uninteresting 無趣的

反 varied 多變的
interesting 有趣的

衍 repeat (v.) 重覆

The information written in this book is repetitive and dull.
這本書裡面的訊息很重複又無聊。

point 相關詞彙：monotonous 無變化的，tedious 冗長乏味的，recurrent 反覆出現的，repeated 重複的，repetitious 反覆的。

The actor was annoyed by the journalist's repetitive questions.
這位演員被記者重複的問題給惹惱了。

---

52 ★ ★ repetition

[͵rɛpɪˋtɪʃən]

ｎ 重複，複製品，背誦

同 retelling 複述

衍 repeat (v.) 重複

Repetition is a tip for mastering anything.
重複是精熟任何事物的訣竅。

The editor commented that some readers might get tired of reading too much repetition.
編輯評論了有些讀者可能會對太多的重複感到厭倦。

53 convey
★
★
[kən`ve]

Ⓥ 運送，傳播，表達
Ⓢ transport 運輸
carry 搬運
bring 攜帶
move 移動

The contemporary writer's book conveys a great sense of family bonds.
當代作家的這本書傳達了家庭連結的強烈感情。

Nowadays, many politicians are more willing to use social media to convey messages.
現在有許多政治人物更加願意使用社群媒體來傳達訊息。

ⓟoint be willing to 意為「願意」，be reluctant to 意為「不願意」。

---

54 serious
★
★
★
[`sɪrɪəs]

ⓐ 嚴重的，危急的，
重要的，嚴肅的
Ⓢ urgent 緊急的
crucial 重要的
vital 重要的
Ⓐ trivial 不重要的
unimportant 不重要的

The movie director looks serious but actually he is quite warm and caring.
電影導演看起來很嚴肅，但他其實很窩心又關愛他人。

The car crash caused serious traffic congestion.
車禍造成嚴重交通堵塞。

ⓟoint 延伸詞彙：car crash = car accident = car collision = traffic collision，意為「車禍」。

---

55 fulfillment
★
★
[fʊl`fɪlmənt]

Ⓝ 完成，實現，滿足（感）
Ⓢ contentment 滿足
self-actualization 自我實現
realization 體現
achievement 完成
accomplishment 成就
Ⓓ fulfill (v.) 履行

Being invited by the international film festival gave the actress a sense of fulfillment.
被國際電影節邀請這件事情，帶給這位女演員一股成就感。

ⓟoint Being invited by the international film festival 為主詞。

The well-known consultant's latest publication is *Career Fulfillment*, which includes specific steps to help readers achieve a sense of fulfillment at work.
那位知名顧問的最新著作是《工作滿足感》，包含詳細的步驟來幫助讀者達成工作上的成就感。

---

56 photographer
★
★
[fə`tɑgrəfə]

Ⓝ 攝影師，照相師
Ⓢ cameraman 攝影師
Ⓓ press-photographer
(n.) 攝影記者

Both professional and amateur photographers can join the competition.
專業及業餘攝影師都可以參加這個比賽。

ⓟoint both A and B 意為「A 和 B 都……」。

The highly acclaimed fashion photographer was interviewed by the journalist.
這名高度被推崇的時裝攝影師接受記者的採訪。

ⓟoint 在多益測驗看到 acclaimed 時，把它想成 famous 或 popular 的意思就可以。

CH 19

傳
播
媒
體

188

57 regard

★
★
★

[rɪˋgɑrd]

v 認為，考慮，看待

同 consider 考慮
view 看待
think of 想到
contemplate 注視
deem 認為

衍 regarding (prep.) 關於

He is regarded as one of the most important contemporary writers.
他被認為是當代最重要的作家之一。

The critic explained why this action movie was highly regarded.
評論家解釋為何這部動作片被高度認可。

---

58 release

★
★
★

[rɪˋlis]

v 釋放，發射，豁免，發表

同 set free 釋放
let go 放開
set / let / turn loose 鬆開
liberate 解放

The young and talented singer just released his latest album.
這位年輕有才華的歌手才剛發行了最新專輯。

point latest = newest，意為「最新的」。

The manager released a statement explaining the reasons for the prompt decision.
經理發表了一份聲明，解釋這個迅速的決定。

---

59 partial

★
★

[ˋpɑrʃəl]

a 局部的，不公平的，偏愛的

同 incomplete 不完整的
qualified 有限制的

反 unbiased 無偏見的
fair 公正的

The critic concluded that the play was just a partial success.
評論家總結說這部劇不太成功。

The tenant was required to make a partial payment before he rented the house.
房客必須要在租房子前先付部分的金額。

point deposit 意為「訂金」，在多益測驗中常用 partial payment 來換句話說。

---

60 current

★
★

[ˋkɝənt]

a 當前的，通用的，現行的

同 contemporary 當代的
present 現在的
modern 現代的

反 past 過去的

The designers attend fashion shows regularly to know the current trends.
設計師定期參加時裝秀以知道最新的趨勢。

The magazine subscriber found out some typos in the current issue.
雜誌訂閱者發現最新一期雜誌的一些錯字。

point 多益測驗雙篇閱讀情境中，會有雜誌訂閱者寫信糾正一些訊息的情境。

61 original
★
★
[əˈrɪdʒən̩l]
ⓐ 最初的，獨創的，原本的
ⓝ 原著，原文，原型
同 primary (a.) 原始的
反 commonplace (a.) 普通的
　 conventional (a.) 常見的
　 unimaginative
　 (a.) 缺乏想像力的
衍 originate (v.) 發源

The original novel is translated into different languages.
原版小說被翻譯成不同語言。

The experienced appraiser can distinguish original paintings from fake ones.
這名經驗豐富的鑑定師可以分辨畫作的真假。

point distinguish A from B 意為「區分 A 和 B」。

---

62 insight
★
[ˈɪnˌsaɪt]
ⓝ 洞察力，深刻的理解
同 perception 感知

The acclaimed novelist's book is full of fascinating insights.
這位備受讚譽的小說家充滿了很棒的想法。

point acclaimed (a.) 讚譽的。

The professor of Sociology provided a new insight into the existing theory.
社會學的教授對現存的理論提供了新觀點。

---

63 bookstore
★
★
[ˈbukˌstor]
ⓝ 書店
同 bookshop 書店（英式）
衍 online bookstore
　 (ph.) 網路書店

The bookstore has been renovated, and all the books are on sale.
書店已經被翻修，所有書都在特價中。

point be on sale 意為「特價中」。

The number of bookstores is decreasing due to the severe competition of online bookstores.
因為網路書店的激烈競爭，實體書店的數量正在遞減中。

point 延伸詞彙：compete (v.) 競爭，competitor (n.) 競爭者。

---

64 beyond
★
★
★
[bɪˈjɑnd]
prep 越過，遲於，
　　　除……之外
ad 在遠處，此外
同 farther (ad.) 更遠地

The breathtaking scenery at the Grand Canyon is beyond description.
大峽谷令人屏息的風景讓人難以言喻。

point be beyond description 意為「無法形容，難以描述」。

The plot is totally beyond most audiences.
這劇情讓許多觀眾無法理解。

point be beyond sb. 意為「令某人無法理解」。

---

65 **withdraw**
★
[wɪð`drɔ]

V 撤退，領錢，提取

同 remove 移除
extract 提取
draw out 取出
pull out 退出

反 deposit 安置，存錢

衍 withdrawal (n.) 撤走

He withdraws money every month to pay his rent and utility bills.
他每個月都會提錢以支付房租和水電雜費。

> point 此句為每個月都會發生的事情，所以用現在式。

Many readers were astonished by the news that the promising young athlete was going to withdraw from the final.
很多讀者對於這名有潛力的年輕運動員即將退出決賽的新聞感到吃驚。

---

66 **sufficient**
★
★
★
[sə`fɪʃənt]

a 足夠的，充分的

同 enough 足夠的
adequate 足夠的
abundant 充足的

反 insufficient 不足的
inadequate 不充分的

The freelance photographer's income is not sufficient to support his own expenditures.
這名自由工作攝影師的收入不夠負擔他自己的支出。

The writer did not have sufficient time to write; therefore, she asked the editor to extend the due date for the final draft.
這名作家沒有足夠的時間寫作，所以她請編輯延後最終稿件的交稿日期。

> point therefore 為副詞，沒有連接的作用，故用分號「;」連接。

---

67 **reveal**
★
★
[rɪ`vil]

V 展現，揭露，洩露

同 display 展示
disclose 揭發
uncover 揭露

反 hide 隱藏
conceal 隱藏

The secretary accidentally revealed the confidential information to other people.
祕書不小心向其他人透露了機密訊息。

> point confidential = secret，意為「機密的」。

The editor was unwilling to reveal the source of the information.
編輯不願意透露訊息來源。

> point be unwilling to 意為「不願意」。

---

68 **pursue**
★
[pɚ`su]

V 追趕，跟隨，繼續進行

同 follow 追隨
chase 追趕
track 追蹤

反 flee 逃走

Most people pursue better lives.
大部分的人追求更好的生活。

After graduating from college, he made up his mind to pursue a career in journalism.
在大學畢業後，他決定從事新聞業。

> point make up one's mind to = decide to，意為「決定做……」。

69 proof
★
★
[pruf]
n 證據，檢驗，考驗
同 evidence 證據
verification 證實
confirmation 確證
certification 證明
testament 證明

The novel is the best proof of his talent.
這本小說就是他才華的最好證明。

If you would like to request a refund, please prepare the proof of purchase, that is, your receipt.
如果你想要求退款的話，請準備好購買證明，也就是你的收據。

(point) that is 意為「也就是」。

---

70 privacy
★
[`praɪvəsɪ]
n 隱居，私生活，隱私
同 isolation 孤立
secret 祕密
衍 private (a.) 私下的

If you share a rental house with others, respect their privacy.
如果你和別人合租房子，要尊重他們的隱私。

(point) others = other people，意為「其他人」。

The main subscribers of that gossip magazine are those who are curious about celebrities' privacy.
八卦雜誌的主要訂閱人為那些好奇名人隱私的人。

(point) 延伸詞彙：subscribe (v.) 訂閱，subscription (n.) 訂閱。

CH 19

傳
播
媒
體

---

71 predictable
★
[prɪ`dɪktəbl]
a 可預言的，可預測的
同 foreseeable 可預見的
anticipated 預料的
foreseen 預知的
反 unpredictable 不可預測的
衍 prediction (n.) 預言

After years of practice, any moves become predictable to the player.
經過多年的練習，任何招數對這個選手來說都是可預期的。

The leading actor's acting was not spot-on and the plot was rather predictable.
男主角的演技不到位，電影劇情很好預測。

(point) spot-on 意為「精準的」。

---

72 exclusion
★
★
[ɪk`skluʒən]
n 排斥，排除在外
同 keeping out 排除
rejection 拒絕
elimination 排除
反 inclusion 包括

People were surprised by her exclusion from the list of nominees.
人們很驚訝她被排除在提名名單之外。

(point) sb. be surprised by... 意為「某人對……感到驚訝」。

The player spends his time practicing basketball, to the exclusion of other interests.
這名球員把所有時間都用在練習籃球上，沒有其他嗜好。

(point) to the exclusion of 意為「（因為努力做某事而）心無旁騖」。

19 傳播媒體

190

---

73 persistence
★
[pɚ`sɪstəns]

n 堅持，固執，持續

同 perseverance 堅持不懈
determination 堅定
endurance 持久

衍 persistent (a) 持續的

He is touched by the leading character's persistence.
他被主角的堅持所感動。

(point) leading character = main character，意為「主角」。

The reader felt the persistence and enthusiasm from the writer's biography.
讀者從作者的自傳中感受到堅持不懈和滿腔熱忱。

---

74 ordinary
★
★
[`ɔrdn͵ɛrɪ]

a 平常的，普通的，平凡的

同 usual 通常的
normal 正常的
general 一般的

反 exceptional 例外的
unusual 稀有的

Nowadays, even ordinary people can make good use of social media to share their opinions.
現在即使是普通人也可以好好利用社群媒體來分享意見。

(point) make good use of 意為「善用」。

It's nothing more than an ordinary neighborhood.
這只不過是個普通的街區。

(point) nothing more than 意為「只不過是」。

---

75 magnificent
★
★
[mæg`nɪfəsənt]

a 宏偉的，華麗的，極美的

同 glorious 壯觀的
superb 宏偉的
awe-inspiring 令人驚嘆的
breathtaking 驚人的

The columnist said it was a magnificent piece of writing.
專欄作家說這是一部文筆很棒的傑作。

You can see the magnificent view of the ocean from your rental apartment.
你可以從你租的公寓中看到壯觀的海景。

(point) 相關詞彙：splendid 壯麗的，spectacular 壯觀的，impressive 印象深刻的，majestic 雄偉的，awesome 令人驚嘆的。

---

76 extraordinary
★
★
[ɪk`strɔrdn͵ɛrɪ]

a 特別的，非凡的，特派的

同 astounding 令人驚奇的
wonderful 極好的

反 commonplace 平凡的
ordinary 普通的

It's an extraordinary coincidence that I bumped into my previous supervisor on my way to the airport.
在我去機場的路上巧遇了前主管，這是一個令人吃驚的巧合。

(point) bump into 意為「巧遇」。

The movie critic pointed out that the actress' acting was extraordinary.
電影評論家指出那名女演員的演技相當出眾。

(point) 相關詞彙：remarkable 非凡的，amazing 驚人的，marvelous 非凡的，stunning 令人震驚的，incredible 驚人的，astonishing 令人驚訝的，exceptional 卓越的。

Question

以下題目完全擬真新制多益 Part 5，請選出最符合句意的選項。

1. We all agreed to ------- John as the employee of the year.
   (A) nominated   (B) nominee   (C) nomination   (D) nominate

2. The critic indicated that the original novel was superior ------- its film version.
   (A) on   (B) to   (C) with   (D) than

3. Have you read the monthly ------- yet?
   (A) exclusion   (B) newsletter   (C) film   (D) energy

4. Many publishers are eager ------- cooperate with the well-known writer.
   (A) to   (B) with   (C) in   (D) on

5. Trend Magazine encourages their subscribers to renew their subscription ------- offering a 10% discount.
   (A) by   (B) issue   (C) on   (D) with

6. The authorities are addressing the ------- right now.
   (A) issue   (B) adventure   (C) repetition   (D) insight

>> 正確答案與解析請翻至下一頁查看

Answer

正確答案與解析

1. 我們都同意提名強為年度最佳員工。
   (A) 提名（過去式）　　　　　　　(B) 被提名人
   (C) 提名 (n.)　　　　　　　　　　(D) 提名（to + 原形動詞）

   正確答案 (D)

2. 評論家指出這部原作小說勝過它的電影版本。
   (B) be superior to... 意為「優於」的意思

   正確答案 (B)

3. 你讀每月的時事通訊了嗎？
   (A) 排除在外　　(B) 內部通訊　　(C) 電影　　(D) 能量

   正確答案 (B)

4. 很多出版社都渴望可以跟那位有名的作家合作。
   (A) be eager to + V 意為「渴望的，急切的」

   正確答案 (A)

5. 潮流雜誌藉由提供九折優惠來鼓勵訂閱者續訂。
   (A) by（藉由）後面須接 Ving

   正確答案 (A)

6. 當局目前正在處理這個問題。
   (A) 議題　　　　(B) 冒險　　　　(C) 重複　　　(D) 觀點

   正確答案 (A)

Chapter 20
日常生活

以下多益必考單字，你認識哪些？

☐ achieve (p.428)　　☐ environment (p.441)　　☐ absorb (p.434)

☐ campus (p.438)　　☐ reflection (p.427)　　☐ proficiency (p.439)

☐ identification (p.427)　　☐ identical (p.426)　　☐ remove (p.443)

☐ common (p.441)　　☐ receive (p.427)　　☐ accident (p.434)

☐ respect (p.443)　　☐ prevent (p.444)　　☐ alter (p.435)

☐ amateur (p.435)　　☐ survive (p.442)　　☐ shortage (p.444)

01 **banquet**
★
★
★
[ˋbæŋkwɪt]

n 宴會，宴請，款待

同 dinner (n.) 宴會
  feast (n.) 盛宴

Johnson Company called to hire us to cater for them in their banquet hall and they would like to know our menu and quote first.
強森公司打來僱用我們在他們的宴席廳辦外燴，但他們想先知道菜單跟估價。

point quote, estimate 皆可表達「估價」。

You are cordially invited to Mr. Mogi's retirement banquet next Monday, and it will be better if you can prepare some remarks for him.
你被誠摯邀請參加茂木先生下週一的退休宴席，如果你可以準備一些話給他，會很棒。

point retirement / farewell banquet (party) 意為「退休餐會」。

02 **prefer**
★
★
★
[prɪˋfɝ]

v 寧願，更喜歡

同 choose 選擇
  fancy 愛好
  favor 偏愛
  select 選擇

衍 preference (n.) 偏愛

Some of my coworkers prefer to consult the on-site health professionals.
我的一些同事偏好向公司內部的醫療專業人士諮詢病情。

point coworker, colleague, associate 都可表達「同事」。

I prefer the simplicity of the countryside but not the hustle and bustle of downtown.
我喜歡鄉下的簡單，勝過市中心的喧囂。

point hustle and bustle 意指「環境喧囂；忙亂」。

03 **dedicate**
★
★
[ˋdɛdəˏket]

v 奉獻，獻出

同 devote 奉獻

衍 dedication (n.) 奉獻

The loyal soldier dedicated his life to his nation.
忠誠的軍人奉獻了他的一生給國家。

The song is dedicated to the composer's beloved daughter.
這首歌是獻給這位名作曲家摯愛的女兒。

point be dedicated to 意為「獻給」。

04 **identical**
★
★
★
[aɪˋdɛntɪkl̩]

a 完全相同的

同 (exactly) the same（完全）一樣的

反 different 不同的

The twins have plenty of identical clothes.
這對雙胞胎有很多一樣的衣服。

The managers from two different departments are identical in their views.
來自兩個不同部門的經理的意見相同。

point 相關詞彙：similar 相像的，alike 相同的。

05 appeal

★

[ə`pil]

Ⅴ 呼籲，懇求，有吸引力，
上訴

The family-oriented comic book appeals to almost all readers of different ages.
這本適合闔家觀賞的漫畫書吸引了幾乎所有年齡層的讀者。
(point) -oriented 意為「以……為導向的」。

During the dry season, the government appeals to the public to save water.
在乾季時，政府呼籲大眾要省水。
(point) 延伸詞彙：rain season 意為「雨季」。

06 identification

★

[aɪˏdɛntəfə`keʃən]

ⁿ 識別，鑑定，身分證明，
有關聯
ⁱᵈ ID 身分證明
recognition 認出
衍 identify (v.) 識別

Please attach a copy of your identification card to the back of the application form.
請把身分證影本貼到申請書的後面。

All visitors without exception must show their identification cards before entering the premises.
所有的訪客毫無例外，都必須在入場前出示身分證。
(point) without exception 意為「毫無例外」。

CH 20

日常生活

07 receive

★
★
★

[rɪ`siv]

Ⅴ 收到，得到，接待
ⁱᵈ accept 接受
acquire 取得
反 give 給予
present 呈獻
衍 receipt (n.) 收據

The applicant just received the acceptance letter.
申請人才剛收到入學接受信。
(point) 相關詞彙：collect 領取，gain 得到，obtain 獲得。

08 reflection

★
★

[rɪ`flɛkʃən]

ⁿ 反射，倒影，想法
ⁱᵈ mirroring 鏡射
反 absorption 吸收
衍 reflect (v.) 反射

The backpacker is watching the reflection of the trees in the lake.
那名背包客正看著湖裡樹的倒影。

Obviously, his unsatisfactory interpersonal relationship is a reflection of his lack of problem-solving skills.
很明顯地，他不盡理想的人際關係反映出他缺少問題解決能力。
(point) interpersonal (a.) 人際的。

日常生活

---

09 **encouragement**
★
[ɪnˈkɝɪdʒmənt]

🔲 鼓勵，獎勵，促進

🔲 motivation 刺激

🔲 discouragement 沮喪
　　dissuasion 勸阻
　　hindering 妨礙

Students need lots of encouragement and feedback from their teachers.
學生需要老師很多的鼓勵及回饋。

point　lots of = a lot of，意為「很多」。

My supervisor's encouragement means a lot to me.
我上司的鼓勵對我來說很重要。

point　相關詞彙：inspiration 鼓舞，incitement 激勵。

---

10 **enroll**
★
★
[ɪnˈrol]

🔲 登記，入學，註冊

🔲 register 登記
　　sign up 註冊
　　apply 申請

🔲 leave 離開
　　drop out 退出，輟學

His nephew enrolled at the bilingual school that was rather popular among the local residents.
他的姪子就讀的雙語學校在當地居民間相當受到歡迎。

point　among 意為「在……之間」。

I called the language center to enroll in the advanced French course.
我打給語言中心報名進階法語班。

---

11 **achieve**
★
★
★
[əˈtʃiv]

🔲 完成，實現，達到

🔲 attain 達到
　　carry out 實現

🔲 fail 失敗

He achieves success by working hard and keeping learning.
他透過努力工作和不斷學習來達到成功。

point　keeping 的 ing 是因為前面的 by 為介係詞，後面要加 ing，而 learning 的 ing 是因為 keep 後面的動詞要加 Ving。

She finally achieved her ambition to become a flight attendant.
她終於實現了成為空服員的夢想。

point　相關詞彙：accomplish 完成，fulfill 完成，reach 達到。

---

12 **heat**
★
[hit]

🔲 熱度，高溫

🔲 把……加熱，使激動

🔲 warm (v.) 使暖和

🔲 chill (v.) 使變冷
　　freeze (v.) 使結冰

🔲 heater (n.) 加熱器

We used microwave to heat yesterday's leftovers.
我們用微波爐加熱昨天的剩菜。

point　leftover (n.) 剩飯；殘留物 (a.) 殘餘的。

The new kettle can heat water faster than the old one.
這個新水壺比舊水壺還能更快加熱水。

13 **progress**

★

['prɑgrɛs]

n 前進，進步，發展

[prə'grɛs]

v 前進，提高，進步

同 advance (v.) 前進

反 regress (v.) 退回

deteriorate (v.) 惡化

衍 progression (n.) 前進

The intern is constantly making progress.

這個實習生不斷地在進步。

point 相關詞彙：development 發展，improvement 改進，breakthrough 突破，growth 成長，advancement 前進。

Restoration work on the old temple is in progress.

老舊廟宇的重建工程正在進行中。

point in progress 意為「正在進行中」。

14 **interior**

★
★

[ɪn'tɪrɪə]

a 內部的，內側的，內地的

n 內部，內側，內心

同 inside (n.) 內部

inner (n.) 內部

internal (a.) 內部的

反 exterior (a.) 外部的

outer(a.) 外面的

The interior decorator has had discussions with his client several times.

這名室內設計師已和他的客戶討論很多次。

The online interior design course will teach you comprehensive knowledge about design.

這個線上室內設計課程將會教導你有關設計的全面性知識。

CH 20

日常生活

15 **furniture**

★
★
★

['fɝnɪtʃə]

n 家具，設備

同 home furnishings 家飾

fittings 家具

The interior designer was asked to decorate the villa with wooden furniture.

室內設計師被要求以木製家具裝潢別墅。

16 **immerse**

★

[ɪ'mɝs]

v 埋頭做，使浸沒

I immersed my clothes in the bleach to get rid of the stain.

我把衣服泡在漂白水裡面去除污漬。

point get rid of 意為「去除」。

17 **affection**
★ [ə`fɛkʃən]
🄝 影響，愛慕，屬性，疾病
🄸 feeling 感情
　　 love 愛
🄰 coldness 冷淡

When you look at the couple's wedding photos, you can feel the groom's affection towards the bride from his eyes.
當你看著那對夫妻的婚禮照片，你可以從新郎的眼神中感受到他對新娘的情感。

(point) significant other 意為「重要他人；另一半」，可為丈夫、太太、男朋友、女朋友或愛人。

Some people don't like to see others display affection in public places, especially when they are single.
有些人不喜歡別人在公共場所公然放閃，尤其是當他們單身時。

(point) 延伸詞彙：married (a.) 已婚的。

---

18 **state**
★ [stet]
★
★ 🄝 狀況，國家，身分
🄸 country 國家
　　 nation 國家
　　 circumstance 情況
　　 condition 狀態

Amy takes her kids to the United State every summer to expose them to an English-speaking environment.
艾咪每年夏天都會帶她的小孩到美國，為了讓他們接觸講英文的環境。

The victims of the nature disaster were in a state of shock.
自然災害的受難者處於驚嚇狀態。

(point) in a state of 意為「在……的狀態」。

---

19 **pleasure**
★ [`plɛʒɚ]
🄝 愉快，樂趣，消遣
🄸 delight 樂事
　　 enjoyment 樂趣
　　 happiness 愉快
　　 joy 歡樂

Reading is one of Roy's few pleasures.
閱讀是羅伊不多的樂趣之一。

I take pleasure in collecting different kinds of basketball shoes.
我喜歡收集不同種類的籃球鞋。

(point) take pleasure in... 意指「樂於……」。

---

20 **hometown**
★ [`hom`taun]
★ 🄝 家鄉，故鄉

The economy of my hometown is based on tourism.
我家鄉的經濟來源是觀光。

There have been a lot of changes in my hometown.
我的家鄉有很多改變。

21 comfortable

★
★
★

[ˋkʌmfɚtəbl]

ⓐ 舒適的，寬裕的，豐富的

圓 easy 寬裕的
cozy 舒適的

衍 comfort (v.) 安慰
comforting (a.) 令人欣慰的

The office was renovated to provide all the staff a more comfortable and delightful working environment.

辦公室被重新整修，以提供所有員工一個更舒適、更令人愉悅的工作環境。

point was renovated 意為「被翻修」，為多益測驗中的常見字，要注意。

She worked really hard before retirement. Now, her life is rather comfortable and stable.

她在退休前工作非常努力。現在，她的生活相當富足且穩定。

22 harbor

★

[ˋhɑrbɚ]

ⓝ 港灣，海港，避難所
ⓥ 庇護，收養，懷有

圓 dock (n.) 碼頭
port (n.) 港口
wharf (n.) 碼頭

Since both of Allen's parents are musicians, he always harbors a wish to be a highly regarded musician.

因為艾倫的父母都是音樂家，他一直都懷著成為著名音樂家的夢想。

point highly regarded 表示「被高度推崇」。

He is against the law by harboring criminals.

他因窩藏罪犯而犯法。

point against 不是動詞，是介係詞，因此前面需要加 be 動詞。

CH 20
日常生活

23 block

★

[blɑk]

ⓝ 塊，街區，阻塞物
ⓥ 阻礙，封鎖，限制

圓 hinder (v.) 妨礙
impede (v.) 阻礙
obstruct (v.) 阻塞

反 aid (v.) 幫助
assist (v.) 協助

If you are looking for the post office, just go straight for two blocks and turn left.

如果你在找郵局，直走兩個街區再左轉。

The application will block pop-ups automatically.

這個應用程式會自動阻擋彈跳出來的廣告。

point pop-ups = pop-up ad，意為「網頁中的廣告」。

24 active

★
★

[ˋæktɪv]

ⓐ 活躍的，積極的，勤奮的

圓 lively 活潑的
vigorous 精力充沛的
alive 活躍的

He is active in social media but not in real life.

他在社群媒體中相當活躍，但在真實生活中卻不是。

As a costume designer, she has an active imagination.

身為一位服裝設計師，她有靈活的想像力。

25 **tow**

★ [to]

v 拖，拉，牽引

n 拖拉，牽引

同 pull (v.) 拉

　 drag (v.) 拉

　 draw (v.) 拖

The tow truck was parked next to the construction site.

拖車停在建地旁邊。

point 延伸詞彙：near 在附近，behind 在後面，in front of 在前面。

A lorry was towing a broken-down car.

一台卡車正拖著一台壞掉的車。

point lorry 與 truck 均指卡車。前者用於英式英語，後者用於美式英語。

---

26 **household**

★ [`haus.hold]

n 一家人，家庭

a 家用的，家喻戶曉的

同 family (n.) 家庭

Mr. Chen is reducing his household expenses right now because he plans to take his family to America next year.

陳先生現在正在減少家庭開銷，因為他計劃明年要帶他家人去美國。

point reduce = decrease，意為「減少」。

The whole household is used to taking a walk after meals.

全家人習慣餐後散步。

point be used to + Ving（現在）習慣……／ used to + V（過去）習慣……。

---

27 **emotion**

★ [ɪ`moʃən]

n 感情，情感，激動

同 feeling 感情

He vented his emotions by painting.

他藉由畫畫發洩感情。

point by + N / Ving 表示「藉由……（管道）」。

I received his thank you card and I can feel his sincere emotion between the lines.

我收到了他的感謝卡，可以從字裡行間感受到他真摯的情感。

point between the lines 表示「字裡行間」。

---

28 **bloom**

★ [blum]

n 花，開花

v 開花，茂盛，繁榮

同 blossom (v.) 開花

　 glow (v.) 鮮豔奪目

He is rather sensitive right now because he is in the bloom of youth.

他現在相當敏感，因為他正處於青春時期。

point in the bloom of youth 意為「青春期」。

After I read through the manual and confirmed with the nursery, I knew that these plants bloom in spring.

在我讀了手冊以及向苗圃確認後，我得知這些植物在春天開花。

29 **housekeeper**
★
['haus.kipɚ]

n 女管家

The housekeeper is a detail-oriented person. She can do whatever the owners expect the house to be.
這個女管家是個注重細節的人。她可以做到房屋主人要求的所有事。

 detail-oriented 意為「注重細節的」，這也會是多益測驗求職廣告中對面試者的要求。

We hired our current housekeeper through the recommendation of a reliable and trustworthy agency.
透過一家可值得信賴的仲介公司的推薦，我們僱用了我們目前的管家。

 延伸詞彙：real estate agency 意為「房地產仲介公司」。

---

30 **janitor**
★
['dʒænɪtɚ]

n 看門人，守衛，管理人

同 custodian 守衛

The janitor cleaned the mess caused by the guests efficiently.
管理員有效率地清理了客人造成的混亂。

 易混淆字：efficiently 意為「有效率地」，effectively 意為「有效地」。

Go to the janitor room if you are looking for brooms.
如果你要找掃把，可以去管理室。

---

31 **accord**
★
[ə'kɔrd]

n 一致，符合，協議
v 使一致，調解，給予
同 agree (v.) 一致
correspond (v.) 符合
反 disagree (v.) 不一致

The committee accorded a scholarship to her because of her excellent academic performance.
委員會因為她優異的學術表現批准給她獎學金。

The president was accorded a warm welcome when he visited this town.
當總統拜訪這個小鎮時，他受到熱烈的歡迎。

---

32 **budge**
★
[bʌdʒ]

v 稍微移動，改變意見
同 move 移動
change position 改變位置

I can't budge the chairs in the park.
我移動不了公園裡的椅子。

 易混淆字：budget (n.) 預算。

His parents will not budge an inch on his request to apply to the law school.
他的父母在他要申請法律學院這個要求上絲毫不肯讓步。

 not budge an inch 意為「一動也不動；毫不改變」。

CH 20
日常生活

20 日常生活

195

33 **absorb**

★
★

[əb`sɔrb]

Ⅴ 吸收，理解，
　使全神貫注，合併

同 soak up 吸取

反 give out 分發

The nursery asked me to put the potted plant near the window so that it can absorb sunlight.
苗圃的人請我把盆栽放在窗戶旁邊，如此一來才能吸收陽光。

point ask sb. to V 意為「請某人做某事」。

The instruction suggests that you massage your face until the lotion is absorbed.
用法說明書建議你按摩你的臉直到乳液被吸收為止。

point suggest + (should) + 原形動詞，意為「建議做……」。

34 **academic**

★
★

[͵ækə`dɛmɪk]

ⓐ 大學的，學術的

ⓝ 教授，學者

同 educational (a.) 教育的
　 instructional (a.) 教學的

反 uneducated (a.) 未受教育的
　 unlearned (a.) 未受教育的

He is excellent in academic-related knowledge but not the daily life common sense.
他很擅長學術相關的知識，而非日常生活常識。

point -related 意為「與……相關的」。

35 **adolescent**

★

[͵ædl`ɛsn̩t]

ⓝ 青少年

ⓐ 青春期的，青少年的，
　幼稚的

同 young (a.) 年輕的
　 youthful (a.) 青年的

衍 adolescence (n.) 青春期

Many adolescents suffer from identity crisis.
很多青少年受認同危機之苦。

point suffer from 意為「受苦／受難於……」。

She was under a lot of peer pressure during her adolescent years.
她在青少年時期承受了很多同儕壓力。

point during + N 意為「在……期間」。

36 **accident**

★
★
★

[`æksədənt]

ⓝ 事故，意外，機遇

同 crash 相撞事故

反 intention 意圖

衍 accident-prone
　 (a.) 特別易出事故的
　 accidental (a.) 意外的

An ambulance came right after a car accident happened at the intersection.
十字路口發生了一場車禍，救護車隨即趕到。

point crossroad 也可表達「十字路口」。

I met with a car accident on my way to work.
我在上班的路上遇到一場車禍。

point meet with an accident 意為「遇到意外事故」。

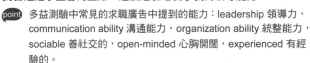

37 **affair**
★
★
[əˈfɛr]

n 事情，事件，事務

同 matter 事情
　thing 事物

Rumor has it that he is having a love affair with his secretary.
謠言說他之前跟他的祕書有緋聞。

point rumor has it that S + V... 意為「謠言說⋯⋯」。

I was the chairman of the Student Affairs Association, and this experience cultivated my leadership.
我曾經是學生會的主席，這個經驗培養了我的領導能力。

point 多益測驗中常見的求職廣告中提到的能力：leadership 領導力，communication ability 溝通能力，organization ability 統整能力，sociable 善社交的，open-minded 心胸開闊，experienced 有經驗的。

38 **alter**
★
★
★
[ˈɔltɚ]

V 改變，修改

同 change 改變
　modify 修改
　amend 修訂
　revise 修改
反 preserve 保存

I had the tailor alter the trousers.
我請裁縫師修改這件長褲。

point have sb. V 意為「請某人做某事」。

To everyone's surprise, they altered their warehouse into a showroom.
讓大家很驚訝的是，他們把倉庫改建成展示間。

point alter... into... 意為「改造成⋯⋯」。

CH 20

日常生活

39 **amateur**
★
★
★
[ˈæməˌtʃur]

n 業餘者，外行，愛好者
a 業餘的，外行的

同 nonprofessional (a.) 外行的
反 professional (a.) 專業的

Both amateurs and professionals can join the competition.
業餘選手和專業選手都可以參加比賽。

Surprisingly, the amateur painter's paintings are far more widespread than other professional ones.
令人訝異地，那位業餘畫家的畫作比其他專業畫家還更廣為流傳。

point far 修飾形容詞比較級，表示「更加」廣為流傳。

40 **bin**
★
[bɪn]

n 箱子，容器，穀倉

同 box 箱子
　can 罐子
　crate 條板箱
　container 容器

Don't litter! Throw garbage in the bins.
不要亂丟垃圾！把垃圾丟到垃圾桶裡。

The company encourages their workers to put paper, glass and cans into separate bins.
公司鼓勵他們的員工把紙、玻璃和罐子放到不同箱子。

point encourage sb. to + V 意為「鼓勵某人做⋯⋯」。

196

20 日常生活

---

41 attorney
★
[əˋtɝnɪ]

n 律師，法定代理人

同 lawyer 律師

He **used to be** an attorney, and now he works as a professor in Chicago University.

他以前是位律師，他現在在芝加哥大學當教授。

point used to + V 表示「過去的事實或習慣」，sb. be used to + Ving 表示「現在的習慣」。

He **acted as** a defense attorney.

他擔任辯護律師。

point act as 意為「擔任」。

---

42 bachelor
★
★
[ˋbætʃələ]

n 學士，單身男子

同 single man 單身男子
   unmarried man 未婚男子
反 married man 已婚男子

Ben's bachelor party will take place next Friday.

班的告別單身派對會在下週五舉行。

point bachelorette party 為「女性的告別單身派對」。

A bachelor's degree in Economics is required for this position.

經濟系學士學位對於這個職位而言是必要的。

point 學歷常在多益測驗中求職廣告的 requirement（必要條件）中提到。

---

43 balcony
★
[ˋbælkənɪ]

n 陽臺，露臺

The **flat** has a good balcony that overlooks the whole city.

這間公寓有個可以俯瞰整個城市的好陽台。

point apartment（美式），flat（英式），皆為「公寓」。

I told the real estate agent that I **preferred** houses with a big balcony.

我告訴房屋仲介我偏好有大陽台的房子。

point 延伸詞彙：preference (n.) 偏好。

---

44 bench
★
[bɛntʃ]

n 長凳

Sitting on the long bench at the riverside, the old couple enjoyed the sunset.

這對老夫妻坐在河邊的長凳，享受著日落。

point 此句為分詞構句，省略了第一個主詞和連接詞。原句為 The couple sat at..., and the couple...。

The wooden bench is broken. Maybe we should replace it with a metal **one**.

這木凳壞了。也許我們要換一個金屬的。

point one 代替 bench。

45 bone
★
[bon]

n 骨頭，骨質，骨骼
同 skull (n.) 頭蓋骨
反 flesh (n.) 肌肉

She boned up on English before applying to the language school in Australia.
申請澳洲的語言學校前她苦讀了英文。
(point) bone up on 意為「苦學；努力攻讀」。

Make sure your shirt is bone dry before you wear it.
一定得讓你的襯衫乾透才能穿。
(point) bone dry 意為「乾透的」。

---

46 bounce
★
★
[bauns]

v 彈回，彈起
n 反彈，彈性，活力
同 spring back (ph.) 彈回
衍 bound (v.) 彈回

The coach was training the player how to bounce the ball quickly.
教練正在教選手如何快速地拍球。

She always bounces back whatever challenges she meets.
不管她遇到什麼挫折，總是能重新振作起來。
(point) whatever 意為「不論什麼」，表常態，使用現在式。

---

47 camp
★
[kæmp]

n 營地，帳篷，陣營
v 紮營，露營，臨時安頓
同 tent (n.) 帳篷

Going camping has become increasingly popular these days.
露營現在逐漸變得熱門。
(point) these days 意為「現今」。

More and more parents view summer camps as an opportunity for their children to experience something new.
有越來越多的父母視夏令營為一個可以讓他們的孩子體驗新事物的機會。
(point) view...as... 意為「視……為……」。

CH 20
日常生活

---

48 university
★
★
★
[ˌjunəˋvɝsətɪ]

n 大學，綜合性大學
同 college 大學
academy 學院
institute 學院
school 學校

He is currently teaching Anthropology at Chicago University.
他目前在芝加哥大學教人類學。

Despite the high prices, the rain gear is especially popular among university students.
儘管價格很高，這個雨具在大學生之中特別受歡迎。
(point) among 意為「在三者之中」，between 意為「在兩者之中」。

日常生活

---

49 campus
★
★ [`kæmpəs]
★ n 校園，大學，學院
同 university 大學
college 大學

There **are** a few buildings **under construction** in the campus now.
現在校園中有些建築正在建造中。
point be under construction 意為「建造中」。

About 40% of the students in this university live in the on-campus housing but not the off-campus housing.
這間大學的學生大約有百分之四十是校內住宿，而不是校外住宿。
point about = approximately，皆可表達「大約」。

---

50 greenhouse
★ [`grin͵haʊs]
n 溫室，暖房
同 glasshouse 溫室

This kind of plant only grows in greenhouses where the **internal** temperature is steady.
這種植物只能種在內部恆溫的溫室。
point 延伸詞彙：external (a.) 外部的。

The government provided people with subsidies to install solar panels **in an attempt to** reduce greenhouse gases.
為了減少溫室氣體，政府提供人們補助金來安裝太陽能面板。
point in an attempt to... 意為「為了……」。

---

51 fertilize
★ [`fɝtl͵aɪz]
v 使肥沃，施肥
衍 fertility (n.) 肥沃

The staff in the nursery taught the customer how to fertilize the potted plant with the product he bought.
苗圃的員工教導顧客如何用他買的產品給盆栽施肥。

The education program introduces how insects fertilize other plants by carrying pollen.
這個教育節目介紹昆蟲如何攜帶花粉使植物授粉。

---

52 fertilizer
★ [`fɝtl͵aɪzɚ]
n 肥料，促進發展者
同 manure 肥料
compost 堆肥

The customer consulted the clerk in the **nursery** on how to use the fertilizer.
顧客向苗圃裡的店員諮詢如何使用肥料。
point nursery (n.) 苗圃；托兒所。

To protect the environment, the farmer tried to decrease the use of chemical fertilizers and pesticides.
為了保護環境，這名農夫試著減少化學肥料及殺蟲劑的使用。

53 **elite**

★ [eˋlit] / [ɪˋlit]

　ⁿ 精英，優秀分子
　ᵃ 精銳的，上等的

Many parents in this district would like to enroll their children in that elite public school.
這區很多家長想要讓自己的孩子就讀那所優秀的公立學校。

Some hold a belief that university education should be an "elite education", while others disagree.
有些人認同大學教育應該是菁英教育，但其他人反對。

54 **unlimited**

★
★ [ʌnˋlɪmɪtɪd]

　ᵃ 無限制的，無數的，遼闊的
　同 extensive 廣大的
　反 limited 有限的
　　 finite 有限的
　　 restricted 有限制的

Natural resources are not unlimited so people have to save as much energy as possible.
自然資源是有限的，因此人們要盡可能地節省能源。

(point) 相關詞彙：limitless 無限的，boundless 無窮的，unbounded 無限的。

Demand for language learning courses appears unlimited.
看來對語言學習課程的需求是沒有止境的。

(point) Demand for language learning courses 為此句的主詞。

55 **proficiency**

★
★ [prəˋfɪʃənsɪ]

　ⁿ 能力
　同 skill 技巧
　　 capacity 能力
　　 competency 能力
　　 adeptness 熟練
　反 incompetence 無能

The experienced teacher knows how to adjust materials according to her students' proficiency levels.
資深的老師知道如何根據學生的能力程度來調整教材。

(point) how to adjust materials according to students' proficiency levels 整句當作 knows 的受詞。

After taking the placement test, test-takers will be informed of their language proficiency levels.
在考完分班考試後，考試者會被通知他們的語言精通程度。

(point) 相關詞彙：mastery 熟練，competence 能力，ability 能力，capability 潛力。

56 **landlord**

★
★ [ˋlændˏlɔrd]

　ⁿ 房東，地主，老闆
　同 host 主人
　　 landlady 女房東
　反 tenant 房客

The tenant renews the rental lease with the landlord every year.
房客跟房東每年續一次租約。

The landlord repainted the walls and fences without informing her tenant.
房東沒有通知她的房客就重漆了牆面和籬笆。

CH 20

日常生活

57 indoor

★
★

[ˋɪn͵dor]

ⓐ 室內的，在室內使用的

⟨反⟩ outdoor 戶外的

In winter, indoor sports and activities are particularly popular.
冬天時，室內運動及活動特別受歡迎。

point 表示時間的介係詞：in + 季節／年；on + 星期幾／特定的日子；at + 時間點。

The professional photographer's speciality is indoor photography.
這名專業攝影師的專長為室內攝影。

point 延伸詞彙：specialist (n.) 專員，specialize in (v.) 專精於。

58 income

★
★
★

[ˋɪn͵kʌm]

ⓝ 收入，收益，所得

⟨同⟩ earnings 收入
salary 薪水
pay 薪俸

⟨反⟩ expenditure 支出

The graphic designer teaches classes in the community college to make extra income.
圖像設計師在社區大學裡教課以賺取額外的收入。

The newlyweds spend 40 percent of their income on mortgage.
這對新婚夫妻花了百分之四十的收入在貸款上。

59 graduate

★
★
★

[ˋgrædʒu͵et]

ⓥ 畢業，取得資格

[ˋgrædʒuɪt]

ⓝ 畢業生（大學、研究所）
ⓐ 畢業了的

⟨衍⟩ grade (n.) 等級
gradual (a.) 逐漸的

Both graduate and undergraduate students can apply for this exchange student program.
碩士生及大學生都可以申請這個交換學生的計畫。

point both... and 意為「兩者皆是」。

The executive assistant has been working for three months since he graduated in July.
這名行政助理自從七月畢業後已經工作三個月了。

point has been working 為現在完成進行式（時間發生較晚），graduated 為過去式（時間發生較早）。

60 environmental

★
★

[ɪn͵vaɪrənˋmɛntl̩]

ⓐ 環境的，有關環境的

⟨同⟩ surrounding 周圍的
ecological 生態的

The environmental protection issue was highlighted in that article.
那篇文章強調了環境保護議題。

The water pollution caused by the chemical plant is the worst environmental disaster in this nation.
化學工廠造成的水汙染是這個國家最嚴重的環境災難。

point caused by the chemical plant 前面省略了 which / that was，用來修飾前面的 pollution。

61 **environment**
★
★ [ɪnˈvaɪrənmənt]
★
🅝 環境，自然環境，包圍
📖 habitat 棲息地
territory 領地
surrounding 環境

The slogan: "Protect the environment for the youth" has raised many people's awareness.
「為我們的年輕一代保護環境」，這個口號已經引起許多人的警覺。

Using environment-friendly products rather than products that contain certain harmful chemicals will be better.
使用對環境友善的產品會比使用含有特定有害化學物質的產品還要好。

 certain (a.) 肯定的；特定的。

62 **common**
★
★ [ˈkɑmən]
★
🅐 普通的，常見的，共同的
📖 usual 通常的
ordinary 普通的
customary 習慣上的
habitual 慣常的
🈺 private 私下的
individual 個人的

It's common for working parents to enroll their children in daycare centers.
在職父母讓小孩加入托嬰中心是相當普遍的。

 it's common for sb. to + V意為「對於某人來說做某事是普遍的」。

The twins have many things in common, such as interest, personality and work.
這對雙胞胎有很多共同點，像是興趣、個性及工作。

point have many things in common 意為「有很多共同點」。have little in common 意為「有很少共同點」。

63 **bookshelf**
★
★ [ˈbʊkˌʃɛlf]
★
🅝 書架，書櫃
📖 shelf 架子
bookstand 書架

The housekeeper dusted the metal bookshelf.
家管擦掉金屬書架上的灰塵。

point dust (n.) 灰塵 (v.) 給……除塵。

Ms. Porter assembled the bookshelves that she bought from the furniture store on her own.
波特小姐自己組裝她從家具店買回來的書架。

 on one's own = by oneself 意為「靠自己」。

64 **apart**
★
★ [əˈpɑrt]
🅐🅓 分開地，相隔地
🅐 分離的
📖 separately (ad.) 分開地
independently (ad.) 獨立地

Even distance can't tear the newlyweds apart.
即使是距離也沒有辦法把這對新婚夫妻拆散。

point newlyweds 有加 -s 為「新婚夫妻」，沒加 -s 時單指新婚的丈夫或妻子。

The watch specialist took the watch apart to change the battery.
手錶專家將手錶拆開以更換電池。

65 **belong**
★
★ [bə'lɔŋ]
★ Ⅴ 合適，屬於，居住

The old wooden closet that once belonged to my grandmother was relatively pricey.
這個曾經屬於我奶奶的木製衣櫥相當昂貴。

(point) pricey = costly (a.) 昂貴的。特別注意 costly 是形容詞，不是副詞。

The student affair association will hold a party to welcome transfer students in an effort to make them feel that they belong.
學生會將會舉辦一個派對來歡迎轉學生，為了讓他們感受到歸屬感。

(point) in an effort to = to，意為「為了……」。

66 **wallpaper**
★ ['wɔl,pepɚ]
Ⅲ 壁紙

With this tool set, you can change wallpaper on your own.
有了這個工具組，你就可以自行更換壁紙。

(point) on your own = by yourself 意為「靠你自己」。

We would like to purchase the wallpaper whose color goes with the carpet.
我們想要買這個顏色和地毯很搭的壁紙。

(point) go with 意為「與……很搭」。

67 **surface**
★ ['sɝfɪs]
★
★ Ⅴ 浮出水面，顯露，加表面層
ⓐ 表面的，水面上的，外觀的
Ⅲ 表面，水面，外觀

The road is being surfaced.
這條路正在被鋪。

(point) 此為多益聽力測驗 Part 1 圖片題中會聽到的句型：進行式＋被動式。

The safety inspector found the surface uneven.
稽查員發覺表面不平整。

68 **survive**
★ [sɚ'vaɪv]
Ⅴ 活下來，倖存，殘留
同 live 活著
反 die 死亡

Some greenhouse plants have a hard time surviving in very cold conditions.
一些在溫室的植物很難在非常寒冷的條件下生存。

(point) have a hard time + Ving 意為「做……有困難」。

The buildings made of fire-resistant materials survived the fire.
用防火材質建造的這棟大樓在這場大火中倖免。

(point) fire-resistant 意為「防火的」。

69 visual
★★
[`vɪʒuəl]
a 視力的，看得見的
衍 vision 視力
sight 視力

Using visual aids can assist your students' learning.
使用視覺道具可以幫助你的學生的學習。

The applicant failed to pass the visual test for pilots.
這位面試者沒能通過專為機師設計的視力測驗。

 fail to + V 意為「做……失敗」。

---

70 sharp
★
[ʃɑrp]
a 鋒利的，明顯的，嚴厲的
同 pointy 尖的
反 blunt 鈍的

Be careful when you cook since the knife is really sharp.
煮菜時請小心，因為刀子很銳利。

People who are suddenly laid off have a hard time getting used to a sharp decline in the standard of living.
突然被解僱的人們很難適應生活水準的驟降。

---

71 respect
★★
[rɪ`spɛkt]
n 敬重，問候，方面
v 尊敬，重視，遵守
同 awe (v.) 敬畏
praise (v.) 讚揚
反 disrespect (v.) 不尊敬
contempt (v.) 輕視

The child was taught to respect the elderly and yield seats to them.
小孩被教導要尊重長者並讓位給他們。

 the elderly 意為「年長者」。

We should respect people who hold different opinions.
我們應該尊重跟我們有不同意見的人們。

 hold different opinions 意為「持有不同意見」。

CH 20
日常生活

---

72 remove
★★★
[rɪ`muv]
v 移動，消除，撤去
同 eliminate 消除
discharge 排出
displace 移開
反 attach 附加
insert 嵌入
add 加入

The leaves on the ground are being removed.
地上的葉子正在被清除。

 are being removed 為進行被動式，意為「正在被移除」。若出現在多益測驗 Part 1 圖片題裡要有人出現才能選。

This new detergent can remove red wine stains from carpets.
這種新的洗潔劑可以去除地毯上的紅酒污漬。

 remove A from B 意為「從 B 中去除 A」。

443

73 shortage

★
★

['ʃɔrtɪdʒ]

n 缺少，不足，匱乏

同 scarcity 缺乏
poverty 缺少
deficiency 不足
lack 缺少

反 abundance 充足

There is a shortage of cheap housing in this commercial area.
這個商業區缺少便宜的住宅。

(point) 延伸詞彙：residential area 意為「住宅區」，industrial area 意為「工業區」。

The dry season has caused a serious water shortage for 2 weeks.
乾旱已經造成兩週嚴重的水源短缺。

(point) rain season 意為「雨季」。high / peak season 意為「旺季」，low / slack season 意為「淡季」。

74 relate

★
★
★

[rɪˈlet]

v 使有聯繫，符合，相處

同 connect (with) 連結
associate (with) 聯繫
link (with) 連結
correlate (with) 關聯

Given that I don't have a similar family background, it's difficult for me to relate to the movie.
有鑑於我沒有相似的家庭背景，因此我很難體會電影情境。

(point) given that + S + V 意為「有鑑於……」。

Rajon is interested in anything relating to interior design.
拉簡對一切和室內設計有關的東西都有興趣。

(point) be interested in 意為「對……感到有興趣」。

75 prevent

★
★
★

[prɪˈvɛnt]

v 防止，預防，妨礙

同 hinder 妨礙
impede 阻礙

反 allow 允許
encourage 鼓勵

衍 preventive (a.) 預防的

The sound of a dripping faucet prevents him from sleeping.
滴水的水龍頭聲音讓他睡不著。

(point) prevent sth. from... 意為「避免某事……；妨礙」。

We could have prevented the accident if we had taken another route.
如果我們走另一條路的話，我們就能避免意外。

(point) 此句為與過去事實相反的假設語氣，代表事實上沒有避免。

76 overlook

★
★
★

[ˌovɚˈluk]

v 忽視，瞭望，檢查

同 neglect 忽視
ignore 忽視

One thing special about this apartment is that its balcony overlooks the river.
這間公寓最特別的一件事就是從陽台可以俯瞰河流。

The experienced attorney never overlooks any details of cases.
有經驗的律師從來不會忽略案件中的細節。

Test 1

● 一、請寫出下列單字的中文意思。

① fertilize ＿＿＿＿＿　⑥ academic ＿＿＿＿＿

② comfortable ＿＿＿＿＿　⑦ visual ＿＿＿＿＿

③ alter ＿＿＿＿＿　⑧ respect ＿＿＿＿＿

④ proficiency ＿＿＿＿＿　⑨ interior ＿＿＿＿＿

⑤ dedicate ＿＿＿＿＿　⑩ environment ＿＿＿＿＿

● 二、請寫出符合下列句意的單字。

① We could have ＿＿＿＿＿ the accident if we had taken another route.
如果我們走另一條路的話，我們就能避免意外。

② Surprisingly, the ＿＿＿＿＿ painter's paintings are far more widespread than other professional ones.
令人訝異地，那位業餘畫家的畫作比其他專業畫家還更廣為流傳。

③ Natural resources are not ＿＿＿＿＿ so people have to save as much energy as possible.
自然資源是有限的，因此人們要盡可能地節省能源。

解答

1. ① 施肥，使土地肥沃　② 舒適的，富足的　③ 改變，修改　④ 熟練，精通　⑤ 奉獻
⑥ 學術的，學校的；學者　⑦ 視覺的，看得見的　⑧ 尊敬，敬意　⑨ 內部的；內部　⑩ 環境，情況
2. ① prevented　② amateur　③ unlimited

Test 2

● 一、請選擇符合下列文意的單字。

> Ⓐ bookshelves　　Ⓑ apply　　　　Ⓒ identification
> Ⓓ achieves　　　Ⓔ landlord　　　Ⓕ receiving

① Please attach a copy of your _____ card to the back of the application form.

② The tenant renews the rental lease with the _____ every year.

③ You're _____ this letter because of the overdue payment.

④ Ms. Porter assembled the _____ that she bought from the furniture on her own.

⑤ He _____ success by working hard and keeping learning.

● 二、請寫出下列片語的中文意思。

① in progress　　　_____　　⑤ between the lines　_____

② in an attempt to　_____　　⑥ hustle and bustle　_____

③ act as　　　　　_____　　⑦ take pleasure in　_____

④ in a state of　　 _____　　⑧ without exception　_____

解答

1. ① C　② E　③ F　④ A　⑤ D
2. ① 正在進行中　② 為了……　③ 擔任　④ 在……的狀態　⑤ 字裡行間　⑥ 環境喧囂；忙亂
　 ⑦ 樂於……　⑧ 毫無例外

MEMO

PSV 0028

一次戰勝新制多益TOEIC必考核心單字

作　　者 — 蔡馨慧 Nicole
主　　編 — 林菁菁、林潔欣
編　　輯 — 黃凱怡
校　　對 — 劉婉瑀
企劃主任 — 葉蘭芳
封面設計 — 江儀玲
內頁設計 — 李宜芝
內頁排版 — 張靜怡

董 事 長 — 趙政岷
出 版 者 — 時報文化出版企業股份有限公司
　　　　　　108019 臺北市和平西路三段 240 號 3 樓
　　　　　　發行專線 — (02) 2306-6842
　　　　　　讀者服務專線 — 0800-231-705・(02) 2304-7103
　　　　　　讀者服務傳真 — (02) 2304-6858
　　　　　　郵撥 — 19344724 時報文化出版公司
　　　　　　信箱 — 10899 臺北華江橋郵局第 99 信箱
時報悅讀網 — http://www.readingtimes.com.tw

法律顧問 — 理律法律事務所　陳長文律師、李念祖律師
印　　刷 — 勁達印刷有限公司
初版一刷 — 2019 年 6 月 21 日
初版十刷 — 2023 年 10 月 16 日
定　　價 — 新臺幣 480 元

版權所有・翻印必究
（缺頁或破損的書，請寄回更換）

時報文化出版公司成立於 1975 年，
並於 1999 年股票上櫃公開發行，於 2008 年脫離中時集團非屬旺中，
以「尊重智慧與創意的文化事業」為信念。

　一次戰勝新制多益 TOEIC 必考核心單字 /
　蔡馨慧 Nicole 作 . -- 初版 . -- 臺北市：時
　報文化，2019.06
　　448 面；17×23 公分 . -- (PSV；0028)
　　ISBN 978-957-13-7819-0 (平裝)

　　1. 多益測驗　2. 詞彙

805.1895　　　　　　　　　　108007493

ISBN 978-957-13-7819-0
Printed in Taiwan